THE NOVELS AND TALES OF
HENRY JAMES

New York Edition

VOLUME XXIV

THE GOLDEN BOWL

VOLUME II

HENRY JAMES

NEW YORK

CHARLES SCRIBNER'S SONS

THE GOLDEN BOWL
VOLUME II

BOOK FOURTH

THE PRINCESS

THE GOLDEN BOWL

I

IT was n't till many days had passed that the Princess began to accept the idea of having done, a little, something she was not always doing, or indeed that of having listened to any inward voice that spoke in a new tone. Yet these instinctive postponements of reflexion were the fruit, positively, of recognitions and perceptions already active; of the sense above all that she had made at a particular hour, made by the mere touch of her hand, a difference in the situation so long present to her as practically unattackable. This situation had been occupying for months and months the very centre of the garden of her life, but it had reared itself there like some strange tall tower of ivory, or perhaps rather some wonderful beautiful but outlandish pagoda, a structure plated with hard bright porcelain, coloured and figured and adorned at the overhanging eaves with silver bells that tinkled ever so charmingly when stirred by chance airs. She had walked round and round it — that was what she felt; she had carried on her existence in the space left her for circulation, a space that sometimes seemed ample and sometimes narrow: looking up all the while at the fair structure that spread itself so amply and rose so high, but never quite making out as yet where she might have entered had she wished. She had n't

wished till now — such was the odd case; and what
was doubtless equally odd besides was that though her
raised eyes seemed to distinguish places that must
serve from within, and especially far aloft, as apert-
ures and outlooks, no door appeared to give access
from her convenient garden level. The great decorated surface had remained consistently impenetrable
and inscrutable. At present however, to her considering mind, it was as if she had ceased merely to circle
and to scan the elevation, ceased so vaguely, so quite
helplessly to stare and wonder: she had caught herself
distinctly in the act of pausing, then in that of lingering, and finally in that of stepping unprecedentedly
near. The thing might have been, by the distance at
which it kept her, a Mahometan mosque, with which
no base heretic could take a liberty; there so hung
about it the vision of one's putting off one's shoes to
enter and even verily of one's paying with one's life
if found there as an interloper. She had n't certainly
arrived at the conception of paying with her life for
anything she might do; but it was nevertheless quite
as if she had sounded with a tap or two one of the rare
porcelain plates. She had knocked in short — though
she could scarce have said whether for admission or
for what; she had applied her hand to a cool smooth
spot and had waited to see what would happen.
Something *had* happened; it was as if a sound, at her
touch, after a little, had come back to her from within;
a sound sufficiently suggesting that her approach had
been noted.

If this image, however, may represent our young
woman's consciousness of a recent change in her life

— a change now but a few days old — it must at the same time be observed that she both sought and found in renewed circulation, as I have called it, a measure of relief from the idea of having perhaps to answer for what she had done. The pagoda in her blooming garden figured the arrangement — how otherwise was it to be named ? — by which, so strikingly, she had been able to marry without breaking, as she liked to put it, with her past. She had surrendered herself to her husband without the shadow of a reserve or a condition and yet had n't all the while given up her father by the least little inch. She had compassed the high felicity of seeing the two men beautifully take to each other, and nothing in her marriage had marked it as more happy than this fact of its having practically given the elder, the lonelier, a new friend. What had moreover all the while enriched the whole aspect of success was that the latter's marriage had been no more measurably paid for than her own. His having taken the same great step in the same free way had n't in the least involved the relegation of his daughter. That it was remarkable they should have been able at once so to separate and so to keep together had never for a moment, from however far back, been equivocal to her; that it was remarkable had in fact quite counted, at first and always, and for each of them equally, as part of their inspiration and their support. There were plenty of singular things they were *not* enamoured of — flights of brilliancy, of audacity, of originality, that, speaking at least for the dear man and herself, were not at all in their line; but they liked to think they had given their life this unusual exten-

5

sion and this liberal form, which many families, many couples, and still more many pairs of couples, would n't have found workable. That last truth had been distinctly brought home to them by the bright testimony, the quite explicit envy, of most of their friends, who had remarked to them again and again that they must, on all the showing, to keep such terms, be people of the highest amiability — equally including in the praise of course Amerigo and Charlotte. It had given them pleasure — as how should n't it ? — to find themselves shed such a glamour; it had certainly, that is, given pleasure to her father and herself, both of them distinguishably of a nature so slow to presume that they would scarce have been sure of their triumph without this pretty reflexion of it. So it was that their felicity had fructified; so it was that the ivory tower, visible and admirable doubtless from any point of the social field, had risen stage by stage. Maggie's actual reluctance to ask herself with proportionate sharpness why she had ceased to take comfort in the sight of it represented accordingly a lapse from that ideal consistency on which her moral comfort almost at any time depended. To remain consistent she had always been capable of cutting down more or less her prior term.

Moving for the first time in her life as in the darkening shadow of a false position, she reflected that she should either not have ceased to be right — that is to be confident — or have recognised that she was wrong; though she tried to deal with herself for a space only as a silken-coated spaniel who has scrambled out of a pond and who rattles the water from his

ears. Her shake of her head, again and again, as she
went, was much of that order, and she had the resource to which, save for the rude equivalent of his
generalising bark, the spaniel would have been a
stranger, of humming to herself hard as a sign that
nothing had happened to her. She had n't, so to
speak, fallen in; she had had no accident nor got wet;
this at any rate was her pretension until after she
began a little to wonder if she might n't, with or without exposure, have taken cold. She could at all events
remember no time at which she had felt so excited,
and certainly none — which was another special
point—that so brought with it as well the necessity for
concealing excitement. This birth of a new eagerness
became a high pastime in her view precisely by reason of the ingenuity required for keeping the thing
born out of sight. The ingenuity was thus a private
and absorbing exercise, in the light of which, might
I so far multiply my metaphors, I should compare
her to the frightened but clinging young mother of an
unlawful child. The idea that had possession of her
would be, by our new analogy, the proof of her mis-
adventure, but likewise all the while only another
sign of a relation that was more to her than anything
on earth. She had lived long enough to make out for
herself that any deep-seated passion has its pangs
as well as its joys, and that we are made by its aches
and its anxieties most richly conscious of it. She had
never doubted of the force of the feeling that bound
her to her husband; but to become aware almost
suddenly that it had begun to vibrate with a violence
that had some of the effect of a strain would, rightly

7

looked at, after all but show that she was, like thousands of women, every day, acting up to the full privilege of passion. Why in the world should n't she, with every right — if on consideration she saw no good reason against it? The best reason against it would have been the possibility of some consequence disagreeable or inconvenient to others — especially to such others as had never incommoded her by the egotism of *their* passions; but if once that danger were duly guarded against the fulness of one's measure amounted to no more than the equal use of one's faculties or the proper playing of one's part. It had come to the Princess, obscurely at first, but little by little more conceivably, that her faculties had n't for a good while been concomitantly used; the case resembled in a manner that of her once-loved dancing, a matter of remembered steps that had grown vague from her ceasing to go to balls. She would go to balls again — that seemed, freely, even crudely, stated, the remedy; she would take out of the deep receptacles in which she had laid them away the various ornaments congruous with the greater occasions and of which her store, she liked to think, was none of the smallest. She would have been easily to be figured for us at this occupation; dipping, at off moments and quiet hours, in snatched visits and by draughty candle-light, into her rich collections and seeing her jewels again a little shyly but all unmistakeably glow. That in fact may pass as the very picture of her semi-smothered agitation, of the diversion she to some extent successfully found in referring her crisis, so far as was possible, to the mere working of her own needs.

It must be added, however, that she would have
been at a loss to determine — and certainly at first —
to which order, that of self-control or that of large
expression, the step she had taken the afternoon of
her husband's return from Matcham with his companion properly belonged. For it had been a step,
distinctly, on Maggie's part, her deciding to do something just then and there which would strike Amerigo
as unusual, and this even though her departure from
custom had merely consisted in her so arranging that
he would n't find her, as he would definitely expect
to do, in Eaton Square. He would have, strangely
enough, as might seem to him, to come back home
for it, and there get the impression of her rather
pointedly, or at least all impatiently and independently, awaiting him. These were small variations and
mild manœuvres, but they went accompanied on
Maggie's part, as we have mentioned, with an infinite
sense of intention. Her watching by his fireside for
her husband's return from an absence might superficially have presented itself as the most natural act
in the world, and the only one, into the bargain, on
which he would positively have reckoned. It fell
by this circumstance into the order of plain matters,
and yet the very aspect by which it was in the event
handed over to her brooding fancy was the fact that
she had done with it all she had designed. She had
put her thought to the proof, and the proof had shown
its edge; this was what was before her, that she was
no longer playing with blunt and idle tools, with
weapons that did n't cut. There passed across her
vision ten times a day the gleam of a bare blade, and

9

at this it was that she most shut her eyes, most knew the impulse to cheat herself with motion and sound. She had merely driven on a certain Wednesday to Portland Place instead of remaining in Eaton Square, and — she privately repeated it again and again — there had appeared beforehand no reason why she should have seen the mantle of history flung by a single sharp sweep over so commonplace a deed. That, all the same, was what had happened; it had been bitten into her mind, just in an hour, that nothing she had ever done would hereafter, in some way yet to be determined, so *count* for her — perhaps not even what she had done in accepting, in their old golden Rome, Amerigo's proposal of marriage. And yet by her little crouching posture there, that of a timid tigress, she had meant nothing recklessly ultimate, nothing clumsily fundamental; so that she called it names, the invidious, the grotesque attitude, holding it up to her own ridicule, reducing so far as she could the *portée* of what had followed it. She had but wanted to get nearer — nearer to something indeed that she could n't, that she would n't, even to herself, describe; and the degree of this achieved nearness was what had been in advance incalculable. Her actual multiplication of distractions and suppressions, whatever it did for her, failed to prevent her living over again any chosen minute — for she could choose them, she could fix them — of the freshness of relation produced by her having administered to her husband the first surprise to which she had ever treated him. It had been a poor thing, but it had been all her own, and the whole passage was back-

wardly there, a great picture hung on the wall of her
daily life for her to make what she would of.

It fell for retrospect into a succession of moments
that were *watchable* still; almost in the manner of the
different things done during a scene on the stage,
some scene so acted as to have left a great impression
on the tenant of one of the stalls. Several of these
moments stood out beyond the others, and those she
could feel again most, count again like the firm pearls
on a string, had belonged more particularly to the
lapse of time before dinner — dinner which had been
so late, quite at nine o'clock, that evening, thanks to
the final lateness of Amerigo's own irruption. These
were parts of the experience — though in fact there
had been a good many of them — between which her
impression could continue sharply to discriminate.
Before the subsequent passages, much later on, it
was to be said, the flame of memory turned to an
equalising glow, that of a lamp in some side-chapel
in which incense was thick. The great moment at
any rate, for conscious repossession, was doubtless
the first: the strange little timed silence which she had
fully gauged, on the spot, as altogether beyond her
own intention, but which — for just how long?
should she ever really know for just how long? —
she could do nothing to break. She was in the smaller
drawing-room, in which she always "sat," and she
had, by calculation, dressed for dinner on finally
coming in. It was a wonder how many things she
had calculated in respect to this small incident —
a matter for the importance of which she had so
quite indefinite a measure. He would be late — he

would be very late; that was the one certainty that seemed to look her in the face. There was still also the possibility that if he drove with Charlotte straight to Eaton Square he might think it best to remain there even on learning she had come away. She had left no message for him on any such chance; this was another of her small shades of decision, though the effect of it might be to keep him still longer absent. He might suppose she would already have dined; he might stay, with all he would have to tell, just on purpose to be nice to her father. She had known him to stretch the point, to these beautiful ends, far beyond that; he had more than once stretched it to the sacrifice of the opportunity for dressing.

If she herself had now avoided any such sacrifice, and had made herself, during the time at her disposal, quite inordinately fresh and quite positively smart, this had probably added, while she waited and waited, to that very tension of spirit in which she was afterwards to find the image of her having crouched. She did her best, quite intensely, by herself, to banish any such appearance; she could n't help it if she could n't read her pale novel — ah that, *par exemple*, was beyond her! — but she could at least sit by the lamp with the book, sit there with her newest frock, worn for the first time, sticking out, all round her, quite stiff and grand; even perhaps a little too stiff and too grand for a familiar and domestic frock, yet marked none the less this time, she ventured to hope, by incontestable intrinsic merit. She had glanced repeatedly at the clock, but had refused herself the weak indulgence of walking up and down, though

the act of doing so, she knew, would make her feel,
on the polished floor, with the rustle and the "hang,"
still more beautifully bedecked. The difficulty was
that it would also make her feel herself still more
sharply in a state; which was exactly what she proposed not to do. The only drops of her anxiety had
been when her thought strayed complacently, with
her eyes, to the front of her gown, which was in a
manner a refuge, a beguilement, especially when she
was able to fix it long enough to wonder if it would
at last really satisfy Charlotte. She had ever been, in
respect to her clothes, rather timorous and uncertain;
for the last year above all she had lived in the light of
Charlotte's possible and rather inscrutable judgement
of them. Charlotte's own were simply the most charming and interesting any woman had ever put on;
there was a kind of poetic justice in her being at last
able in this particular, thanks to means, thanks quite
to omnipotence, freely to exercise her genius. But
Maggie would have described herself as, in these connexions, constantly and intimately "torn"; conscious
on one side of the impossibility of copying her companion and conscious on the other of the impossibility
of sounding her, independently, to the bottom. Yes,
it was one of the things she should go down to her
grave without having known — how Charlotte, after
all had been said, *really* thought her stepdaughter
looked under any supposedly ingenious personal experiment. She had always been lovely about the stepdaughter's material braveries — had done for her
the very best with them; but there had ever fitfully
danced at the back of Maggie's head the suspicion

13

THE GOLDEN BOWL

that these expressions were mercies, not judgements, embodying no absolute but only a relative frankness. Had n't Charlotte, with so perfect a critical vision, if the truth were known, given her up as hopeless — hopeless by a serious standard, and thereby invented for her a different and inferior one, in which, as the only thing to be done, she patiently and soothingly abetted her? Had n't she in other words assented in secret despair, perhaps even in secret irritation, to her being ridiculous? — so that the best now possible was to wonder once in a great while whether one might n't give her the surprise of something a little less out of the true note than usual. Something of this kind was the question that Maggie, while the absentees still delayed, asked of the appearance she was endeavouring to present; but with the result repeatedly again that it only went and lost itself in the thick air that had begun more and more to hang, for our young woman, over her accumulations of the unanswered. They were *there*, these accumulations; they were like a roomful of confused objects, never as yet "sorted," which for some time now she had been passing and re-passing, along the corridor of her life. She passed it when she could without opening the door; then, on occasion, she turned the key to throw in a fresh contribution. So it was that she had been getting things out of the way. They rejoined the rest of the confusion; it was as if they found their place, by some instinct of affinity, in the heap. They knew in short where to go, and when she at present by a mental act once more pushed the door open she had practically a sense of method and experience. What she

14

should never know about Charlotte's thought — she tossed *that* in. It would find itself in company, and she might at last have been standing there long enough to see it fall into its corner. The sight moreover would doubtless have made her stare, had her attention been more free — the sight of the mass of vain things, congruous, incongruous, that awaited every addition. It made her in fact, with a vague gasp, turn away, and what had further determined this was the final sharp extinction of the inward scene by the outward. The quite different door had opened and her husband was there.

It had been as strange as she could consent afterwards to think it; it had been essentially what had made the abrupt bend in her life: he had come back, had followed her from the other house, *visibly* uncertain — this was written in the face he for the first minute showed her. It had been written only for those seconds, and it had appeared to go, quickly, after they began to talk; but while it lasted it had been written large, and though she did n't quite know what she had expected of him she felt she had n't expected the least shade of embarrassment. What had made the embarrassment — she called it embarrassment so as to be able to assure herself she put it at the very worst — what had made the particular look was his thus distinguishably wishing to see how he should find her. Why *first?* — that had later on kept coming to her; the question dangled there as if it were the key to everything. With the sense of it, on the spot, she had felt overwhelmingly that she was significant, that so she must instantly strike him, and that this had a kind of violence beyond what she had intended. It was in fact even at the moment not absent from her view that he might easily have made an abject fool of her — at least for the time. She had indeed for just ten seconds been afraid of some such turn: the uncertainty in his face had become so, the next thing, an uncertainty in the very air. Three words of impatience the least bit loud, some outbreak of "What in the world are you 'up to,' and what do you mean?" any note of that sort would instantly have brought her low — and this all the more that heaven knew she had n't in any manner designed to be high. It was such a trifle, her small breach with custom, or at any rate with his natural presumption, that all magnitude of wonder had already had, before one could deprecate the shadow of it, the effect of a complication. It had made for him some difference that she could n't measure, this meeting him at home and alone instead of elsewhere and with others, and back and back it kept coming to her that the blankness he showed her before he was able to *see* might, should she choose to insist on it, have a meaning — have, as who should say, an historic value — beyond the importance of momentary expressions in general. She had naturally had on the spot no ready notion of what he might want to see; it was enough for a ready notion, not to speak of a beating heart, that he *did* see, that he saw his wife in her own drawing-room at the hour when she would most properly be there.

He had n't in any way challenged her, it was true, and, after those instants during which she now believed him to have been harbouring the impression of something unusually prepared and pointed in her attitude and array, he had advanced upon her smiling and smiling, and thus, without hesitation at the last, had taken her into his arms. The hesitation had been at the first, and she at present saw that he had surmounted it without her help. She had given him no help; for if on the one hand she could n't speak for hesitation, so on the other — and especially as he did n't ask her — she could n't explain why she was agitated. She had known it all the while down to her toes, known it in his presence with fresh intensity, and if he had uttered but a question it would have pressed in her the spring of recklessness. It had been strange that the most natural thing of all to say to him should have had that appearance; but she was more than ever conscious that *any* appearance she had would come round more or less straight to her father, whose life was now so quiet, on the basis accepted for it, that the least alteration of his consciousness, even in the possible sense of enlivenment, would make their precious equilibrium waver. *That* was at the bottom of her mind, that their equilibrium was everything, and that it was practically precarious, a matter of a hair's breadth for the loss of the balance. It was the equilibrium, or at all events her conscious fear about it, that had brought her heart into her mouth; and the same fear was on either side in the silent look she and Amerigo had exchanged. The happy balance that demanded this amount of consideration was truly thus, as by its own confession, a delicate matter; but that her husband had also *his* habit of anxiety and his general caution only brought them after all more closely together. It would have been most beautifully therefore in the name of the equilibrium, and in that of her joy at their feeling so exactly the same about it, that she might have spoken if she had permitted the truth on the subject of her behaviour to ring out — on the subject of that poor little behaviour which was for the moment so very limited a case of eccentricity.

"'Why, why' have I made this evening such a point of our not all dining together? Well, because I 've all day been so wanting you alone that I finally could n't bear it and that there did n't seem any great reason why I should try to. *That* came to me — funny as it may at first sound, with all the things we 've so wonderfully got into the way of bearing for each other. You 've seemed these last days — I don't know what: more absent than ever before, too absent for us merely to go on so. It 's all very well, and I perfectly see how beautiful it is, all round; but there comes a day when something snaps, when the full cup, filled to the very brim, begins to flow over. That 's what has happened to my need of you — the cup, all day, has been too full to carry. So here I am with it, spilling it over you — and just for the reason that 's the reason of my life. After all I 've scarcely to explain that I 'm as much in love with you now as the first hour; except that there are some hours — which I know when they come, because they almost frighten me — that show me I 'm even more so. They come of themselves — and ah they 've been coming! After all, after all —!" Some such words as those were what *did n't* ring out, yet it was as if even the unuttered

18

sound had been quenched here in its own quaver. It was where utterance would have broken down by its very weight if he had let it get so far. Without that extremity, at the end of a moment, he had taken in what he needed to take — that his wife was *testifying*, that she adored and missed and desired him. "After all, after all," since she put it so, she was right. That was what he had to respond to; that was what, from the moment that, as has been said, he "saw," he had to treat as the most pertinent thing possible. He held her close and long, in expression of their personal reunion — this obviously was one way of doing so. He rubbed his cheek tenderly and with a deep vague murmur against her face, that side of her face she was not pressing to his breast. That was not less obviously another way, and there were ways enough in short for his extemporised ease, for the good humour she was afterwards to find herself thinking of as his infinite tact. This last was partly no doubt because the question of tact might be felt as having come up at the end of a quarter of an hour during which he had liberally talked and she had genially questioned. He had told her of his day, the happy thought of his roundabout journey with Charlotte, all their cathedral-hunting adventure, and how it had turned out rather more of an affair than they expected. The moral of it was at any rate that he was tired verily, and must have a bath and dress — to which end she would kindly excuse him for the shortest time possible. She was to remember afterwards something that had passed between them on this — how he had looked, for her, during an instant, at the door, before going out, how he had met her asking him, in hesitation first, then quickly in decision, whether she could n't help him by going up with him. He had perhaps also for a moment hesitated, but he had declined her offer, and she was to preserve, as I say, the memory of the smile with which he had opined that at that rate they would n't dine till ten o'clock and that he should go straighter and faster alone. Such things, as I say, were to come back to her — they played through her full after-sense like lights on the whole impression; the subsequent parts of the experience were not to have blurred their distinctness. One of these subsequent parts, the first, had been the not inconsiderable length, to her later and more analytic consciousness, of this second wait for her husband's reappearance. She might certainly, with the best will in the world, had she gone up with him, have been more in his way than not, since people could really almost always hurry better without help than with it. Still she could hardly have made him take more time than he struck her as actually taking, though it must indeed be added that there was now in this much-thinking little person's state of mind no mere crudity of impatience. Something had happened, rapidly, with the beautiful sight of him and with the drop of her fear of having annoyed him by making him go to and fro. Subsidence of the fearsome, for Maggie's spirit, was always at first positive emergence of the sweet, and it was long since anything had been so sweet to her as the particular quality suddenly given by her present emotion to the sense of possession.

II

AMERIGO was away from her again, as she sat there, as she walked there without him — for she had, with the difference of his presence in the house, ceased to keep herself from moving about; but the hour was filled nevertheless with the effect of his nearness, and above all with the effect, strange in an intimacy so established, of an almost renewed vision of the facts of his aspect. She had seen him last but five days since, yet he had stood there before her as if restored from some far country, some long voyage, some combination of dangers or fatigues. This unquenchable variety in his appeal to her interest, what did it mean but that — reduced to the flatness of mere statement — she was married by good fortune to an altogether dazzling person ? That was an old old story, but the truth of it shone out to her like the beauty of some family picture, some mellow portrait of an ancestor, that she might have been looking at, almost in surprise, after a long intermission. The dazzling person was upstairs and she was down, and there were moreover the other facts of the selection and decision that this demonstration of her own had required, and of the constant care that the equilibrium involved; but she had all the same never felt so absorbingly married, so abjectly conscious of a master of her fate. He could do what he would with her; in fact what was actually happening was that he was actually doing it.

"What he would," what he *really* would — only that
quantity itself escaped perhaps, in the brightness of
the high harmony, familiar naming and discussing.
It was enough of a recognition for her that, whatever
the thing he might desire, he would always absolutely
bring it off. She knew at this moment without a
question, with the fullest surrender, how he had
brought off in her, by scarce more than a single allusion, a perfect flutter of tenderness. If he had come
back tired, tired from his long day, the exertion had
been literally in her service and her father's. They
two had sat at home in peace, the Principino between
them, the complications of life kept down, the bores
sifted out, the large ease of the home preserved, *because* of the way the others held the field and braved
the weather. Amerigo never complained — any more
than for that matter Charlotte did; but she seemed to
see to-night as she had never yet quite done that their
business of social representation, conceived as they
conceived it, beyond any conception of her own and
conscientiously carried out, was an affair of living
always in harness. She remembered Fanny Assingham's old judgement, that friend's description of her
father and herself as not living at all, as not knowing
what to do or what might be done for them; and there
came back to her with it an echo of the long talk
they had had together, one September day at Fawns,
under the trees, when she put before him this dictum
of Fanny's.

That occasion might have counted for them — she
had already often made the reflexion — as the first
step in an existence more intelligently arranged. It

had been an hour from which the chain of causes and consequences was definitely traceable — so many things, and at the head of the list her father's marriage, having appeared to her to flow from Charlotte's visit to Fawns, and that event itself having flowed from the memorable talk. But what perhaps most came out in the light of these concatenations was that it had been for all the world as if Charlotte had been "had in," as the servants always said of extra help, because they had thus suffered it to be pointed out to them that if their family coach lumbered and stuck the fault was in its lacking its complement of wheels. Having but three, as they might say, it had wanted another, and what had Charlotte done from the first but begin to act, on the spot, and ever so smoothly and beautifully, as a fourth? Nothing had been immediately more manifest than the greater grace of the movement of the vehicle — as to which, for the completeness of her image, Maggie was now supremely to feel how every strain had been lightened for herself. So far as *she* was one of the wheels she had but to keep in her place; since the work was done for her she felt no weight, and it was n't too much to acknowledge that she had scarce to turn round. She had a long pause before the fire during which she might have been fixing with intensity her projected vision, have been conscious even of its taking an absurd, a fantastic shape. She might have been watching the family coach pass and noting that somehow Amerigo and Charlotte were pulling it while she and her father were not so much as pushing. They were seated inside together, dandling the Principino and holding him up to the

windows to see and be seen, like an infant positively
royal; so that the exertion was *all* with the others.
Maggie found in this image a repeated challenge;
again and yet again she paused before the fire: after
which, each time, in the manner of one for whom a
strong light has suddenly broken, she gave herself
to livelier movement. She had seen herself at last,
in the picture she was studying, suddenly jump from
the coach; whereupon, frankly, with the wonder of the
sight, her eyes opened wider and her heart stood still
for a moment. She looked at the person so acting as if
this person were somebody else, waiting with intensity
to see what would follow. The person had taken a
decision — which was evidently because an impulse
long gathering had at last felt a sharpest pressure.
Only how was the decision to be applied? — what in
particular would the figure in the picture do? She
looked about her, from the middle of the room, under
the force of this question, as if *there* exactly were the
field of action involved. Then as the door opened
again she recognised, whatever the action, the form,
at any rate, of a first opportunity. Her husband had
reappeared — he stood before her refreshed, almost
radiant, quite reassuring. Dressed, anointed, fragrant,
ready above all for his dinner, he smiled at her over
the end of their delay. It was as if her opportunity
had depended on his look — and now she saw that it
was good. There was still for the instant something
in suspense, but it passed more quickly than on his
previous entrance. He was already holding out his
arms.

It was for hours and hours later on as if she had

somehow been lifted aloft, were floated and carried on some warm high tide beneath which stumbling-blocks had sunk out of sight. This came from her being again for the time in the enjoyment of confidence, from her knowing, as she believed, what to do. All the next day and all the next she appeared to herself to know it. She had a plan, and she rejoiced in her plan: this consisted of the light that, suddenly breaking into her restless reverie, had marked the climax of that vigil. It had come to her as a question — "What if I've abandoned *them*, you know? What if I've accepted too passively the funny form of our life?" There would be a process of her own by which she might do differently in respect to Amerigo and Charlotte — a process quite independent of any process of theirs. Such a solution had but to rise before her to affect her, to charm her, with its simplicity, an advantageous simplicity she had been stupid for so long not to have been struck by; and the simplicity meanwhile seemed proved by the success that had already begun to attend her. She had only had herself to do something to see how promptly it answered. This consciousness of its having answered with her husband was the uplifting sustaining wave. He had "met" her — she so put it to herself; met her with an effect of generosity and of gaiety in especial, on his coming back to her ready for dinner, which she wore in her breast as the token of an escape for them both from something not quite definite but clearly much less good. Even at that moment in fact her plan had begun to work; she had been, when he brightly reappeared, in the act of plucking it out of

the heart of her earnestness — plucking it, in the
garden of thought, as if it had been some full-blown
flower that she could present to him on the spot. Well,
it was the flower of participation, and as that, then
and there, she held it out to him, putting straightway
into execution the idea, so needlessly, so absurdly obscured, of her *sharing* with him, whatever the enjoyment, the interest, the experience might be — and
sharing also for that matter with Charlotte.

She had thrown herself at dinner into every feature
of the recent adventure of the companions, letting him
see without reserve that she wished to hear everything
about it, and making Charlotte in particular, Charlotte's judgement of Matcham, Charlotte's aspect,
her success there, her effect traceably produced, her
clothes inimitably worn, her cleverness gracefully
displayed, her social utility, in fine, brilliantly ex-
emplified, the subject of endless enquiry. Maggie's
enquiry was most sympathetic, moreover, for the
whole happy thought of the cathedral-hunt, which
she was so glad they had entertained and as to the
pleasant results of which, down to the cold beef and
bread-and-cheese, the queer old smell and the dirty
tablecloth at the inn, Amerigo was good-humouredly
responsive. He had looked at her across the table
more than once, as if touched by the humility of this
welcome offered to impressions at second-hand, the
amusements, the large freedoms only of others — as
if recognising in it something fairly exquisite; and
at the end, while they were alone, before she had rung
for a servant, he had renewed again his condonation
of the little irregularity, such as it was, on which she

had ventured. They had risen together to come upstairs; he had been talking at the last about some of
the people, at the very last of all about Lady Castledean and Mr. Blint; after which she had once more
broken ground on the matter of the "type" of
Gloucester. It brought her, as he came round the
table to join her, yet another of his kind conscious
stares, one of the looks, visibly beguiled but at the
same time not invisibly puzzled, with which he had
already shown his sense of this charming grace of her
curiosity. It was as if he might for a moment be
going to say: "You need n't *pretend*, dearest, quite
so hard, need n't think it necessary to care quite so
much!" — it was as if he stood there before her with
some such easy intelligence, some such intimate reassurance, on his lips. Her answer would have been
all ready — that she was n't in the least pretending;
and she looked up at him, while he took her hand,
with the maintenance, the real persistence, of her lucid
little plan in her eyes. She wanted him to understand
from that very moment that she was going to be *with*
him again, quite with *them*, together, as she doubtless
had n't been since the "funny" changes — that was
really all one could call them — into which they had
each, as for the sake of the others, too easily and too
obligingly slipped. They had taken too much for
granted that their life together required, as people in
London said, a special "form" — which was very
well so long as the form was kept only for the outside
world and was made no more of among themselves
than the pretty mould of an iced pudding, or something of that sort, into which, to help yourself, you

did n't hesitate to break with the spoon. So much as *that* she would, with an opening, have allowed herself furthermore to observe; she wanted him to understand how her scheme embraced Charlotte too; so that if he had but uttered the acknowledgement she judged him on the point of making — the acknowledgement of his catching at her brave little idea for their case — she would have found herself, as distinctly, voluble almost to eloquence.

What befell however was that even while she thus waited she felt herself present at a process taking place rather deeper within him than the occasion, on the whole, appeared to require — a process of weighing something in the balance, of considering, deciding, dismissing. He had guessed that she was there with an idea, there in fact by reason of her idea; only this, oddly enough, was what at the last stayed his words. She was helped to these perceptions by his now looking at her still harder than he had yet done — which really brought it to the turn of a hair for her that she did n't make sure his notion of her idea was the right one. It was the turn of a hair because he had possession of her hands and was bending toward her, ever so kindly, as if to see, to understand more, or possibly give more — she did n't know which; and that had the effect of simply putting her, as she would have said, in his power. She gave up, let her idea go, let everything go; her one consciousness was that he was taking her again into his arms. It was not till afterwards that she discriminated as to this; felt how the act operated with him *instead* of the words he had n't uttered — operated in his view as probably better than any words, as always better in fact at any time than anything. Her acceptance of it, her response to it, inevitable, foredoomed, came back to her later on as a virtual assent to the assumption he had thus made that there was really nothing such a demonstration did n't anticipate and did n't dispose of, and also that the spring acting within herself might well have been beyond any other the impulse legitimately to provoke it. It made, for any issue, the third time since his return that he had drawn her to his breast; and at present, holding her to his side as they left the room, he kept her close for their moving into the hall and across it, kept her for their slow return together to the apartments above. He had been right, overwhelmingly right, as to the felicity of his tenderness and the degree of her sensibility, but even while she felt these things sweep all others away she tasted of a sort of terror of the weakness they produced in her. It was still for her that she had positively something to do, and that she must n't be weak for this, must much rather be strong. For many hours after, none the less, she remained weak — if weak it was; though holding fast indeed to the theory of her success, since her agitated overture had been after all so unmistakeably met.

She recovered soon enough on the whole the sense that this left her Charlotte always to deal with — Charlotte who at any rate, however *she* might meet overtures, must meet them at the worst more or less differently. Of that inevitability, of such other ranges of response as were open to Charlotte, Maggie took the measure in approaching her, on the morrow of her

return from Matcham, with the same show of desire
to hear all her story. She wanted the whole picture
from her, as she had wanted it from her companion,
and, promptly, in Eaton Square, whither, without the
Prince, she repaired almost ostentatiously for the purpose, this purpose only, she brought her repeatedly
back to the subject, both in her husband's presence
and during several scraps of independent colloquy.
Before her father, instinctively, Maggie took the
ground that his wish for interesting echoes would be
not less than her own — allowing, that is, for everything his wife would already have had to tell him, for
such passages between them as might have occurred
since the evening before. Joining them after luncheon, reaching them, in her desire to proceed with
the application of her idea, before they had quitted the
breakfast-room, the scene of their midday meal, she
referred, in her parent's presence, to what she might
have lost by delay, she expressed the hope that there
would be an anecdote or two left for her to pick up.
Charlotte was dressed to go out, and her husband,
it appeared, rather positively prepared not to; he
had left the table but was seated near the fire with
two or three of the morning papers and the residuum
of the second and third posts on a stand beside him —
more even than the usual extravagance, as Maggie's
glance made out, of circulars, catalogues, advertise-
ments, announcements of sales, foreign envelopes and
foreign handwritings that were as unmistakeable as
foreign clothes. Charlotte, at the window, looking
into the side-street that abutted on the Square, might
have been watching for their visitor's advent before

withdrawing; and in the light, strange and coloured, like that of a painted picture, which fixed the impression for her, objects took on values not hitherto so fully shown. It was the effect of her quickened sensibility; she knew herself again in presence of a problem, in need of a solution for which she must intensely work: that consciousness, lately born in her, had been taught the evening before to accept a temporary lapse, but had quickly enough again, with her getting out of her own house and her walking across half the town — for she had come from Portland Place on foot — found breath still in its lungs.

It exhaled this breath in a sigh faint and unheard; her tribute, while she stood there before speaking, to realities looming through the golden mist that had already begun to be scattered. The conditions facing her had yielded for the time to the golden mist — had considerably melted away; but there they were again, definite, and it was for the next quarter of an hour as if she could have counted them one by one on her fingers. Sharp to her above all was the renewed attestation of her father's comprehensive acceptances, which she had so long regarded as of the same quality with her own, but which, so distinctly now, she should have the complication of being obliged to deal with separately. They had n't yet struck her as absolutely extraordinary — which had made for her lumping them with her own, since her view of her own had but so lately begun to change; though it instantly stood out for her that there was really no new judgement of them she should be able to show without attracting in some degree his attention, without per-

haps exciting his surprise and making thereby, for
the situation she shared with him, some difference.
She was reminded and warned by the concrete image; and for a minute Charlotte's face, immediately
presented to her, affected her as searching her own
to see the reminder tell. She had not less punctually
kissed her stepmother, and then had bent over her
father, from behind, and laid her cheek upon him;
little amenities tantamount heretofore to an easy
change of guard — Charlotte's own frequent, though
always cheerful, term of comparison for this process
of transfer. Maggie figured thus as the relieving
sentry, and so smoothly did use and custom work for
them that her mate might even on this occasion, after
acceptance of the pass-word, have departed without
irrelevant and, in strictness, unsoldierly gossip. This
was not, none the less, what happened; inasmuch as
if our young woman had been floated over her first
impulse to break the existing charm at a stroke, it
yet took her but an instant to sound at any risk the
note she had been privately practising. If she had
practised it the day before, at dinner, on Amerigo,
she knew but the better how to begin for it with Mrs.
Verver, and it immensely helped her for that matter to
be able at once to speak of the Prince as having done
more to quicken than to soothe her curiosity. Frankly
and gaily she had come to ask — to ask what, in their
unusually prolonged campaign, the two had achieved.
She had got out of her husband, she admitted, what
she could, but husbands were never the persons who
answered such questions ideally. He had only made
her more curious, and she had arrived early this way

in order to miss as little as possible of Charlotte's story.

"Wives, papa," she said, "are always much better reporters — though I grant," she added for Charlotte, "that fathers are n't much better than husbands. He never," she smiled, "tells me more than a tenth of what you tell him; so I hope you have n't told him everything yet, since in that case I shall probably have lost the best part of it." Maggie went, she went — she felt herself going; she reminded herself of an actress who had been studying a part and rehearsing it, but who suddenly, on the stage, before the footlights, had begun to improvise, to speak lines not in the text. It was this very sense of the stage and the footlights that kept her up, made her rise higher: just as it was the sense of action that logically involved some platform — action quite positively for the first time in her life, or, counting in the previous afternoon, for the second. The platform remained for three or four days thus sensibly under her feet, and she had all the while with it the inspiration of quite remarkably, of quite heroically improvising. Preparation and practice had come but a short way; her part opened out and she invented from moment to moment what to say and to do. She had but one rule of art — to keep within bounds and not lose her head; certainly she might see for a week how far that would take her. She said to herself in her excitement that it was perfectly simple: to bring about a difference, touch by touch, without letting either of the three, and least of all her father, so much as suspect her hand. If they should suspect they would want a reason, and the humiliating truth was that she was n't ready with a reason — not, that is, with what she would have called a reasonable one. She thought of herself, instinctively, beautifully, as having dealt, all her life, at her father's side and by his example, only in reasonable reasons; and what she would really have been most ashamed of would be to produce for *him*, in this line, some inferior substitute. Unless she were in a position to plead definitely that she was jealous she should be in no position to plead decently that she was dissatisfied. This latter condition would be a necessary implication of the former; without the former behind it it would *have* to fall to the ground. So had the case wonderfully been arranged for her; there was a card she could play, but there was only one, and to play it would be to end the game. She felt herself — as at the small square green table between the tall old silver candlesticks and the neatly arranged counters — her father's playmate and partner; and what it constantly came back to in her mind was that for her to ask a question, to raise a doubt, to reflect in any degree on the play of the others, would be to break the charm. The charm she had to call it, since it kept her companion so constantly engaged, so perpetually seated and so contentedly occupied. To say anything at all would be in fine to have to say *why* she was jealous; and she could in her private hours but stare long, with suffused eyes, at that impossibility.

By the end of a week, the week that had begun especially with her morning hour in Eaton Square between her father and his wife, her consciousness of being beautifully treated had become again verily

greater than her consciousness of anything else; and
I must add moreover that she at last found herself
rather oddly wondering what else, as a consciousness,
could have been quite so overwhelming. Charlotte's
response to the experiment of being more with her
ought, as she very well knew, to have stamped the
experiment with the feeling of success; so that if the
success itself seemed a boon less substantial than the
original image of it, it enjoyed thereby a certain analogy with our young woman's aftertaste of Amerigo's
own determined demonstrations. Maggie was to have
retained, for that matter, more than one aftertaste,
and if I have spoken of the impressions fixed in her
as soon as she had so insidiously taken the field, a
definite note must be made of her perception, during
those moments, of Charlotte's prompt uncertainty.
She had shown, no doubt — she could n't not have
shown — that she had arrived with an idea; quite
exactly as she had shown her husband the night before that she was awaiting him with a sentiment.
This analogy in the two situations was to keep up for
her the remembrance of a kinship of expression in the
two faces — in respect to which all she as yet professed
to herself was that she had affected them, or at any
rate the sensibility each of them so admirably covered, in the same way. To make the comparison at
all was, for Maggie, to return to it often, to brood
upon it, to extract from it the last dregs of its interest
— to play with it in short nervously, vaguely, inces-
santly, as she might have played with a medallion
containing on either side a cherished little portrait
and suspended round her neck by a gold chain of a

firm fineness that no effort would ever snap. The miniatures were back to back, but she saw them for ever face to face, and when she looked from one to the other she found in Charlotte's eyes the gleam of the momentary "What does she really want?" that had come and gone for her in the Prince's. So again she saw the other light, the light touched into a glow both in Portland Place and in Eaton Square, as soon as she had betrayed that she wanted no harm — wanted no greater harm of Charlotte, that is, than to take in that she meant to go out with her. She had been present at that process as personally as she might have been present at some other domestic incident — the hanging of a new picture say, or the fitting of the Principino with his first little trousers.

She remained present accordingly all the week, so charmingly and systematically did Mrs. Verver now welcome her company. Charlotte had but wanted the hint, and what was it but the hint after all that during the so subdued but so ineffaceable passage in the breakfast-room she had seen her take? It had been taken moreover not with resignation, not with qualifications or reserves, however bland; it had been taken with avidity, with gratitude, with a grace of gentleness that supplanted explanations. The very liberality of this accommodation might indeed have appeared in the event to give its own account of the matter — as if it had fairly written the Princess down as a person of variations and had accordingly conformed but to a rule of tact in accepting these caprices for law. The caprice actually prevailing happened to be that the advent of one of the ladies anywhere

should, till the fit had changed, become the sign unfailingly of the advent of the other; and it was emblazoned in rich colour on the bright face of this
period that Mrs. Verver only wished to know on any
occasion what was expected of her, only held herself
there for instructions, in order even to better them
if possible. The two young women, while the passage
lasted, became again very much the companions of
other days, the days of Charlotte's prolonged visits to
the admiring and bountiful Maggie, the days when
equality of condition for them had been all the result
of the latter's native vagueness about her own advantages. The earlier elements flushed into life again,
the frequency, the intimacy, the high pitch of accompanying expression — appreciation, endearment, confidence; the rarer charm produced in each by this
active contribution to the felicity of the other: all
enhanced furthermore — enhanced or qualified, who
should say which? — by a new note of diplomacy,
almost of anxiety, just sensible on Charlotte's part in
particular; of intensity of observance, in the matter
of appeal and response, in the matter of making sure
the Princess might be disposed or gratified, that
resembled an attempt to play again, with more refinement, at disparity of relation. Charlotte's attitude had in short its moments of flowering into pretty
excesses of civility, self-effacements in the presence
of others, sudden little formalisms of suggestion
and recognition, that might have represented her
sense of the duty of not "losing sight" of a social dis-
tinction. This impression came out most for Maggie
when, in their easier intervals, they had only them-

selves to regard, and when her companion's inveteracy
of never passing first, of not sitting till she was seated,
of not interrupting till she appeared to give leave, of
not forgetting too familiarly that in addition to being
important she was also sensitive, had the effect of
throwing over their intercourse a kind of silver tissue
of decorum. It hung there above them like a canopy
of state, a reminder that though the lady-in-waiting
was an established favourite, safe in her position, a
little queen, however good-natured, was always a little
queen and might with small warning remember it.

And yet another of these concomitants of feverish
success all the while was the perception that in another
quarter too things were being made easy. Charlotte's
alacrity in meeting her had in one sense operated
slightly overmuch as an intervention: it had begun to
reabsorb her at the very hour of her husband's showing her that to be all there, as the phrase was, he likewise only required — as one of the other phrases was
too — the straight tip. She had heard him talk about
the straight tip in his moods of amusement at English slang, in his remarkable displays of assimilative
power, power worthy of better causes and higher inspirations; and he had taken it from her at need in a
way that, certainly in the first glow of relief, had made
her brief interval seem large. Then, however immediately, and even though superficially, there had declared itself a readjustment of relations to which she
was, once more, practically a little sacrificed. "I must
do everything," she had said, "without letting papa
see what I do — at least till it's done!" but she scarce
knew how she proposed even for the next few days to

blind or beguile this participant in her life. What had
in fact promptly enough happened, she presently
recognised, was that if her stepmother had beautifully
taken possession of her, and if she had virtually been
rather snatched again thereby from her husband's
side, so on the other hand this had with as little delay
entailed some very charming assistance for her in
Eaton Square. When she went home with Charlotte,
from whatever happy demonstration, for the benefit
of the world in which they supposed themselves to
live, that there was no smallest reason why their
closer association should n't be public and acclaimed
— at these times she regularly found that Amerigo
had come either to sit with his father-in-law in the
absence of the ladies or to make on his side precisely
some such display of the easy working of the family
life as would represent the equivalent of her excursions with Charlotte. Under this particular impression it was that everything in Maggie most melted
and went to pieces — everything, that is, that belonged to her disposition to challenge the perfection
of their common state. It divided them again, that
was true, this particular turn of the tide — cut them
up afresh into pairs and parties; quite as if a sense
for the equilibrium was what, between them all, had
most power of insistence; quite as if Amerigo himself
were all the while at bottom equally thinking of it and
watching it. But as against that he was making her
father not miss her, and he could have rendered neither of them a more excellent service. He was acting
in short on a cue, the cue given him by observation;
it had been enough for him to see the shade of change

in *her* behaviour: his instinct for relations, the most exquisite conceivable, prompted him immediately to meet and match the difference, to play somehow into its hands. That was what it was, she renewedly felt, to have married a man who was sublimely a gentleman; so that in spite of her not wanting to translate *all* their delicacies into the grossness of discussion she yet found again and again in Portland Place moments for saying: "If I did n't love you, you know, for yourself, I should still love you for *him*." He looked at her after such speeches as Charlotte looked in Eaton Square when she called *her* attention to his benevolence: through the dimness of the almost musing smile that took account of her extravagance, harmless though it might be, as a tendency to reckon with. "But my poor child," Charlotte might under this pressure have been on the point of replying, "that's the way nice people *are*, all round — so that why should one be surprised about it? We're all nice together — as why should n't we be? If we had n't been we would n't have gone far — and I consider that we've gone very far indeed. Why should you 'take on' as if you were n't a perfect dear yourself, capable of all the sweetest things? — as if you had n't in fact grown up in an atmosphere, the atmosphere of all the good things that I recognised, even of old, as soon as I came near you, and that you've allowed me now, between you, to make so blessedly my own." Mrs. Verver might in fact have but just failed to make another point, a point charmingly natural to her as a grateful and irreproachable wife. "It is n't a bit wonderful, I may also remind you, that your husband should find, when opportunity permits, worse things to do than to go about with mine. I happen, love, to appreciate my husband — I happen perfectly to understand that his acquaintance should be culti-vated and his company enjoyed."

Some such happily-provoked remarks as these from Charlotte at the other house had been in the air, but we have seen how there was also in the air, for our young woman, as an emanation from the same, a dis-tilled difference of which the very principle was to keep down objections and retorts. That impression came back — it had its hours of doing so; and it may interest us on the ground of its having prompted in Maggie a final reflexion, a reflexion out of the heart of which a light flashed for her like a great flower grown in a night. As soon as this light had spread a little it produced in some quarters a surprising dis-tinctness, made her of a sudden ask herself why there should have been even for three days the least ob-scurity. The perfection of her success, decidedly, was like some strange shore to which she had been noise-lessly ferried and where, with a start, she found herself quaking at the thought that the boat might have put off again and left her. The word for it, the word that flashed the light, was that they were *treating* her, that they were proceeding with her — and for that matter with her father — by a plan that was the exact coun-terpart of her own. It was n't from her they took their cue, but — and this was what in particular made her sit up — from each other; and with a depth of unanimity, an exact coincidence of inspiration, that when once her attention had begun to fix it struck her

as staring out at her in recovered identities of behaviour, expression and tone. They had a view of her
situation, and of the possible forms her own consciousness of it might take — a view determined by
the change of attitude they had had ever so subtly
to recognise in her on their return from Matcham.
They had had to read into this small and all-but-sup-
pressed variation a mute comment — on they did n't
quite know what; and it now arched over the Princess's head like a vault of bold span that important
communication between them on the subject could n't
have failed of being immediate. This new perception
bristled for her, as we have said, with odd intimations,
but questions unanswered played in and out of it as
well — the question for instance of why such promptitude of harmony *should* have been important. Ah
when she began to recover piece by piece the process
became lively; she might have been picking small
shining diamonds out of the sweepings of her ordered
house. She bent, in this pursuit, over her dust-bin; she
challenged to the last grain the refuse of her innocent
economy. Then it was that the dismissed vision of
Amerigo that evening in arrest at the door of her
salottino while her eyes, from her placed chair, took
him in — then it was that this immense little memory
gave out its full power. Since the question was of
doors she had afterwards, she now saw, shut it out;
she had responsibly shut in, as we have understood,
shut in there with her sentient self, only the fact of
his reappearance and the plenitude of his presence.
These things had been testimony after all to super-
sede any other, for on the spot, even while she looked,

the warmly-washing wave had travelled far up the strand. She had subsequently lived for hours she could n't count under the dizzying smothering welter — positively in submarine depths where everything came to her through walls of emerald and mother-of-pearl; though indeed she had got her head above them, for breath, when face to face with Charlotte again on the morrow in Eaton Square. Meanwhile, none the less, as was so apparent, the prior, the prime impression had remained, in the manner of a spying servant, on the other side of the barred threshold; a witness availing himself in time of the lightest pretext to re-enter. It was as if he had found this pretext in her observed necessity of comparing — comparing the obvious common elements in her husband's and her stepmother's ways of now "taking" her. With or without her witness, at any rate, she was led by comparison to a sense of the quantity of earnest intention operating, and operating so harmoniously, between her companions; and it was in the mitigated midnight of these approximations that she had discerned the promise of her dawn.

It was a worked-out scheme for their not wounding her, for their behaving to her quite nobly; to which each had in some winning way induced the other to contribute, and which therefore, so far as that went, proved she had become with them a subject of intimate study. Quickly, quickly, on a certain alarm taken, eagerly and anxiously, before they *should*, without knowing it, wound her, they had signalled from house to house their clever idea, the idea by which for all these days her own idea had been profiting. They had built her in with their purpose — which was why, above her, a vault seemed more heavily to arch; so that she sat there in the solid chamber of her helplessness as in a bath of benevolence artfully prepared for her, over the brim of which she could but just manage to see by stretching her neck. Baths of benevolence were very well, but at least, unless one were a patient of some sort, a nervous eccentric or a lost child, one usually was n't so immersed save by one's request. It was n't in the least what *she* had requested. She had flapped her little wings as a symbol of desired flight, not merely as a plea for a more gilded cage and an extra allowance of lumps of sugar. Above all she had n't complained, not by the quaver of a syllable — so what wound in particular had she shown her fear of receiving? What wound *had* she received — as to which she had exchanged the least word with them? If she had ever whined or moped they might have had some reason; but she would be hanged — she conversed with herself in strong language — if she had been from beginning to end anything but pliable and mild. It all came back in consequence to some required process of their own, a process operating quite positively as a precaution and a policy. They had got her into the bath and, for consistency with themselves — which was with each other — must keep her there. In that condition she would n't interfere with the policy, which was established, which was arranged. Her thought over this arrived at a great intensity — had indeed its pauses and timidities, but always to take afterwards a further and lighter spring. The ground was well-nigh

covered by the time she had made out her husband
and his colleague as directly interested in preventing
her freedom of movement. Policy or no policy, it was
they themselves who were arranged. She must be
kept in position so as not to *dis*arrange them. It fitted
immensely together, the whole thing, as soon as she
could give them a motive; for, strangely as it had by
this time begun to appear to herself, she had n't hitherto imagined them sustained by an ideal distinguishably different from her own. Of course they were
arranged — all four arranged; but what had the basis
of their life been precisely but that they were arranged
together? Ah! Amerigo and Charlotte were arranged
together, but she — to confine the matter only to herself — was arranged apart. It rushed over her, the
full sense of all this, with quite another rush from that
of the breaking wave of ten days before; and as her
father himself seemed not to meet the vaguely-clutch-
ing hand with which, during the first shock of complete perception, she tried to steady herself, so she felt
very much alone.

III

THERE had been from far back — that is from the
Christmas-time on — a plan that the parent and the
child should "do something lovely" together, and
they had recurred to it on occasion, nursed it and
brought it up theoretically, though without as yet
quite allowing it to put its feet to the ground. The
most it had done was to try a few steps on the drawing-room carpet with much attendance on either side,
much holding up and guarding, much anticipation in
fine of awkwardness or accident. Their companions,
by the same token, had constantly assisted at the per-
formance, following the experiment with sympathy
and gaiety, and never so full of applause, Maggie now
made out for herself, as when the infant project had
kicked its little legs most wildly — kicked them, for
all the world, across the Channel and half the Con-
tinent, kicked them over the Pyrenees and innocently
crowed out some rich Spanish name. She asked herself at present if it had been a "real" belief that they
were but wanting, for some such adventure, to snatch
their moment; whether either had at any instant seen
it as workable, save in the form of a toy to dangle
before the other, that they should take flight, without
wife or husband, for one more look, "before they
died," at the Madrid pictures, as well as for a drop of
further weak delay in respect to three or four possible
prizes, privately offered, rarities of the first water,

responsibly reported on and profusely photographed, still patiently awaiting their noiseless arrival in retreats to which the clue had not otherwise been given away. The vision dallied with during the duskier days in Eaton Square had stretched to the span of three or four weeks of springtime for the total adventure, three or four weeks in the very spirit, after all, of their regular life, as their regular life had been persisting; full of shared mornings, afternoons, evenings, walks, drives, "looks-in" at old places on vague chances; full also in especial of that purchased social ease, the sense of the comfort and credit of their house, which had essentially the perfection of something paid for, but which "came" on the whole so cheap that it might have been felt as costing — as costing the parent and child — nothing. It was for Maggie to wonder at present if she had been sincere about their going, to ask herself whether she would have stuck to their plan even if nothing had happened.

Her view of the impossibility of sticking to it now may give us the measure of her sense that everything had happened. A difference had been made in her relation to each of her companions, and what it compelled her to say to herself was that to behave as she might have behaved before would be to act for Amerigo and Charlotte with the highest hypocrisy. She saw in these days that a journey abroad with her father would, more than anything else, have amounted, on his part and her own, to a last expression of an ecstasy of confidence, and that the charm of the idea in fact had been in some such sublimity. Day after day she put off the moment of "speaking," as she inwardly and very comprehensively called it—speaking, that is, to her father; and all the more that she was ridden by a strange suspense as to his himself breaking silence. She gave him time, gave him, during several days, that morning, that noon, that night, and the next and the next and the next; even made up her mind that if he stood off longer it would be proof conclusive that he too was n't at peace. They would then have been all successfully throwing dust in each other's eyes; and it would be at last as if they must turn away their faces, since the silver mist that protected them had begun to grow sensibly thin. Finally, at the end of April, she decided that if he should say nothing for another period of twenty-four hours she must take it as showing that they were, in her private phraseology, lost; so little possible sincerity could there be in pretending to care for a journey to Spain at the approach of a summer that already promised to be hot. Such a proposal on his lips, such an extravagance of optimism, would be *his* way of being consistent — for that he did n't really want to move, or to move further, at the worst, than back to Fawns again, could only signify that he was n't contented at heart. What he wanted at any rate and what he did n't want were in the event put to the proof for Maggie just in time to give her a fresh wind. She had been dining, with her husband, in Eaton Square on the occasion of hospitality offered by Mr. and Mrs. Verver to Lord and Lady Castledean. The propriety of some demonstration of this sort had been for many days before our group, the question reduced to the mere issue of which of the two houses should first take

48

the field. The issue had been easily settled — in the manner of every issue referred in any degree to Amerigo and Charlotte: the initiative obviously belonged to Mrs. Verver, who had gone to Matcham while Maggie had stayed away, and the evening in Eaton Square might have passed for a demonstration all the more personal that the dinner had been planned on "intimate" lines. Six other guests only, in addition to the host and the hostess of Matcham, made up the company, and each of these persons had for Maggie the interest of an attested connexion with the Easter revels at that visionary house. Their common memory of an occasion that had clearly left behind it an ineffaceable charm — this air of beatific reference, less subdued in the others than in Amerigo and Charlotte, lent them, together, an inscrutable comradeship against which the young woman's imagination broke in a small vain wave.

It wasn't that she wished she had been of the remembered party and possessed herself of its secrets; for she didn't care about its secrets — she could concern herself at present absolutely with no secret but her own. What occurred was simply that she became aware, at a stroke, of the quantity of further nourishment required by her own, and of the amount of it she might somehow extract from these people; whereby she rose of a sudden to the desire to possess and use them, even to the extent of braving, of fairly defying, of directly exploiting, or possibly quite enjoying, under cover of an evil duplicity, the felt element of curiosity with which they regarded her. Once she was conscious of the flitting wing of this last im-

49

pression — the perception, irresistible, that she was something for *their* queer experience, just as they were something for hers — there was no limit to her conceived design of not letting them escape. She went and went, again, to-night, after her start was taken; went positively as she had felt herself going, three weeks before, on the morning when the vision of her father and his wife awaiting her together in the breakfast-room had been so determinant. In this other scene it was Lady Castledean who was determinant, who kindled the light, or at all events the heat, and who acted on the nerves; Lady Castledean whom she knew she so oddly did n't like, in spite of reasons upon reasons, the biggest diamonds on the yellowest hair, the longest lashes on the prettiest falsest eyes, the oldest lace on the most violet velvet, the rightest manner on the wrongest assumption. Her ladyship's assumption was that she kept, at every moment of her life, every advantage — it made her beautifully soft, very nearly generous; so she did n't distinguish the little protuberant eyes of smaller social insects, often endowed with such a range, from the other decorative spots on their bodies and wings. Maggie had liked, in London and in the world at large, so many more people than she had thought it right to fear, right even to so much as judge, that it positively quickened her fever to have to recognise in this case such a lapse of all the sequences. It was only that a charming clever woman wondered about her — that is wondered about her as Amerigo's wife, and wondered moreover with the intention of kindness and the spontaneity almost of surprise.

The point of view — that one — was what she read in their free contemplation, in that of the whole eight; there was something in Amerigo to be explained, and she was passed about, all tenderly and expertly, like a dressed doll held, in the right manner, by its firmly-stuffed middle, for the account she could give. She might have been made to give it by pressure of her stomach; she might have been expected to articulate with a rare imitation of nature, "Oh yes, I'm *here* all the while; I'm also in my way a solid little fact and I cost originally a great deal of money: cost, that is, my father, for my outfit, and let in my husband for an amount of pains — toward my training — that money would scarce represent." Well, she *would* meet them in some such way, and she translated her idea into action, after dinner, before they dispersed, by engaging them all unconventionally, almost violently, to dine with her in Portland Place just as they were, if they did n't mind the same party, which was the party she wanted. Oh she was going, she was going — she could feel it afresh; it was a good deal as if she had sneezed ten times or had suddenly burst into a comic song. There were breaks in the connexion, as there would be hitches in the process; she did n't yet wholly see what they would do for her, nor quite how herself she should handle them; but she was dancing up and down, beneath her propriety, with the thought that she had at least begun something — she so fairly liked to feel that she was a point for convergence of wonder. It was n't after all either that *their* wonder so much signified — that of the cornered six whom it glimmered before her that she might still live to drive about like a flock of sheep: the intensity of her consciousness, its sharpest savour, was in the theory of her having diverted, having, as they said, captured, the attention of Amerigo and Charlotte, at neither of whom all the while did she so much as once look. She had pitched them in with the six, for that matter, so far as they themselves were concerned; they had dropped, for the succession of minutes, out of contact with their function — had in short, startled and impressed, abandoned their post. "They're paralysed, they're paralysed!" she commented deep within; so much it helped her own apprehension to hang together that they should suddenly lose their bearings.

Her grasp of appearances was thus out of proportion to her view of causes; but it came to her then and there that if she could only get the facts of appearance straight, only jam them down into their place, the reasons lurking behind them, kept uncertain for the eyes by their wavering and shifting, would n't perhaps be able to help showing. It was n't of course that the Prince and Mrs. Verver marvelled to see her civil to their friends; it was rather precisely that civil was just what she was n't: she had so departed from any such custom of delicate approach — approach by the permitted note, the suggested "if," the accepted vagueness — as would enable the people in question to put her off if they wished. And the profit of her plan, the effect of the violence she was willing to let it go for, was exactly in their *being* the people in question, people she had seemed to be rather shy of before and for whom she suddenly opened her mouth so

wide. Later on, we may add, with the ground soon
covered by her agitated but resolute step, it was to
cease to matter what people they were or were n't; but
meanwhile the particular sense of them that she had
taken home to-night had done her the service of
seeming to break the ice where that formation was
thickest. Still more unexpectedly, the service might
have been the same for her father; inasmuch as immediately, when every one had gone, he did exactly
what she had been waiting for and despairing of —
and did it, as he did everything, with a simplicity that
left any purpose of sounding him deeper, of drawing him out further, of going, in his own frequent
phrase, "behind" what he said, nothing whatever to
do. He brought it out straight, made it bravely and
beautifully irrelevant, save for the plea of what they
should lose by breaking the charm: "I guess we won't
go down there after all, will we, Mag? — just when
it's getting so pleasant here." That was all, with nothing to lead up to it; but it was done for her at a stroke,
and done not less, more rather, for Amerigo and Charlotte, on whom the immediate effect, as she secretly,
as she almost breathlessly measured it, was prodigious.
Everything now so fitted for her to everything else
that she could feel the effect as prodigious even while
sticking to her policy of giving the pair no look.
There were thus some five wonderful minutes during
which they loomed, to her sightless eyes, on either
side of her, larger than they had ever loomed before,
larger than life, larger than thought, larger than any
danger or any safety. There was thus a space of
time in fine, fairly vertiginous for her, during which

she took no more account of them than if they were n't in the room.

She had never never treated them in any such way — not even just now, when she had plied her art upon the Matcham band; her present manner was an intenser exclusion, and the air was charged with their silence while she talked with her other companion as if she had nothing but him to consider. He had given her the note, amazingly, by his allusion to the pleasantness — that of such an occasion as his successful dinner — which might figure as their bribe for renouncing; so that it was all as if they were speaking selfishly, counting on a repetition of just such extensions of experience. Maggie achieved accordingly an act of unprecedented energy, threw herself into her father's presence as by the absolute consistency with which she held his eyes; saying to herself, at the same time that she smiled and talked and inaugurated her system, "What does he mean by it? That's the question — what does he *mean?*" but studying again all the signs in him that recent anxiety had made familiar and counting the stricken minutes on the part of the others. It was in their silence that the others loomed, as she felt; she had had no measure, she afterwards knew, of this duration, but it drew out and out — really to what would have been called in simpler conditions awkwardness — as if she herself were stretching the cord. Ten minutes later, however, in the homeward carriage, to which her husband, cutting delay short, had proceeded at the first announcement, ten minutes later she was to stretch it almost to breaking. The Prince had permitted her to linger much less, before his move to the door, than they usually lingered at the gossiping close of such evenings; which she, all responsive, took as a sign of his impatience to modify for her the odd effect of his not having, and of Charlotte's not having, instantly acclaimed the issue of the question debated or, more exactly, settled before them. He had had time to become aware of this possible impression in her, and his virtually urging her into the carriage was connected with his feeling that he must take action on the new ground. A certain ambiguity in her would absolutely have tormented him; but he had already found something to soothe and correct — as to which she had on her side a shrewd notion of what it would be. She was herself for that matter prepared, and was also, of a truth, as she took her seat in the brougham, amazed at her preparation. It allowed her scarce an interval; she brought it straight out.

"I was certain that was what father would say if I should leave him alone. I *have* been leaving him alone, and you see the effect. He hates now to move — he likes too much to be with us. But if you see the effect" — she felt herself magnificently keeping it up —"perhaps you don't see the cause. The cause, my dear, is too lovely."

Her husband, on taking his place beside her, had, during a minute or two, for her watching sense, neither said nor done anything; he had been, for that sense, as if thinking, waiting, deciding: yet it was still before he spoke that he, as she felt it to be, definitely acted. He put his arm round her and drew her close — indulged in the demonstration, the long firm embrace by his single arm, the infinite pressure of her whole person to his own, that such opportunities had so often suggested and prescribed. Held accordingly and, as she could but too intimately feel, exquisitely solicited, she had said the thing she was intending and desiring to say and as to which she felt, even more than she felt anything else, that whatever he might do she must n't be irresponsible. Yes, she was in his exerted grasp, and she knew what that was; but she was at the same time in the grasp of her conceived responsibility, and the extraordinary thing was that of the two intensities the second was presently to become the sharper. He took his time for it meanwhile, but he met her speech after a fashion. "The cause of your father's deciding not to go?"

"Yes, and of my having wanted to let it act for him quietly — I mean without my insistence." She had, in her compressed state, another pause, and it made her feel as if she were immensely resisting. Strange enough was this sense for her, and altogether new, the sense of possessing, by miraculous help, some advantage that, absolutely then and there, in the carriage, as they rolled, she might either give up or keep. Strange, inexpressibly strange —so distinctly she saw that if she did give it up she should somehow give up everything for ever. And what her husband's grasp really meant, as her very bones registered, was that she *should* give it up: it was exactly for this that he had resorted to unfailing magic. He *knew how* to resort to it — he could be on occasion, as she had lately more than ever learned, so munificent a lover: all of which was precisely a part

56

of the character she had never ceased to regard in him as princely, a part of his large and beautiful ease, his genius for charm, for intercourse, for expression, for life. She should have but to lay her head back on his shoulder with a certain movement to make it definite for him that she did n't resist. To this as they went every throb of her consciousness prompted her—every throb, that is, but one, the throb of her deeper need to know where she "really" was. By the time she had uttered the rest of her idea therefore she was still keeping her head and intending to keep it; though she was also staring out of the carriage-window with eyes into which the tears of suffered pain had risen, happily perhaps indistinguishable in the dusk. She was making an effort that horribly hurt her, and as she could n't cry out her eyes swam in her silence. With them, all the same, through the square opening beside her, through the grey panorama of the London night, she achieved the feat of not losing sight of what she wanted; and her lips helped and protected her by being able to be gay. "It's not to leave *you*, my dear — for that he'll give up anything; just as he would go off anywhere, I think, you know, if you would go with him. I mean you and he alone," Maggie pursued with her gaze out of her window.

For which Amerigo's answer again took him a moment. "Ah the dear old boy! You'd like me to propose him something —?"

"Well, if you think you could bear it."

"And leave," the Prince asked, "you and Charlotte alone?"

"Why not?" Maggie had also to wait a minute,

57

but when she spoke it came clear. "Why should n't Charlotte be just one of *my* reasons — my not liking to leave her? She has always been so good, so perfect, to me — but never so wonderfully as just now. We have somehow been more together — thinking for the time almost only of each other; it has been quite as in old days." And she proceeded consummately, for she felt it as consummate: "It's as if we had been missing each other, had got a little apart — though going on so side by side. But the good moments, if one only waits for them," she hastened to add, "come round of themselves. Moreover you've seen for yourself, since you've made it up so to father; feeling for yourself in your beautiful way every difference, every air that blows; not having to be told or pushed, only being perfect to live with, through your habit of kindness and your exquisite instincts. But of course you've seen, all the while, that both he and I have deeply felt how you've managed; managed that he has n't been too much alone and that I on my side have n't appeared to — what you might call — neglect him. This is always," she continued, "what I can never bless you enough for; of all the good things you've done for me you've never done anything better." She went on explaining as for the pleasure of explaining — even though knowing he must recognise, as a part of his easy way too, her description of his large liberality. "Your taking the child down yourself, those days, and your coming each time to bring him away — nothing in the world, nothing you could have invented, would have kept father more under the charm. Besides, you know how you've

always suited him and how you've always so beautifully let it seem to him that he suits you. Only it has
been these last weeks as if you wished — just in order
to please him — to remind him of it afresh. So there
it is," she wound up; "it's your doing. You've produced your effect — that of his wanting not to be,
even for a month or two, where you're not. He
doesn't want to bother or bore you — *that*, I think,
you know, he never has done; and if you'll only give
me time I'll come round again to making it my care,
as always, that he shan't. But he can't bear you out of
his sight."

She had kept it up and up, filling it out, crowding
it in; and all really without difficulty, for it was, every
word of it, thanks to a long evolution of feeling, what
she had been primed to the brim with. She made the
picture, forced it upon him, hung it before him; remembering happily how he had gone so far, one day,
supported by the Principino, as to propose the Zoo in
Eaton Square, to carry with him there, on the spot,
under this pleasant inspiration, both his elder and his
younger companion, with the latter of whom he had
taken the tone that they were introducing Granddaddy, Granddaddy nervous and rather funking it,
to lions and tigers more or less at large. Touch by
touch she thus dropped into her husband's silence the
truth about his good nature and his good manners;
and it was this demonstration of his virtue precisely
that added to the strangeness, even for herself, of her
failing as yet to yield to him. It would be a question
but of the most trivial act of surrender, the vibration
of a nerve, the mere movement of a muscle; but the

act grew important between them just through her
doing perceptibly nothing, nothing but talk in the
very tone that would naturally have swept her into
tenderness. She knew more and more — every lapsing minute taught her — how he might by a single
rightness make her cease to watch him; that rightness,
a million miles removed from the queer actual, falling
so short, which would consist of his breaking out to
her diviningly, indulgently, with the last happy inconsequence. "Come away with me somewhere, *you* —
and then we need n't think, we need n't even talk, of
anything, of any one else": five words like that would
answer her, would break her utterly down. But they
were the only ones that would so serve. She waited
for them, and there was a supreme instant when by
the testimony of all the rest of him she seemed to feel
them in his heart and on his lips; only they did n't
sound, and as that made her wait again so it made her
more intensely watch. This in turn showed her that
he too watched and waited, and how much he had
expected something that he now felt would n't come.
Yes, it would n't come if he did n't answer her, if he
but said the wrong things instead of the right. If he
could say the right everything would come — it hung
by a hair that everything might crystallise for their
recovered happiness at his touch. This possibility
glowed at her however for fifty seconds only then to
turn cold, and as it fell away from her she felt the chill
of reality and knew again, all but pressed to his heart
and with his breath upon her cheek, the slim rigour
of her attitude, a rigour beyond that of her natural
being. They at last had silences that were almost

crudities of mutual resistance — silences that persisted through his felt effort to treat her recurrence to the part he had lately played, to interpret all the sweetness of her so talking to him, as a manner of making love to him. Ah it was no such manner, heaven knew, for Maggie; she could make love, if this had been in question, better than that! On top of which it came to her presently to say, keeping in with what she had already spoken: "Except of course that, for the question of going off somewhere, he'd go readily, quite delightedly, with you. I verily believe he'd like to have you for a while to himself."

"Do you mean he thinks of proposing it?" the Prince after a moment sounded.

"Oh no — he does n't ask, as you must so often have seen. But I believe he'd go 'like a shot,' as you say, if you were to suggest it."

It had the air, she knew, of a kind of condition made, and she had asked herself while she spoke if it would n't cause his arm to let her go. The fact that it did n't suggested to her that she had made him of a sudden still more intensely think, think with such concentration that he could do but one thing at once. And it was precisely as if the concentration had the next moment been proved in him. He took a turn inconsistent with the superficial impression — a jump that made light of their approach to gravity and represented for her the need in him to gain time. This she made out was his drawback — that the warning from her had come to him and had come to Charlotte after all too suddenly. That they were in face of it rearranging, that they *had* to rearrange, was all before her again; yet to do as they would like they must enjoy a snatch, longer or shorter, of recovered independence. Amerigo was for the instant but doing as he *did n't* like, and it was as if she were watching his effort without disguise. "What's your father's idea this year then about Fawns? Will he go at Whitsuntide and will he then stay on?"

Maggie went through the form of thought. "He'll really do, I imagine, as he has in so many ways so often done before; do whatever may seem most agreeable to yourself. And there's of course always Charlotte to be considered. Only their going early to Fawns, if they do go," she said, "need n't in the least entail your and my going."

"Ah," Amerigo echoed, "it need n't in the least entail your and my going?"

"We can do as we like. What they may do need n't trouble us, since they're by good fortune perfectly happy together."

"Oh," the Prince returned, "your father's never so happy as with you near him to enjoy his being so."

"Well, I may enjoy it," said Maggie, "but I'm not the cause of it."

"You're the cause," her husband declared, "of the greater part of everything that's good among us." But she received this tribute in silence, and the next moment he pursued: "If Mrs. Verver has arrears of time with you to make up, as you say, she'll scarcely do it — or *you* scarcely will — by our cutting, your and my cutting, too loose."

"I see what you mean," Maggie mused.

He let her for a little give her attention to it; after

which, "Shall I just quite of a sudden," he asked, "propose him a journey?"

Maggie cast about her, but she brought forth the fruit of reflexion. "It would have the merit that Charlotte then *would* be with me — with me I mean so much more. Also that I should n't, by choosing such a time for going away, seem unconscious and ungrateful, seem not to respond, seem in fact rather to wish to shake her off. I should respond on the contrary most markedly — by being here alone with her for a month."

"And would you like to be here alone with her for a month?"

"I could do with it beautifully. Or we might even," she said quite gaily, "go together down to Fawns."

"You could be so very content without me?" the Prince presently threw out.

"Yes, my own dear — if you could be content for a while with father. That would keep me up. I might for the time," she went on, "go to stay there with Charlotte; or, better still, she might come to Portland Place."

"Oho!" said the Prince with cheerful vagueness.

"I should feel, you see," she continued, "that the two of us were showing the same sort of kindness."

Amerigo thought. "The two of us? Charlotte and I?"

Maggie again took a moment. "You and I, darling."

"I see, I see" — he promptly understood. "And what reason shall I give — give I mean your father?"

63

"For asking him to go off? Why the very simplest
— if you conscientiously can. The desire," said
Maggie, "to be agreeable to him. Just that only."

Something in this reply made her husband again
reflect. "'Conscientiously'? Why should n't I conscientiously? It would n't, by your own contention,"
he developed, "represent any surprise for him. I
must strike him sufficiently as, at the worst, the last
person in the world to wish to do anything to hurt
him."

Ah there it was again, for Maggie — the note
already sounded, the note of the felt need of not working harm! Why this precautionary view, she asked
herself afresh, when her father had complained, at the
very least, as little as herself? With their stillness
together so perfect, what had suggested so, around
them, the attitude of sparing them? Her inner vision
fixed it once more, this attitude, saw it in the others
as vivid and concrete, extended it straight from her
companion to Charlotte. Before she was well aware
accordingly she had echoed in this intensity of thought
Amerigo's last words. "You 're the last person in the
world to wish to do anything to hurt him."

She heard herself, heard her tone, after she had
spoken, and heard it the more that, for a minute after,
she felt her husband's eyes on her face, very close, too
close for her to see him. He was looking at her because he was struck, and looking hard — though his
answer when it came was straight enough. "Why
is n't that just what we 've been talking about —
that I 've affected you as fairly studying his comfort
and his pleasure? He might show his sense of it,"

the Prince went on, "by proposing to *me* an excursion."

"And you'd go with him?" Maggie immediately asked.

He hung fire but an instant. *"Per Dio!"*

She also had her pause, but she broke it — since gaiety was in the air — with an intense smile. "You can say that safely because the proposal's one that he won't make of his own motion."

She could n't have narrated afterwards — and in fact was at a loss to tell herself — by what transition, what rather marked abruptness of change in their personal relation, their drive came to its end with a kind of interval established, almost confessed to, between them. She felt it in the tone with which he repeated after her "'Safely' — ?"

"Safely as regards being thrown with him perhaps after all in such a case too long. He's a person to think you might easily feel yourself to be. So it won't," Maggie said, "come from father. He's too modest."

Their eyes continued to meet on it from corner to corner of the brougham. "Oh your modesty, between you — !" But he still smiled for it. "So that unless I insist — ?"

"We shall simply go on as we are."

"Well, we're going on beautifully," he answered — though by no means with the effect it would have had if their mute transaction, that of attempted capture and achieved escape, had n't taken place. As Maggie said nothing none the less to gainsay his remark, it was open to him to find himself the next moment conscious of still another idea. "I wonder if it *would* do. I mean for me to break in."

"'To break in' — ?"

"Between your father and his wife. But there would be a way," he said — "we can make Charlotte ask him." And then as Maggie herself now wondered, echoing it again: "We can suggest to her to suggest to him that he shall let me take him off."

"Oh!" said Maggie.

"Then if he asks her why I so suddenly break out she'll be able to tell him the reason."

They were stopping, and the footman, who had alighted, had rung at the house-door. "That you think it would be so charming?"

"That I think it would be so charming. That we've persuaded *her* will be convincing."

"I see," Maggie went on while the footman came back to let them out. "I see," she said again; though she felt a little disconcerted. What she really saw of a sudden was that her stepmother might report her as above all concerned for the proposal, and this brought her back her need that her father should n't think her concerned in any degree for anything. She alighted the next instant with a slight sense of defeat; her husband, to let her out, had passed before her and, a little in advance, awaited her on the edge of the low terrace, a step high, that preceded their open entrance, on either side of which one of their servants stood. The sense of a life tremendously ordered and fixed rose before her, and there was something in Amerigo's very face, while his eyes again met her own through the dusky lamplight, that was like a conscious reminder of it. He had answered her distinctly just before, and it appeared to leave her nothing to say. It was almost as if, having planned for the last word, she saw him himself enjoying it. It was almost as if — in the strangest way in the world — he were paying her back by the production of a small pang, that of a new uneasiness, for the way she had slipped from him during their drive.

IV

MAGGIE'S new uneasiness might have had time to drop, inasmuch as she not only was conscious, during several days that followed, of no fresh indication for it to feed on, but was even struck, in quite another way, with an augmentation of the symptoms of that difference she had taken it into her head to work for. She recognised by the end of a week that if she had been in a manner caught up her father had been not less so — with the effect of her husband's and his wife's closing in together round them and of their all having suddenly begun, as a party of four, to lead a life gregarious, and from that reason almost hilarious, so far as the easy sound of it went, as never before. It might have been an accident and a mere coincidence — so at least she said to herself at first; but a dozen chances that furthered the whole appearance had risen to the surface, pleasant pretexts, oh certainly pleasant, as pleasant as Amerigo in particular could make them, for associated undertakings, quite for shared adventures, for its always turning out amusingly that they wanted to do very much the same thing at the same time and in the same way. Funny all this was, to some extent, in the light of the fact that the father and daughter, for so long, had expressed so few positive desires; yet it would be sufficiently natural that if Amerigo and Charlotte *had* at last got a little tired of each other's company they should find their relief not

so much in sinking to the rather low level of their
companions as in wishing to pull the latter into the
train in which they so constantly moved. "We're in
the train," Maggie mutely reflected after the dinner
in Eaton Square with Lady Castledean; "we've suddenly waked up in it and found ourselves rushing
along very much as if we had been put in during sleep
— shoved like a pair of labelled boxes into the van.
And since I wanted to 'go' I'm certainly going," she
might have added; "I'm moving without trouble —
they're doing it all for us: it's wonderful how they
understand and how perfectly it succeeds." For that
was the thing she had most immediately to acknowledge: it seemed as easy for them to make a quartette
as it had formerly so long appeared for them to make
a pair of couples — this latter being thus a discovery
too absurdly belated. The only point at which day
after day the success appeared at all qualified was
represented, as might have been said, by her irresistible impulse to give her father a clutch when the train
indulged in one of its occasional lurches. Then —
there was no denying it — his eyes and her own met;
so that they were themselves doing active violence, as
against the others, to that very spirit of union, or at
least to that very achievement of change, which she
had taken the field to invoke.

The maximum of change was reached no doubt the
day the Matcham party dined in Portland Place; the
day really perhaps of Maggie's maximum of social
glory, in the sense of its showing for her own occasion,
her very own, with every one else extravagantly rally-
ing and falling in, absolutely conspiring to make her

its heroine. It was as if her father himself, always with more initiative as a guest than as a host, had dabbled too in the conspiracy; and the impression was not the more vague for the presence of the Assinghams, likewise very much caught-up now, after something of a lull, by the side-wind of all the rest of the motion, and giving our young woman, so far at least as Fanny was concerned, the sense of some special intention of encouragement and applause. Fanny, who had n't been present at the other dinner, thanks to a preference entertained and expressed by Charlotte, made a splendid show at this one in new orange-coloured velvet with multiplied turquoises, not less than with a confidence as different as possible, her hostess inferred, from her too-marked betrayal of a belittled state at Matcham. Maggie was not indifferent to her own opportunity to redress this balance — which seemed for the hour part of a general rectification; she liked making out for herself that on the high level of Portland Place, a spot exempt on all sorts of grounds from jealous jurisdictions, her friend could feel as "good" as any one and could in fact at moments almost appear to take the lead in recognition and celebration, so far as the evening might conduce to intensify the lustre of the little Princess. Mrs. Assingham produced on her the impression of giving her constantly her cue for this; and it was in truth partly by her help, intelligently, quite gratefully accepted, that the little Princess in Maggie was drawn out and emphasised. She could n't definitely have said how it happened, but she felt herself for the first time in her career living up to the public and popular notion of such a personage, as it pressed upon her from all round; rather wondering inwardly too while she did so at that strange mixture in things through which the popular notion could be evidenced for her by such supposedly great ones of the earth as the Castledeans and their kind. Fanny Assingham might really have been there at all events, like one of the assistants in the ring at the circus, to keep up the pace of the sleek revolving animal on whose back the lady in short spangled skirts should brilliantly caper and posture. That was all, doubtless: Maggie had forgotten, had neglected, had declined, to be the little Princess on anything like the scale open to her; but now that the collective hand had been held out to her with such alacrity, so that she might skip up into the light even, as seemed to her modest mind, with such a show of pink stocking and such an abbreviation of white petticoat, she could strike herself as perceiving, under arched eyebrows, where her mistake had been. She had invited for the later hours after her dinner a fresh contingent, the whole list of her apparent London acquaintance — which was again a thing in the manner of little princesses for whom the princely art was a matter of course. That was what she was learning to do, to fill out as a matter of course her appointed, her expected, her imposed character; and, though there were latent considerations that somewhat interfered with the lesson, she was having to-night an inordinate quantity of practice, none of it so successful as when, quite wittingly, she directed it at Lady Castledean, who was reduced by it at last to an unprecedented state of passivity. The perception of this high result

71

caused Mrs. Assingham fairly to flush with responsive joy; she glittered at her young friend from moment to moment quite feverishly; it was positively as
if her young friend had in some marvellous sudden
supersubtle way become a source of succour to herself,
become beautifully divinely retributive. The intensity
of the taste of these registered phenomena was in fact
that somehow, by a process and through a connexion
not again to be traced, she so practised at the same
time on Amerigo and Charlotte — with only the
drawback, her constant check and second-thought,
that she concomitantly practised perhaps still more
on her father.

This last was a danger indeed that for much of the
ensuing time had its hours of strange beguilement —
those at which her sense for precautions so suffered
itself to lapse that she felt her communion with him
more intimate than any other. It *could n't* but pass
between them that something singular was happening
— so much as this she again and again said to herself;
whereby the comfort of it was there after all to be
noted just as much as the possible peril, and she could
think of the couple they formed together as groping,
with sealed lips but with mutual looks that had never
been so tender, for some freedom, some fiction, some
figured bravery, under which they might safely talk of
it. The moment was to come — and it finally came
with an effect as penetrating as the sound that follows
the pressure of an electric button — when she read the
least helpful of meanings into the agitation she had
created. The merely specious description of their case
would have been that, after being for a long time, as

a family, delightfully, uninterruptedly happy, they
had still had a new felicity to discover; a felicity for
which, blessedly, her father's appetite and her own in
particular had been kept fresh and grateful. This
livelier march of their intercourse as a whole was the
thing that occasionally determined in him the clutching instinct we have glanced at; very much as if he had
said to her in default of her breaking silence first:
"Everything's remarkably pleasant, is n't it? — but
where for it after all are we? up in a balloon and
whirling through space or down in the depths of the
earth, in the glimmering passages of a gold-mine?"
The equilibrium, the precious condition, lasted in
spite of rearrangement; there had been a fresh dis-
tribution of the different weights, but the balance
persisted and triumphed: all of which was just the
reason why she was forbidden, face to face with the
companion of her adventure, the experiment of a test.
If they balanced they balanced — she had to take
that; it deprived her of every pretext for arriving,
by however covert a process, at what he thought.

But she had her hours thus of feeling supremely
linked to him by the rigour of their law, and when it
came over her that all the while the wish on his side
to spare her might be what most worked with him, this
very fact of their seeming to have nothing "inward"
really to talk about wrapped him up for her in a kind
of sweetness that was wanting, as a consecration, even
in her yearning for her husband. She was powerless
however, was only more utterly hushed, when the interrupting flash came, when she would have been all
ready to say to him: "Yes, this is by every appearance

the best time we've had yet; but don't you see all the same how they must be working together for it and how my very success, my success in shifting our beautiful harmony to a new basis, comes round to being *their* success, above all; their cleverness, their amiability, their power to hold out, their complete possession in short of our life?" For how could she say as much as that without saying a great deal more? without saying "They'll do everything in the world that suits us, save only one thing — prescribe a line for us that will make them separate." How could she so much as imagine herself even faintly murmuring that without putting into his mouth the very words that would have made her quail? "Separate, my dear? Do you want them to separate? Then you want *us* to — you and me? For how can the one separation take place without the other?" That was the question that in spirit she had heard him ask — with its dread train moreover of involved and connected enquiries. Their own separation, his and hers, was of course perfectly thinkable, but only on the basis of the sharpest of reasons. Well, the sharpest, the very sharpest would be that they could no longer afford, as it were, he to let his wife, she to let her husband, "run" them in such compact formation. And say they accepted this account of their situation as a practical finality, acting upon it and proceeding to a division, would no sombre ghosts of the smothered past on either side show across the widening strait pale unappeased faces, or raise in the very passage deprecating denouncing hands?

Meanwhile, however such things might be, she was

to have occasion to say to herself that a deeper
treachery would perhaps lurk in recoveries and re-
assurances. She was to feel alone again, as she had
felt at the issue of her high tension with her husband
during their return from meeting the Castledeans in
Eaton Square. The evening in question had left her
with a larger alarm, but then a lull had come — the
alarm after all was yet to be confirmed. There came an
hour inevitably when she knew with a chill what she
had feared and why; it had taken, this hour, a month
to arrive, but to find it before her was thoroughly to
recognise it, for it showed her sharply what Amerigo
had meant in alluding to a particular use that they
might make of Charlotte for their reaffirmed harmony and prosperity. The more she thought, at present, of the tone he had employed to express their enjoyment of this resource, the more it came back to her
as the product of a conscious art of dealing with her.
He had been conscious at the moment of many things
— conscious even not a little of desiring and thereby
of needing to see what she would do in a given case.
The given case would be that of her being to a certain
extent, as she might fairly make it out, *menaced* —
horrible as it was to impute to him any intention represented by such a word. Why it was that to speak
of making her stepmother intervene, as they might
call it, in a question that seemed just then and there
quite peculiarly their own business — why it was that
a turn so familiar and so easy should at the worst
strike her as charged with the spirit of a threat, was
an oddity disconnected for her temporarily from its
grounds, the adventure of an imagination within her

75

that possibly had lost its way. That precisely was
doubtless why she had learned to wait, as the weeks
passed by, with a fair, or rather indeed with an excessive, imitation of resumed serenity. There had been
no prompt sequel to the Prince's equivocal light, and
that made for patience; yet she was none the less to
have to admit after many days that the bread he had
cast on the waters had come home and that she should
thus be justified of her old apprehension. The consequence of this in turn was a renewed pang in presence of his remembered ingenuity. To be ingenious
with *her*—what *did n't*, what might n't that mean when
she had so absolutely never at any point of contact
with him put him by as much as the value of a penny
to the expense of sparing, doubting, fearing her, of
having in any way whatever to reckon with her? The
ingenuity had been in his simply speaking of their
use of Charlotte as if it were common to them in an
equal degree, and his triumph on the occasion had
been just in the simplicity. She could n't — and he
knew it — say what was true: "Oh you 'use' her, and
I use her, if you will, yes; but we use her ever so differently and separately — not at all in the same way
or degree. There's nobody we really use together but
ourselves, don't you see? — by which I mean that
where our interests are the same I can so beautifully,
so exquisitely serve you for everything, and you can so
beautifully, so exquisitely serve me. The only person
either of us needs is the other of us; so why as a matter of course in such a case as this drag in Charlotte?"

She could n't so challenge him because it would
have been — and there she was paralysed — the *note*.

76

It would have translated itself on the spot for his ear
into jealousy, and from reverberation to repercussion
would have reached her father's exactly in the form of
a cry piercing the stillness of peaceful sleep. It had
been for many days almost as difficult for her to catch
a quiet twenty minutes with her father as it had formerly been easy; there had been in fact of old — the
time, so strangely, seemed already far away — an inevitability in her longer passages with him, a sort of
domesticated beauty in the calculability round about
them of everything. But at present Charlotte was
almost always there when Amerigo brought her to
Eaton Square, where Amerigo was constantly bringing her; and Amerigo was almost always there when
Charlotte brought her husband to. Portland Place,
where Charlotte was constantly bringing *him*. The
fractions of occasions, the chance minutes that put
them face to face, had as yet of late contrived to count
but little between them either for the sense of opportunity or for that of exposure, inasmuch as the life-
long rhythm of their intercourse made against all cur-
sory handling of deep things. They had never availed
themselves of any given quarter of an hour to gossip
about fundamentals; they moved slowly through
large still space; they could be silent together, at any
time, beautifully, with much more comfort than hur-
riedly expressive. It appeared indeed to have become
true that their common appeal measured itself for
vividness just by this economy of sound; they might
have been talking "at" each other when they talked
with their companions, but these latter were assuredly
not in any directer way to gain light on the current

phase of their relation. Such were some of the reasons for which Maggie suspected fundamentals, as I have called them, to be rising, by a new movement, to the surface — suspected it one morning late in May, when her father presented himself in Portland Place alone. He had his pretext — of that she was fully aware: the Principino, two days before, had shown signs, happily not persistent, of a feverish cold and had notoriously been obliged to spend the interval at home. This was ground, ample ground, for punctual enquiry; but what it wasn't ground for, she quickly found herself reflecting, was his having managed in the interest of his visit to dispense so unwontedly — as their life had recently come to be arranged — with his wife's attendance. It had so happened that she herself was for the hour exempt from her husband's, and it will at once be seen that the hour had a quality all its own when I note that, remembering how the Prince had looked in to say he was going out, the Princess whimsically wondered if their respective *sposi* might n't frankly be meeting, whimsically hoped indeed they were temporarily so disposed of. Strange was her need at moments to think of them as not attaching an excessive importance to their repudiation of the general practice that had rested only a few weeks before on such a consecrated rightness. Repudiations surely were not in the air — they had none of them come to that; for was n't she at this minute testifying directly against them by her own behaviour? When she should confess to fear of being alone with her father, to fear of what he might then — ah with such a slow painful motion as she had a

78

horror of!—say to her, *then* would be time enough
for Amerigo and Charlotte to confess to not liking to
appear to foregather.

She had this morning a wonderful consciousness
both of dreading a particular question from him and
of being able to check, yes even to disconcert magnificently by her apparent manner of receiving it, any
restless imagination he might have about its importance. The day, bright and soft, had the breath of
summer; it made them talk, to begin with, of Fawns,
of the way Fawns invited — Maggie aware the while
that in thus regarding with him the sweetness of its
invitation to one couple just as much as to another
her humbugging smile grew very nearly convulsive.
That was it, and there was truly relief of a sort in
taking it in: she was humbugging him already, by absolute necessity, as she had never never done in her
life — doing it up to the full height of what she had
allowed for. The necessity, in the great dimly-shining
room where, declining for his reasons to sit down, he
moved about in Amerigo's very footsteps, the necessity affected her as pressing upon her with the very
force of the charm itself; of the old pleasantness
between them so candidly playing up there again; of
the positive flatness of their tenderness, a surface all
for familiar use, quite as if generalised from the long
succession of tapestried sofas, sweetly faded, on which
his theory of contentment had sat, through unmeas-
ured pauses, beside her own. She *knew* from this instant, knew in advance and as well as anything would
ever teach her, that she must never intermit for a soli-
tary second her so highly undertaking to prove there

79

was nothing the matter with her. She of a sudden saw everything she might say or do in the light of that undertaking, established connexions from it with any number of remote matters, struck herself for instance as acting all in its interest when she proposed their going out, in the exercise of their freedom and in homage to the season, for a turn in the Regent's Park. This resort was close at hand, at the top of Portland Place, and the Principino, beautifully better, had already proceeded there under high attendance: all of which considerations were defensive for Maggie, all of which became to her mind part of the business of cultivating continuity.

Upstairs, while she left him to put on something to go out in, the thought of his waiting below for her, in possession of the empty house, brought with it, sharply if briefly, one of her abrupt arrests of consistency, the brush of a vain imagination almost paralysing her often for the minute before her glass — the vivid look, in other words, of the particular difference his marriage had made. The particular difference seemed at such instants the loss, more than anything else, of their old freedom, their never having had to think, where they were together concerned, of any one, of anything but each other. It had n't been *her* marriage that did it; that had never, for three seconds, suggested to either of them that they must act diplomatically, must reckon with another presence — no, not even with her husband's. She groaned to herself while the vain imagination lasted, "*Why* did he marry ? ah why *did* he ?" and then it came up to her more than ever that nothing could have been more

beautiful than the way in which, till Charlotte came
so much more closely into their life, Amerigo had n't
interfered. What she had gone on owing him for this
mounted up again to her eyes like a column of figures
— or call it even if one would a house of cards: it was
her father's wonderful act that had tipped the house
down and made the sum wrong. With all of which,
immediately after her question, her "Why did he,
why did he?" rushed back inevitably the confound-
ing, the overwhelming wave of the knowledge of his
reason. "He did it for *me*, he did it for me," she
moaned, "he did it exactly that our freedom — meaning, beloved man, simply and solely mine — should be
greater instead of less; he did it, divinely, to liberate
me so far as possible from caring what became of
him." She found time upstairs, even in her haste, as
she had repeatedly found time before, to let the wonderments involved in these recognitions flash at her
with their customary effect of making her blink: the
question in especial of whether she might find her
solution in acting, herself, in the spirit of what he
had done, in forcing her "care" really to grow as
much less as he had tried to make it. Thus she felt
the whole weight of their case drop afresh upon her
shoulders, was confronted unmistakeably with the
prime source of her haunted state. It all came from
her not having been able not to mind — not to mind
what became of him; not having been able, without
anxiety, to let him go his way and take his risk and
lead his life. She had made anxiety her stupid little
idol; and absolutely now, while she stuck a long pin
a trifle fallaciously into her hat — she had, with an

approach to irritation, told her maid, a new woman whom she had lately found herself thinking of as abysmal, that she did n't want her — she tried to focus the possibility of some understanding between them in consequence of which he should cut loose.

Very near indeed it looked, any such possibility! — that consciousness too had taken its turn by the time she was ready; all the vibration, all the emotion of this present passage being precisely in the very sweetness of their lapse back into the conditions of the simpler time, into a queer resemblance between the aspect and the feeling of the moment and those of numberless other moments that were sufficiently far away. She had been quick in her preparation, in spite of the flow of the tide that sometimes took away her breath; but a pause once more was still left for her to make, a pause, at the top of the stairs, before she came down to him, in the span of which she asked herself if it were n't thinkable, from the perfectly practical point of view, that she should simply sacrifice him. She did n't go into the detail of what sacrificing him would mean — she did n't need to; so distinct was it, in one of her restless lights, that there he was awaiting her, that she should find him walking up and down the drawing-room in the warm fragrant air to which the open windows and the abundant flowers contributed; slowly and vaguely moving there and looking very slight and young and superficially manageable, almost as much like her child, putting it a little freely, as like her parent; with the appearance about him above all of having perhaps arrived just on purpose to *say* it to her himself in so many words: "Sacrifice

me, my own love; do sacrifice me, do sacrifice me!"
Should she want to, should she insist on it, she might
verily hear him bleating it at her, all conscious and
all accommodating, like some precious spotless ex-
ceptionally intelligent lamb. The positive effect of the
intensity of this figure however was to make her shake
it away in her resumed descent; and after she had
rejoined him, after she had picked him up, she was to
know the full pang of the thought that her impossibility was *made*, absolutely, by his consciousness, by
the lucidity of his intention: this she felt while she
smiled there for him again all hypocritically; while
she drew on fair fresh gloves; while she interrupted
the process first to give his necktie a slightly smarter
twist and then to make up to him for her hidden madness by rubbing her nose into his cheek according to
the tradition of their frankest levity. From the instant she should be able to convict him of intending,
every issue would be closed and her hypocrisy would
have to redouble. The only way to sacrifice him would
be to do so without his dreaming what it might be
for. She kissed him, she arranged his cravat, she
dropped remarks, she guided him out, she held his
arm, not to be led, but to lead him, and taking it
to her by much the same intimate pressure she had
always used, when a little girl, to mark the insepar-
ability of her doll — she did all these things so that he
should sufficiently fail to dream of what they might
be for.

V

THERE was nothing to show that her effort in any degree fell short till they got well into the Park and he struck her as giving, unexpectedly, the go-by to any serious search for the Principino. The way they sat down a while in the sun was a sign of that; his dropping with her into the first pair of sequestered chairs they came across and waiting a little, after they were placed, as if now at last she might bring out, as between them, something more specific. It made her but feel the more sharply how the specific, in almost any direction, was utterly forbidden her — how the use of it would be, for all the world, like undoing the leash of a dog eager to follow up a scent. It would come out, the specific, where the dog would come out; would run to earth somehow the truth — for she was believing herself in relation to the truth! — at which she must n't so much as indirectly point. Such at any rate was the fashion in which her passionate prudence played over possibilities of danger, reading symptoms and betrayals into everything she looked at and yet having to make it evident even while she recognised them that she did n't wince. There were moments between them, in their chairs, when he might have been watching her guard herself and trying to think of something new that would trip her up. There were pauses during which, with her affection as sweet and still as the sunshine, she might yet, as at some hard game over a

table for money, have been defying him to fasten on
her the least little complication of consciousness. She
was afterwards positively proud of the great style in
which she had kept this up; later on, at the hour's end,
when they had retraced their steps to find Amerigo
and Charlotte awaiting them at the house, she was
able to say to herself that truly she had put her plan
through; even though once more setting herself the
difficult task of making their relation, every minute
of the time, not fall below the standard of that other
hour in the treasured past which hung there behind
them like a framed picture in a museum, a high-water-
mark for the history of their old fortune; the summer
evening in the park at Fawns, when, side by side under
the trees just as now, they had let their happy confidence lull them with its most golden tone. There had
been the possibility of a trap for her at present in the
very question of their taking up anew that residence;
wherefore she had n't been the first to sound it, in
spite of the impression from him of his holding off to
see what she would do. She was saying to herself in
secret: "*Can* we again, in this form, migrate there?
Can I, for myself, undertake it? face all the intenser
keeping-up and stretching-out, indefinitely, impossibly,
that our conditions in the country, as we've established and accepted them, would stand for?" She had
positively lost herself in this inward doubt — so much
she was subsequently to remember; but remembering
then too that her companion, though perceptibly perhaps as if not to be eager, had broken the ice very
much as he had broken it in Eaton Square after the
banquet to the Castledeans.

Her mind had taken a long excursion, wandered far into the vision of what a summer at Fawns, with Amerigo and Charlotte still more eminently in presence against that higher sky, would bring forth. Was n't her father meanwhile only pretending to talk of it ? just as she was in a manner pretending to listen ? He got off it finally, at all events, for the transition it could n't well help thrusting out at him; it had amounted exactly to an arrest of her private excursion by the sense that he had begun to *imitate* — oh as never yet! — the ancient tone of gold. It had verily come from him at last, the question of whether she thought it would be *very* good — but very good indeed — that he should leave England for a series of weeks on some pretext with the Prince. Then it had been that she was to know her husband's "menace" had n't really dropped, since she was face to face with the effect of it. Ah the effect of it had occupied all the rest of their walk, had stayed out with them and come home with them, besides making it impossible that they should n't presently feign to recollect how rejoining the child had been their original purpose. Maggie's uneffaced note was that it had, at the end of five minutes more, driven them to that endeavour as to a refuge, and caused them afterwards to rejoice, as well, that the boy's irrepressibly importunate company, in due course secured and enjoyed, with the extension imparted by his governess, a person expectant of consideration, constituted a cover for any awkwardness. For that was what it had all come to, that the dear man had spoken to her to *try* her — quite as he had been spoken to himself by Charlotte with the same

86

fine idea. The Princess took it in on the spot, firmly grasping it; she heard them together, her father and his wife, dealing with the queer case. "The Prince tells me that Maggie has a plan for your taking some foreign journey with him, and as he likes to do everything she wants he has suggested my speaking to you for it as the thing most likely to make you consent. So I do speak — see? — being always so eager myself, as you know, to meet Maggie's wishes. I speak, but without quite understanding this time what she has in her head. Why *should* she of a sudden at this particular moment desire to ship you off together and remain here alone with me? The compliment's all to me, I admit, and you must decide quite as you like. The Prince is quite ready, evidently, to do his part — but you'll have it out with him. That is you'll have it out with *her*." Something of that kind was what, in her mind's ear, Maggie heard — and this, after his waiting for her to appeal to him directly, was her father's invitation to her to have it out. Well, as she could say to herself all the rest of the day, that was what they did while they continued to sit there in their penny chairs, that was what they *had* done as much as they would now ever, ever, have out anything. The measure of this at least had been given, that each would fight to the last for the protection, for the perversion, of any real anxiety. She had confessed instantly, with her humbugging grin, not flinching by a hair, meeting his eyes as mildly as he met hers, she had confessed to her fancy that they might both, he and his son-in-law, have welcomed such an escapade, since they had both been so long so furiously domestic.

She had almost cocked her hat under the inspiration of this opportunity to hint how a couple of spirited young men, reacting from confinement and sallying forth arm-in-arm, might encounter the agreeable in forms that would strike them for the time at least as novel. She had felt for fifty seconds, with her eyes all so sweetly and falsely in her companion's, horribly vulgar; yet without minding it either — such luck should she have if to be nothing worse than horribly vulgar would see her through. "And I thought Amerigo might like it better," she had said, "than wandering off alone."

"Do you mean that he won't go unless I take him?"

She had considered here, and never in her life had she considered so promptly and so intently. If she really put it that way her husband, challenged, might belie the statement; so that what would *that* do but make her father wonder, make him perhaps ask straight out, why she was exerting pressure? She could n't of course afford to be suspected for an instant of exerting pressure; which was why she was obliged only to make answer: "Would n't that be just what you must have out with *him?*"

"Decidedly — if he makes me the proposal. But he has n't made it yet."

Oh once more how she was to feel she had smirked! "Perhaps he's too shy!"

"Because you're so sure he so really wants my company?"

"I think he has thought you might like it."

"Well, I should —!" But with this he looked away from her, and she held her breath to hear him either ask if she wished him to address the question to Amerigo straight, or enquire if she should be greatly disappointed by his letting it drop. What had "settled" her, as she was privately to call it, was that he had done neither of these things, and had thereby markedly stood off from the risk involved in trying to draw out her reason. To attenuate on the other hand this appearance, and quite as if to fill out the too large receptacle made so musingly by his abstention, he had himself presently given her a reason — had positively spared her the effort of asking whether he judged Charlotte not to have approved. He had taken everything on himself — *that* was what had settled her. She had had to wait very little more to feel with this how much he was taking. The point he made was his lack of any eagerness to put time and space, on any such scale, between himself and his wife. He was n't so unhappy with her — far from it, and Maggie was to hold that he had grinned back, paternally, through his rather shielding glasses, in easy emphasis of this — as to be able to hint that he required the relief of absence. Therefore unless it was for the Prince himself —!

"Oh I don't think it would have been for Amerigo himself. Amerigo and I," Maggie had said, "perfectly rub on together."

"Well then there we are."

"I see" — and she had again with sublime blandness assented. "There we are."

"Charlotte and I too," her father had gaily proceeded, "perfectly rub on together." With which he had appeared for a little to be making time. "To put it only so," he had mildly and happily added — "to

89

put it only so!" He had spoken as if he might easily put it much better, yet as if the humour of contented understatement fairly sufficed for the occasion. He had played then either all consciously or all unconsciously into Charlotte's hands; and the effect of this was to render trebly oppressive Maggie's conviction of Charlotte's plan. She had done what she wanted, his wife had — which was also what Amerigo had made her do. She had kept her test, Maggie's test, from becoming possible, and had applied instead a test of her own. It was exactly as if she had known her stepdaughter would fear to be summoned to say, under the least approach to cross-examination, why any change was desirable; and it was for our young woman herself, still more prodigiously, as if her father had been capable of calculations to match, of judging it important that he should n't be brought to demand of her what was the matter with her. Why otherwise, with such an opportunity, had n't he demanded it? Always from calculation — that was why, that was why. He was terrified of the retort he might have invoked: "What, my dear, if you come to that, is the matter with *you?*" When a minute later on he had followed up his last note by a touch or two designed still further to conjure away the ghost of the anomalous, at that climax verily she would have had to be dumb to the question. "There seems a kind of charm, does n't there? on our life — and quite as if just lately it had got itself somehow renewed, had waked up refreshed. A kind of wicked selfish prosperity perhaps, as if we had grabbed everything, fixed everything, down to the last lovely object for the last glass case of the last corner, left over, of my old show. That's the only take-off, that it has made us perhaps lazy, a wee bit languid — lying like gods together, all careless of mankind."

"Do you consider that we're languid?" — that form of rejoinder she had jumped at for the sake of its pretty lightness. "Do you consider that we're careless of mankind? — living as we do in the biggest crowd in the world and running about always pursued and pursuing."

It had made him think indeed a little longer than she had meant; but he came up again, as she might have said, smiling. "Well, I don't know. We get nothing but the fun, do we?"

"No," she had hastened to declare; "we certainly get nothing but the fun."

"We do it all," he had remarked, "so beautifully."

"We do it all so beautifully." She had n't denied this for a moment. "I see what you mean."

"Well, I mean too," he had gone on, "that we have n't no doubt enough the sense of difficulty."

"Enough? Enough for what?"

"Enough not to be selfish."

"I don't think *you* are selfish," she had returned — and had managed not to wail it.

"I don't say it's me particularly — or that it's you or Charlotte or Amerigo. But we're selfish together — we move as a selfish mass. You see we want always the same thing," he had gone on — "and that holds us, that binds us, together. We want each other," he had further explained; "only wanting it, each time, *for* each other. That's what I call the happy spell; but it's also a little — possibly — the immorality."

"'The immorality'?" she had pleasantly echoed.

"Well, we're tremendously moral for ourselves — that is for each other; and I won't pretend that I know exactly at whose particular personal expense you and I for instance are happy. What it comes to, I dare say, is that there's something haunting — as if it were a bit uncanny — in such a consciousness of our general comfort and privilege. Unless indeed," he had rambled on, "it's only I to whom, fantastically, it says so much. That's all I mean at any rate — that it's 'sort of' soothing; as if we were sitting about on divans, with pigtails, smoking opium and seeing visions. 'Let us then be up and doing' — what is it Longfellow says? That seems sometimes to ring out; like the police breaking in — into our opium-den — to give us a shake. But the beauty of it is at the same time that we *are* doing; we're doing, that is, after all, what we went in for. We're working it, our life, our chance, whatever you may call it, as we saw it, as we felt it, from the first. We *have* worked it, and what more can you do than that? It's a good deal for me," he had wound up, "to have made Charlotte so happy — to have so perfectly contented her. *You*, from a good way back, were a matter of course — I mean your being all right; so I need n't mind your knowing that my great interest since then has rather inevitably been in making sure of the same success, very much to your advantage as well, for Charlotte. If we've worked our life, our idea really, as I say — if at any rate I can sit here and say that I've worked my share of it — it has

not been what you may call least by our having put
Charlotte so at her ease. *That* has been soothing, all
round; that has curled up as the biggest of the blue
fumes, or whatever they are, of the opium. Don't you
see what a cropper we would have come if she *had n't*
settled down as she has?" And he had concluded by
turning to Maggie as for something she might n't
really have thought of. "You, darling, in that case,
I verily believe, would have been the one to hate it
most."

"To hate it —?" Maggie had invoked vagueness.

"To hate our having, with our tremendous intentions, *not* brought it off. And I dare say I should have
hated it for you even more than for myself."

"That's not unlikely perhaps when it was for me,
after all, that you did it."

He had hesitated, but only a moment. "I never
told you so."

"Well, Charlotte herself soon enough told me."

"But I never told *her*," her father had answered.

"Are you very sure?" she had presently asked.

"Well, I like to think how thoroughly I was taken
with her, and how right I was, and how fortunate,
to have that for my basis. I told her all the good
I thought of her."

"Then that," Maggie had returned, "was precisely
part of the good. I mean it was precisely part of it
that she could so beautifully understand."

"Yes — understand everything."

"Everything — and in particular your reasons.
Her telling me — that showed me how she had understood."

They were face to face again now, and she saw she had made his colour rise; it was as if he were still finding in her eyes the concrete image, the enacted scene, of her passage with Charlotte, which he was actually hearing of for the first time and as to which it would have been natural he should question her further. His forbearance to do so would but mark precisely the complication of his fears. "What she does like," he finally said, "is the way it has succeeded."

"Your marriage?"

"Yes — my whole idea. The way I've been justified. That's the joy I give her. If for *her* either it had failed —!" That however wasn't worth talking about; he had broken off. "You think then you could now risk Fawns?"

"'Risk' it?"

"Well, morally — from the point of view I was talking of; that of our sinking deeper into sloth. Our selfishness somehow seems at its biggest down there."

Maggie had allowed him the amusement of her not taking this up. "Is Charlotte," she had simply asked, "really ready?"

"Oh if you and I and Amerigo are. Whenever one corners Charlotte," he had developed more at his ease, "one finds that she only wants to know what *we* want. Which is what we got her for!"

"What we got her for — exactly!" And so for a little, even though with a certain effect of oddity in their more or less successful ease, they left it; left it till Maggie made the remark that it was all the same wonderful her stepmother should be willing, before the season was out, to exchange so much company for so much comparative solitude.

"Ah," he had then made answer, "that's because her idea, I think, this time, is that we shall have more people, more than we've hitherto had, in the country. Don't you remember that *that*, originally, was what we were to get her for?"

"Oh yes — to give us a life." Maggie had gone through the form of recalling this, and the light of their ancient candour, shining from so far back, had seemed to bring out some things so strangely that, with the sharpness of the vision, she had risen to her feet. "Well, with a 'life' Fawns will certainly do." He had remained in his place while she looked over his head; the picture, in her vision, had suddenly swarmed. The vibration was that of one of the lurches of the mystic train in which, with her companion, she was travelling; but she was having to steady herself this time before meeting his eyes. She had measured indeed the full difference between the move to Fawns because each of them now knew the others wanted it and the pairing-off, for a journey, of her husband and her father, which nobody knew that either wanted. "More company" at Fawns would be effectually enough the key in which her husband and her stepmother were at work; there was truly no question but that she and her father must accept any array of visitors. No one could try to marry him now. What he had just said was a direct plea for that, and what was the plea itself but an act of submission to Charlotte? He had, from his chair, been noting her look, but he had the next minute also risen, and then

95

it was they had reminded each other of their having come out for the boy. Their junction with him and with his companion successfully effected, the four had moved home more slowly and still more vaguely; yet with a vagueness that permitted of Maggie's reverting an instant to the larger issue. "If we have people in the country then, as you were saying, do you know for whom my first fancy would be? You may be amused, but it would be for the Castledeans."

"I see. But why should I be amused?"

"Well, I mean I am myself. I don't think I like her — and yet I like to see her: which, as Amerigo says, is 'rum.'"

"But don't you feel she's very handsome?" her father enquired.

"Yes, but it is n't for that."

"Then what is it for?"

"Simply that she may be *there* — just there before us. It's as if she may have a value — as if something may come of her. I don't in the least know what, and she rather irritates me meanwhile. I don't even know, I admit, why — but if we see her often enough I may find out."

"Does it matter so very much?" her companion had asked while they moved together.

She had hesitated. "You mean because you do rather like her?"

He on his side too had waited a little, but then he had taken it from her. "Yes, I guess I do rather like her."

Which she accepted for the first case she could recall of their not being affected by a person in the same way. It came back therefore to his pretending; but she had gone far enough, and to add to her appearance of levity she further observed that though they were so far from a novelty she should also immediately desire at Fawns the presence of the Assinghams. That put everything on a basis independent of explanations; yet it was extraordinary at the same time how much, once in the country again with the others, she was going, as they used to say at home, to need the presence of the good Fanny. It was the strangest thing in the world, but it was as if Mrs. Assingham might in a manner mitigate the intensity of her consciousness of Charlotte. It was as if the two would balance, one against the other; as if it came round again in that fashion to her idea of the equilibrium. It would be like putting this friend into her scale to make weight — into the scale with her father and herself. Amerigo and Charlotte would be in the other; therefore it would take the three of them to keep that one straight. And as this played all duskily in her mind it had received from her father, with a sound of suddenness, a luminous contribution. "Ah rather! *Do* let's have the Assinghams."

"It would be to have them," she had said, "as we used so much to have them. For a good long stay in the old way and on the old terms: 'as regular boarders' Fanny used to call it. That is if they'll come."

"As regular boarders on the old terms — that's what I should like too. But I guess they'll come," her companion had added in a tone into which she had read meanings. The main meaning was that he felt he was going to require them quite as much as she was. His recognition of the new terms as different from the old, what was that practically but a confession that something had happened, and a perception that, interested in the situation she had helped to create, Mrs. Assingham would be by so much as this concerned in its inevitable development ? It amounted to an intimation, off his guard, that he should be thankful for some one to turn to. If she had wished covertly to sound him he had now in short quite given himself away, and if she had even at the start needed anything more to settle her here assuredly was enough. He had hold of his small grandchild as they retraced their steps, swinging the boy's hand and not bored, as he never was, by his always bristling, like a fat little porcupine, with shrill interrogation-points — so that, secretly, while they went, she had wondered again if the equilibrium might n't have been more real, might n't above all have demanded less strange a study, had it only been on the books that Charlotte should give him a Principino of his own. She had repossessed herself now of his other arm, only this time she was drawing him back, gently, helplessly back to what they had tried for the hour to get away from — just as he was consciously drawing the child and as high Miss Bogle on her left, representing the duties of home, was complacently drawing *her*. The duties of home, when the house in Portland Place reappeared, showed even from a distance as vividly there before them. Amerigo and Charlotte had come in — that is Amerigo had, Charlotte rather having come out — and the pair were perched together in the balcony, he bareheaded, she divested of her jacket, her mantle or whatever, but crowned with a brilliant brave hat, responsive to the balmy day, which Maggie immediately "spotted" as new, as insuperably original, as worn, in characteristic generous harmony, for the first time; all evidently to watch for the return of the absent, to be there to take them over again as punctually as possible. They were gay, they were amused, in the pleasant morning; they leaned across the rail and called down their greeting, lighting up the front of the great black house with an expression that quite broke the monotony, that might almost have shocked the decency, of Portland Place. The group on the pavement stared up as at the peopled battlements of a castle; even Miss Bogle, who carried her head most aloft, gaped a little, through the interval of space, as toward truly superior beings. There could scarce have been so much of the open mouth since the dingy waifs on Christmas Eve had so lamentably chanted for pennies — the time when Amerigo, insatiable for English customs, had come out with a gasped "Santissima Vergine!" to marvel at the depositaries of this tradition and purchase a reprieve. Maggie's individual gape was inevitably again for the thought of how the pair would be at work. *104340*

VI

SHE had not again for weeks had Mrs. Assingham
so effectually in presence as on the afternoon of that
lady's return from the Easter party at Matcham; but
the intermission was made up as soon as the date
of the migration to Fawns — that of the more or less
simultaneous adjournment of the two houses — began
to be discussed. It had struck her promptly that
this renewal with an old friend of the old terms she
had talked of with her father was the one opening for
her spirit that would n't too much advertise or betray
her. Even her father, who had always, as he would
have said, "believed in" their ancient ally, would n't
necessarily suspect her of invoking Fanny's aid toward
any special enquiry — and least of all if Fanny would
only act as Fanny so easily might. Maggie's measure
of Fanny's ease would have been agitating to Mrs.
Assingham had it been all at once revealed to her —
as for that matter it was soon destined to become even
on a comparatively graduated showing. Our young
woman's idea in particular was that her safety, her
escape from being herself suspected of suspicion,
would proceed from this friend's power to cover, to
protect and, as might be, even showily to represent her
— represent, that is, her relation to the form of the life
they were all actually leading. This would doubtless
be, as people said, a large order; but that Mrs. Assingham existed substantially or could somehow be made

prevailingly to exist for her private benefit was the
finest flower Maggie had plucked from among the sug-
gestions sown, like abundant seed, on the occasion of
the entertainment offered in Portland Place to the
Matcham company. Mrs. Assingham had that night,
rebounding from dejection, bristled with bravery
and sympathy; she had then absolutely, she had perhaps recklessly, for herself, betrayed the deeper and
darker consciousness — an impression it would now be
late for her inconsistently to attempt to undo. It was
with a wonderful air of giving out all these truths that
the Princess at present approached her again; making
doubtless at first a sufficient scruple of letting her know
what in especial she asked of her, yet not a bit ashamed,
as she in fact quite expressly declared, of Fanny's discerned foreboding of the strange uses she might perhaps have for her. Quite from the first really Maggie
said extraordinary things to her, such as "You can
help me, you know, my dear, when nobody else can";
such as "I almost wish, upon my word, that you had
something the matter with you, that you had lost your
health or your money or your reputation (forgive me,
love!) so that I might be with you as much as I want,
or keep you with *me*, without exciting comment, without exciting any other remark than that such kind-
nesses are 'like' me." We have each our own way
of making up for our unselfishness, and Maggie, who
had no small self at all as against her husband or her
father and only a weak and uncertain one as against
her stepmother, would verily at this crisis have seen
Mrs. Assingham's personal life or liberty sacrificed
without a pang.

The attitude that the appetite in question maintained in her was to draw peculiar support moreover from the current aspects and agitations of her victim. This personage struck her in truth as ready for almost anything; as not perhaps effusively protesting, yet as wanting with a restlessness of her own to know what *she* wanted. And in the long run — which was none so long either — there was to be no difficulty, as happened, about that. It was as if, for all the world, Maggie had let her see that she held her, that she made her, fairly responsible for something; not, to begin with, dotting all the i's nor hooking together all the links, but treating her, without insistence, rather with caressing confidence, as there to see and to know, to advise and to assist. The theory, visibly, had patched itself together for her that the dear woman had somehow from the early time had a hand in *all* their fortunes, so that there was no turn of their common relations and affairs that could n't be traced back in some degree to her original affectionate interest. On this affectionate interest the good lady's young friend now built before her eyes — very much as a wise or even as a mischievous child, playing on the floor, might pile up blocks, skilfully and dizzily, with an eye on the face of a covertly-watching elder. When the blocks tumbled down they but acted after the nature of blocks; yet the hour would come for their rising so high that the structure would have to be noticed and admired. Mrs. Assingham's appearance of unreservedly giving herself involved meanwhile on her own side no separate recognitions: her face of almost anxious attention was directed altogether to her young friend's so vivid felicity; it suggested that she took for granted at the most certain vague recent enhancements of that state. If the Princess now, more than before, was going and going, she was prompt to publish that she beheld her go, that she had always known she *would*, sooner or later, and that any appeal for participation must more or less contain and invite the note of triumph. There was a blankness in her blandness, assuredly, and very nearly an extravagance in her generalising gaiety; a precipitation of cheer particularly marked whenever they met again after short separations: meetings during the first flush of which Maggie sometimes felt reminded of other looks in other faces; of two strangely unobliterated impressions above all, the physiognomic light that had played out in her husband at the shock — she had come at last to talk to herself of the "shock" — of his first vision of her on his return from Matcham and Gloucester, and the wonder of Charlotte's beautiful bold wavering glance when, the next morning in Eaton Square, this old friend had turned from the window to begin to deal with her.

If she had dared to think of it so crudely she would have said that Fanny was afraid of her, afraid of something she might say or do, even as for their few brief seconds Amerigo and Charlotte had been — which made exactly an expressive element common to the three. The difference however was that this look had in the dear woman its oddity of a constant renewal, whereas it had never for the least little instant again peeped out of the others. Other looks, other lights, radiant and steady, with the others, had taken its place, reaching a climax so short a time ago, that morning of the appearance of the pair on the balcony of her house to overlook what she had been doing with her father; when their general interested brightness and beauty, attuned to the outbreak of summer, had seemed to shed down warmth and welcome and the promise of protection. They were conjoined not to do anything to startle her — and now at last so completely that, with experience and practice, they had almost ceased to fear their liability. Mrs. Assingham on the other hand, deprecating such an accident not less, had yet less assurance through having less control. The high pitch of her cheer accordingly, the tentative adventurous expressions, of the would-be smiling order, that preceded her approach even like a squad of skirmishers, or whatever they were called, moving ahead of the baggage-train — these things had at the end of a fortnight brought a dozen times to our young woman's lips a challenge that had the cunning to await its right occasion, but of the relief of which, as a demonstration, she meanwhile felt no little need. "You've such a dread of my possibly complaining to you that you keep pealing all the bells to drown my voice; but don't cry out, my dear, till you're hurt — and above all ask yourself how I can be so wicked as to complain. What in the name of all that's fantastic can you dream that I have to complain *of?*" Such enquiries the Princess temporarily succeeded in repressing, and she did so, in a measure, by the aid of her wondering if this ambiguity with which her friend affected her would n't be at present a good deal like the ambiguity with which she herself must frequently

affect her father. She wondered how she should enjoy
on *his* part such a take-up as she but just succeeded
from day to day in sparing Mrs. Assingham, and that
made for her trying to be as easy with this associate
as Mr. Verver, blessed man, all indulgent but all
inscrutable, was with his daughter. She had none the
less extracted from her a vow in respect to the time
that if the Colonel might be depended on they would
spend at Fawns; and nothing came home to her more
in this connexion or inspired her with a more intimate interest than her sense of absolutely seeing her
interlocutress forbear to observe that Charlotte's view
of a long visit even from such allies was there to be
reckoned with.

Fanny stood off from that proposition as visibly to
the Princess, and as consciously to herself, as she might
have backed away from the edge of a chasm into which
she feared to slip; a truth that contributed again to
keep before our young woman her own constant danger of advertising subtle processes. That Charlotte
should have begun to be restrictive about the Assinghams — which she had never, and for a hundred obviously good reasons, been before — this in itself was
a fact of the highest value for Maggie, and of a value
enhanced by the silence in which Fanny herself so
much too unmistakeably dressed it. What gave it
quite thrillingly its price was exactly the circumstance
that it thus opposed her to her stepmother more act-
ively — if she was to back up her friends for holding
out — than she had ever yet been opposed; though of
course with the involved result of the fine chance given
Mrs. Verver to ask her husband for explanations. Ah

from the moment she should be definitely *caught* in opposition there would be naturally no saying how much Charlotte's opportunities might multiply. What would become of her father, she hauntedly asked, if his wife, on the one side, should begin to press him to call his daughter to order, and the force of old habit — to put it only at that — should dispose him not less effectively to believe in this young person at any price? There she was, all round, imprisoned in the circle of the reasons it was impossible she should give — certainly give *him*. The house in the country was his house, and thereby was Charlotte's; it was her own and Amerigo's only so far as its proper master and mistress should profusely place it at their disposal. Maggie felt of course that she saw no limit to her father's profusion, but this could n't be even at the best the case with Charlotte's, whom it would never be decent, when all was said, to reduce to fighting for her preferences. There were hours truly when the Princess saw herself as not unarmed for battle if battle might only take place without spectators.

This last advantage for her was however too sadly out of the question; her sole strength lay in her being able to see that if Charlotte would n't "want" the Assinghams it would be because that sentiment too would have motives and grounds. She had all the while command of one way of meeting any objection, any complaint, on his wife's part, reported to her by her father; it would be open to her to retort to his possible "What are your reasons, my dear?" by a lucidly-produced "What are hers, love, please? — is n't that what we had better know? May n't her reasons be a dislike, beautifully founded, of the presence and thereby of the observation of persons who perhaps know about her things it's inconvenient to her they should know?" That hideous card she might in mere logic play — being at this time, at her still swifter private pace, intimately familiar with all the fingered pasteboard in her pack. But she could play it only on the forbidden issue of sacrificing him; the issue so forbidden that it involved even a horror of finding out if he would really have consented to be sacrificed. What she must do she must do by keeping her hands off him; and nothing meanwhile, as we see, had less in common with *that* scruple than such a merciless manipulation of their yielding beneficiaries as her spirit so boldly revelled in. She saw herself in this connexion without detachment — saw others alone with intensity; otherwise she might have been struck, fairly have been amused, by her free assignment of the pachydermatous quality. If *she* could face the awkwardness of the persistence of her friends at Fawns in spite of Charlotte, she somehow looked to them for an inspiration of courage that would improve upon her own. They were in short not only themselves to find a plausibility and an audacity, but were somehow by the way to pick up these forms for her, Maggie, as well. And she felt indeed that she was giving them scant time longer when one afternoon in Portland Place she broke out with an irrelevance that was merely superficial.

"What awfulness, in heaven's name, is there between them? What do you believe, what do you *know?*"

Oh if she went by faces her visitor's sudden white-
ness at this might have carried her far! Fanny Assingham turned pale for it, but there was something
in such an appearance, in the look it put into the eyes,
that renewed Maggie's conviction of what this companion had been expecting. She had been watching
it come, come from afar, and now that it was there,
after all, and the first convulsion over, they would
doubtless soon find themselves in a more real relation.
It was there because of the Sunday luncheon they had
partaken of alone together; it was there, as strangely
as one would, because of the bad weather, the cold per-
verse June rain, that was making the day wrong; it
was there because it stood for the whole sum of the
perplexities and duplicities among which our young
woman felt herself lately to have picked her steps; it
was there because Amerigo and Charlotte were again
paying together alone a "week-end" visit which it had
been Maggie's plan infernally to promote — just to see
if this time they really would; it was there because
she had kept Fanny, on her side, from paying one she
would manifestly have been glad to pay, and had made
her come instead, stupidly, vacantly, boringly, to
luncheon; all in the spirit of celebrating the fact that
the Prince and Mrs. Verver had thus put it into her
own power to describe them exactly as they were. It
had abruptly occurred in truth that Maggie required
the preliminary help of determining *how* they were;
though on the other hand before her guest had answered her question everything in the hour and the
place, everything in all the conditions, affected her as
crying it out. Her guest's stare of ignorance above

all — that of itself first cried it out. "'Between them'? What do you mean?"

"Anything there should n't be, there should n't have *been* — all this time. Do you believe there is — or what's your idea?"

Fanny's idea was clearly, to begin with, that her young friend had taken her breath away; but she looked at her very straight and very hard. "Do you speak from a suspicion of your own?"

"I speak at last from a torment. Forgive me if it comes out. I've been thinking for months and months, and I've no one to turn to, no one to help me to make things out; no impression but my own, don't you see? to go by."

"You've been thinking for months and months?" — Mrs. Assingham took it in. "But *what* then, dear Maggie, have you been thinking?"

"Well, horrible things — like a little beast that I perhaps am. That there may be something — something wrong and dreadful, something they cover up."

The elder woman's colour had begun to come back; she was able, though with a visible effort, to face the question less amazedly. "You imagine, poor child, that the wretches are in love? Is that it?"

But Maggie for a minute only stared back at her. "Help me to find out *what* I imagine. I don't know — I've nothing but my perpetual anxiety. Have *you* any? — do you see what I mean? If you'll tell me truly, that at least, one way or the other, will do something for me."

Fanny's look had taken a peculiar gravity — a fulness with which it seemed to shine. "Is what it comes to that you're jealous of Charlotte?"

"Do you mean whether I hate her?"—and Maggie thought. "No; not on account of father."

"Ah," Mrs. Assingham returned, "that isn't what one would suppose. What I ask is if you're jealous on account of your husband."

"Well," said Maggie presently, "perhaps that may be all. If I'm unhappy I'm jealous; it must come to the same thing; and with you at least I'm not afraid of the word. If I'm jealous, don't you see? I'm tormented," she went on—"and all the more if I'm helpless. And if I'm both helpless *and* tormented I stuff my pocket-handkerchief into my mouth, I keep it there, for the most part, night and day, so as not to be heard too indecently moaning. Only now, with you, at last, I can't keep it longer; I've pulled it out and here I am fairly screaming at you. They're away," she wound up, "so they can't hear; and I'm by a miracle of arrangement not at luncheon with father at home. I live in the midst of miracles of arrangement, half of which I admit are my own; I go about on tiptoe, I watch for every sound, I feel every breath, and yet I try all the while to seem as smooth as old satin dyed rose-colour. Have you ever thought of me," she asked, "as really feeling as I do?"

Her companion, conspicuously, required to be clear. "Jealous, unhappy, tormented—? No," said Mrs. Assingham; "but at the same time—and though you may laugh at me for it!—I'm bound to confess I've never been so awfully sure of what I may call knowing you. Here you are indeed, as you say—such a deep little person! I've never imagined your existence poisoned, and since you wish to know if I consider it need be I've not the least difficulty in speaking on the spot. Nothing decidedly strikes me as more unnecessary."

For a minute after this they remained face to face; Maggie had sprung up while her friend sat enthroned, and, after moving to and fro in her intensity, now paused to receive the light she had invoked. It had accumulated, considerably, by this time, round Mrs. Assingham's ample presence, and it made, even to our young woman's own sense, a medium in which she could at last take a deeper breath. "I've affected you, these months — and these last weeks in especial — as quiet and natural and easy?"

But it was a question that took, not imperceptibly, some answering. "You've never affected me, from the first hour I beheld you, as anything but — in a way all your own — absolutely good and sweet and beautiful. In a way, as I say," Mrs. Assingham almost caressingly repeated, "just all your very own — nobody else's at all. I've never thought of you but as *outside* of ugly things, so ignorant of any falsity or cruelty or vulgarity as never to have to be touched by them or to touch them. I've never mixed you up with them; there would have been time enough for that if they had seemed to be near you. But they haven't — if that's what you want to know."

"You've only believed me contented then because you've believed me stupid?"

Mrs. Assingham had a free smile now for the length of this stride, dissimulated though it might be

in a graceful little frisk. "If I had believed you stupid
I should n't have thought you interesting, and if I
had n't thought you interesting I should n't have noted
whether I 'knew' you, as I 've called it, or not. What
I 've always been conscious of is your having concealed about you somewhere no small amount of
character; quite as much in fact," Fanny smiled,
"as one could suppose a person of your size able
to carry. The only thing was," she explained, "that
thanks to your never calling one's attention to it, I
had n't made out much more about it, and should
have been vague above all as to *where* you carried it
or kept it. Somewhere *under*, I should simply have
said — like that little silver cross you once showed me,
blest by the Holy Father, that you always wear, out
of sight, next your skin. That relic I 've had a glimpse
of" — with which she continued to invoke the privilege of humour. "But the precious little innermost, say
this time little golden personal nature of you — blest
by a greater power I think even than the Pope — *that*
you 've never consentingly shown me. I 'm not sure
you 've ever consentingly shown it to any one. You 've
been in general too modest."

Maggie, trying to follow, almost achieved a little
fold of her forehead. "I strike you as modest to-day
— modest when I stand here and scream at you ?"

"Oh your screaming, I 've granted you, is something
new. I must fit it on somewhere. The question is,
however," Mrs. Assingham further proceeded, "of
what the deuce I can fit it on *to*. Do you mean," she
asked, "to the fact of our friends' being, from yesterday to to-morrow, at a place where they may more or

less irresponsibly meet?" She spoke with the air of putting it as badly for them as possible. "Are you thinking of their being there alone — of their having consented to be?" And then as she had waited without result for her companion to say: "But is n't it true that — after you had this time again, at the eleventh hour, said *you* would n't — they would really much rather not have gone?"

"Yes — they would certainly much rather not have gone. But I wanted them to go."

"Then, my dear child, what in the world is the matter?"

"I wanted to see if they *would*. And they 've had to," Maggie added. "It was the only thing."

Her friend appeared to wonder. "From the moment you and your father backed out?"

"Oh I don't mean go for those people. I mean go for us. For father and me," Maggie went on. "Because now they know."

"They 'know'?" Fanny Assingham quavered.

"That I 've been for some time past taking more notice. Notice of the queer things in our life."

Maggie saw her companion for an instant on the point of asking her what these queer things might be; but Mrs. Assingham had the next minute brushed by that ambiguous opening and taken, as she evidently felt, a better one. "And is it for that you did it? I mean gave up the visit."

"It 's for that I did it. To leave them to themselves — as they less and less want, or at any rate less and less venture to appear to want, to be left. As they had for so long arranged things," the Princess went on, "you see they sometimes have to be." And then, as if baffled by the lucidity of this, Mrs. Assingham for a little said nothing: "Now do you think I'm modest?"

With time however Fanny could brilliantly think anything that would serve. "I think you're wrong. That, my dear, is my answer to your question. It demands assuredly the straightest I can make. I see no 'awfulness'—I suspect none. I'm deeply distressed," she added, "that you should do anything else."

It drew again from Maggie a long look. "You've never even imagined anything?"

"Ah God forbid!—for it's exactly as a woman of imagination that I speak. There's no moment of my life at which I'm not imagining something; and it's thanks to that, darling," Mrs. Assingham pursued, "that I figure the sincerity with which your husband, whom *you* see as viciously occupied with your stepmother, is interested, is tenderly interested, in his admirable adorable wife." She paused a minute as to give her friend the full benefit of this — as to Maggie's measure of which however no sign came; and then, poor woman, haplessly, she crowned her effort. "He would n't hurt a hair of your head."

It had produced in Maggie at once, and apparently in the intended form of a smile, the most extraordinary expression. "Ah there it is!"

But her guest had already gone on. "And I'm absolutely certain that Charlotte would n't either."

It kept the Princess, with her strange grimace, standing there. "No — Charlotte would n't either. That's how they've had again to go off together. They've been afraid not to—lest it should disturb me,

114

aggravate me, somehow work upon me. As I insisted
that they must, that we could n't all fail — though
father and Charlotte had n't really accepted; as I did
this they had to yield to the fear that their showing as
afraid to move together would count for them as the
greater danger: which would be the danger, you see,
of my feeling myself wronged. Their least danger,
they know, is in going on with all the things that I 've
seemed to accept and that I 've given no indication at
any moment of not accepting. Everything that has
come up for them has come up, in an extraordinary
manner, without my having by a sound or a sign
given myself away — so that it 's all as wonderful as
you may conceive. They move at any rate among the
dangers I speak of — between that of their doing too
much and that of their not having any longer the confidence or the nerve, or whatever you may call it, to
do enough." Her tone might by this time have shown
a strangeness to match her smile; which was still
more marked as she wound up: "And that 's how
I make them do what I like!"

It had an effect on Mrs. Assingham, who rose with
the deliberation that from point to point marked the
widening of her grasp. "My dear child, you 're amazing."

"Amazing — ?"

"You 're terrible."

Maggie thoughtfully shook her head. "No; I 'm
not terrible, and you don't think me so. I do strike
you as surprising, no doubt — but surprisingly mild.
Because — don't you see? — I *am* mild. I can bear
anything."

"Oh 'bear'!" Mrs. Assingham fluted.

"For love," said the Princess.

Fanny hesitated. "Of your father?"

"For love," Maggie repeated.

It kept her friend watching. "Of your husband?"

"For love," Maggie said again.

It was for the moment as if the distinctness of this might have determined in her companion a choice between two or three highly different alternatives. Mrs. Assingham's rejoinder at all events — however much or however little it was a choice — was presently a triumph. "Speaking with this love of your own then, have you undertaken to convey to me that you believe your husband and your father's wife to be in act and in fact lovers of each other?" And then as the Princess did n't at first answer: "Do you call such an allegation as that 'mild'?"

"Oh I 'm not pretending to be mild to *you*. But I 've told you, and moreover you must have seen for yourself, how much so I 've been to them."

Mrs. Assingham, more brightly again, bridled. "Is that what you call it when you make them, for terror as you say, do as you like?"

"Ah there would n't be any terror for them if they had nothing to hide."

Mrs. Assingham faced her — quite steady now. "Are you really conscious, love, of what you 're saying?"

"I 'm saying that I 'm bewildered and tormented, and that I 've no one but you to speak to. I 've thought, I 've in fact been sure, that you 've seen for

116

yourself how much this is the case. It's why I've believed you would meet me halfway."

"Halfway to what? To denouncing," Fanny asked, "two persons, friends of years, whom I've always immensely admired and liked, and against whom I have n't the shadow of a charge to make?"

Maggie looked at her with wide eyes. "I had much rather you should denounce *me* than denounce them. Denounce me, denounce me," she said, "if you can see your way." It was exactly what she appeared to have argued out with herself. "If conscientiously you can denounce me; if conscientiously you can revile me; if conscientiously you can put me in my place for a low-minded little pig —!"

"Well?" said Mrs. Assingham consideringly, as she paused for emphasis.

"I think I shall be saved."

Her friend took it for a minute however by carrying thoughtful eyes, eyes verily portentous, over her head. "You say you've no one to speak to, and you make a point of your having so disguised your feelings — not having, as you call it, given yourself away. Have you then never seen it not only as your right, but as your bounden duty, worked up to such a pitch, to speak to your husband?"

"I've spoken to him," said Maggie.

Mrs. Assingham stared. "Ah then it is n't true that you've made no sign."

Maggie had a silence. "I've made no trouble. I've made no scene. I've taken no stand. I've neither reproached nor accused him. You'll say there's a way in all that of being nasty enough."

"Oh!" dropped from Fanny as if she could n't help it.

"But I don't think — strangely enough — that he regards me as nasty. I think that at bottom — for that *is*," said the Princess, "the strangeness — he's sorry for me. Yes, I think that deep within he pities me."

Her companion wondered. "For the state you've let yourself get into?"

"For not being happy when I've so much to make me so."

"You've everything," said Mrs. Assingham with alacrity. Yet she remained for an instant embarrassed as to a further advance. "Yet I don't understand how, if you've done nothing —"

An impatience from Maggie had checked her. "I've not done absolutely 'nothing.'"

"But what then —?"

"Well," she went on after a minute, "he knows what I've done."

It produced on Mrs. Assingham's part, her whole tone and manner exquisitely aiding, a hush not less prolonged and the very duration of which inevitably gave it something of the character of an equal recognition. "And what then has *he* done?"

Maggie took again a minute. "He has been splendid."

"'Splendid'? Then what more do you want?"

"Ah what you see!" said Maggie. "Not to be afraid."

It made her guest again hang fire. "Not to be afraid really to speak?"

"Not to be afraid *not* to speak."

Mrs. Assingham considered further. "You can't even to Charlotte?" But as, at this, after a look at her, Maggie turned off with a movement of suppressed despair, she checked herself and might have been watching her, for all the difficulty and the pity of it, vaguely move to the window and the view of the dull street. It was almost as if she had had to give up, from failure of responsive wit in her friend — the last failure she had feared — the hope of the particular relief she had been working for. Mrs. Assingham resumed the next instant however in the very tone that seemed most to promise her she should have to give up nothing. "I see, I see; you'd have in that case too many things to consider." It brought the Princess round again, proving itself thus the note of comprehension she wished most to clutch at. "*Don't* be afraid."

Maggie took it where she stood — which she was soon able to signify. "Thank you."

It very properly encouraged her counsellor. "What your idea imputes is a criminal intrigue carried on, from day to day, amid perfect trust and sympathy, not only under your eyes, but under your father's. That's an idea it's impossible for me for a moment to entertain."

"Ah there you are then! It's exactly what I wanted from you."

"You're welcome to it!" Mrs. Assingham breathed.

"You never *have* entertained it?" Maggie pursued.

"Never for an instant," said Fanny with her head very high.

Maggie took it again, yet again as wanting more. "Pardon my being so horrid. But by all you hold sacred?"

Mrs. Assingham faced her. "Ah my dear, upon my positive word as an honest woman."

"Thank you then," said the Princess.

So they remained a little; after which, "But do you believe it, love?" Fanny enquired.

"I believe *you*."

"Well, as I've faith in *them* it comes to the same thing."

Maggie, at this last, appeared for a moment to think again; but she embraced the proposition. "The same thing."

"Then you're no longer unhappy?" her guest urged, coming more gaily toward her.

"I doubtless shan't be a great while."

But it was now Mrs. Assingham's turn to want more. "I've convinced you it's impossible?"

She had held out her arms, and Maggie, after a moment meeting her, threw herself into them with a sound that had its oddity as a sign of relief. "Impossible, impossible," she emphatically, more than emphatically, replied; yet the next minute she had burst into tears over the impossibility, and a few seconds later, pressing, clinging, sobbing, had even caused them to flow, audibly, sympathetically and perversely, from her friend.

VII

THE understanding appeared to have come to be that
the Colonel and his wife were to present themselves
toward the middle of July for the "good long visit" at
Fawns on which Maggie had obtained from her father
that he should genially insist; as well as that the couple
from Eaton Square should welcome there earlier in the
month, and less than a week after their own arrival,
the advent of the couple from Portland Place. "Oh
we shall give you time to breathe!" Fanny remarked,
in reference to the general prospect, with a gaiety that
announced itself as heedless of criticism, to each
member of the party in turn; sustaining and bracing
herself by her emphasis, pushed even to an amiable
cynicism, of the confident view of these punctualities
of the Assinghams. The ground she could best occupy,
to her sense, was that of her being moved, as in this
connexion she had always been moved, by the admitted grossness of her avidity, the way the hospitality
of the Ververs met her convenience and ministered to
her ease, destitute as the Colonel had kept her, from
the first, of any rustic retreat, any leafy bower of her
own, any fixed base for the stale season now at hand.
She had explained at home, she had repeatedly re-
explained, the terms of her dilemma, the real difficulty
of her, or — as she now put it — of their, position.
When the pair could do nothing else, in Cadogan
Place, they could still talk of marvellous little Maggie,
and of the charm, the sinister charm, of their having

to hold their breath to watch her; a topic the moment-
ous midnight discussion at which we have been present was so far from having exhausted. It came up,
irrepressibly, at all private hours; they had planted it
there between them, and it grew, from day to day, in
a manner to make their sense of responsibility almost
yield to their sense of fascination. Mrs. Assingham
declared at such moments that in the interest of this
admirable young thing — to whom, she also declared,
she had quite "come over" — she was ready to pass
with all the world else, even with the Prince himself,
the object, inconsequently, as well, of her continued,
her explicitly shameless appreciation, for a vulgar in-
delicate pestilential woman, showing her true character in an abandoned old age. The Colonel's confessed
attention had been enlisted, we have seen, as never
yet, under pressure from his wife, by any guaranteed
imbroglio; but this, she could assure him she perfectly
knew, was not a bit because he was sorry for her, was
touched by what she had let herself in for, but because
when once they had been opened he could n't keep his
eyes from resting complacently, resting almost intelligently, on the Princess. If he was in love with *her*
now, however, so much the better; it would help them
both not to wince at what they would have to do for
her. Mrs. Assingham had come back to that whenever he groaned or grunted; she had at no beguiled
moment — since Maggie's little march *was* positively
beguiling — let him lose sight of the grim necessity
awaiting them. "We shall have, as I 've again and
again told you, to lie for her — to lie till we 're black
in the face."

"To lie 'for' her?" The Colonel often, at these hours, as from a vague vision of old chivalry in a new form, wandered into apparent lapses from lucidity.

"To lie *to* her, up and down, and in and out — it comes to the same thing. It will consist just as much of lying to the others too: to the Prince about one's belief in *him;* to Charlotte about one's belief in *her;* to Mr. Verver, dear sweet man, about one's belief in every one. So we've work cut out — with the biggest lie, on top of all, being that we *like* to be there for such a purpose. We hate it unspeakably — I'm more ready to be a coward before it, to let the whole thing, to let every one, selfishly and pusillanimously slide, than before any social duty, any felt human call, that has ever forced me to be decent. I speak at least for myself. For you," she had added, "as I've given you so perfect an opportunity to fall in love with Maggie, you'll doubtless find your account in being so much nearer to her."

"And what do you make," the Colonel could, at this, always imperturbably enough ask, "of the account you yourself will find in being so much nearer to the Prince; of your confirmed, if not exasperated, infatuation with whom — to say nothing of my weak good nature about it—you give such a pretty picture?"

To the picture in question she had in fact been always able contemplatively to return. "The difficulty of my enjoyment of that is, don't you see? that I'm making, in my loyalty to Maggie, a sad hash of his affection for me."

"You find means to call it then, this whitewashing of his crime, being 'loyal' to Maggie?"

"Oh about that particular crime there's always much to say. It's always more interesting to us than any other crime — it has at least *that* for it. But of course I call everything I have in mind at all being loyal to Maggie. Being loyal to her is more than anything else helping her with her father — which is what she most wants and needs."

The Colonel had had it before, but he could apparently never have too much of it. "Helping her 'with' him — ?"

"Helping her against him then. Against what we've already so fully talked of — its having to be recognised between them that he doubts. That's where my part is so plain — to see her through, to see her through to the end." Exaltation, for the moment, always lighted Mrs. Assingham's reference to this plainness; yet she at the same time seldom failed, the next instant, to qualify her view of it. "When I talk of my obligation as clear I mean that it's absolute; for just *how*, from day to day and through thick and thin, to keep the thing up is, I grant you, another matter. There's one way, luckily, nevertheless, in which I'm strong. I can so perfectly count on her."

The Colonel seldom failed here, as from the insidious growth of an excitement, to wonder, to encourage. "Not to see you're lying?"

"To stick to me fast, whatever she sees. If I stick to her — that is to my own poor struggling way, under providence, of watching over them *all* — she'll stand by me to the death. She won't give me away. For you know she easily can."

This, regularly, was the most lurid turn of their

road; but Bob Assingham, with each journey, met it as for the first time. "Easily?"

"She can utterly dishonour me with her father. She can let him know that I was aware at the time of his marriage — as I had been aware at the time of her own — of the relations that had pre-existed between his wife and her husband."

"And how can she do so if, up to this minute, by your own statement, she's herself in ignorance of your knowledge?"

It was a question that Mrs. Assingham had ever, for dealing with, a manner to which repeated practice had given almost a grand effect; very much as if she was invited by it to say that about this exactly she proposed to do her best lying. But she said, and with full lucidity, something quite other: it could give itself a little the air still of a triumph over his coarseness. "By acting immediately with the blind resentment with which, in her place, ninety-nine women out of a hundred would act; and by so making Mr. Verver in turn act with the same natural passion, the passion of ninety-nine men out of a hundred. They've only to agree about me," the poor lady said; "they've only to feel at one over it, feel bitterly practised upon, cheated and injured; they've only to denounce me to each other as false and infamous, for me to be quite irretrievably dished. Of course it's I who have been, and who continue to be cheated — cheated by the Prince and Charlotte; but they're not obliged to give me the benefit of that, or to give either of us the benefit of anything. They'll be within their rights to lump us all together as a false cruel conspiring crew and, if they can find the right facts to support them, get rid of us root and branch."

This on each occasion put the matter so at the worst that repetition even scarce controlled the hot flush with which she was compelled to see the parts of the whole history, all its ugly consistency and its temporary gloss, hang together. She enjoyed invariably the sense of making her danger present, of making it real, to her husband, and of his almost turning pale when their eyes met at this possibility of their compromised state and their shared discredit. The beauty was that, as under a touch of one of the ivory notes at the left of the keyboard, he sounded out with the short sharpness of the dear fond stupid uneasy man. "Conspiring — so far as *you* were concerned — to what end?"

"Why to the obvious end of getting the Prince a wife — at Maggie's expense. And then to that of getting Charlotte a husband at Mr. Verver's."

"Of rendering friendly services, yes — which have produced, as it turns out, complications. But from the moment you did n't do it *for* the complications, why should n't you have rendered them?"

It was extraordinary for her always, in this connexion, how, with time given him, he fell to speaking better for her than she could, in the presence of her clear-cut image of the "worst," speak for herself. Troubled as she was she thus never wholly failed of her amusement by the way. "Oh is n't what I may have meddled 'for' — so far as it can be proved I did meddle — open to interpretation; by which I mean to Mr. Verver's and Maggie's? May n't they see my motive, in the light of that appreciation, as the wish to be decidedly more friendly to the others than to the victimised father and daughter?" She positively liked to keep it up. "May n't they see my motive as the determination to serve the Prince, in any case and at any price, first; to 'place' him comfortably; in other words to find him his fill of money? May n't it have all the air for them of a really equivocal sinister bargain between us — something quite unholy and *louche*?"

It infallibly produced in the poor Colonel the echo. "'Louche,' love —?"

"Why, have n't you said as much yourself? — have n't you put your finger on that awful possibility?"

She had a way now with his felicities that made him enjoy being reminded of them. "In speaking of your having always had such a 'mash' —?"

"Such a mash, precisely, for the man I was to help to put so splendidly at his ease. A motherly mash an impartial look at it would show it only as likely to have been — but we 're not talking of course about impartial looks. We 're talking of good innocent people deeply worked upon by a horrid discovery and going much further in their view of the lurid, as such people almost always do, than those who have been wider awake all round from the first. What I was to have got from my friend, in such a view, in exchange for what I had been able to do for him — well, that would have been an equivalent, of a kind best known to myself, for me shrewdly to consider." And she easily lost herself each time in the anxious satisfaction of filling out the picture. It would have been seen, it would have been heard of before, the case of the woman a man does n't want, or of whom he 's tired, or for whom he has no use but *such* uses, and who 's capable, in her infatuation, in her passion, of promoting his interests with other women rather than lose sight of him, lose touch of him, cease to have to do with him at all. *Cela s'est vu*, my dear; and stranger things still — as I need n't tell *you!* Very good then," she wound up; "there 's a perfectly possible conception of the behaviour of your sweet wife; since, as I say, no imagination 's so lively, once it 's started, as that of really agitated lambs. Lions are nothing to them, for lions are sophisticated, are *blasés*, are brought up from the first to prowling and mauling. It does give us, you 'll admit, something to think about. My relief is luckily, however, in what I finally do think."

He was well enough aware by this time of what she finally did think, but he was n't without a sense again also for his amusement by the way. It would have made him, for a spectator of these passages between the pair, resemble not a little the artless child who hears his favourite story told for the twentieth time and enjoys it exactly because he knows what is next to happen. "What of course will pull them up if they turn out to have less imagination than you assume is the profit you can have found in furthering Mrs. Verver's marriage. You were n't at least in love with Charlotte."

"Oh," Mrs. Assingham, at this, always brought out, "my hand in that is easily accounted for by my desire to be agreeable to *him*."

"To Mr. Verver?"

"To the Prince — by preventing her in that way

from taking, as he was in danger of seeing her do, some husband with whom he would n't be able to open, to keep open, so large an account as with his father-in-law. I've brought her near him, kept her within his reach, as she could never have remained either as a single woman or as the wife of a different man."

"Kept her, on that sweet construction, to be his mistress?"

"Kept her, on that sweet construction, to be his mistress." She brought it out grandly — it had always so, for her own ear as well as, visibly, for her husband's, its effect. "The facilities in the case, thanks to the particular conditions, being so quite ideal."

"Down even to the facility of your minding everything so little — from your own point of view — as to have supplied him with the enjoyment of *two* beautiful women."

"Down even to *that* — to the monstrosity of my folly. But not," Mrs. Assingham added, "'two' of anything. One beautiful woman — and one beautiful fortune. That's what a creature of pure virtue exposes herself to when she suffers her pure virtue, suffers her sympathy, her disinterestedness, her exquisite sense for the lives of others, to carry her too far. *Voilà*."

"I see. It's the way the Ververs have you."

"It's the way the Ververs 'have' me. It's in other words the way they would be able to make such a show to each other of having me — if Maggie were n't so divine."

"She lets you off?" He never failed to insist on all this to the very end; which was how he had become so versed in what she finally thought.

"She lets me off. So that now, horrified and contrite at what I've done, I may work to help her out. And Mr. Verver," she was fond of adding, "lets me off too."

"Then you do believe he knows?"

It determined in her always there, with a significant pause, a deep immersion in her thought. "I believe he'd let me off if he did know — so that I might work to help *him* out. Or rather, really," she went on, "that I might work to help Maggie. That would be his motive, that would be his condition, in forgiving me; just as hers for me in fact, her motive and her condition, are my acting to spare her father. But it's with Maggie only that I'm directly concerned; nothing ever — not a breath, not a look, I'll guarantee — shall I have, whatever happens, from Mr. Verver himself. So it is therefore that I shall probably by the closest possible shave escape the penalty of my crimes."

"You mean being held responsible."

"I mean being held responsible. My advantage will be that Maggie's such a trump."

"Such a trump that, as you say, she'll stick to you."

"Stick to me, on our understanding — stick to me. For our understanding's signed and sealed." And to brood over it again was ever for Mrs. Assingham to break out again with exaltation. "It's a grand high compact. She has solemnly promised."

"But in words — ?"

"Oh yes, in words enough — since it's a matter of words. To keep up *her* lie so long as I keep up mine."

"And what do you call 'her' lie?"

"Why the pretence that she believes me. Believes they're innocent."

"She positively believes then they're guilty? She has arrived at that, she's really content with it, in the absence of proof?"

It was here each time that Fanny Assingham most faltered; but always at last to get the matter for her own sense and with a long sigh sufficiently straight. "It isn't a question of belief or of proof, absent or present; it's inevitably with her a question of natural perception, of insurmountable feeling. She irresistibly *knows* that there's something between them. But she hasn't 'arrived' at it, as you say, at all; that's exactly what she hasn't done, what she so steadily and intensely refuses to do. She stands off and off, so as not to arrive; she keeps out to sea and away from the rocks, and what she most wants of me is to keep at a safe distance with her — as I, for my own skin, only ask not to come nearer." After which, invariably, she let him have it all. "So far from wanting proof — which she must get, in a manner, by my siding with her — she wants *dis*proof, as against herself, and has appealed to me, so extraordinarily, to side against her. It's really magnificent when you come to think of it, the spirit of her appeal. If I'll but cover them up brazenly *enough*, the others, so as to show, round and about them, as happy as a bird, she on her side will do what she can. If I'll keep them quiet, in a word, it will enable her to gain time — time as against any idea of her father's — and so somehow come out. If I'll take care of Charlotte in particular she'll take care of the Prince; and it's beautiful and wonderful, really pathetic and exquisite, to see what she feels time may do for her."

"Ah but what does she call, poor little thing, 'time'?"

"Well, this summer at Fawns to begin with. She can live as yet of course but from hand to mouth; but she has worked it out for herself, I think, that the very danger of Fawns, superficially looked at, may practically amount to a greater protection. *There* the lovers — if they *are* lovers! — will have to mind. They'll feel it for themselves, unless things are too utterly far gone with them."

"And things are *not* too utterly far gone with them?"

She had inevitably, poor woman, her hesitation for this, but she put down her answer as for the purchase of some absolutely indispensable article she would have put down her last shilling. "No."

It made him always grin at her. "Is *that* a lie?"

"Do you think you're worth lying to? If it weren't the truth for me," she added, "I wouldn't have accepted for Fawns. I *can*, I believe, keep the wretches quiet."

"But how — at the worst?"

"Oh 'the worst' — don't talk about the worst! I can keep them quiet at the best, I seem to feel, simply by our being there. It will work from week to week of itself. You'll see."

He was willing enough to see, but he desired to provide —! "Yet if it doesn't work?"

"Ah that's talking about the worst!"

Well, it might be; but what were they doing from

morning to night at this crisis but talk? "Who'll keep the others?"

"The others —?"

"Who'll keep *them* quiet? If your couple have had a life together they can't have had it completely without witnesses, without the help of persons, however few, who must have some knowledge, some idea about them. They've had to meet, secretly, protectedly, they've had to arrange; for if they have n't met and have n't arranged and have n't thereby in some quarter or other had to give themselves away, why are we piling it up so? Therefore if there's evidence up and down London —"

"There must be people in possession of it? Ah it is n't all," she always remembered, "up and down London. Some of it must connect them — I mean," she musingly added, "it naturally *would* — with other places; with who knows what strange adventures, opportunities, dissimulations? But whatever there may have been it will also all have been buried on the spot. Oh they've known *how* — too beautifully! But nothing all the same is likely to find its way to Maggie of itself."

"Because every one who may have anything to tell, you hold, will have been so squared?" And then inveterately, before she could say — he enjoyed so much coming to this: "What will have squared Lady Castledean?"

"The consciousness" — she had never lost her promptness — "of having no stones to throw at any one else's windows. She has enough to do to guard her own glass. That was what she was doing," Fanny said, "that last morning at Matcham when all of us went off and she kept the Prince and Charlotte over. She helped them simply that she might herself be helped — if it was n't perhaps rather, with her ridiculous Mr. Blint, that *he* might be. They put in together therefore of course that day; they got it clear — and quite under her eyes; inasmuch as they did n't become traceable again, as we know, till late in the evening." On this historic circumstance Mrs. Assingham was always ready afresh to brood; but she was no less ready, after her brooding, devoutly to add: "Only we know nothing whatever else — for which all our stars be thanked!"

The Colonel's gratitude was apt to be less marked. "What did they do for themselves, anyway, from the moment they got that free hand to the moment (long after dinner-time, have n't you told me?) of their turning up at their respective homes?"

"Well, it's none of your business!"

"I don't speak of it as mine, but it's only too much theirs. People are always traceable, in England, when tracings are required. Something sooner or later happens; somebody sooner or later breaks the holy calm. Murder will out."

"Murder will — but this is n't murder. Quite the contrary perhaps! I verily believe," she had her moments of adding, "that for the amusement of the row you'd prefer an explosion."

This however was a remark he seldom noticed; he wound up for the most part, after a long contemplative smoke, with a transition from which no exposed futility in it had succeeded in weaning him. "What

I can't for my life make out is your idea of the old boy."

"Charlotte's too inconceivably funny husband? I *have* no idea."

"I beg your pardon — you've just shown it. You never speak of him but *as* too inconceivably funny."

"Well, he is," she always confessed. "That is he may be, for all I know, too inconceivably great. But that's not an idea. It represents only my weak necessity of feeling that he's beyond me — which is n't an idea either. You see he may be stupid too."

"Precisely — there you are."

"Yet on the other hand," she always went on, "he may be sublime : sublimer even than Maggie herself. He may in fact have already been. But we shall never know." With which her tone betrayed perhaps a shade of soreness for the single exemption she did n't yearningly welcome. "*That* I can see."

"Oh I say —!" It came to affect the Colonel himself with a sense of privation.

"I 'm not sure even that Charlotte will."

"Oh my dear, what Charlotte does n't know —!"

But she brooded and brooded. "I 'm not sure even that the Prince will." It seemed privation in short for them all. "They 'll be mystified, confounded, tormented. But they won't *know* — and all their possible putting their heads together won't make them. That," said Fanny Assingham, "will be their punishment." And she ended, ever, when she had come so far, at the same pitch. "It will probably also — if I get off with so little — be mine."

135

"And what," her husband liked to ask, "will be mine?"

"Nothing — you're not worthy of any. One's punishment is in what one feels, and what will make ours effective is that we *shall* feel." She was splendid with her "ours"; she flared up with this prophecy. "It will be Maggie herself who will mete it out."

"Maggie — ?"

"*She'll* know — about her father; everything. Everything," she repeated. On the vision of which each time Mrs. Assingham, as with the presentiment of an odd despair, turned away from it. "But she'll never tell us."

VIII

If Maggie had n't so firmly made up her mind never to say, either to her good friend or to any one else, more than she meant about her father, she might have found herself betrayed into some such overflow during the week spent in London with her husband after the others had adjourned to Fawns for the summer. This was because of the odd element of the unnatural imparted to the so simple fact of their brief separation by the assumptions resident in their course of life hitherto. She was used, herself, certainly, by this time, to dealing with odd elements; but she dropped instantly even from such peace as she had patched up, when it was a question of feeling that her unpenetrated parent might be alone with them. She thought of him as alone with them when she thought of him as alone with Charlotte — and this, strangely enough, even while fixing her sense to the full on his wife's power of preserving, quite of enhancing, every felicitous appearance. Charlotte had done that — under immeasureably fewer difficulties indeed — during the numerous months of their hymeneal absence from England, the period prior to that wonderful reunion of the couples, in the interest of the larger play of all the virtues of each, which was now bearing, for Mrs. Verver's stepdaughter at least, such remarkable fruit. It was the present so much briefer interval in a situation, possibly in a relation, so changed — it was the new terms of her problem that would tax Charlotte's art. The Princess could pull herself up repeatedly by remembering that the real "relation" between her father and his wife was a thing she knew nothing about and that in strictness was not of her concern; but she none the less failed to keep quiet, as she would have called it, before the projected image of their ostensibly happy isolation. Nothing could have had less of the quality of quietude than a certain queer wish that fitfully flickered up in her, a wish that usurped perversely the place of a much more natural one. If Charlotte, while she was about it, could only have been *worse!* — that idea Maggie fell to invoking instead of the idea that she might desirably have been better. For, exceedingly odd as it was to feel in such ways, she believed she might n't have worried so much if she did n't somehow make her stepmother out, under the beautiful trees and among the dear old gardens, as lavish of fifty kinds of confidence and twenty kinds, at least, of gentleness. Gentleness and confidence were certainly the right thing as from a charming woman to her husband, but the fine tissue of reassurance woven by this lady's hands and flung over her companion as a light muffling veil, formed precisely a wrought transparency through which she felt her father's eyes continually rest on herself. The reach of his gaze came to her straighter from a distance; it showed him as still more conscious, down there alone, of the suspected, the felt elaboration of the process of their not alarming nor hurting him. She had herself now, for weeks and weeks, and all unwinkingly, traced the extension of this pious effort; but her perfect success in giving no sign — she did herself *that* credit—would have been an achievement quite wasted if Mrs. Verver should make with him those mistakes of proportion, one set of them too abruptly, too incoherently designed to correct another set, that she had made with his daughter. However, if she *had* been worse, poor woman, who should say that her husband would to a certainty have been better?

One groped noiselessly among such questions, and it was actually not even definite for the Princess that her own Amerigo, left alone with her in town, had arrived at the golden mean of non-precautionary gallantry which would tend by his calculation to brush private criticism from its last perching-place. The truth was, in this connexion, that she had different sorts of terrors, and there were hours when it came to her that these days were a prolonged repetition of that night-drive, of weeks before, from the other house to their own, when he had tried to charm her by his sovereign personal power into some collapse that would commit her to a repudiation of consistency. She was never alone with him, it was to be said, without her having sooner or later to ask herself what had already become of her consistency; yet at the same time so long as she breathed no charge she kept hold of a remnant of appearance that could save her from attack. Attack, real attack from him as he would conduct it, was what she above all dreaded; she was so far from sure that under that experience she might n't drop into some depth of weakness, might n't show him some shortest way with her that he would know how to use again. Therefore since she had given him as yet no moment's pretext for pretending to her that she had either lost faith or suffered by a feather's weight in happiness, she left him, it was easy to reason, with an immense advantage for all waiting and all tension. She wished him for the present to "make up" to her for nothing. Who could say to what making-up might lead, into what consenting or pretending or destroying blindness it might plunge her? She loved him too helplessly still to dare to open the door by an inch to his treating her as if either of them had wronged the other. Something or somebody — and who, at this, which of them all? — would inevitably, would in the gust of momentary selfishness, be sacrificed to that; whereas what she intelligently needed was to know where she was going. Knowledge, knowledge, was a fascination as well as a fear; and a part precisely of the strangeness of this juncture was the way her apprehension that he would break out to her with some merely general profession was mixed with her dire need to forgive him, to reassure him, to respond to him, on no ground that she did n't fully measure. To do these things it must be clear to her what they were *for;* but to act in that light was by the same effect to learn horribly what the other things had been. He might tell her only what he wanted, only what would work upon her by the beauty of his appeal; and the result of the direct appeal of *any* beauty in him would be her helpless submission to his terms. All her temporary safety, her hand-to-mouth success, accordingly, was in his neither perceiving nor divining this, thanks to such means as she could take to prevent him; take, literally from hour to hour, during these days of more unbroken exposure. From hour to hour she fairly expected some sign of his having decided on a jump. "Ah yes, it *has* been as you think; I've strayed away, I've fancied myself free, given myself in other quantities, with larger generosities, because I thought you were different — different from what I now see. But it was only, only, because I did n't know — and you must admit that you gave me scarce reason enough. Reason enough, I mean, to keep clear of my mistake; to which I confess, for which I'll do exquisite penance, which you can help me now, I too beautifully feel, to get completely over."

That was what, while she watched herself, she potentially heard him bring out; and while she carried to an end another day, another sequence and yet another of their hours together, without his producing it, she felt herself occupied with him beyond even the intensity of surrender. She was keeping her head for a reason, for a cause; and the labour of this detachment, with the labour of her forcing the pitch of it down, held them together in the steel hoop of an intimacy compared with which artless passion would have been but a beating of the air. Her greatest danger, or at least her greatest motive for care, was the obsession of the thought that if he actually did suspect, the fruit of his attention to her could n't help being a sense of the growth of her importance. Taking the measure with him, as she had taken it

with her father, of the prescribed reach of her hypocrisy, she saw how it would have to stretch even
to her seeking to prove that she was *not*, all the same,
important. A single touch from him — oh she should
know it in case of its coming!—any brush of his hand,
of his lips, of his voice, inspired by recognition of her
probable interest as distinct from pity for her virtual
gloom, would hand her over to him bound hand and
foot. Therefore to be free, to be free to act other
than abjectly for her father, she must conceal from
him the validity that, like a microscopic insect pushing a grain of sand, she was taking on even for herself.
She could keep it up with a change in sight, but she
could n't keep it up for ever; so that one extraordinary effect of their week of untempered confronta-
tion, which bristled with new marks, was to make
her reach out in thought to their customary companions and calculate the kind of relief that rejoining them would bring. She was learning almost from
minute to minute to be a mistress of shades — since
always when there were possibilities enough of intimacy there were also by that fact, in intercourse,
possibilities of iridescence; but she was working
against an adversary who was a master of shades
too and on whom if she did n't look out she should
presently have imposed a consciousness of the nature
of their struggle. To feel him in fact, to think of his
feeling himself, her adversary in things of this fineness — to see him at all in short brave a name that
would represent him as in opposition — was already
to be nearly reduced to a visible smothering of her
cry of alarm. Should he guess they were having in

their so occult manner a *high* fight, and that it was
she, all the while, in her supposed stupidity, who
had made it high and was keeping it high — in the
event of his doing this before they could leave town
she should verily be lost.

The possible respite for her at Fawns would come
from the fact that observation in him there would
inevitably find some of its directness diverted. This
would be the case if only because the remarkable
strain of her father's placidity might be thought of
as likely to claim some larger part of his attention.
Besides which there would be always Charlotte herself to draw him off. Charlotte would help him again
doubtless to study anything, right or left, that might
be symptomatic; but Maggie could see that this very
fact might perhaps contribute in its degree to protect the secret of her own fermentation. It is n't even
incredible that she may have discovered the gleam
of a comfort that was to broaden in the conceivable
effect on the Prince's spirit, on his nerves, on his finer
irritability, of some of the very airs and aspects, the
light graces themselves, of Mrs. Verver's too perfect competence. What it would most come to after
all, she said to herself, was a renewal for him of
the privilege of watching that lady watch *her*. Very
well then: with the elements really so mixed in him
how long would he go on enjoying mere spectator-
ship of that act? For she had by this time made up
her mind that in Charlotte's company he deferred to
Charlotte's easier art of mounting guard. Would n't
he get tired — to put it only at that — of seeing her
always on the rampart, erect and elegant, with her

lace-flounced parasol now folded and now shouldered, march to and fro against a gold-coloured east or west? Maggie had truly gone far for a view of the question of this particular reaction, and she was n't incapable of pulling herself up with the rebuke that she counted her chickens before they were hatched. How sure she should have to be of so many things before she might thus find a weariness in Amerigo's expression and a logic in his weariness!

One of her dissimulated arts for meeting their tension meanwhile was to interweave Mrs. Assingham as plausibly as possible with the parts and parcels of their surface, to bring it about that she should join them of an afternoon when they drove together or if they went to look at things — looking at things being almost as much a feature of their life as if they were bazaar-opening royalties. Then there were such combinations, later in the day, as her attendance on them, and the Colonel's as well, for such whimsical matters as visits to the opera no matter who was singing and sudden outbreaks of curiosity about the British drama. The good couple from Cadogan Place could always unprotestingly dine with them and "go on" afterwards to such publicities as the Princess cultivated the boldness of now perversely preferring. It may be said of her that during these passages she plucked her sensations by the way, detached nervously the small wild blossoms of her dim forest, so that she could smile over them at least with the spacious appearance, for her companions, for her husband above all, of bravely, of altogether frivolously, going a-maying. She had her intense, her smothered excitements, some of which were almost inspirations; she had in particular the extravagant, positively at moments the amused, sense of *using* her friend to the topmost notch, accompanied with the high luxury of not having to explain. Never, no never should she have to explain to Fanny Assingham again — who, poor woman, on her own side, would be charged, it might be for ever, with that privilege of the higher ingenuity. She put it all off on Fanny, and the dear thing herself might henceforth appraise the quantity. More and more magnificent now in her blameless egoism, Maggie asked no questions of her, and thus only signified the greatness of the opportunity she gave her. She did n't care for what devotions, what dinners of their own the Assinghams might have been "booked"; that was a detail, and she could think without wincing of the ruptures and rearrangements to which her service condemned them. It all fell in beautifully moreover; so that, as hard at this time, in spite of her fever, as a little pointed diamond, the Princess showed something of the glitter of consciously possessing the constructive, the creative hand. She had but to have the fancy of presenting herself, of presenting her husband, in a certain high and convenient manner, to make it natural they should go about with their gentleman and their lady. To what else but this exactly had Charlotte during so many weeks of the earlier season worked her up? — herself assuming and discharging, so far as might be, the character and office of one of those revolving subordinate presences that float in the wake of greatness.

The precedent was therefore established and the group normally constituted. Mrs. Assingham meanwhile, at table, on the stairs, in the carriage or the opera-box, might — with her constant overflow of expression, for that matter, and its singularly resident character where men in especial were concerned — look across at Amerigo in whatever sense she liked: it was n't of that Maggie proposed to be afraid. She might warn him, she might rebuke him, she might reassure him, she might — if it were impossible not to — absolutely make love to him; even this was open to her, as a matter simply between *them*, if it would help her to answer for the impeccability she had guaranteed. And Maggie desired in fact only to strike her as acknowledging the efficacy of her aid when she mentioned to her one evening a small project for the morrow, privately entertained — the idea, irresistible, intense, of going to pay at the Museum a visit to Mr. Crichton. Mr. Crichton, as Mrs. Assingham could easily remember, was the most accomplished and obliging of public functionaries, whom every one knew and who knew every one — who had from the first in particular lent himself freely, and for the love of art and history, to becoming one of the steadier lights of Mr. Verver's adventurous path. The custodian of one of the richest departments of the great national collection of precious things, he could feel for the sincere private collector and urge him on his way even when condemned to be present at his capture of trophies sacrificed by the country to parliamentary thrift. He carried his amiability to the point of saying that since London, under pettifogging views, *had* to miss from time to time its rarest opportunities, he was almost consoled to see such lost causes invariably wander at last one by one, with the tormenting tinkle of their silver bells, into the wondrous, the already famous fold beyond the Mississippi. There was a charm in his "almosts" that was not to be resisted, especially after Mr. Verver and Maggie had grown sure — or almost again — of enjoying the monopoly of them; and on this basis of envy changed to sympathy by the more familiar view of the father and the daughter, Mr. Crichton had at both houses, though especially in Eaton Square, learned to fill out the responsive and suggestive character. It was at his invitation, Fanny well recalled, that Maggie, one day, long before, and under her own attendance precisely, had, for the glory of the name she bore, paid a visit to one of the ampler shrines of the supreme exhibitory temple, an alcove of shelves charged with the gold-and-brown, gold-and-ivory, of old Italian bindings and consecrated to the records of the Prince's race. It had been an impression that penetrated, that remained; yet Maggie had sighed ever so prettily at its having to be so superficial. She was to go back some day, to dive deeper, to linger and taste; in spite of which, however, Mrs. Assingham could n't recollect perceiving that the visit had been repeated. This second occasion had given way, for a long time, in her happy life, to other occasions — all testifying in their degree to the quality of her husband's blood, its rich mixture and its many remarkable references; after which, no doubt, the charming piety involved had grown, on still further grounds, bewildered and faint.

It now appeared none the less that some renewed conversation with Mr. Crichton had breathed on the faintness revivingly, and Maggie mentioned her purpose as a conception of her very own, to the success of which she designed to devote her morning. Visits of gracious ladies, under his protection, lighted up rosily, for this perhaps most flower-loving and honey-sipping member of the great Bloomsbury hive, its packed passages and cells; and though not sworn of the province toward which his friend had found herself, according to her appeal to him, yearning again, nothing was easier for him than to put her in relation with the presiding urbanities. So it had been settled, Maggie said to Mrs. Assingham, and she was to dispense with Amerigo's company. Fanny was to remember later on that she had at first taken this last fact for one of the finer notes of her young woman's detachment, imagined she must be going alone because of the shade of irony that in these ambiguous days her husband's personal presence might be felt to confer practically on any tribute to his transmitted significance. Then as the next moment she felt it clear that so much plotted freedom was virtually a refinement of reflexion, an impulse to commemorate afresh whatever might still survive of pride and hope, her sense of ambiguity happily fell and she congratulated her companion on having anything so exquisite to do and on being so exquisitely in the humour to do it. After the occasion had come and gone she was confirmed in her optimism; she made out in the even-

ing that the hour spent among the projected lights,
the annals and illustrations, the parchments and
portraits, the emblazoned volumes and the murmured commentary, had been for the Princess en-
larging and inspiring. Maggie had said to her some
days before, very sweetly but very firmly, "Invite us
to dine, please, for Friday, and have any one you like
or you can — it does n't in the least matter whom";
and the pair in Cadogan Place had bent to this man-
date with a docility not in the least ruffled by all that
it took for granted.

It provided for an evening — this had been Maggie's
view; and she lived up to her view, in her friend's
eyes, by treating the occasion, more or less explicitly,
as new and strange. The good Assinghams had feasted
in fact at the two other boards on a scale so dispro-
portionate to the scant solicitations of their own that
it was easy to make a joke of seeing how they fed at
home, how they met, themselves, the question of
giving to eat. Maggie dined with them, in short,
and arrived at making her husband appear to dine,
much in the manner of a pair of young sovereigns
who have, in the frolic humour of the golden years
of reigns proposed themselves to a pair of faithfully-
serving subjects. She showed an interest in their ar-
rangements, an enquiring tenderness almost for their
economies; so that her hostess not unnaturally, as
they might have said, put it all down — the tone and
the freedom of which she set the example — to the
effect wrought in her afresh by one of the lessons
learned in the morning at the altar of the past.
Had n't she picked it up from an anecdote or two

offered again to her attention that there were for
princesses of such a line more ways than one of being
a heroine? Maggie's way to-night was to surprise
them all, truly, by the extravagance of her affability.
She was doubtless not positively boisterous; yet,
though Mrs. Assingham, as a bland critic, had never
doubted her being graceful, she had never seen her
put so much of it into being what might have been
called assertive. It was all a tune to which Fanny's
heart could privately palpitate: her guest was happy,
happy as a consequence of something that had occurred, but she was making the Prince not lose a
ripple of her laugh, though not perhaps always enabling him to find it absolutely not foolish. Foolish
in public beyond a certain point he was scarce the
man to brook his wife's being thought to be; so that
there hovered before their friend the possibility of some
subsequent scene between them, in the carriage or
at home, of slightly sarcastic enquiry, of promptly invited explanation; a scene that according as Maggie
should play her part in it might or might n't precipitate developments. What made these appearances
practically thrilling meanwhile was this mystery —
a mystery, it was clear, to Amerigo himself — of the
incident or the influence that had so peculiarly determined them.

The lady of Cadogan Place was to read deeper,
however, within three days, and the page was turned
for her on the eve of her young confidant's leaving
London. The awaited migration to Fawns was to
take place on the morrow, and it was known meanwhile to Mrs. Assingham that their party of four

were to dine that night, at the American Embassy,
with another and a larger party; so that the elder
woman had a sense of surprise on receiving from the
younger, under date of six o'clock, a telegram re-
questing her immediate attendance. "Please come
to me at once; dress early, if necessary, so that we
shall have time: the carriage, ordered for us, will take
you back first." Mrs. Assingham, on quick deliberation, dressed, though not perhaps with full lucidity,
and by seven o'clock was in Portland Place, where
her friend, "upstairs," and described to her on her
arrival as herself engaged in dressing, instantly received her. She knew on the spot, poor Fanny, as
she was afterwards to declare to the Colonel, that her
feared crisis had popped up as at the touch of a spring,
that her impossible hour was before her. Her impossible hour was the hour of its coming out that
she had known of old so much more than she had
ever said; and she had often put it to herself in apprehension, she tried to think even in preparation,
that she should recognise the approach of her doom
by a consciousness akin to that of the blowing open
of a window on some night of the highest wind and
the lowest thermometer. It would be all in vain to
have crouched so long by the fire; the glass would
have been smashed, the icy air would fill the place.
If the air in Maggie's room then, on her going up,
was n't as yet quite the polar blast she had expected,
it was none the less perceptibly such an atmosphere
as they had n't hitherto breathed together. The
Princess, she noted, was completely dressed — that
business was over; it added indeed to the effect of

her importantly awaiting the assistance she had summoned, of her showing a deck cleared, so to speak,
for action. Her maid had already left her, and she
presented herself, in the large clear room, where everything was admirable, but where nothing was out of
place, as for the first time in her life rather "bedizened." Was it that she had put on too many things,
overcharged herself with jewels, wore in particular
more of them than usual, and bigger ones, in her
hair? — a question her visitor presently answered by
attributing this appearance largely to the bright red
spot, red as some monstrous ruby, that burned in
either of her cheeks. These two items of her aspect
had promptly enough their own light for Mrs.
Assingham, who made out by it that nothing more
pathetic could be imagined than the refuge and disguise her agitation had instinctively asked of the arts
of dress, multiplied to extravagance, almost to inco-
herence. She had had visibly her idea—that of not
betraying herself by inattentions into which she had
never yet fallen, and she stood there circled about and
furnished forth, as always, in a manner that testified to
her perfect little personal processes. It had ever been
her sign that she was for all occasions *found* ready,
without loose ends or exposed accessories or unre-
moved superfluities; a suggestion of the swept and
garnished, in her whole splendid yet thereby more or
less encumbered and embroidered setting, that reflected her small still passion for order and symmetry,
for objects with their backs to the walls, and spoke
even of some probable reference in her American
blood to dusting and polishing New England grand-

mothers. If her apartment was "princely," in the clearness of the lingering day, she looked as if she had been carried there prepared, all attired and decorated, like some holy image in a procession, and left precisely to show what wonder she could work under pressure. Her friend felt — how could she not? — as the truly pious priest might feel when confronted, behind the altar, before the festa, with his miraculous Madonna. Such an occasion would be grave, in general, with all the gravity of what he might look for. But the gravity of to-night would be of the rarest; what he might look for would depend so on what he could give.

IX

"Something very strange has happened, and I think you ought to know it."

Maggie spoke this indeed without extravagance, yet with the effect of making her guest measure anew the force of her appeal. It was their definite understanding: whatever Fanny knew Fanny's faith would provide for. And she knew accordingly at the end of five minutes what the extraordinary in the late occurrence had consisted of, and how it had all come of Maggie's achieved hour, under Mr. Crichton's protection, at the Museum. He had desired, Mr. Crichton, with characteristic kindness, after the wonderful show, after offered luncheon at his contiguous lodge, a part of the place, to see her safely home; especially on his noting, in attending her to the great steps, that she had dismissed her carriage; which she had done really just for the harmless amusement of taking her way alone. She had known she should find herself, as the consequence of such an hour, in a sort of exalted state, under the influence of which a walk through the London streets would be exactly what would suit her best; an independent ramble, impressed excited contented, with nothing to mind and nobody to talk to and shop-windows in plenty to look at if she liked: a low taste, of the essence, it was to be supposed, of her nature, that she had of late for so many reasons been unable to gratify.

She had taken her leave with her thanks — she knew
her way quite enough; it being also sufficiently the
case that she had even a shy hope of not going too
straight. To wander a little wild was what would
truly amuse her; so that, keeping clear of Oxford
Street and cultivating an impression as of parts she
did n't know, she had ended with what she had more
or less been plotting for, an encounter with three
or four shops — an old bookseller's, an old print-
monger's, a couple of places with dim antiquities in
the window — that were not as so many of the other
shops, those in Sloane Street say; a hollow parade
which had long since ceased to beguile. There had
remained with her moreover an allusion of Charlotte's, of some months before — seed dropped into
her imagination in the form of a casual speech about
there being in Bloomsbury such "funny little fascinat-
ing" places and even sometimes such unexpected
finds. There could perhaps have been no stronger
mark than this sense of well-nigh romantic opportunity — no livelier sign of the impression made on
her, and always so long retained, so watchfully nursed,
by any observation of Charlotte's, however lightly
thrown off. And then she had felt somehow more
at her ease than for months and months before; she
did n't know why, but her time at the Museum, oddly,
had done it; it was as if she had n't come into so
many noble and beautiful associations, nor secured
them also for her boy, secured them even for her
father, only to see them turn to vanity and doubt,
turn possibly to something still worse. "I believed
in him again as much as ever, and I *felt* how I be-

lieved in him," she said with bright fixed eyes; "I felt it in the streets as I walked along, and it was as if that helped me and lifted me up, my being off by myself there, not having for the moment to wonder and watch; having on the contrary almost nothing on my mind."

It was so much as if everything would come out right that she had fallen to thinking of her father's birthday, had given herself this as a reason for trying what she could pick up for it. They would keep it at Fawns, where they had kept it before — since it would be. the twenty-first of the month; and she might n't have another chance of making sure of something to offer him. There was always of course the impossibility of finding him anything, the least bit "good," that he would n't already long ago in his rummagings have seen himself — and only not to think a quarter good enough; this however was an old story, and one could n't have had any fun with him but for his sweet theory that the individual gift, the friendship's offering, was by a rigorous law of nature a foredoomed aberration, and that the more it *was* so the more it showed, and the more one cherished it for showing, how friendly it had been. The infirmity of art was the candour of affection, the grossness of pedigree the refinement of sympathy; the ugliest objects in fact as a general thing were the bravest, the tenderest mementoes, and, as such, figured in glass cases apart, worthy doubtless of the home but not worthy of the temple — dedicated to the grimacing, not to the clear-faced gods. She herself, naturally, through the past years, had come to

be much represented in those receptacles; against the
thick locked panes of which she still liked to flatten
her nose, finding in its place each time everything
she had on successive anniversaries tried to believe
he might pretend at her suggestion to be put off with
or at least to think curious. She was now ready to
try it again: they had always, with his pleasure in
her pretence and her pleasure in his, with the funny
betrayal of the sacrifice to domestic manners on
either side, played the game so happily. To this
end, on her way home, she had loitered everywhere;
quite too deludedly among the old books and the old
prints, which had yielded nothing to her purpose,
but with a strange inconsequence in one of the other
shops, that of a small antiquarian, a queer little foreign
man who had shown her a number of things, shown
her finally something that, struck with it as rather
a rarity and thinking it would, compared to some of
her ventures, quite superlatively do, she had bought
— bought really, when it came to that, for a price.
"It appears now it won't do at all," said Maggie;
"something has happened since that puts it quite out
of the question. I had only my day of satisfaction in
it, but I feel at the same time, as I keep it here before
me, that I would n't have missed it for the world."
She had talked, from the first of her friend's entrance,
coherently enough, even with a small quaver that
overstated her calm; but she held her breath every few
seconds as if for deliberation and to prove she did n't
pant — all of which marked for Fanny the depth of
her commotion: her reference to her thought about
her father, about her chance to pick up something

that might divert him, her mention in fine of his fortitude under presents, having meanwhile naturally, it should be said, much less an amplitude of insistence on the speaker's lips than a power to produce on the part of the listener herself the prompt response and full comprehension of memory and sympathy, of old amused observation. The picture was filled out by the latter's fond fancy. But Maggie was at any rate under arms; she knew what she was doing and had already her plan — a plan for making, for allowing as yet, "no difference"; in accordance with which she would still dine out, and not with red eyes nor convulsed features nor neglected items of appearance, nor anything that would raise a question. Yet there was some knowledge that exactly to this support of her not breaking down she desired, she required, possession of; and with the sinister rise and fall of lightning unaccompanied by thunder it played before Mrs. Assingham's eyes that she herself should have, at whatever risk or whatever cost, to supply her with the stuff of her need. All our friend's instinct was to hold off from this till she should see what the ground would bear; she would take no step nearer unless *intelligibly* to meet her, and, awkward though it might be to hover there only pale and distorted, with mere imbecilities of vagueness, there was a quality of bald help in the fact of not as yet guessing what such an ominous start could lead to. She caught, however, after a second's thought, at the Princess's allusion to her lost reassurance.

"You mean you were so at your ease on Monday — the night you dined with us?"

"I was very happy then," said Maggie.

"Yes — we thought you so gay and so brilliant." Fanny felt it feeble, but she went on. "We were so *glad* you were happy."

Maggie stood a moment, at first only looking at her. "You thought me all right, eh?"

"Surely, dearest; we thought you all right."

"Well, I dare say it was natural; but in point of fact I never was more wrong in my life. For all the while if you please this was brewing."

Mrs. Assingham indulged, as nearly as possible to luxury, her vagueness. "'This' — ?"

"*That!*" replied the Princess, whose eyes, her companion now saw, had turned to an object on the chimney-piece of the room, of which, among so many precious objects — the Ververs, wherever they might be, always revelled peculiarly in matchless old mantel ornaments — her visitor had n't taken heed.

"Do you mean the gilt cup?"

"I mean the gilt cup."

The piece now recognised by Fanny as new to her own vision was a capacious bowl, of old-looking, rather strikingly yellow gold, mounted by a short stem on an ample foot which held a central position above the fireplace, where, to allow it the better to show, a clearance had been made of other objects, notably of the Louis-Seize clock that accompanied the candelabra. This latter trophy ticked at present on the marble slab of a commode that exactly matched it in splendour and style. Mrs. Assingham took it, the bowl, as a fine thing; but the question was obviously not of its intrinsic value, and she kept off

from it, admiring it at a distance. "But what has
that to do — ?"

"It has everything. You'll see." With which again
however for the moment Maggie attached to her
strange wide eyes. "He knew her before — before I
had ever seen him."

"'He' knew — ?" But Fanny, while she cast
about her for the links she missed, could only echo it.

"Amerigo knew Charlotte — more than I ever
dreamed."

Fanny felt then it was stare for stare. "But surely
you always knew they had met."

"I did n't understand. I knew too little. Don't
you see what I mean?" the Princess asked.

Mrs. Assingham wondered during these instants
how much she even now knew; it had taken a minute
to perceive how gently she was speaking. With that
perception of its being no challenge of wrath, no
heat of the deceived soul, but only a free exposure
of the completeness of past ignorance, inviting derision even if it must, the elder woman felt first a
strange barely credible relief: she drew in, as if it
had been the warm summer scent of a flower, the
sweet certainty of not meeting, any way she should
turn, any consequence of judgement. She should n't
be judged — save by herself; which was her own
wretched business. The next moment however at
all events she inwardly blushed not for her immediate cowardice: she had thought of herself, thought
of "getting off," before so much as thinking — that
is of pitifully seeing — that she was in presence of an
appeal that was *all* an appeal, that utterly accepted

its necessity. "In a general way, dear child, yes. But not — a — in connexion with what you've been telling me."

"They were intimate, you see. Intimate," said the Princess.

Fanny continued to face her, taking from her excited eyes this history, so dim and faint for all her anxious emphasis, of the far-away other time. "There's always the question of what one considers —!"

"What one considers intimate? Well, I know what I consider intimate now. Too intimate," said Maggie, "to let me know anything about it."

It was quiet — yes; but not too quiet for Fanny Assingham's capacity to wince. "Only compatible with letting *me*, you mean?" She had asked it after a pause, but turning again to the new ornament of the chimney and wondering even while she took relief from it at this gap in her experience. "But here are things, my dear, of which my ignorance is perfect."

"They went about together — they're known to have done it. And I don't mean only before — I mean after."

"After?" said Fanny Assingham.

"Before we were married — yes; but after we were engaged."

"Ah I've known nothing about that!" And she said it with a braver assurance — clutching with comfort at something that was apparently new to her.

"That bowl," Maggie went on, "is, so strangely — too strangely almost to believe at this time of day

— the proof. They were together all the while — up to the very eve of our marriage. Don't you remember how just before that she came back so unexpectedly from America?"

The question had for Mrs. Assingham — and whether all consciously or not — the oddest pathos of simplicity. "Oh yes, dear, of course I remember how she came back from America — and how she stayed with *us*, and what view one had of it."

Maggie's eyes still all the time pressed and penetrated; so that during a moment just here she might have given the little flare, have made the little pounce, of asking what then "one's" view had been. To the small flash of this eruption Fanny stood for her minute wittingly exposed; but she saw it as quickly cease to threaten — quite saw the Princess, even though in all her pain, refuse, in the interest of their strange and exalted bargain, to take advantage of the opportunity for planting the stab of reproach, the opportunity thus coming all of itself. She saw her — or believed she saw her — look at her chance for straight denunciation, look at it and then pass it by; and she felt herself with this fact hushed well-nigh to awe at the lucid higher intention that no distress could confound and that no discovery — since it was, however obscurely, a case of "discovery" — could make less needful. These seconds were brief — they rapidly passed; but they lasted long enough to renew our friend's sense of her own extraordinary undertaking, the function again imposed on her, the answerability again drilled into her, by this intensity of intimation. She was reminded of the

terms on which she was let off — her quantity of
release having made its sufficient show in that recall
of her relation to Charlotte's old reappearance; and
deep within the whole impression glowed — ah so
inspiringly when it came to that! — her steady view,
clear from the first, of the beauty of her companion's
motive. It was like a fresh sacrifice for a larger conquest — "Only see me through *now*, do it in the face
of this and in spite of it, and I leave you a hand of
which the freedom is n't to be said!" The aggravation of fear — or call it apparently of knowledge —
had jumped straight into its place as an aggravation
above all for her father; the effect of this being but
to quicken to passion her reasons for making his
protectedness, or in other words the forms of his
ignorance, still the law of her attitude and the key
to her solution. She kept as tight hold of these reasons and these forms, in her confirmed horror, as the
rider of a plunging horse grasps his seat with his knees
and she might absolutely have been putting it to her
guest that she believed she could stay on if they
should only "meet" nothing more. Though ignorant still of what she *had* definitely met Fanny yearned,
within, over her spirit; and so, no word about it
said, passed, through mere pitying eyes, a vow to
walk ahead and, at cross-roads, with a lantern for
the darkness and wavings-away for unadvised traf-
fic, look out for alarms. There was accordingly no
wait in Maggie's reply. "They spent together hours
— spent at least a morning — the certainty of which
has come back to me now, but that I did n't dream
of at the time. That cup there has turned witness —

by the most wonderful of chances. That's why, since it has been here, I've stood it out for my husband to see; put it where it would meet him almost immediately if he should come into the room. I've wanted it to meet him," she went on, "and I've wanted him to meet *it*, and to be myself present at the meeting. But that has n't taken place as yet; often as he has lately been in the way of coming to see me here — yes in particular lately — he has n't showed to-day." It was with her managed quietness more and more that she talked — an achieved coherence that helped her evidently to hear and to watch herself; there was support, and thereby an awful harmony, but which meant a further guidance, in the facts she could add together. "It's quite as if he had an instinct — something that has warned him off or made him uneasy. He does n't understand, naturally, what has happened, but guesses, with his beautiful cleverness, that something has, and is n't in a hurry to be confronted with it. So in his vague fear he keeps off."

"But being meanwhile in the house — ?"

"I've no idea — not having seen him to-day, by exception, since before luncheon. He spoke to me then," the Princess freely explained, "of a ballot, of great importance, at a club — for somebody, some personal friend, I think, who's coming up and is supposed to be in danger. To make an effort for him he thought he had better lunch there. You see the efforts he *can* make"—for which Maggie found a smile that went to her friend's heart. "He's in so many ways the kindest of men. But it was hours ago."

Mrs. Assingham thought. "The more danger then of his coming in and finding me here. I don't know, you see, what you now consider that you've ascertained; nor anything of the connexion with it of that object that you declare so damning." Her eyes rested on this odd acquisition and then quitted it, went back to it and again turned from it: it was inscrutable in its rather stupid elegance, and yet, from the moment one had thus appraised it, vivid and definite in its domination of the scene. Fanny could no more overlook it now than she could have overlooked a lighted Christmas-tree; but nervously and all in vain she dipped into her mind for some floating reminiscence of it. At the same time that this attempt left her blank she understood a good deal, she even not a little shared, the Prince's mystic apprehension. The golden bowl put on, under consideration, a sturdy, a conscious perversity; as a "document," somehow, it was ugly, though it might have a decorative grace. "His finding me here in presence of it might be more flagrantly disagreeable — for all of us — than you intend or than would necessarily help us. And I must take time truly to understand what it means."

"You're safe, as far as that goes," Maggie returned; "you may take it from me that he won't come in and that I shall only find him waiting for me below when I go down to the carriage."

Fanny Assingham took it from her, took it and more. "We're to sit together at the Ambassador's then — or at least you two are — with this new complication thrust up before you and all unexplained;

and to look at each other with faces that pretend for the ghastly hour not to be seeing it?"

Maggie looked at *her* with a face that might have been the one she was preparing. "'Unexplained,' my dear? Quite the contrary — explained: fully, intensely, admirably explained, with nothing really to add. My own love" — she kept it up — "I don't want anything *more*. I've plenty to go upon and to do with as it is."

Fanny Assingham stood there in her comparative darkness, with her links verily still missing; and the most acceptable effect of this was, singularly, as yet, a cold fear of getting nearer the fact. "But when you come home —? I mean he'll come up with you again. Won't he see it then?"

On which Maggie gave her, after an instant's visible thought, the strangest of slow headshakes. "I don't know. Perhaps he'll never see it — if it only stands there waiting for him. He may never again," said the Princess, "come into this room."

Fanny more deeply wondered. "Never again? Oh —!"

"Yes, it may be. How do I know? With *this!*" she quietly went on.

She hadn't looked again at the incriminating piece, but there was a marvel to her friend in the way the little word representing it seemed to express and include for her the whole of her situation. "Then you intend not to speak to him —?"

Maggie waited. "To 'speak' —?"

"Well, about your having it and about what you consider that it represents."

"Oh I don't know that I shall speak — if he does n't. But his keeping away from me because of that — what will that *be* but to speak? He can't say or do more. It won't be for me to speak," Maggie added in a different tone, one of the tones that had already so penetrated her guest. "It will be for me to listen."

Mrs. Assingham turned it over. "Then it all depends on that object that you regard, for your reasons, as evidence?"

"I think I may say that *I* depend on it. I can't," said Maggie, "treat it as nothing now."

Mrs. Assingham, at this, went closer to the cup on the chimney — quite liking to feel that she did so, moreover, without going closer to her companion's vision. She looked at the precious thing — if precious it was — found herself in fact eyeing it as if, by her dim solicitation, to draw its secret from it rather than suffer the imposition of Maggie's knowledge. It was brave and firm and rich, with its bold deep hollow; and, without this queer torment about it, would, thanks to her love of plenty of yellow, figure to her as an enviable ornament, a possession really desirable. She did n't touch it, but if after a minute she turned away from it the reason was, rather oddly and suddenly, in her fear of doing so. "Then it all depends on the bowl? I mean your future does? For that's what it comes to, I judge."

"What it comes to," Maggie presently returned, "is what that thing has put me, so almost miraculously, in the way of learning: how far they had originally gone together. If there was so much between them before, there can't — with all the other appearances — not be a great deal more now." And she went on and on; she steadily made her points. "If such things were already then between them they make all the difference for possible doubt of what may have been between them since. If there had been nothing before there might be explanations. But it makes to-day too much to explain. I mean to explain away," she said.

Fanny Assingham was there to explain away — of this she was duly conscious; for that at least had been true up to now. In the light, however, of Maggie's demonstration the quantity, even without her taking as yet a more exact measure, might well seem larger than ever. Besides which, with or without exactness, the effect of each successive minute in the place was to put her more in presence of what Maggie herself saw. Maggie herself saw the truth, and that was really while they remained there together enough for Mrs. Assingham's relation to it. There was a force in the Princess's mere manner about it that made the detail of what she knew a matter of minor importance. Fanny had in fact something like a momentary shame over her own need of asking for this detail. "I don't pretend to repudiate," she said after a little, "my own impressions of the different times I suppose you speak of; any more," she added, "than I can forget what difficulties and, as it constantly seemed to me, what dangers, every course of action — whatever I should decide upon — made for me. I tried, I tried hard, to act for the best. And, you know," she next pursued while at the sound of her own statement a slow courage and even a faint warmth of conviction came back to her — "and, you know, I believe it's what I shall turn out to have done."

This produced a minute during which their interchange, though quickened and deepened, was that of silence only and the long, charged look; all of which found virtual consecration when Maggie at last spoke. "I'm sure you tried to act for the best."

It kept Fanny Assingham again a minute in silence. "I never thought, dearest, you were n't an angel."

Not however that this alone was much help! "It was up to the very eve, you see," the Princess went on — "up to within two or three days of our marriage. That, *that*, you know —!" And she broke down for strangely smiling.

"Yes, as I say, it was while she was with me. But I did n't know it. That is," said Fanny Assingham, "I did n't know of anything in particular." It sounded weak — that she felt; but she had really her point to make. "What I mean is that I don't *know*, for knowledge, now, anything I did n't then. That's how I am." She still however floundered. "I mean it's how I *was*."

"But don't they, how you were and how you are," Maggie asked, "come practically to the same thing?" The elder woman's words had struck her own ear as in the tone, now mistimed, of their recent but all too factitious understanding, arrived at in hours when, as there was nothing susceptible of proof, there was nothing definitely to disprove. The situation had changed by — well, by whatever there was, by the outbreak of the definite; and this could keep Maggie at least firm. She was firm enough as she pursued. "It was *on* the whole thing that Amerigo married me." With which her eyes had their turn again at her damnatory piece. "And it was on that — it was on that!" But they came back to her visitor. "And it was on it all that father married *her*."

Her visitor took it as might be. "They both married — ah that you must believe! — with the highest intentions."

"Father did certainly!" And then at the renewal of this consciousness it all rolled over her. "Ah to thrust such things on *us*, to do them here between us and with us day after day and in return, in return —! To do it to *him* — to him, to him!"

Fanny hesitated. "You mean it's for him you most suffer?" And then as the Princess, after a look, but turned away, moving about the room — which made the question somehow seem a blunder — "I ask," she continued, "because I think everything, everything we now speak of, may be for him really, may be *made* for him, quite as if it had n't been."

But Maggie had the next moment faced about as if without hearing her. "Father did it for *me* — did it all and only for me."

Mrs. Assingham, with a certain promptness, threw up her head; but she faltered again before she spoke. "Well —!"

It was only an intended word, but Maggie showed after an instant that it had reached her. "Do you mean that that's the reason, that that's *a* reason —?"

Fanny at first however, feeling the response in this, did n't say all she meant; she said for the moment something else instead. "He did it for you — largely at least for you. And it was for you that I did, in my smaller interested way — well, what I could do. For I could do something," she continued; "I thought I saw your interest as he himself saw it. And I thought I saw Charlotte's. I believed in her."

"And *I* believed in her," said Maggie.

Mrs. Assingham waited again; but she presently pushed on. "She believed then in herself."

"Ah?" Maggie murmured.

Something exquisite, faintly eager, in the prompt simplicity of it, supported her friend further. "And the Prince believed. His belief was real. Just as he believed in himself."

Maggie spent a minute in taking it from her. "He believed in himself?"

"Just as I too believed in him. For I absolutely did, Maggie." To which Fanny then added: "And I believe in him yet. I mean," she subjoined — "well, I mean I *do*."

Maggie again took it from her; after which she was again restlessly set afloat. Then when this had come to an end: "And do you believe in Charlotte yet?"

Mrs. Assingham had a demur that she felt she could now afford. "We'll talk of Charlotte some other day. They both at any rate thought themselves safe at the time."

"Then why did they keep from me everything I might have known?"

Her friend bent upon her the mildest eyes. "Why did I myself keep it from you?"

"Oh you were n't obliged for honour."

"Dearest Maggie," the poor woman broke out on this, "you *are* divine!"

"They pretended to love me," the Princess went on. "And they pretended to love *him*."

"And pray what was there that I didn't pretend?"

"Not at any rate to care for me as you cared for Amerigo and for Charlotte. They were much more interesting — it was perfectly natural. How couldn't you like Amerigo?" Maggie continued.

Mrs. Assingham gave it up. "How couldn't I, how couldn't I?" Then with a fine freedom she went all her way. "How *can't* I, how can't I?"

It fixed afresh Maggie's wide eyes on her. "I see — I see. Well, it's beautiful for you to be able to. And of course," she added, "you wanted to help Charlotte."

"Yes" — Fanny considered it — "I wanted to help Charlotte. But I wanted also, you see, to help you — by not digging up a past that I believed, with so much on top of it, solidly buried. I wanted, as I still want," she richly declared, "to help every one."

It set Maggie once more in movement — movement which however spent itself again with a quick emphasis. "Then it's a good deal my fault — if everything really began so well?"

Fanny Assingham met it as she could. "You've been only too perfect. You've thought only too much —"

But the Princess had already caught at the words. "Yes — I've thought only too much!" Yet she appeared to continue for the minute full of that fault.

She had it in fact, by this prompted thought, all before her. "Of him, dear man, of *him* —!"

Her friend, able to take in thus directly her vision of her father, watched her with a new suspense. *That* way might safety lie — it was like a wider chink of light. "He believed—with a beauty!—in Charlotte."

"Yes, and it was I who had made him believe. I did n't mean to at the time so much, for I had no idea then of what was coming. But I did it, I did it!" the Princess declared.

"With a beauty — ah with a beauty you too!" Mrs. Assingham insisted.

Maggie at all events was seeing for herself — it was another matter. "The thing was that he made her think it would be so possible."

Fanny again hesitated. "The Prince made her think — ?"

Maggie stared — she had meant her father. But her vision seemed to spread. "They both made her think. She would n't have thought without them."

"Yet Amerigo's good faith," Mrs. Assingham insisted, "was perfect. And there was nothing, all the more," she added, "against your father's."

The remark kept Maggie for a moment still. "Nothing perhaps but his knowing that she knew."

"'Knew' — ?"

"That he was doing it so much for me. To what extent," she suddenly asked of her friend, "do you think he was aware she knew?"

"Ah who can say what passes between people in such a relation? The only thing one can be sure of is that he was generous." And Mrs. Assingham conclusively smiled. "He doubtless knew as much as was right for himself."

"As much, that is, as was right for her."

"Yes then — as was right for her. The point is," Fanny declared, "that whatever his knowledge it made all the way it went for his good faith."

Maggie continued to gaze, and her friend now fairly waited on her successive movements. "Is n't the point, very considerably, that his good faith must have been his faith in her taking almost as much interest in me as he himself took?"

Fanny Assingham thought. "He recognised, he adopted, your long friendship. But he founded on it no selfishness."

"No," said Maggie with still deeper consideration: "he counted her selfishness out almost as he counted his own."

"So you may say."

"Very well," Maggie went on; "if he had none of his own, he invited her, may have expected her, on her side, to have as little. And she may only since have found that out."

Mrs. Assingham looked blank. "Since —?"

"And he may have become aware," Maggie pursued, "that she has found it out. That she has taken the measure, since their marriage," she explained, "of how much he had asked of her — more say than she had understood at the time. He may have made out at last how such a demand was in the long run to affect her."

"He may have done many things," Mrs. Assingham responded; "but there's one thing he certainly won't have done. He'll never have shown that he expected of her a quarter as much as she must have understood he was to give."

"I've often wondered," Maggie mused, "what Charlotte really understood. But it's one of the things she has never told me."

"Then as it's one of the things she has never told me either we shall probably never know it, and we may regard it as none of our business. There are many things," said Mrs. Assingham, "that we shall never know."

Maggie took it in with a long reflexion. "Never."

"But there are others," her friend went on, "that stare us in the face and that — under whatever difficulty you may feel you labour — may now be enough for us. Your father has been extraordinary."

It had been as if Maggie were feeling her way, but she rallied to this with a rush. "Extraordinary."

"Magnificent," said Fanny Assingham.

Her companion held tight to it. "Magnificent."

"Then he'll do for himself whatever there may be to do. What he undertook for you he'll do to the end. He did n't undertake it to break down; in what — quiet patient exquisite as he is — did he *ever* break down? He had never in his life proposed to himself to have failed, and he won't have done it on this occasion."

"Ah this occasion!" — and Maggie's wail showed her of a sudden thrown back on it. "Am I in the least sure that, with everything, he even knows what it is? And yet am I in the least sure he does n't?"

175

"If he does n't then so much the better. Leave him alone."

"Do you mean give him up?"

"Leave *her*," Fanny Assingham went on. "Leave her *to* him."

Maggie looked at her darkly. "Do you mean leave him to *her*? After this?"

"After everything. Are n't they, for that matter, intimately together now?"

"'Intimately' —? How do I know?"

But Fanny kept it up. "Are n't you and your husband — in spite of everything?"

Maggie's eyes still further if possible dilated. "It remains to be seen!"

"If you 're not then where 's your faith?"

"In my husband —?"

Mrs. Assingham but for an instant hesitated. "In your father. It all comes back to that. Rest on it."

"On his ignorance?"

Fanny met it again. "On whatever he may offer you. *Take* that."

"Take it —?" Maggie stared.

Mrs. Assingham held up her head. "And be grateful." On which for a minute she let the Princess face her. "Do you see?"

"I see," said Maggie at last.

"Then there you are." But Maggie had turned away, moving to the window as if still to keep something in her face from sight. She stood there with her eyes on the street while Mrs. Assingham's reverted to that complicating object on the chimney as to which her condition, so oddly even to herself, was that both of recurrent wonder and recurrent protest. She went over to it, looked at it afresh and yielded now to her impulse to feel it in her hands. She laid them on it, lifting it up, and was surprised thus with the weight of it — she had seldom handled so much massive gold. That effect itself somehow prompted her to further freedom and presently to saying: "I don't believe in this, you know."

It brought Maggie round to her. "Don't believe in it? You will when I tell you."

"Ah tell me nothing! I won't have it," said Mrs. Assingham. She kept the cup in her hand, held it there in a manner that gave Maggie's attention to her, she saw the next moment, a quality of excited suspense. This suggested to her oddly that she had, with the liberty she was taking, an air of intention, and the impression betrayed by her companion's eyes grew more distinct on the latter's part in a word of warning.

"It's of value, but its value's impaired, I've learned, by a crack."

"A crack? — in the gold — ?"

"It isn't gold." With which, Maggie somewhat strangely smiled. "That's the point."

"What is it then?"

"It's glass — and cracked, under the gilt, as I say, at that."

"Glass? — of this weight?"

"Well," said Maggie, "it's crystal — and was once I suppose precious. But what," she then asked, "do you mean to do with it?"

She had come away from her window, one of the

three by which the wide room, enjoying an advantageous "back," commanded the western sky and caught a glimpse of the evening flush; while Mrs. Assingham, possessed of the bowl and possessed too of this indication of a flaw, approached another for the benefit of the slowly-fading light. Here, thumbing the singular piece, weighing it, turning it over and growing suddenly more conscious, above all, of an irresistible impulse, she presently spoke again. "A crack? Then your whole idea has a crack."

Maggie, by this time at some distance from her, waited a moment. "If you mean by my idea the knowledge that has come to me that —"

But Fanny, with decision, had already taken her up. "There's only one knowledge that concerns us — one fact with which we can have anything to do."

"Which one then?"

"The fact that your husband has never, never, never —!" But the very gravity of this statement, while she raised her eyes to her friend across the room, made her for an instant hang fire.

"Well, never what?"

"Never been half so interested in you as now. But don't you, my dear, really feel it?"

Maggie took her time. "Oh I think what I've told you helps me to feel it. His having to-day given up even his forms; his keeping away from me; his not having come." And she shook her head as against all easy glosses. "It *is* because of that, you know."

"Well, then if it's because of this —!" And Fanny Assingham, who had been casting about her and whose inspiration decidedly had come, raised

the cup in her two hands, raised it positively above
her head and from under it solemnly smiled at the
Princess as a signal of intention. So for an instant, full
of her thought and of her act, she held the precious
vessel, and then with due note taken of the margin of
the polished floor, bare fine and hard in the embrasure
of her window, dashed it boldly to the ground, where
she had the thrill of seeing it lie shattered with the
violence of the crash. She had flushed with the force
of her effort as Maggie had flushed with wonder at
the sight, and this high reflexion in their faces was
all that passed between them for a minute more.
After which, "Whatever you meant by it — and I
don't want to know *now* — has ceased to exist," Mrs.
Assingham said.

"And what in the world, my dear, *did* you mean
by it?" That clear vibration of the touched spring
rang out as the first effect of Fanny's speech. It broke
upon the two women's absorption with a sharpness
almost equal to the smash of the crystal, for the door
of the room had been opened by the Prince without
their taking heed. He had apparently had time
moreover to catch the conclusion of Fanny's act;
his eyes attached themselves, through the large
space allowing just there, as happened, a free view,
to the shining fragments at this lady's feet. His
question had been addressed to his wife, but he
moved his eyes immediately afterwards to those of
her visitor, whose own then held them in a manner
of which neither party had been capable, doubtless,
for mute penetration, since the hour spent by him
in Cadogan Place on the eve of his marriage and the

afternoon of Charlotte's reappearance. Something now again became possible for these communicants under the intensity of their pressure, something that took up that tale and that might have been a redemption of pledges then exchanged. This rapid play of suppressed appeal and disguised response lasted indeed long enough for more results than one; quite enough for Mrs. Assingham to measure the feat of quick self-recovery, possibly therefore of recognition still more immediate, accompanying Amerigo's vision and estimate of the evidence with which she had been — so admirably, she felt as she looked at him — inspired to deal. She looked at him and looked at him — there were so many things she wanted on the spot to say. But Maggie was looking too — and was moreover looking at them both; so that these things, for the elder woman, very quickly reduced themselves to one. She met his question — not too late, since it had by their silence remained in the air. Gathering herself to go, leaving the golden bowl split into three pieces on the ground, she simply referred him to his wife. She should see them later, they would all meet soon again; and meanwhile, as to what Maggie had meant — she said, in her turn, from the door — why Maggie herself was doubtless by this time ready to tell him.

X

LEFT with her husband Maggie however for the time said nothing; she only felt on the spot a strong, sharp wish not to see his face again till he should have had a minute to arrange it. She had seen it enough for her temporary clearness and her next movement — seen as it showed during the stare of surprise that followed his entrance. Then it was that she knew how hugely expert she had been made — made for judging it quickly — by the vision of it, indelibly registered for reference, that had flashed a light into her troubled soul the night of his late return from Matcham. The expression worn by it at that juncture for however few instants had given her a sense of its possibilities, one of the most relevant of which might have been playing up for her, before the consummation of Fanny Assingham's retreat, just long enough to be recognised. What she had recognised in it was *his* recognition, the result of his having been forced, by the flush of their visitor's attitude and the unextinguished report of her words, to take account of the flagrant signs of the accident, of the incident, on which he had unexpectedly dropped. He had not unnaturally failed to see this occurrence represented by the three fragments of an object apparently valuable which lay there on the floor and which even across the width of the room, his kept interval, reminded him, unmistakeably though confusedly, of something known, some other unfor-

181

gotten image. That was a mere shock, that was a pain — as if Fanny's violence had been a violence redoubled and acting beyond its intention, a violence calling up the hot blood as a blow across the mouth might have called it. Maggie knew as she turned away from him that she did n't want his pain; what she wanted was her own simple certainty — not the red mark of conviction flaming there in his beauty. If she could have gone on with bandaged eyes she would have liked that best; if it were a question of saying what she now apparently should have to, and of taking from him what he would say, any blindness that might wrap it would be the nearest approach to a boon.

She went in silence to where her friend — never in intention visibly so much her friend as at that moment — had braced herself to so amazing an energy, and there under Amerigo's eyes she picked up the shining pieces. Bedizened and jewelled, in her rustling finery, she paid, with humility of attitude, this prompt tribute to order — only to find however that she could carry but two of the fragments at once. She brought them over to the chimney-piece, to the conspicuous place occupied by the cup before Fanny's appropriation of it, and after laying them carefully down went back for what remained, the solid detached foot. With this she returned to the mantel-shelf, placing it with deliberation in the centre and then for a minute occupying herself as with the attempt to fit the other morsels together. The split determined by the latent crack was so sharp and so neat that if there had been anything to hold them the bowl might still quite beautifully, a few steps away, have passed for uninjured. As there was however nothing to hold them but Maggie's hands during the few moments the latter were so employed, she could only lay the almost equal parts of the vessel carefully beside their pedestal and leave them thus before her husband's eyes. She had proceeded without words, but quite as if with a sought effect — in spite of which it had all seemed to her to take a far longer time than anything she had ever so quickly accomplished. Amerigo said nothing either — though it was true his silence had the gloss of the warning she doubtless appeared to admonish him to take: it was as if her manner hushed him to the proper observation of what she was doing. He should have no doubt of it whatever: she *knew*, and her broken bowl was proof that she knew — yet the least part of her desire was to make him waste words. He would have to think — this she knew even better still; and all she was for the present concerned with was that he should be aware. She had taken him for aware all day, or at least for obscurely and instinctively anxious — as to that she had just committed herself to Fanny Assingham; but what she had been wrong about was the effect of his anxiety. His fear of staying away, as a marked symptom, had at least proved greater than his fear of coming in; he had come in even at the risk of bringing it with him — and ah what more did she require now than her sense, established within the first minute or two, that he *had* brought it, however he might be steadying himself against dangers of betrayal by some wrong word, and that it was shut in there between them, the successive moments throbbing under it the while as the pulse of fever throbs under the doctor's thumb?

Maggie's sense accordingly in his presence was that though the bowl had been broken her reason had n't; the reason for which she had made up her mind, the reason for which she had summoned her friend, the reason for which she had addressed the place to her husband's eyes; it was all one reason, and as her intense little clutch held the matter what had happened by Fanny's act and by his apprehension of it had n't in the least happened to *her*, but absolutely and directly to himself, as he must proceed to take in. There it was that her wish for time interposed — time for Amerigo's use, not for hers, since she for ever so long now, for hours and hours as they seemed, had been living with eternity; with which she would continue to live. She wanted to say to him "Take it, take it, take all you need of it; arrange yourself so as to suffer least, or to be at any rate least distorted and disfigured. Only *see*, see that *I* see, and make up your mind on this new basis at your convenience. Wait — it won't be long — till you can confer again with Charlotte, for you'll do it much better then, more easily to both of us. Above all don't show me, till you've got it well under, the dreadful blur, the ravage of suspense and embarrassment produced, and produced by my doing, in your personal serenity, your incomparable superiority." After she had squared again her little objects on the chimney she was within an ace, in fact, of turning on him with that appeal; besides its being lucid for her all the while that the occasion was passing, that they were dining out, that he was n't

dressed, and that, though she herself was, she was yet
in all probability so horribly red in the face and so
awry in many ways with agitation, that in view of
the Ambassador's company, of possible comments
and constructions, she should need before her glass
some restoration of appearances.

Amerigo meanwhile after all could clearly make
the most of her having enjoined on him to wait — suggested it by the positive pomp of her dealings with the
smashed cup; to wait, that is, till she should pronounce
as Mrs. Assingham had promised for her. This delay again certainly tested her presence of mind —
though that strain was not what presently made her
speak. Keep her eyes for the time from her husband's as she might, she soon found herself much more
drivingly conscious of the strain on his own wit.
There was even a minute, when her back was turned
to him, during which she knew once more the strangeness of her desire to spare him, a strangeness that had
already fifty times brushed her, in the depth of her
trouble, as with the wild wing of some bird of the air
who might blindly have swooped for an instant into
the shaft of a well, darkening there by his momentary flutter the far-off round of sky. It was extraordinary, this quality in the taste of her wrong which
made her completed sense of it seem rather to soften
than to harden, and it was the more extraordinary the
more she had to recognise it; for what it came to was
that seeing herself finally sure, knowing everything,
having the fact, in all its abomination, so utterly before her that there was nothing else to add — what it
came to was that merely by being *with* him there in

silence she felt within her the sudden split between conviction and action. They had begun to cease on the spot, surprisingly, to be connected; conviction, that is, budged no inch, only planting its feet the more firmly in the soil — but action began to hover like some lighter and larger but easier form, excited by its very power to keep above ground. It would be free, it would be independent, it would go in — would n't it ? — for some prodigious and superior adventure of its own. What would condemn it, so to speak, to the responsibility of freedom — this glimmered on Maggie even now — was the possibility, richer with every lapsing moment, that her husband would have on the whole question a new need of her, a need which was in fact being born between them in these very seconds. It struck her truly as so new that he would have felt hitherto none to compare with it at all; would indeed absolutely by this circumstance be *really* needing her for the first time in their whole connexion. No, he had used her, he had even exceedingly enjoyed her, before this; but there had been no precedent for that character of a proved necessity to him which she was rapidly taking on. The immense advantage of this particular clue moreover was that she should have now to arrange, to alter, to falsify nothing; should have to be but consistently simple and straight. She asked herself with concentration, while her back was still presented, what would be the very ideal of that method; but the next instant it had all come to her and she had turned round on him for the application. "Fanny Assingham broke it — knowing it had a crack and that it would go if she used sufficient force.

She thought, when I had told her, that that would be the best thing to do with it — thought so from her own point of view. That had n't been at all my idea, but she acted before I understood. I had on the contrary," she explained, "put it here in full view exactly that you might see it."

He stood with his hands in his pockets; he had carried his eyes to the fragments on the chimney-piece, and she could already distinguish the element of relief, absolutely of succour, in his acceptance from her of the opportunity to consider the fruits of their friend's violence — every added inch of reflexion and delay having the advantage, from this point on, of counting for him double. It had operated within her now to the last intensity, her glimpse of the precious truth that by her helping him, helping him to help himself, as it were, she should help him to help *her*. Had n't she fairly got into his labyrinth with him? — was n't she indeed in the very act of placing herself there for him at its centre and core, whence, on that definite orientation and by an instinct all her own, she might securely guide him out of it? She offered him thus assuredly a kind of support that was n't to have been imagined in advance and that moreover required — ah most truly! — some close looking at before it could be believed in and pronounced void of treachery. "Yes, look, look," she seemed to see him hear her say even while her sounded words were other — "look, look, both at the truth that still survives in that smashed evidence and at the even more remarkable appearance that I 'm not such a fool as you supposed me. Look at the possibility that since I *am* different

there may still be something in it for you — if you 're
capable of working with me to get that out. Consider
of course as you must the question of what you may
have to surrender on your side, what price you may
have to pay, whom you may have to pay *with*, to set
this advantage free; but take in at any rate that there
is something for you if you don't too blindly spoil your
chance for it." He went no nearer the damnatory
pieces, but he eyed them from where he stood with
a degree of recognition just visibly less to be dissimulated; all of which represented for her a certain traceable process. And her uttered words meanwhile
were different enough from those he might have in-
serted between the lines of her already-spoken. "It 's
the golden bowl, you know, that you saw at the little
antiquario's in Bloomsbury so long ago — when you
went there with Charlotte, when you spent those hours
with her, unknown to me, a day or two before our marriage. It was shown you both, but you did n't take it;
you left it for me, and I came upon it, extraordinarily,
through happening to go into the same shop on Monday last; in walking home, in prowling about to pick
up some small old thing for father's birthday after my
visit to the Museum, my appointment there with Mr.
Crichton, of which I told you. It was shown me and
I was struck with it and took it — knowing nothing
about it at the time. What I now know I've learned
since — I learned this afternoon, a couple of hours ago;
receiving from it naturally a great impression. So
there it is — in its three pieces. You can handle them
— don't be afraid — if you want to make sure the
thing *is* the thing you and Charlotte saw together. Its

having come apart makes an unfortunate difference
for its beauty, its artistic value, but none for anything
else. Its other value is just the same — I mean that of
its having given me so much of the truth about you. I
don't therefore so much care what becomes of it now
— unless perhaps you may yourself, when you come
to think, have some good use for it. In that case,"
Maggie wound up, "we can easily take the pieces
with us to Fawns."

It was wonderful how she felt, by the time she had
seen herself through this narrow pass, that she had
really achieved something — that she was in fine
emerging with the prospect a little less contracted.
She had done for him, that is, what her instinct enjoined; had laid a basis not merely momentary on
which he could meet her. When by the turn of his
head he did finally meet her this was the last thing
that glimmered out of his look; but it none the less
came into sight as a betrayal of his distress and
almost as a question of his eyes; so that for still
another minute before he committed himself there occurred between them a kind of unprecedented moral
exchange over which her superior lucidity presided.
It was not however that when he did commit himself
the show was promptly portentous. "But what in the
world has Fanny Assingham had to do with it?"

She could verily, out of all her smothered soreness,
almost have smiled: this enquiry so affected her as
giving the whole thing up to her. But it left her only
to go the straighter. "She has had to do with it that
I immediately sent for her and that she immediately
came. She was the first person I wanted to see —

because I knew she'd know. Know more about what I had learned, I mean, than I could make out for myself. I made out as much as I could for myself — that I also wanted to have done; but it did n't in spite of everything take me very far, and she has really been a help. Not so much as she would like to be — not so much as, poor dear, she just now tried to be; yet she has done her very best for you — never forget that! — and has kept me along immeasurably better than I should have been able to come without her. She has gained me time; and that, these three months, don't you see? has been everything."

She had said "Don't you see?" on purpose, and was to feel the next moment that it had acted. "'These three months'?" the Prince asked.

"Counting from the night you came home so late from Matcham. Counting from the hours you spent with Charlotte at Gloucester; your visit to the cathedral — which you won't have forgotten describing to me in so much detail. For that was the beginning of my being sure. Before it I had been sufficiently in doubt. Sure," Maggie developed, "of your having, and of your having for a long time had, *two* relations with Charlotte."

He stared, a little at sea, as he took it up. "'Two' — ?"

Something in the tone of it gave it a sense, or an ambiguity, almost foolish — leaving Maggie to feel as in a flash how such a consequence, a foredoomed infelicity, partaking of the ridiculous even in one of the cleverest, might be of the very essence of the penalty of wrong-doing. "Oh you may have had fifty — had the same relation with her fifty times! It's of the number of *kinds* of relation with her that I speak — a number that does n't matter really so long as there was n't only the one kind father and I supposed. One kind," she went on, "was there before us; we took that fully for granted, as you saw, and accepted it. We never thought of there being another kept out of our sight. But after the evening I speak of I knew there was something else. As I say, I had before that my idea — which you never dreamed I had. From the moment I speak of it had more to go upon, and you became yourselves, you and she, vaguely yet uneasily conscious of the difference. But it's within these last hours that I've most seen where we are; and as I've been in communication with Fanny Assingham about my doubts, so I wanted to let her know my certainty — with the determination of which however you must understand she has had nothing to do. She defends you," Maggie remarked.

He had given her all his attention, and, with this impression for her again that he was in essence fairly reaching out to her for time — time, only time, she could sufficiently imagine, and to whatever strangeness, that he absolutely liked her to talk, even at the cost of his losing almost everything else by it. It was still for a minute as if he waited for something worse; wanted everything that was in her to come out, any definite fact, anything more precisely nameable, so that he too — as was his right — should know where he was. What stirred in him above all, while he followed in her face the clear train of her speech, must have been the impulse to take up something she put before him that he was yet afraid directly to touch. He wanted to make free with it, but had to keep his hands off, for reasons he had already understood; and the discomfort of his privation yearned at her out of his eyes with an announcing gleam of the fever, the none too tolerable chill, of specific recognition. She affected him as speaking more or less for her father as well, and his eyes might have been trying to hypnotise her into giving him the answer without his asking the question. "Had *he* his idea, and has he now, with you, anything more?" — those were the words he had to hold himself from not speaking and that she would as yet certainly do nothing to make easy. She felt with her sharpest thrill how he was straitened and tied, and with the miserable pity of it her present conscious purpose of keeping him so could none the less perfectly accord. To name her father on any such basis of anxiety and compunction would be to do the impossible thing, to do neither more nor less than give Charlotte away. Visibly, palpably, traceably, he stood off from this, moved back from it as from an open chasm now suddenly perceived, but which had been, between the two, with so much, so strangely much else, quite uncalculated. Verily it towered before her, this history of their confidence. They had built strong and piled high — based as it was on such appearances — their conviction that, thanks to her native complacencies of so many sorts, she would always, quite to the end and through and through, take them as nobly sparing her. Amerigo was at any rate having the sensation of a particular ugliness to avoid, a particular difficulty to count with, that practically found him as unprepared as if he had been, like his wife, an abjectly simple person. And she meanwhile, however abjectly simple, was further discerning for herself that, whatever he might have to take from her — she being, on her side, beautifully free — he absolutely would n't be able for any qualifying purpose to name Charlotte either. As his father-in-law's wife Mrs. Verver rose between them there, for the time, in august and prohibitive form; to protect her, defend her, explain about her, was at the least to bring her into the question — which would be by the same stroke to bring her husband. But this was exactly the door Maggie would n't open to him; on all of which she was the next moment asking herself if, thus warned and embarrassed, he were n't fairly writhing in his pain. He writhed, on that hypothesis, some seconds more, for it was n't till then that he had chosen between what he could do and what he could n't.

"You're apparently drawing immense conclusions from very small matters. Won't you perhaps feel in fairness that you're striking out, triumphing, or whatever I may call it, rather too easily — feel it when I perfectly admit that your smashed cup there does come back to me? I frankly confess now to the occasion and to having wished not to speak of it to you at the time. We took two or three hours together by arrangement; it *was* on the eve of my marriage — at the moment you say. But that put it on the eve of yours too, my dear — which was directly the point. It was desired to find for you, at the eleventh hour, some small wedding-present — a hunt, for something worth giving you, and yet possible from other points of view as well, in which it seemed I could be of use. You were naturally not to be told — precisely because it was all *for* you. We went forth together and we looked; we rummaged about and, as I remember we called it, we prowled; then it was that, as I freely recognise, we came across that crystal cup — which I'm bound to say, upon my honour, I think it rather a pity Fanny Assingham, from whatever good motive, should have treated so ill." He had kept his hands in his pockets; he turned his eyes again, but more complacently now, to the ruins of the precious vessel; and Maggie could feel him exhale into the achieved quietness of his explanation a long deep breath of comparative relief. Behind everything, beneath everything it was somehow a comfort to him at last to be talking with her — and he seemed to be proving to himself that he *could* talk. "It was at a little shop in Bloomsbury — I think I could go to the place now. The man understood Italian, I remember; he wanted awfully to work off his bowl. But I did n't believe in it and we did n't take it."

Maggie had listened with an interest that wore all the expression of candour. "Oh you left it for me. But what did you take?"

He looked at her; first as if he were trying to remember, then as if he might have been trying to forget. "Nothing, I think — at that place."

"What did you take then at any other? What did you get me — since that was your aim and end — for a wedding-gift?"

"Did n't we get you anything?" The Prince had

his shade of surprise — he continued very nobly to bethink himself.

Maggie waited a little; she had for some time now kept her eyes on him steadily, but they wandered at this to the fragments on her chimney. "Yes; it comes round after all to your having got me the bowl. I myself was to come upon it, the other day, by so wonderful a chance; was to find it in the same place and to have it pressed upon me by the same little man, who does, as you say, understand Italian. I did 'believe in it,' you see — must have believed in it somehow instinctively; for I took it as soon as I saw it. Though I did n't know at all then," she added, "what I was taking *with* it."

The Prince paid her an instant the visible deference of trying to imagine what this might have been. "I agree with you that the coincidence is extraordinary — the sort of thing that happens mainly in novels and plays. But I don't see, you must let me say, the importance or the connexion —"

"Of my having made the purchase where you failed of it?" She had quickly taken him up; but she had, with her eyes on him once more, another drop into the order of her thoughts, to which, through whatever he might say, she was still adhering. "It's not my having gone into the place at the end of four years that makes the strangeness of the coincidence; for don't such chances as that in London easily occur? The strangeness," she lucidly said, "is in what my purchase was to represent to me after I had got it home; which value came," she explained, "from the wonder of my having found such a friend."

"'Such a friend'?" As a wonder assuredly her husband could but take it.

"As the little man in the shop. He did for me more than he knew — I owe it to him. He took an interest in me," Maggie said; "and, taking that interest, he recalled your visit, he remembered you and spoke of you to me."

On which the Prince passed the comment of a sceptical smile. "Ah but, my dear, if extraordinary things come from people's taking an interest in you —"

"My life in that case," she asked, "must be very agitated? Well, he liked me, I mean — very particularly. It's only so I can account for my afterwards hearing from him — and in fact he gave me that to-day," she pursued, "he gave me it frankly, as his reason."

"To-day?" the Prince enquiringly echoed.

But she was singularly able — it had been marvellously "given" her, she afterwards said to herself — to abide, for her light, for her clue, by her own order. "I inspired him with sympathy — there you are! But the miracle is that he should have a sympathy to offer that could be of use to me. That was really the oddity of my chance," the Princess proceeded — "that I should have been moved, in my ignorance, to go precisely to *him*."

He saw her so keep her course that it was as if he could at the best but stand aside to watch her and let her pass; he only made a vague demonstration that was like an ineffective gesture. "I'm sorry to say any ill of your friends, and the thing was a long time ago;

besides which there was nothing to make me recur to
it. But I remember the man's striking me as a horrid little beast."

She gave a slow headshake — as if, no, after consideration, not *that* way were an issue. "I can only think
of him as kind, for he had nothing to gain. He had
in fact only to lose. It was what he came to tell me
— that he had asked me too high a price, more than
the object was really worth. There was a particular
reason which he had n't mentioned and which had
made him consider and repent. He wrote for leave to
see me again — wrote in such terms that I saw him
here this afternoon."

"Here?" — it made the Prince look about him.

"Downstairs — in the little red room. While he
was waiting he looked at the few photographs that
stand about there and recognised two of them.
Though it was so long ago, he remembered the visit
made him by the lady and the gentleman, and that
gave him his connexion. It gave me mine, for he remembered everything and told me everything. You
see you too had produced your effect; only, unlike you,
he had thought of it again — he *had* recurred to it. He
told me of your having wished to make each other
presents — but of that's not having come off. The
lady was greatly taken with the piece I had bought of
him, but you had your reason against receiving it from
her, and you had been right. He'd think that of you
more than ever now," Maggie went on; "he'd see how
wisely you had guessed the flaw and how easily the
bowl could be broken. I had bought it myself, you
see, for a present — he knew I was doing that. This

was what had worked in him — especially after the price I had paid."

Her story had dropped an instant; she still brought it out in small waves of energy, each of which spent its force; so that he had an opportunity to speak before this force was renewed. But the quaint thing was what he now said. "And what, pray, *was* the price?"

She paused again a little. " It was high certainly — for those fragments. I think I feel as I look at them there rather ashamed to say."

The Prince then again looked at them; he might have been growing used to the sight. "But shall you at least get your money back?"

"Oh I'm far from wanting it back — I feel so that I'm getting its worth." With which, before he could reply, she had a quick transition. "The great fact about the day we're talking of seems to me to have been quite remarkably that no present was then made me. If your undertaking had been for that, that was not at least what came of it."

"You received then nothing at all?" The Prince looked vague and grave, almost retrospectively concerned.

"Nothing but an apology for empty hands and empty pockets; which was made me — as if it mattered a mite! — ever so frankly, ever so beautifully and touchingly."

This Amerigo heard with interest, yet not with confusion. "Ah of course you could n't have minded!" Distinctly, as she went on, he was getting the better of the mere awkwardness of his arrest; quite as if making out that he need *suffer* arrest from her now — be-

fore they should go forth to show themselves in the
world together—in no greater quantity than an occasion ill-chosen at the best for a scene might decently
make room for. He looked at his watch; their engage-
ment remained all the while before him. "But I don't
make out, you see, what case against me you rest —"

"On everything I'm telling you? Why the whole
case — the case of your having for so long so successfully deceived me. The idea of your finding something for me — charming as that would have been —
was what had least to do with your taking a morning
together at that moment. What had really to do with
it," said Maggie, "was that you *had* to: you could n't
not, from the moment you were again face to face.
And the reason of that was that there had been so much
between you before — before *I* came between you at
all."

Her husband had been for these last moments moving about under her eyes; but at this, as to check any
show of impatience, he again stood still. "You've
never been more sacred to me than you were at that
hour — unless perhaps you've become so at this one."

The assurance of his speech, she could note, quite
held up its head in him; his eyes met her own so for
the declaration that it was as if something cold and
momentarily unimaginable breathed upon her, from
afar off, out of his strange consistency. She kept her
direction still however under that. "Oh the thing
I've known best of all is that you've never wanted
together to offend us. You've wanted quite intensely
not to, and the precautions you've had to take for it
have been for a long time one of the strongest of my

impressions. That, I think," she added, "is the way I've best known."

"'Known'?" he repeated after a moment.

"Known. Known that you were older friends, and so much more intimate ones, than I had any reason to suppose when we married. Known there were things that had n't been told me — and that gave their meaning little by little to other things that were before me."

"Would they have made a difference in the matter of our marriage," the Prince presently asked, "if you *had* known them?"

She took her time to think. "I grant you not — in the matter of *ours*." And then as he again fixed her with his hard yearning, which he could n't keep down: "The question is so much bigger than that. You see how much what I know makes of it for me." That was what acted on him, this iteration of her knowledge, into the question of the validity of the various bearings of which he could n't on the spot trust himself to pretend in any high way to go. What her claim, as she made it, represented for him — that he could n't help betraying if only as a consequence of the effect of the word itself, her repeated distinct "know, know," on his nerves. She was capable of being sorry for his nerves at a time when he should need them for dining out, pompously, rather responsibly, without his heart in it; yet she was n't to let that prevent her using, with all economy, so precious a chance for supreme clearness. "I did n't force this upon you, you must recollect, and it probably would n't have happened for you if you had n't come in."

"Ah," said the Prince, "I was liable to come in, you know."

"I did n't think you were this evening."

"And why not?"

"Well," she answered, "you have many liabilities — of different sorts." With which she recalled what she had said to Fanny Assingham. "And then you 're so deep."

It produced in his features, despite his control of them, one of those quick plays of expression, the shade of a grimace, that testified as nothing else did to his race. "It 's you, cara, who are deep."

Which after an instant she had accepted from him; she could so feel at last that it was true. "Then I shall have need of it all."

"But what would you have done," he was by this time asking, "if I *had n't* come in?"

"I don't know." She had cast about. "What would you?"

"Oh *io* — that is n't the question. I depend on you. I go on. You 'd have spoken to-morrow?"

"I think I 'd have waited."

"And for what?" he asked.

"To see what difference it would make for myself. My possession at last, I mean, of real knowledge."

"Oh!" said the Prince.

"My only point now, at any rate," she went on, "is the difference, as I say, that it may make for *you*. Your knowing was — from the moment you did come in — all I had in view." And she sounded it again — he should have it once more. "Your knowing that I 've ceased —"

201

"That you've ceased — ?" With her pause in fact she had fairly made him press her for it.

"Why to be as I was. *Not* to know."

It was once more then after a little that he had had to stand receptive; yet the singular effect of this was that there was still something of the same sort he was made to want. He had another hesitation, but at last this odd quantity showed. "Then does any one else know?"

It was as near as he could come to naming her father, and she kept him at that distance. "Any one — ?"

"Any one I mean but Fanny Assingham."

"I should have supposed you had had by this time particular means of learning. I don't see," she said, "why you ask me."

Then after an instant — and only after an instant as she saw — he made out what she meant; and it gave her all strangely enough the still further light that Charlotte, for herself, knew as little as he had known. The vision loomed in this light, it fairly glared for the few seconds — the vision of the two others alone together at Fawns, and Charlotte, as one of them, having gropingly to go on, always not knowing and not knowing! The picture flushed at the same time with all its essential colour — that of the so possible identity of her father's motive and principle with her own. *He* was "deep," as Amerigo called it, so that no vibration of the still air should reach his daughter; just as she had earned that description by making and by, for that matter, intending still to make, her care for his serenity, or at any rate for the firm outer shell of his dignity, all marvellous enamel, her paramount law. More strangely even than anything else her husband seemed to speak now but to help her in this. "I know nothing but what you tell me."

"Then I've told you all I intended. Find out the rest —!"

"Find it out —?" He waited.

She stood before him a moment—it took that time to go on. Depth upon depth of her situation, as she met his face, surged and sank within her; but with the effect somehow once more that they rather lifted her than let her drop. She had her feet somewhere through it all—it was her companion absolutely who was at sea. And she kept her feet; she pressed them to what was beneath her. She went over to the bell beside the chimney and gave a ring that he could but take as a summons of her maid. It stopped everything for the present; it was an intimation to him to go and dress. But she had to insist. "Find out for yourself!"

BOOK FIFTH

I

AFTER the little party was again constituted at Fawns
—which had taken, for completeness, some ten days
—Maggie naturally felt herself still more possessed
in spirit of everything that had last happened in London. There was a phrase that came back to her from
old American years: she was having, by that idiom,
the time of her life—she knew it by the perpetual
throb of this sense of possession, which was almost
too violent either to recognise or to hide. It was as
if she had come out—that was her most general
consciousness; out of a dark tunnel, a dense wood,
or even simply a smoky room, and had thereby at
least for going on the advantage of air in her lungs.
It was as if she were somehow at last gathering in the
fruits of patience; she had either been really more
patient than she had known at the time, or had been
so for longer: the change brought about by itself as
great a difference of view as the shift of an inch in
the position of a telescope. It was her telescope in
fact that had gained in range—just as her danger
lay in her exposing herself to the observation by the
more charmed and therefore the more reckless use
of this optical resource. Not under any provocation
to produce it in public was her unremitted rule; but
the difficulties of duplicity had not shrunk while the
need of that course had doubled. Humbugging,
which she had so practised with her father, had been

a comparatively simple matter on the basis of mere doubt; but the ground to be covered was now greatly larger, and she felt not unlike some young woman of the theatre who, engaged for a minor part in the play and having mastered her cues with anxious effort, should find herself suddenly promoted to leading lady and expected to appear in every act of the five. She had made much to her husband, that last night, of her "knowing"; but it was exactly this quantity she now knew that, from the moment she could only dissimulate it, added to her responsibility and made of the latter *all* a mere question of having something precious and precarious in charge. There was no one to help her with it — not even Fanny Assingham now; this good friend's presence having been doomed to become, with that climax of their last interview in Portland Place, a severely simplified function. She had her use, oh yes, a thousand times; but it could only consist henceforth in her quite conspicuously touching at no point whatever — assuredly at least with Maggie — the matter they had discussed. She was there inordinately as a value, but as a value only for the clear negation of everything. She was exactly their general sign of unimpaired beatitude — and she was to live up to that somewhat arduous character, poor thing, as she might. She might privately lapse from it, if she must, with Amerigo, or with Charlotte — only not of course ever, so much as for the wink of an eye, with the master of the house. Such lapses would be her own affair, which Maggie at present could take no thought of. She treated her young friend meanwhile, it was to be said, to no betrayal of such wavering; so that from the moment of her alighting at the door with the Colonel everything went on between them at concert pitch. What had she done that last evening in Maggie's room but bring the husband and wife more together than, as would seem, they had ever been? Therefore what indiscretion should n't she show by attempting to go behind the grand appearance of her success? — which would be to court a doubt of her beneficent work. She knew accordingly nothing but harmony, she diffused restlessly nothing but peace — an extravagant expressive aggressive peace, not incongruous after all with the solid calm of the place; a kind of helmeted trident-shaking *pax Britannica.*

The peace, it must be added, had become, as the days elapsed, a peace quite generally animated and peopled — thanks to that fact of the presence of "company" in which Maggie's ability to preserve an appearance had learned from so far back to find its best resource. It was n't inconspicuous, it was in fact striking, that this resource just now seemed to meet in the highest degree every one's need: quite as if every one were, by the multiplication of human objects in the scene, by the creation, by the confusion of fictive issues, hopeful of escaping somebody else's notice. It had reached the point in truth that the collective bosom might have been taken to heave with the knowledge of the descent upon adjacent shores, for a short period, of Mrs. Rance and the Lutches, still united, and still so divided, for conquest: the sense of the party showed at least, oddly enough, as favourable to the fancy of the quaint turn that some near "week-end" might derive from their reappearance. This measured for Maggie the ground they had all travelled together since that unforgotten afternoon of the none so distant year, that determinant September Sunday when, sitting with her father in the park, as in commemoration of the climax both of their old order and of their old danger, she had proposed to him that they should "call in" Charlotte — call her in as a specialist might be summoned to an invalid's chair. Was n't it a sign of something rather portentous, their being ready to be beholden as for a diversion to the once despised Kitty and Dotty? That had already had its application, in truth, to her invocation of the Castledeans and several other members again of the historic Matcham week, made before she left town, and made, always consistently, with an idea — since she was never henceforth to approach these people without an idea, and since that lurid element of their intercourse grew and grew for her with each occasion. The flame with which it burned afresh during these particular days, the way it held up the torch to everything, to everything that *might* have occurred as the climax of revels springing from traditions so vivified — this by itself justified her private motive and reconsecrated her diplomacy. She had already produced by the aid of these people something of the effect she sought—that of being "good" for whatever her companions were good for, and of not asking either of them to give up any one or anything for her sake. There was moreover frankly a sharpness of point in it that she enjoyed; it gave an accent to the truth she wished to illustrate — the truth that the surface of her recent life, thick-sown with the flower of earnest endeavour, with every form of the unruffled and the undoubting, suffered no symptom anywhere to peep out. It was as if under her pressure neither party could get rid of the complicity, as it might be figured, of the other; as if in a word she saw Amerigo and Charlotte committed, for fear of betrayals on their own side, to a kind of wan consistency on the subject of Lady Castledean's "set," and this latter group by the same stroke compelled to assist at attestations the extent and bearing of which they rather failed to grasp and which left them indeed, in spite of hereditary high spirits, a trifle bewildered and even a trifle scared.

They made none the less at Fawns for number, for movement, for sound — they played their parts during a crisis that must have hovered for them, in the long passages of the old house, after the fashion of the established ghost, felt, through the dark hours, as a constant possibility, rather than have menaced them in the form of a daylight bore, one of the perceived outsiders who are liable to be met in the drawing-room or to be sat next to at dinner. If the Princess moreover had failed of her occult use for so much of the machinery of diversion, she would still have had a sense not other than sympathetic for the advantage now extracted from it by Fanny Assingham's bruised philosophy. This good friend's relation to it was actually the *revanche*, she sufficiently indicated, of her obscured lustre at Matcham, where

she had known her way about so much less than
most of the others. She knew it at Fawns, through
the pathless wild of the right tone, positively better
than any one, Maggie could note for her; and her
revenge had the magnanimity of a brave pointing
out of it to every one else, a wonderful irresistible
conscious and almost compassionate patronage. Here
was a house, she triumphantly caused it to be noted,
in which she so bristled with values that some of them
might serve, by her amused willingness to share, for
such of the temporarily vague, among her fellow
guests, such of the dimly disconcerted, as had lost the
key to their own. It may have been partly through
the effect of this especial strain of community with her
old friend that Maggie found herself one evening
moved to take up again their dropped directness of
reference. They had remained downstairs together
late; the other women of the party had filed, singly
or in couples, up the "grand" staircase on which,
from the equally grand hall, these retreats and ad-
vances could always be pleasantly observed; the men
had apparently taken their way to the smoking-
room; while the Princess, in possession thus of a rare
reach of view, had lingered as if to enjoy it. Then she
saw that Mrs. Assingham was remaining a little —
and as for the appreciation of her enjoyment; upon
which they stood looking at each other across the
cleared prospect until the elder woman, only vaguely
expressive and tentative now, came nearer. It was
like the act of asking if there were anything she
could yet do, and that question was answered by
her immediately feeling, on this closer view, as she

212

had felt when presenting herself in Portland Place after Maggie's last sharp summons. Their understanding was taken up by these new snatched moments where that occasion had left it.

"He has never told her I know. Of that I'm at last satisfied." And then as Mrs. Assingham opened wide eyes: "I've been in the dark since we came down, not understanding what he has been doing or intending — not making out what can have passed between them. But within a day or two I've begun to suspect, and this evening, for reasons — oh too many to tell you! — I've been sure, since it explains. *Nothing* has passed between them — that's what has happened. It explains," the Princess repeated with energy; "it explains, it explains!" She spoke in a manner that her auditor was afterwards to describe to the Colonel, oddly enough, as that of the quietest excitement; she had turned back to the chimney-place, where, in honour of a damp day and a chill night, the piled logs had turned to flame and sunk to embers; and the evident intensity of her vision for the fact she imparted made Fanny Assingham wait upon her words. It explained, this striking fact, more indeed than her companion, though conscious of fairly gaping with good will, could swallow at once. The Princess however, as for indulgence and confidence, quickly filled up the measure. "He has n't let her know that I know — and clearly does n't mean to. He has made up his mind; he'll say nothing about it. Therefore as she's quite unable to arrive at the knowledge by herself she has no idea how much I'm really in possession. She believes," said Maggie, "and, so far as her own conviction goes, she *knows*, that I'm not in possession of anything. And that somehow for my own help seems to me immense."

"Immense, my dear!" Mrs. Assingham applausively murmured, though not quite even as yet seeing all the way. "He's keeping quiet then on purpose?"

"On purpose." Maggie's lighted eyes at least looked further than they had ever looked. "He'll *never* tell her now."

Fanny wondered; she cast about her; most of all she admired her little friend, in whom this announcement was evidently animated by an heroic lucidity. She stood there, in her full uniform, like some small erect commander of a siege, an anxious captain who has suddenly got news, replete with importance for him, of agitation, of division within the place. This importance breathed upon her comrade. "So you're all right?"

"Oh *all* right's a good deal to say. But I seem at least to see as I have n't before where I am with it."

Fanny bountifully brooded; there was a point left vague. "And you have it from *him?*—your husband himself has told you?"

"'Told' me —?"

"Why what you speak of. It is n't of an assurance received from him then that you do speak?"

At which Maggie had continued to stare. "Dear me, no. Do you suppose I've asked him for an assurance?"

"Ah you have n't?" Her companion smiled.

"That's what I supposed you might mean. Then, darling, what *have* you — ?"

"Asked him for ? I've asked him for nothing."

But this in turn made Fanny stare. "Then nothing, that evening of the Embassy dinner, passed between you ?"

"On the contrary everything passed."

"Everything — ?"

"Everything. I told him what I knew — and I told him how I knew it."

Mrs. Assingham waited. "And that was all ?"

"Was n't it quite enough ?"

"Oh love," she bridled, "that's for you to have judged !"

"Then I *have* judged," said Maggie — "I did judge. I made sure he understood — then I let him alone."

Mrs. Assingham wondered. "But he did n't explain — ?"

"Explain ? Thank God, no !" Maggie threw back her head as with horror at the thought, then the next moment added : "And I did n't either."

The decency of pride in it shed a cold little light — yet as from heights at the base of which her companion rather panted. "But if he neither denies nor confesses — ?"

"He does what's a thousand times better — he lets it alone. He does," Maggie went on, "as he *would* do ; as I see now I was quite sure he would. He lets *me* alone."

Fanny Assingham turned it over. "Then how do you know so where, as you say, you 'are' ?"

"Why just *by* that. I put him in possession of the difference; the difference made about me by the fact that I had n't been after all — though with a wonderful chance, I admitted, helping me — too stupid to have arrived at knowledge. He had to see that I'm changed for him — quite changed from the idea of me that he had so long been going on with. It became a question then of his really taking in the change — and what I now see is that he's doing so."

Fanny followed as she could. "Which he shows by letting you, as you say, alone?"

Maggie looked at her a minute. "And by letting *her*."

Mrs. Assingham did what she might to embrace it — checked a little however by a thought that was the nearest approach she could have, in this almost too large air, to an inspiration. "Ah but does Charlotte let *him*?"

"Oh that's another affair — with which I've practically nothing to do. I dare say however she does n't." And the Princess had a more distant gaze for the image evoked by the question. "I don't in fact well see how she *can*. But the point for me is that he understands."

"Yes," Fanny Assingham cooed, "understands—?"

"Well, what I want. I want a happiness without a hole in it big enough for you to poke in your finger."

"A brilliant perfect surface — to begin with at least. I see."

"The golden bowl — as it *was* to have been." And Maggie dwelt musingly on this obscured figure.

"The bowl with all our happiness in it. The bowl without the crack."

For Mrs. Assingham too the image had its force, and the precious object shone before her again, reconstituted plausible presentable. But was n't there still a piece missing? "Yet if he lets you alone and you only let him — ?"

"May n't our doing so, you mean, be noticed? — may n't it give us away? Well, we hope not — we try not — we take such care. We alone know what 's between us — we and you; and have n't you precisely been struck, since you 've been here," Maggie asked, "with our making so good a show?"

Her friend hesitated. "To your father?"

But it made her hesitate too; she would n't speak of her father directly. "To every one. To *her* — now that you understand."

It held poor Fanny again in wonder. "To Charlotte — yes: if there 's so much beneath it for you and if it 's all such a plan. That makes it hang together — it makes *you* hang together." She fairly exhaled her admiration. "You 're like nobody else — you 're extraordinary."

Maggie met it with appreciation, but with a reserve. "No, I 'm not extraordinary — but I *am*, for every one, quiet."

"Well, that 's just what *is* extraordinary. 'Quiet' is more than *I* am, and you leave me far behind." With which again for an instant Mrs. Assingham frankly brooded. "'Now that I understand,' you say — but there 's one thing I don't understand." And the next minute, while her companion waited, she had mentioned it. "How can Charlotte after all not have pressed him, not have attacked him about it? How can she not have asked him — asked him on his honour, I mean — if you know?"

"How can she 'not'? Why of course," said the Princess limpidly, "she *must!*"

"Well then — ?"

"Well then you think he must have told her? Why exactly what I mean," said Maggie, "is that he will have done nothing of the sort; will, as I say, have maintained the contrary."

Fanny Assingham weighed it. "Under her direct appeal for the truth?"

"Under her direct appeal for the truth."

"Her appeal to his honour?"

"Her appeal to his honour. That's my point."

Fanny Assingham braved it. "For the truth as from him to *her?*"

"From him to any one."

Mrs. Assingham's face lighted. "He'll simply, he'll insistently have lied?"

Maggie brought it out roundly. "He'll simply, he'll insistently have lied."

It held again her companion, who next, however, with a single movement, throwing herself on her neck, overflowed. "Oh if you knew how you help me!"

Maggie had liked her to understand so far as this was possible, but hadn't been slow to see afterwards how the possibility was limited, when one came to think, by mysteries she was not to sound. This inability in her was indeed not remarkable, inasmuch as the Princess herself, as we have seen, was only now in a position to boast of touching bottom. Maggie inwardly lived in a consciousness that she could but partly open even to so good a friend and her own visitation of the fuller expanse of which was for that matter still going on. They had been duskier still, however, these recesses of her imagination — that, no doubt, was what might at present be said for them. She had looked into them on the eve of her leaving town almost without penetration: she had made out in those hours, and also of a truth during the days which immediately followed, little more than the strangeness of a relation having for its chief mark — whether to be prolonged or not — the absence of any "intimate" result of the crisis she had invited her husband to recognise. They had dealt with this crisis again face to face, very briefly, the morning after the scene in her room — but with the odd consequence of her having appeared merely to leave it on his hands. He had received it from her as he might have received a bunch of keys or a list of commissions — attentive to her instructions about them, but only putting them for the time very carefully and safely into his pocket. The instructions had seemed from day to day to make so little difference for his behaviour — that is for his speech or his silence; to produce as yet so little of the fruit of action. He had taken from her on the spot in a word, before going to dress for dinner, all she then had to give — after which, on the morrow, he had asked her for more, a good deal as if she might have renewed her supply during the night; but he had had at his command for this latter purpose an air of extraordinary detachment and discretion, an air amounting really

to an appeal which, if she could have brought herself
to describe it vulgarly, she would have noted as cool,
just as he himself would have described it in any one
else as "cheeky"; a suggestion that she should trust
him on the particular ground since she did n't on the
general. Neither his speech nor his silence struck her
as signifying more or signifying less, under this pressure, than they had seemed to signify for weeks past;
yet if her sense had n't been absolutely closed to the
possibility in him of any thought of wounding her she
might have taken his undisturbed manner, the perfection of his appearance of having recovered himself,
for one of those intentions of high impertinence by the
aid of which great people, *les grands seigneurs*, persons of her husband's class and type, always know
how to re-establish a violated order.

It was her one purely good fortune that she could
feel thus sure impertinence — to *her* at any rate —
was not among the arts on which he proposed to
throw himself; for though he had in so almost mysti-
fying a manner, replied to nothing, denied nothing,
explained nothing, apologised for nothing, he had
somehow conveyed to her that this was not because
of any determination to treat her case as not "worth"
it. There had been consideration, on both occasions,
in the way he had listened to her — even though at
the same time there had been extreme reserve; a
reserve indeed, it was also to be remembered, qualified by the fact that on their second and shorter interview in Portland Place, and quite at the end of this
passage, she had imagined him positively proposing to
her a temporary accommodation. It had been but the

matter of something in the depths of the eyes he finally
fixed upon her, and she had found in it, the more she
kept it before her, the tacitly-offered sketch of a working arrangement. "Leave me my reserve; don't question it — it's all I have just now, don't you see? so
that, if you'll make me the concession of letting me
alone with it for as long a time as I require I promise
you something or other, grown under cover of it, even
though I don't yet quite make out what, as a return for
your patience." She had turned away from him with
some such unspoken words as that in her ear, and indeed she *had* to represent to herself that she had spir-
itually heard them, had to listen to them still again, to
explain her particular patience in face of his particular
failure. He had n't so much as pretended to meet for
an instant the question raised by her of her accepted
ignorance of the point in time, the period before their
own marriage, from which his intimacy with Charlotte dated. As an ignorance in which he and Charlotte had been personally interested — and to the
pitch of consummately protecting, for years, each
other's interest — as a condition so imposed upon her
the fact of its having ceased might have made it on the
spot the first article of his defence. He had vouch-
safed it however nothing better than his longest stare
of postponed consideration. That tribute he had
coldly paid it, and Maggie might truly herself have
been stupefied, had n't she had something to hold
on by, at her own present ability, even provisional, to
make terms with a chapter of history into which she
could but a week before not have dipped without a
mortal chill. At the rate at which she was living she

was getting used hour by hour to these extensions of view; and when she asked herself at Fawns to what single observation of her own, of those offered him in London, the Prince had had an affirmation to oppose, she but just failed to focus the small strained wife of the moments in question as some panting dancer of a difficult step who had capered, before the footlights of an empty theatre, to a spectator lounging in a box. Her best comprehension of Amerigo's success in not committing himself was in her recall meanwhile of the enquiries he had made of her on their only return to the subject, and which he had in fact explicitly provoked their return in order to make. He had had it over with her again, the so distinctly remarkable incident of her interview at home with the little Bloomsbury shopman. This anecdote, for him, had, not altogether surprisingly, required some straighter telling, and the Prince's attitude in presence of it had represented once more his nearest approach to a cross-examination. The difficulty in respect to the little man had been for the question of his motive — his motive in writing first, in the spirit of retraction, to a lady with whom he had made a most advantageous bargain, and in then coming to see her so that his apology should be personal. Maggie had felt her explanation weak, but there were the facts, and she could give no other. Left alone after the transaction with the knowledge that his visitor designed the object bought of him as a birthday-gift to her father — for Maggie confessed freely to having chattered to him almost as to a friend — the vendor of the golden bowl had acted on a scruple rare enough in vendors of any class

and almost unprecedented in the thrifty children of
Israel. He had n't liked what he had done and what
he had above all made such a "good thing" of having
done; at the thought of his purchaser's good faith and
charming presence, opposed to that flaw in her acquisition which would make it verily, as an offering
to a loved parent, a thing of sinister meaning and evil
effect, he had known conscientious, he had known
superstitious visitings, had given way to a whim all
the more remarkable to his own commercial mind,
no doubt, from its never having troubled him in other
connexions. She had recognised the oddity of her
adventure and left it to show for what it was. She
had n't been unconscious on the other hand that if it
had n't touched Amerigo so nearly he would have
found in it matter for some amused reflexion. He
had uttered an extraordinary sound, something between a laugh and a howl, on her saying, as she had
made a point of doing: "Oh most certainly he *told*
me his reason was because he 'liked' me!" — though
she remained in doubt of whether that inarticulate
comment had been provoked most by the familiar-
ities she had offered or by those that, so pictured, she
had had to endure. That the partner of her bargain
had yearned to see her again, that he had plainly
jumped at a pretext for it, this also she had frankly
expressed herself to the Prince as having, in no snub-
bing, no scandalised, but rather in a positively appre-
ciative and indebted spirit, not delayed to make out.
He had wished ever so seriously to return her a part
of her money, and she had wholly declined to receive
it; and then he had uttered his hope that she had n't,

at all events, already devoted the crystal cup to the beautiful purpose so kindly and so fortunately named to him. It was n't a thing for a present to a person she was fond of, for she would n't wish to give a present that would bring ill luck. That had come to him —so that he could n't rest, and he should feel better now that he had told her. His having led her to act in ignorance was what he should have been ashamed of; and if she would pardon, gracious lady as she was, all the liberties he had taken, she might make of the bowl any use in life but that one.

It was after this that the most extraordinary incident of all of course had occurred — his pointing to the two photographs with the remark that those were persons he knew, and that, more wonderful still, he had made acquaintance with them years before precisely over the same article. The lady, on that occasion, had taken up the fancy of presenting it to the gentleman, and the gentleman, guessing and dodging ever so cleverly, had declared that he would n't for the world receive an object under such suspicion. He himself, the little man had confessed, would n't have minded — about *them;* but he had never forgotten either their talk or their faces, the impression altogether made by them, and, if she really wished to know now what had perhaps most moved him, it was the thought that she should ignorantly have gone in for a thing not good enough for other buyers. He had been immensely struck—that was another point — with this accident of their turning out after so long friends of hers too: they had disappeared, and this was the only light he had ever had upon them. He had

flushed up quite red with his recognition, with all his
responsibility — had declared that the connexion
must have had, mysteriously, something to do with
the impulse he had obeyed. And Maggie had made, to
her husband, while he again stood before her, no
secret of the shock, for herself, so suddenly and violently received. She had done her best, even while
taking it full in the face, not to give herself away;
but she would n't answer—no, she would n't—for
what she might in her agitation have made her in-
formant think. He might think what he would —
there had been three or four minutes during which,
while she asked him question upon question, she had
doubtless too little cared. And he had spoken, for his
remembrance, as fully as she could have wished; he
had spoken, oh delightedly, for the "terms" on which
his other visitors had appeared to be with each other,
and in fact for that conviction of the nature and degree
of their intimacy under which, in spite of precautions,
they had n't been able to help leaving him. He had
observed and judged and not forgotten; he had been
sure they were great people, but no, ah no, distinctly,
had n't "liked" them as he liked the Signora Prin-
cipessa. Certainly — she had created no vagueness
about that — he had been in possession of her name
and address for sending her both her cup and her account. But the others he had only always wondered
about — he had been sure they would never come
back. And as to the time of their visit he could place
it positively to a day — by reason of a transaction of
importance, recorded in his books, that had occurred
but a few hours later. He had left her in short defin-

itely rejoicing that he had been able to make up to her for not having been quite "square" over their little business by rendering her so unexpectedly the service of this information. His joy moreover was — as much as Amerigo would! — a matter of the personal interest with which her kindness, gentleness, grace, her charming presence and easy humanity and familiarity, had inspired him. All of which while, in thought, Maggie went over it again and again — oh over any imputable rashness of her own immediate passion and pain as well as over the rest of the straight little story she had after all to tell — might very conceivably make a long sum for the Prince to puzzle out.

There were meanwhile, after the Castledeans and those invited to meet them had gone and before Mrs. Rance and the Lutches had come, three or four days during which she was to learn the full extent of her need not to be penetrable; and then it was indeed that she felt all the force and threw herself upon all the help of the truth she had confided several nights earlier to Fanny Assingham. She had known it in advance, had warned herself of it while the house was full: Charlotte had designs upon her of a nature best known to herself and was only waiting for the better opportunity of their finding themselves less companioned. This consciousness had been exactly at the bottom of Maggie's wish to multiply their spectators; there were moments for her positively, moments of planned postponement, of evasion scarcely less disguised than studied, during which she turned over with anxiety the different ways — there being two or three possible ones — in which her young stepmother might, at need, seek to work upon her. Amerigo's not having "told" her of his passage with his wife gave, for Maggie, altogether a new aspect to Charlotte's consciousness and condition — an aspect with which, for apprehension, for wonder, and even at moments, inconsequently enough, for something like compassion, the Princess had now to reckon. She sought to discover — for she was capable of that — what he had *meant* by keeping the sharer of his guilt in the dark about a matter touching her otherwise so nearly; what he had meant, that is, for this unmistakeably mystified personage herself. Maggie could imagine what he had meant for *her* — all sorts of thinkable things, whether things of mere "form" or things of sincerity, things of pity or things of prudence: he had meant for instance in all probability, primarily, to conjure away any such appearance of a changed relation between the two women as his father-in-law might notice and follow up. It would have been open to him however, given the pitch of their intimacy, to avert this danger by some more conceivable course with Charlotte; since an earnest warning, in fact the full freedom of alarm, that of his insisting to her on the peril of suspicion incurred and on the importance accordingly of outward peace at any price, would have been the course really most conceivable. Instead of warning and advising he had reassured and deceived her; so that our young woman, who had been from far back, by the habit of her nature, as much on her guard against sacrificing others as if she felt the great trap of life mainly to be set for one's doing so, now found herself attaching her fancy to that side of the situation of the exposed pair which involved for themselves at least the sacrifice of the least fortunate.

She never at present thought of what Amerigo might be intending without the reflexion, by the same stroke, that, whatever this quantity, he was leaving still more to her own ingenuity. He was helping her, when the thing came to the test, only by the polished, possibly almost too polished, surface his manner to his wife wore for an admiring world; and that surely was entitled to scarce more than the praise of negative diplomacy. He was keeping his manner right, as she had related to Mrs. Assingham; the case would have been beyond calculation if on top of everything he had allowed it to go wrong. She had hours of exaltation indeed when the meaning of all this pressed in upon her as a tacit vow from him to abide without question by whatever she should be able to achieve or think fit to prescribe. Then it was that even while holding her breath for the awe of it she truly felt almost able enough for anything. It was as if she had passed in a time incredibly short from being nothing for him to being all; it was as if, rightly noted, every turn of his head, every tone of his voice, in these days, *might* mean that there was but one way in which a proud man reduced to abjection could hold himself. During those of Maggie's vigils in which that view loomed largest the image of her husband thus presented to her gave out a beauty for the revelation of which she struck herself as paying, if anything, all too little. To make sure of it—to make sure of the beauty shining out of the humility and of the humility lurking in all the pride of his presence—she would

have gone the length of paying more yet, of paying
with difficulties and anxieties compared to which those
actually before her might have been as superficial as
headaches or rainy days.

The point at which these exaltations dropped however was the point at which it was apt to come over
her that if her complications had been greater the
question of paying would have been limited still less
to the liabilities of her own pocket. The complications were verily great enough, whether for ingenuities or sublimities, so long as she had to come back to
it so often that Charlotte could all the while only be
struggling with secrets beyond any guessing. It was
odd how that certainty again and again determined
and coloured her wonderments of detail; the question
for instance of *how* Amerigo, in snatched opportunities of conference, put the haunted creature off with
false explanations, met her particular challenges and
evaded — if that was what he did do! — her particular demands. Even the conviction that Charlotte was
but awaiting some chance really to test her trouble
upon her lover's wife left Maggie's sense meanwhile
open as to the sight of gilt wires and bruised wings,
the spacious but suspended cage, the home of eternal
unrest, of pacings, beatings, shakings all so vain, into
which the baffled consciousness helplessly resolved
itself. The cage was the deluded condition, and Maggie, as having known delusion — rather! — understood the nature of cages. She walked round Charlotte's — cautiously and in a very wide circle; and
when inevitably they had to communicate she felt
herself comparatively outside and on the breast of

nature: she saw her companion's face as that of a prisoner looking through bars. So it was that through bars, bars richly gilt but firmly though discreetly planted, Charlotte finally struck her as making a grim attempt; from which at first the Princess drew back as instinctively as if the door of the cage had suddenly been opened from within.

II

THEY had been alone that evening — alone as a party of six, and four of them, after dinner, under suggestion not to be resisted, sat down to "bridge" in the smoking-room. They had passed together to that apartment on rising from table, Charlotte and Mrs. Assingham alike indulgent always to tobacco and in fact practising an emulation which, as Fanny said, would, for herself, had the Colonel not issued an interdict based on the fear of her stealing his cigars, have stopped only at the short pipe. Here cards had with inevitable promptness asserted their rule, the game forming itself, as had often happened before, of Mr. Verver with Mrs. Assingham for partner and of the Prince with Mrs. Verver. The Colonel, who had then asked of Maggie licence to relieve his mind of a couple of letters for the earliest post out on the morrow, was addressing himself to this task at the other end of the room, and the Princess herself had welcomed the comparatively hushed hour — for the bridge-players were serious and silent — much in the mood of a tired actress who has the good fortune to be "off," while her mates are on, almost long enough for a nap on the property sofa in the wing. Maggie's nap, had she been able to snatch forty winks, would have been of the spirit rather than of the sense; yet as she subsided, near a lamp, with the last salmon-coloured French periodical, she was to fail, for refreshment, even of that sip of independence.

There was no question for her, as she found, of closing her eyes and getting away; they strayed back to
life, in the stillness, over the top of her Review; she
could lend herself to none of those refinements of the
higher criticism with which its pages bristled; she was
there, where her companions were, there again and
more than ever there; it was as if of a sudden they
had been made, in their personal intensity and their
rare complexity of relation, freshly importunate to her.
It was the first evening there had been no one else.
Mrs. Rance and the Lutches were due the next day;
but meanwhile the facts of the situation were upright
for her round the green cloth and the silver flambeaux;
the fact of her father's wife's lover facing his mistress;
the fact of her father sitting, all unsounded and un-
blinking, between them; the fact of Charlotte keeping
it up, keeping up everything, across the table, with
her husband beside her; the fact of Fanny Assingham,
wonderful creature, placed opposite to the three and
knowing more about each, probably, when one came
to think, than either of them knew of either. Erect
above all for her was the sharp-edged fact of the relation of the whole group, individually and collectively,
to herself—herself so speciously eliminated for the
hour, but presumably more present to the attention of
each than the next card to be played.

Yes, under that imputation, to her sense, they sat—
the imputation of wondering, beneath and behind all
their apparently straight play, if she were n't really
watching them from her corner and consciously, as
might be said, holding them in her hand. She was
asking herself at last how they could bear it—for,

though cards were as nought to her and she could follow no move, so that she was always on such occasions
out of the party, they struck her as conforming alike,
in the matter of gravity and propriety, to the stiff
standard of the house. Her father, she knew, was a
high adept, one of the greatest—she had been ever,
in her stupidity, his small, his sole despair; Amerigo
excelled easily, as he understood and practised every
art that could beguile large leisure; Mrs. Assingham
and Charlotte, moreover, were accounted as "good"
as members of a sex incapable of the nobler consistency could be. Therefore evidently they were n't, all
so up to their usual form, merely passing it off, whether
for her or for themselves; and the amount of enjoyed
or at least achieved security represented by so complete a conquest of appearances was what acted on
her nerves precisely with a kind of provocative force.
She found herself for five minutes thrilling with the
idea of the prodigious effect that, just as she sat there
near them, she had at her command; with the sense
that if she were but different—oh ever so different!
—all this high decorum would hang by a hair. There
reigned for her absolutely during these vertiginous
moments that fascination of the monstrous, that
temptation of the horribly possible, which we so often
trace by its breaking out suddenly, lest it should go
further, in unexplained retreats and reactions.

After it had been thus vividly before her for a little
that, springing up under her wrong and making them
all start, stare and turn pale, she might sound out their
doom in a single sentence, a sentence easy to choose
among several of the lurid—after she had faced that

blinding light and felt it turn to blackness she rose from her place, laying aside her magazine, and moved slowly round the room, passing near the card-players and pausing an instant behind the chairs in turn. Silent and discreet she bent a vague mild face upon them as if to signify that little as she followed their doings she wished them well; and she took from each, across the table, in the common solemnity, an upward recognition which she was to carry away with her on her moving out to the terrace a few minutes later. Her father and her husband, Mrs. Assingham and Charlotte, had done nothing but meet her eyes; yet the difference in these demonstrations made each a separate passage—which was all the more wonderful since, with the secret behind every face, they had alike tried to look at her *through* it and in denial of it.

It all left her, as she wandered off, with the strangest of impressions—the sense, forced upon her as never yet, of an appeal, a positive confidence, from the four pairs of eyes, that was deeper than any negation and that seemed to speak on the part of each for some relation to be contrived by her, a relation with herself, which would spare the individual the danger, the actual present strain, of the relation with the others. They thus tacitly put it upon her to be disposed of, the whole complexity of their peril, and she promptly saw why: because she was there, and there just *as* she was, to lift it off them and take it; to charge herself with it as the scapegoat of old, of whom she had once seen a terrible picture, had been charged with the sins of the people and had gone forth into the desert to sink under his burden and die. That indeed was n't *their* design and their interest, that she should sink under hers; it would n't be their feeling that she should do anything but live, live on somehow for their benefit, and even as much as possible in their company, to keep proving to them that they had truly escaped and that she was still there to simplify. This idea of her simplifying, and of their combined struggle, dim as yet but steadily growing, toward the perception of her adopting it from them, clung to her while she hovered on the terrace, where the summer night was so soft that she scarce needed the light shawl she had picked up. Several of the long windows of the occupied rooms stood open to it, and the light came out in vague shafts and fell upon the old smooth stones. The hour was moonless and starless and the air heavy and still—which was why, in her evening dress, she need fear no chill and could get away, in the outer darkness, from that provocation of opportunity which had assaulted her, within on her sofa, as a beast might have leaped at her throat.

Nothing in fact was stranger than the way in which, when she had remained there a little, her companions, watched by her through one of the windows, actually struck her as almost consciously and gratefully safer. They might have been—really charming as they showed in the beautiful room, and Charlotte certainly, as always, magnificently handsome and supremely distinguished—they might have been figures rehearsing some play of which she herself was the author; they might even, for the happy appearance they continued to present, have been such figures as would by the strong note of character in each fill any author with the certitude of success, especially of their own histrionic.

They might in short have represented any mystery
they would; the point being predominantly that the
key to the mystery, the key that could wind and un-
wind it without a snap of the spring, was there in her
pocket — or rather, no doubt, clasped at this crisis in
her hand and pressed, as she walked back and forth,
to her breast. She walked to the end and far out of
the light; she returned and saw the others still where
she had left them; she passed round the house and
looked into the drawing-room, lighted also, but empty
now, and seeming to speak the more in its own voice of
all the possibilities she controlled. Spacious and splendid, like a stage again awaiting a drama, it was a scene
she might people, by the press of her spring, either
with serenities and dignities and decencies, or with
terrors and shames and ruins, things as ugly as those
formless fragments of her golden bowl she was trying
so hard to pick up.

She continued to walk and continued to pause; she
stopped afresh for the look into the smoking-room,
and by this time — it was as if the recognition had of
itself arrested her — she saw as in a picture, with the
temptation she had fled from quite extinct, why it was
she had been able to give herself from the first so little
to the vulgar heat of her wrong. She might fairly, as
she watched them, have missed it as a lost thing; have
yearned for it, for the straight vindictive view, the
rights of resentment, the rages of jealousy, the pro-
tests of passion, as for something she had been cheated
of not least: a range of feelings which for many women
would have meant so much, but which for *her* husband's wife, for her father's daughter, figured nothing

236

nearer to experience than a wild eastern caravan, looming into view with crude colours in the sun, fierce pipes in the air, high spears against the sky, all a thrill, a natural joy to mingle with, but turning off short before it reached her and plunging into other defiles. She saw at all events why horror itself had almost failed her; the horror that, foreshadowed in advance, would by her thought have made everything that was unaccustomed in her cry out with pain; the horror of finding evil seated all at its ease where she had only dreamed of good; the horror of the thing hideously *behind*, behind so much trusted, so much pretended, nobleness, cleverness, tenderness. It was the first sharp falsity she had known in her life, to touch at all or be touched by; it had met her like some bad-faced stranger surprised in one of the thick-carpeted corridors of a house of quiet on a Sunday afternoon; and yet, yes, amazingly, she had been able to look at terror and disgust only to know that she must put away from her the bitter-sweet of their freshness. The sight, from the window, of the group so constituted, *told* her why, told her how, named to her, as with hard lips, named straight *at* her, so that she must take it full in the face, that other possible relation to the whole fact which alone would bear upon her irresistibly. It was extraordinary: they positively brought home to her that to feel about them in any of the immediate, inevitable, assuaging ways, the ways usually open to innocence outraged and generosity betrayed, would have been to give them up, and that giving them up was, marvellously, not to be thought of. She had never, from the first hour of her state of acquired conviction, given them up so little as now; though she was, no doubt, as the consequence of a step taken a few minutes later, to invoke the conception of doing that, if might be, even less. She had resumed her walk — stopping here and there, while she rested on the cool smooth stone balustrade, to draw it out; in the course of which, after a little, she passed again the lights of the empty drawing-room and paused again for what she saw and felt there.

It was not at once however that this became quite concrete; that was the effect of her presently making out that Charlotte was in the room, launched and erect there in the middle and looking about her; that she had evidently just come round to it, from her card-table, by one of the passages — with the expectation to all appearance of joining her stepdaughter. She had pulled up at seeing the great room empty — Maggie not having passed out, on leaving the group, in a manner to be observed. So definite a quest of her, with the bridge-party interrupted or altered for it, was an impression that fairly assailed the Princess and to which something of attitude and aspect, of the air of arrested pursuit and purpose, in Charlotte, together with the suggestion of her next vague movements, quickly added its meaning. This meaning was that she had decided, that she had been infinitely conscious of Maggie's presence before, that she knew she should at last find her alone, and that she wanted her, for some reason, enough to have presumably called on Bob Assingham for aid. He had taken her chair and let her go, and the arrangement was for Maggie a signal proof of her earnestness; of the energy in fact, that, though superficially commonplace in a situation in which people were n't supposed to be watching each other, was what affected our young woman on the spot as a breaking of bars. The splendid shining supple creature was out of the cage, was at large; and the question now almost grotesquely rose of whether she might n't by some art, just where she was and before she could go further, be hemmed in and secured. It would have been for a moment, in this case, a matter of quickly closing the windows and giving the alarm— with poor Maggie's sense that though she could n't know what she wanted of her it was enough for trepidation that at these firm hands anything should be wanted: to say nothing of the sequel in the form of a flight taken again along the terrace even under the shame of the confessed feebleness of such evasions on the part of an outraged wife. It was to this feebleness, none the less, that the outraged wife had presently resorted; the most that could be said for her being, as she felt while she finally stopped short and at a distance, that she could at any rate resist her abjection sufficiently not to sneak into the house by another way and safely reach her room. She had literally caught herself in the act of dodging and ducking, and it told her there vividly, in a single word, what she had all along been most afraid of.

She had been afraid of the particular passage with Charlotte that would determine her father's wife to take him into her confidence as she could n't possibly as yet have done, to prepare for him a statement of her wrong, to lay before him the infamy of what she was apparently suspected of. This, should she have made

up her mind to do it, would rest on a calculation the
thought of which strangely evoked other possibilities
and visions. It would show her as sufficiently believing in her grasp of her husband to be able to assure
herself that with his daughter thrown on the defensive,
with Maggie's cause and Maggie's word in fine against
her own, it was n't Maggie's that would most certainly
carry the day. Such a glimpse of her conceivable
idea, which would be founded on reasons all her own,
reasons of experience and assurance impenetrable
to others but intimately familiar to herself — such a
glimpse opened out wide as soon as it had come into
view; for if so much as this was still firm ground between the elder pair, if the beauty of appearances had
been so consistently preserved, it was only the golden
bowl as Maggie herself knew it that had been broken,
The breakage stood not for any wrought discomposure
among the triumphant three — it stood merely for the
dire deformity of her attitude toward them. She was
unable at the minute, of course, fully to measure the
difference thus involved for her, and it remained inevitably an agitating image, the way it might be held
over her that if she did n't of her own prudence satisfy
Charlotte as to the reference, in her mocking spirit, of
so much of the unuttered and unutterable, of the constantly and unmistakeably implied, her father would
be invited without further ceremony to recommend
her to do so. But *any* confidence, *any* latent operating
insolence, that Mrs. Verver should, thanks to her large
native resources, continue to be possessed of and to
hold in reserve, glimmered suddenly as a possible
working light and seemed to offer, for meeting her, a

new basis and something like a new system. Maggie felt truly a rare contraction of the heart on making out the next instant what the new system would probably have to be — and she had practically done that before perceiving that the thing she feared had already taken place. Charlotte, extending her search, appeared now to define herself vaguely in the distance; of this after an instant the Princess was sure, though the darkness was thick, for the projected clearness of the smoking-room windows had presently contributed its help. Her friend came slowly into that circle — having also, for herself, by this time, not indistinguishably discovered that Maggie was on the terrace. Maggie, from the end, saw her stop before one of the windows to look at the group within, and then saw her come nearer and pause again, still with a considerable length of the place between them.

Yes, Charlotte had seen she was watching her from afar, and had stopped now to put her further attention to the test. Her face was fixed on her, through the night; she was the creature who had escaped by force from her cage, yet there was in her whole motion assuredly, even as so dimly discerned, a kind of portentous intelligent stillness. She had escaped with an intention, but with an intention the more definite that it could so accord with quiet measures. The two women at all events only hovered there, for these first minutes, face to face over their interval and exchanging no sign; the intensity of their mutual look might have pierced the night, and Maggie was at last to start with the scared sense of having thus yielded to doubt, to dread, to hesitation, for a time that, with no other proof needed, would have completely given her away. How long had she stood staring?—a single minute or five? Long enough in any case to have felt herself absolutely take from her visitor something that the latter threw upon her, irresistibly, by this effect of silence, by this effect of waiting and watching, by this effect, flagrantly, of timing her indecision and her fear. If then, scared and hanging back, she had, as was so evident, sacrificed all past pretences, it would have been with the instant knowledge of an immense advantage gained that Charlotte finally saw her come on. Maggie came on with her heart in her hands; she came on with the definite prevision, throbbing like the tick of a watch, of a doom impossibly sharp and hard, but to which, after looking at it with her eyes wide open, she had none the less bowed her head. By the time she was at her companion's side, for that matter, by the time Charlotte had, without a motion, without a word, simply let her approach and stand there, her head was already on the block, so that the consciousness that everything had gone blurred all perception of whether or no the axe had fallen. Oh the "advantage," it was perfectly enough, in truth, with Mrs. Verver; for what was Maggie's own sense but that of having been thrown over on her back with her neck from the first half-broken and her helpless face staring up? That position only could account for the positive grimace of weakness and pain produced there by Charlotte's dignity.

"I've come to join you—I thought you'd be here."

"Oh yes, I'm here," Maggie heard herself return a little flatly.

242

"It's too close indoors."

"Very — but close even here." Charlotte was still
and grave — she had even uttered her remark about
the temperature with an expressive weight that verged
upon solemnity; so that Maggie, reduced to looking
vaguely about at the sky, could only feel her not fail
of her purpose. "The air's heavy as if with thunder —
I think there'll be a storm." She made the suggestion
to carry off an awkwardness — which was a part always of her companion's gain; but the awkwardness
didn't diminish in the silence that followed. Charlotte had said nothing in reply; her brow was dark as
with a fixed expression, and her high elegance, her
handsome head and long straight neck testified
through the dusk to their inveterate completeness
and noble erectness. It was as if what she had come
out to do had already begun, and when, as a consequence, Maggie had said helplessly "Don't you want
something? won't you have my shawl?" everything
might have crumbled away in the comparative pov-
erty of the tribute. Mrs. Verver's rejection of it had
the brevity of a sign that they hadn't closed in for idle
words, just as her dim serious face, uninterruptedly
presented until they moved again, might have figured
the success with which she watched all her message
penetrate. They presently went back the way she had
come, but she stopped Maggie again within range
of the smoking-room window and made her stand
where the party at cards would be before her. Side by
side for three minutes they fixed this picture of quiet
harmonies, the positive charm of it and, as might have
been said, the full significance — which, as was now

brought home to Maggie, could be no more after all than a matter of interpretation, differing always for a different interpreter. As she herself had hovered in sight of it a quarter of an hour before, it would have been a thing for her to show Charlotte — to show in righteous irony, in reproach too stern for anything but silence. But now it was she who was being shown it, and shown it by Charlotte, and she saw quickly enough that as Charlotte showed it so she must at present submissively seem to take it.

The others were absorbed and unconscious, either silent over their game or dropping remarks unheard on the terrace; and it was to her father's quiet face, discernibly expressive of nothing that was in his daughter's mind, that our young woman's attention was most directly given. His wife and his daughter were both closely watching him, and to which of them, could he have been notified of this, would his raised eyes first, all impulsively, have responded? in which of them would he have felt it most important to destroy — for *his* clutch at the equilibrium — any germ of uneasiness? Not yet since his marriage had Maggie so sharply and so formidably known her old possession of him as a thing divided and contested. She was looking at him by Charlotte's leave and under Charlotte's direction; quite in fact as if the particular way she should look at him were prescribed to her; quite even as if she had been defied to look at him in any other. It came home to her too that the challenge was n't, as might be said, in his interest and for his protection, but pressingly, insistently in Charlotte's, for that of *her* security at any price. She might verily by this dumb demonstration have been naming to Maggie the price, naming it as a question for Maggie herself, a sum of money that she properly was to find. She must remain safe and Maggie must pay —what she was to pay with being her own affair.

Straighter than ever thus the Princess again felt it all put upon her, and there was a minute, just a supreme instant, during which there burned in her a wild wish that her father would only look up. It throbbed for these seconds as a yearning appeal to him — she would chance it, that is, if he would but just raise his eyes and catch them, across the larger space, standing in the outer dark together. Then he might be affected by the sight, taking them as they were; he might make some sign — she scarce knew what — that would save *her;* save her from being the one this way to pay all. He might somehow show a preference — distinguishing between them; might out of pity for her signal to her that this extremity of her effort for him was more than he asked. That represented Maggie's one little lapse from consistency — the sole small deflexion in the whole course of her scheme. It had come to nothing the next minute, for the dear man's eyes had never moved, and Charlotte's hand, promptly passed into her arm, had already, had very firmly drawn her on — quite for that matter as from some sudden, some equal perception on her part too of the more ways than one in which their impression could appeal. They retraced their steps along the rest of the terrace, turning the corner of the house, and presently came abreast of the other windows, those of the pompous drawing-room still lighted and still empty. Here Charlotte again paused, and it was again as if she were pointing out what Maggie had observed for herself, the very look the place had of being vivid in its stillness, of having, with all its great objects as ordered and balanced as for a formal reception, been appointed for some high transaction, some real affair of state. In presence of this opportunity she faced her companion once more; she traced in her the effect of everything she had already communicated; she signified with the same success that the terrace and the sullen night would bear too meagre witness to the completion of her idea. Soon enough then, within the room, under the old lustres of Venice and the eyes of the several great portraits, more or less contemporary with these, that awaited on the walls of Fawns their final far migration — soon enough Maggie found herself staring, and at first all too gaspingly, at the grand total to which each separate demand Mrs. Verver had hitherto made upon her, however she had made it, now amounted.

"I've been wanting — and longer than you'd perhaps believe — to put a question to you for which no opportunity has seemed to me yet quite so good as this. It would have been easier perhaps if you had struck me as in the least disposed ever to give me one. I have to take it now, you see, as I find it." They stood in the centre of the immense room, and Maggie could feel that the scene of life her imagination had made of it twenty minutes before was by this time sufficiently peopled. These few straight words filled it to its uttermost reaches, and nothing, either, was now absent from her consciousness of the part she

was 'called on to play in it. Charlotte had marched
straight in, dragging her rich train; she rose there
beautiful and free, her whole aspect and action attuned to the firmness of her speech. Maggie had kept
the shawl she had taken out with her, and, clutching
it tight in her nervousness, drew it round her as if
huddling in it for shelter, covering herself with it for
humility. She looked out as from under an improvised hood — the sole headgear of some poor woman
at somebody's proud door; she waited even like the
poor woman; she met her friend's eyes with recognitions she could n't suppress. She might sound it as
she could —"What question then?"— everything
in her, from head to foot, crowded it upon Charlotte
that she knew. She knew too well — that she was
showing; so that successful vagueness, to save some
scrap of her dignity from the imminence of her defeat,
was already a lost cause, and the one thing left was if
possible, at any cost, even that of stupid inconsequence, to try to look as if she were n't afraid. If she
could but appear at all not afraid she might appear
a little not ashamed — that is not ashamed to *be*
afraid, which was the kind of shame that could be
fastened on her, it being fear all the while that moved
her. Her challenge at any rate, her wonder, her terror
— the blank blurred surface, whatever it was, that she
presented — became a mixture that ceased to signify;
for to the accumulated advantage by which Charlotte
was at present sustained her next words themselves
had little to add. "Have you any ground of complaint of me? Is there any wrong you consider I 've
done you? I feel at last that I 've a right to ask you."

247

Their eyes had to meet on it, and to meet long; Maggie's avoided at least the disgrace of looking away. "What makes you want to ask it?"

"My natural desire to know. You've done that for so long little justice."

Maggie waited a moment. "For so long? You mean you've thought — ?"

"I mean, my dear, that I've seen. I've seen, week after week, that *you* seemed to be thinking — of something that perplexed or worried you. Is it anything for which I'm in any degree responsible?"

Maggie summoned all her powers. "What in the world *should* it be?"

"Ah that's not for me to imagine, and I should be very sorry to have to try to say! I'm aware of no point whatever at which I may have failed you," said Charlotte; "nor of any at which I may have failed any one in whom I can suppose you sufficiently interested to care. If I've been guilty of some fault I've committed it all unconsciously, and am only anxious to hear from you honestly about it. But if I've been mistaken as to what I speak of —the difference, more and more marked, as I've thought, in all your manner to me — why obviously so much the better. No form of correction received from you could give me greater satisfaction."

She spoke, it struck her companion, with rising, with extraordinary ease; as if hearing herself say it all, besides seeing the way it was listened to, helped her from point to point. She saw she was right — that this *was* the tone for her to take and the thing for her to do, the thing as to which she was probably feeling that she had in advance, in her delays and uncertainties, much exaggerated the difficulty. The difficulty was small, and it grew smaller as her adversary continued to shrink; she was not only doing as she wanted, but had by this time effectively done it and hung it up. All of which but deepened Maggie's sense of the sharp and simple need now of seeing her through to the end. "'If' you've been mistaken, you say?"—and the Princess but barely faltered. "You *have* been mistaken."

Charlotte looked at her splendidly hard. "You're perfectly sure it's *all* my mistake?"

"All I can say is that you've received a false impression."

"Ah then—so much the better! From the moment I *had* received it I knew I must sooner or later speak of it—for that, you see, is systematically my way. And now," Charlotte added, "you make me glad I've spoken. I thank you very much."

It was strange how for Maggie too with this the difficulty seemed to sink. Her companion's acceptance of her denial was like a general pledge not to keep things any worse for her than they essentially had to be; it positively helped her to build up her falsehood—to which accordingly she contributed another block. "I've affected you evidently—quite accidentally—in some way of which I've been all unaware. I've *not* felt at any time that you've wronged me."

"How could I come within a mile," Charlotte enquired, "of such a possibility?"

Maggie, with her eyes on her more easily now,

made no attempt to say; she said after a little something more to the present point. "I accuse you — I accuse you of nothing."

"Ah that's lucky!"

Charlotte had brought this out with the richness almost of gaiety; and Maggie, to go on, had to think with her own intensity of Amerigo — to think how he on his side had had to go through with his lie to her, how it was for his wife he had done so, and how his doing so had given her the clue and set her the example. He must have had his own difficulty about it, and she was n't after all falling below him. It was in fact as if, thanks to her hovering image of him confronted with this admirable creature even as she was confronted, there glowed upon her from afar, yet straight and strong, a deep explanatory light which covered the last inch of the ground. He had given her something to conform to, and she had n't unintelligently turned on him, "gone back on" him, as he would have said, by not conforming. They were together thus, he and she, close, close together — whereas Charlotte, though rising there radiantly before her, was really off in some darkness of space that would steep her in solitude and harass her with care. The heart of the Princess swelled accordingly even in her abasement; she had kept in tune with the right, and something certainly, something that might resemble a rare flower snatched from an impossible ledge, would, and possibly soon, come of it for her. The right, the right — yes, it took this extraordinary form of humbugging, as she had called it, to the end. It was only a question of not by a hair's breadth de-

flecting into the truth. So supremely was she braced.
"You must take it from me that your anxiety rests
quite on a misconception. You must take it from me
that I've never at any moment fancied I could suffer
by you." And marvellously she kept it up — not only
kept it up but improved on it. "You must take it from
me that I've never thought of you but as beautiful,
wonderful and good. Which is all, I think, that you
can possibly ask."

Charlotte held her a moment longer: she needed
—not then to have appeared only tactless — the last
word. "It's much more, my dear, than I dreamed
of asking. I only wanted your denial."

"Well then you have it."

"Upon your honour?"

"Upon my honour."

And she made a point even, our young woman,
of not turning away. Her grip of her shawl had
loosened — she had let it fall behind her; but she
stood there for anything more and till the weight
should be lifted. With which she saw soon enough
what more was to come. She saw it in Charlotte's
face and felt it make between them, in the air, a chill
that completed the coldness of their conscious per-
jury. "Will you kiss me on it then?"

She could n't say yes, but she did n't say no;
what availed her still however was to measure in her
passivity how much too far Charlotte had come to
retreat. But there was something different also, something for which, while her cheek received the prodigious kiss, she had her opportunity — the sight of
the others, who, having risen from their cards to join

the absent members of their party, had reached the open door at the end of the room and flagrantly stopped short in presence of the demonstration that awaited them. Her husband and her father were in front, and Charlotte's embrace of her —which was n't to be distinguished for them either, she felt, from her embrace of Charlotte—took on with their arrival a high publicity.

III

HER father had asked her three days later and in an interval of calm how she was affected, in the light of their reappearance and of their now perhaps richer fruition, by Dotty and Kitty and by the once formidable Mrs. Rance; and the consequence of this enquiry had been for the pair just such another stroll together away from the rest of the party and off into the park as had asserted its need to them on the occasion of the previous visit of these anciently more agitating friends—that of their long talk on a sequestered bench beneath one of the great trees, when the particular question had come up for them the then purblind discussion of which at their enjoyed leisure Maggie had formed the habit of regarding as the "first beginning" of their present situation. The whirligig of time had thus brought round for them again, on their finding themselves face to face while the others were gathering for tea on the terrace, the same odd impulse quietly to "slope"—so Adam Verver himself, as they went, familiarly expressed it—that had acted in its way of old; acted for the distant autumn afternoon and for the sharpness of their since so outlived crisis. It might have been funny to them now that the presence of Mrs. Rance and the Lutches —and with symptoms too at that time less developed —had once for their anxiety and their prudence constituted a crisis; it might have been funny that these ladies could ever have figured to their imagination as a symbol of dangers vivid enough to precipitate the need of a remedy. This amount of entertainment and assistance they were indeed disposed to extract from their actual impressions; they had been finding it for months past, by Maggie's view, a resource and a relief to talk, with an approach to intensity, when they met, of all the people they were n't really thinking of and did n't really care about, the people with whom their existence had begun almost to swarm; and they closed in at present round the spectres of their past, as they permitted themselves to describe the three ladies, with a better imitation of enjoying their theme than they had been able to achieve, certainly, during the stay for instance of the Castledeans. The Castledeans were a new joke comparatively, and they had had—always to Maggie's view —to teach themselves the way of it; whereas the Detroit, the Providence party, rebounding so from Providence, from Detroit, was an old and ample one, of which the most could be made and as to which a humorous insistence could be guarded.

Sharp and sudden moreover this afternoon had been their well-nigh confessed desire just to rest together a little as from some strain long felt but never named; to rest as who should say shoulder to shoulder and hand in hand, each pair of eyes so yearningly — and indeed what could it be but so wearily ? — closed as to render the collapse safe from detection by the other pair. It was positively as if in short the inward felicity of their being once more, perhaps only for half an hour, simply daughter and father had glimmered out for them and they had picked up the pretext that would make it easiest. They were husband and wife — oh so immensely! — as regards other persons; but after they had dropped again on their old bench, conscious that the party on the terrace, augmented as in the past by neighbours, would do beautifully without them, it was wonderfully like their having got together into some boat and paddled off from the shore where husbands and wives, luxuriant complications, made the air too tropical. In the boat they were father and daughter, and poor Dotty and Kitty supplied abundantly, for their situation, the oars or the sail. Why, into the bargain, for that matter — this came to Maggie — could n't they always live, so far as they lived together, in a boat? She felt in her face with the question the breath of a possibility that soothed her; they needed only *know* each other henceforth in the unmarried relation. That other sweet evening in the same place he had been as unmarried as possible —which had kept down, so to speak, the quantity of change in their state. Well then that other sweet evening was what the present sweet evening would resemble; with the quite calculable effect of an exquisite inward refreshment. They *had* after all, whatever happened, always and ever each other; each other —that was the hidden treasure and the saving truth —to do exactly what they would with: a provision full of possibilities. Who could tell as yet what, thanks to it, they would n't have done before the end?

They had meanwhile been tracing together, in the

golden air that toward six o'clock of a July afternoon hung about the massed Kentish woods, several features of the social evolution of her old playmates, still beckoned on, it would seem, by unattainable ideals, still falling back, beyond the sea, to their native seats, for renewals of the moral, financial, conversational — one scarce knew what to call it — outfit, and again and for ever reappearing like a tribe of Wandering Jewesses. Our couple had finally exhausted however the study of these annals — not to say animals — and Maggie was to take up after a drop a different matter, or one at least with which the immediate connexion was not at first apparent. "Were you amused at me just now — when I wondered what other people could wish to struggle for? Did you think me," she asked with some earnestness —"well, fatuous?"

"'Fatuous'?" —he seemed at a loss.

"I mean sublime in *our* happiness — as if looking down from a height. Or rather sublime in our general position — that's what I mean." She spoke as from the habit of her anxious conscience—something that disposed her frequently to assure herself for her human commerce of the state of the "books" of the spirit. "Because I don't at all want," she explained, "to be blinded or made 'sniffy' by any sense of a social situation." Her father listened to this declaration as if the precautions of her general mercy could still, as they betrayed themselves, have surprises for him — to say nothing of a charm of delicacy and beauty; he might have been wishing to see how far she could go and where she would, all touchingly to him, arrive. But she waited a little—as if made nervous precisely by feeling him depend too much on what she said. They were avoiding the serious, standing off anxiously from the real, and they fell again and again, as if to disguise their precaution itself, into the tone of the time that came back to them from their other talk, when they had shared together this same refuge. "Don't you remember," she went on, "how, when they were here before, I broke it to you that I was n't so very sure we ourselves had the thing itself?"

He did his best to do so. "Had you meant a social situation?"

"Yes—after Fanny Assingham had first broken it to me that at the rate we were going we should never have one."

"Which was what put us on Charlotte?" Oh yes, they had had it over quite often enough for him easily to remember.

Maggie had another pause — taking it from him that he now could both affirm and admit without wincing that they had been at their critical moment "put" on Charlotte. It was as if this recognition had been threshed out between them as fundamental to the honest view of their success. "Well," she continued, "I recall how I felt, about Kitty and Dotty, that even if we had already then been more 'placed,' or whatever you may call what we are now, it still would n't have been an excuse for wondering why others could n't obligingly leave me more exalted by having themselves smaller ideas. For those," she said, "were the feelings we used to have."

"Oh yes," he responded philosophically — "I remember the feelings we used to have."

Maggie appeared to wish to plead for them a little in tender retrospect — as if they had been also respectable. "It was bad enough, I thought, to have no sympathy in your heart when you *had* a position. But it was worse to be sublime about it — as I was so afraid, as I'm in fact still afraid of being — when it wasn't even there to support one." And she put forth again the earnestness she might have been taking herself as having outlived; became for it — which was doubtless too often even now her danger — almost sententious. "One must always, whether or no, have some imagination of the states of others — of what they may feel deprived of. However," she added, "Kitty and Dotty couldn't imagine we were deprived of anything. And now, and now—!" But she stopped as for indulgence to their wonder and envy.

"And now they see still more that we can have got everything and kept everything and yet not be proud."

"No, we're not proud," she answered after a moment. "I'm not sure we're quite proud enough." Yet she changed the next instant that subject too. She could only do so however by harking back — as if it had been a fascination. She might have been wishing, under this renewed, this still more suggestive visitation, to keep him with her for remounting the stream of time and dipping again, for the softness of the water, into the contracted basin of the past. "We talked about it — we talked about it; you don't remember so well as I. You too did n't know—and it was beautiful of you; like Kitty and Dotty you too thought we had a position, and were surprised when *I* thought we ought to have told them we were n't doing for them what they supposed. In fact," Maggie pursued, "we're not doing it now. We're not, you see, really introducing them. I mean not to the people they want."

"Then what do you call the people with whom they're now having tea?"

It made her quite spring round. "That's just what you asked me the other time—one of the days there was somebody. And I told you I did n't call anybody anything."

"I remember — that such people, the people we made so welcome, did n't 'count'; that Fanny Assingham knew they did n't." She had awakened, his daughter, the echo; and on the bench there, as before, he nodded his head amusedly, he kept nervously shaking his foot. "Yes, they were only good enough —the people who came —for *us*. I remember," he said again: "that was the way it all happened."

"That was the way — that was the way. And you asked me," Maggie added, "if I did n't think we ought to tell them. Tell Mrs. Rance in particular I mean that we had been entertaining her up to then under false pretences."

"Precisely—but you said she would n't have understood."

"To which you replied that in that case you were like her. *You* did n't understand."

"No, no—but I remember how, about our having

259

in our benighted innocence no position, you quite crushed me with your explanation."

"Well then," said Maggie with every appearance of delight, "I'll crush you again. I told you that you by yourself had one — there was no doubt of that. You were different from me — you had the same one you always had."

"And *then* I asked you," her father concurred, "why in that case you hadn't the same."

"Then indeed you did." He had brought her face round to him before, and this held it, covering him with its kindled brightness, the result of the attested truth of their being able thus in talk to live again together. "What I replied was that I had lost my position by my marriage. That one — I know how I saw it — would never come back. I had done something *to* it — I didn't quite know what; given it away somehow and yet not as then appeared really got my return. I had been assured — always by dear Fanny — that I *could* get it, only I must wake up. So I was trying, you see, to wake up — trying very hard."

"Yes — and to a certain extent you succeeded; as also in waking me. But you made much," he said, "of your difficulty." To which he added: "It's the only case I remember, Mag, of your ever making *any-thing* of a difficulty."

She kept her eyes on him a moment. "That I was so happy as I was?"

"That you were so happy as you were."

"Well, you admitted" — Maggie kept it up — "that that was a good difficulty. You confessed that our life did seem to be beautiful."

He thought a moment. "Yes — I may very well have confessed it, for so it did seem to me." But he guarded himself with his dim, his easier smile. "What do you want to put on me now?"

"Only that we used to wonder — that we were wondering then — if our life was n't perhaps a little selfish."

This also for a time, much at his leisure, Adam Verver retrospectively fixed. "Because Fanny Assingham thought so?"

"Oh no; she never thought, she could n't think, if she would, anything of that sort. She only thinks people are sometimes fools," Maggie developed; "she does n't seem to think so much about their being wrong — wrong, that is, in the sense of being wicked. She does n't," the Princess further adventured, "quite so much mind their being wicked."

"I see — I see." And yet it might have been for his daughter that he did n't so very vividly see. "Then she only thought *us* fools?"

"Oh no — I don't say that. I'm speaking of our being selfish."

"And that comes under the head of the wickedness Fanny condones?"

"Oh I don't say she *condones* — !" A scruple in Maggie raised its crest. "Besides, I'm speaking of what was."

Her father showed however, after a little, that he had n't been reached by this discrimination; his thoughts were resting for the moment where they had settled. "Look here, Mag," he said reflectively — "I ain't selfish. I'll be blowed if I'm selfish."

Well, Maggie, if he *would* talk of that, could also pronounce. "Then, father, *I* am."

"Oh shucks!" said Adam Verver, to whom the vernacular, in moments of deepest sincerity, could thus come back. "I'll believe it," he presently added, "when Amerigo complains of you."

"Ah it's just he who's my selfishness. I'm selfish, so to speak, *for* him. I mean," she continued, "that he's my motive — in everything."

Well, her father could from experience fancy what she meant. "But has n't a girl a right to be selfish about her husband?"

"What I *don't* mean," she observed without answering, "is that I'm jealous of him. But that's his merit — it's not mine."

Her father again seemed amused at her. "You *could be* — otherwise?"

"Oh how can I talk," she asked, "of 'otherwise'? It *is n't*, luckily for me, otherwise. If everything were different" — she further presented her thought — "of course everything *would* be." And then again as if that were but half: "My idea is this, that when you only love a little you're naturally not jealous — or are only jealous also a little, so that it does n't matter. But when you love in a deeper and intenser way, then you're in the very same proportion jealous; your jealousy has intensity and, no doubt, ferocity. When however you love in the most abysmal and unutterable way of all — why then you're beyond everything, and nothing can pull you down."

Mr. Verver listened as if he had nothing on these high lines to oppose. "And that's the way *you* love?"

For a minute she failed to speak, but at last she answered: "It was n't to talk about that. I do *feel* however beyond everything — and as a consequence of that, I dare say," she added with a turn to gaiety, "seem often not to know quite *where* I am."

The mere fine pulse of passion in it, the suggestion as of a creature consciously floating and shining in a warm summer sea, some element of dazzling sapphire and silver, a creature cradled upon depths, buoyant among dangers, in which fear or folly or sinking otherwise than in play was impossible — something of all this might have been making once more present to him, with his discreet, his half-shy assent to it, her probable enjoyment of a rapture that he in his day had presumably convinced no great number of persons either of his giving or of his receiving. He sat a while as if he knew himself hushed, almost admonished, and not for the first time; yet it was an effect that might have brought before him rather what she had gained than what he had missed. Besides, who but himself really knew what *he*, after all, had n't, or even had, gained? The beauty of her condition was keeping him at any rate, as he might feel, in sight of the sea, where, though his personal dips were over, the whole thing could shine at him and the air and the plash and the play become for him too a sensation. That could n't be fixed upon him as missing; since if it was n't personally floating, if it was n't even sitting in the sand, it could yet pass very well for breathing the bliss, in a communicated irresistible way — for tasting the balm. It could pass further for knowing — for knowing that without

263

him nothing might have been: which would have been missing least of all. "I guess I've never been jealous," he finally remarked. And it said more to her, he had occasion next to perceive, than he was intending; for it made her, as by the pressure of a spring, give him a look that seemed to tell of things she could n't speak.

But she at last tried for one of them. "Oh it's you, father, who are what I call beyond everything. Nothing can pull *you* down."

He returned the look as with the sociability of their easy communion, though inevitably throwing in this time a shade of solemnity. He might have been seeing things to say and others, whether of a type presumptuous or not, doubtless better kept back. So he settled on the merely obvious. "Well then we make a pair. We're all right."

"Oh we're all right!" A declaration launched not only with all her discriminating emphasis, but confirmed by her rising with decision and standing there as if the object of their small excursion required accordingly no further pursuit. At this juncture, however — with the act of their crossing the bar to get, as might be, into port — there occurred the only approach to a betrayal of their having had to beat against the wind. Her father kept his place, and it was as if she had got over first and were pausing for her consort to follow. If they were all right, they were all right; yet he seemed to hesitate and wait for some word beyond. His eyes met her own suggestively, and it was only after she had contented herself with simply smiling at him, smiling ever so fixedly, that he spoke, for the remaining importance of it, from the bench; where he leaned back, raising his face to her, his legs thrust out a trifle wearily and his hands grasping either side of the seat. They had beaten against the wind and she was still fresh; they had beaten against the wind and he, as at the best the more battered vessel, perhaps just vaguely drooped. But the effect of their silence was that she appeared to beckon him on, and he might have been fairly alongside of her when at the end of another minute he found their word. "The only thing is that as for ever putting up again with your pretending that you're selfish —!"

At this she helped him out with it. "You won't take it from me?"

"I won't take it from you."

"Well of course you won't, for that's your way. It doesn't matter and it only proves —! But it doesn't matter either what it proves. I'm at this very moment," she declared, "frozen stiff with selfishness."

He faced her a while longer in the same way; it was strangely as if, by this sudden arrest, by their having, in their acceptance of the unsaid, or at least their reference to it, practically given up pretending — it was as if they were "in" for it, for something they had been ineffably avoiding, but the dread of which was itself in a manner a seduction, just as any confession of the dread was by so much an allusion. Then she seemed to see him let himself go. "When a person's of the nature you speak of there are always other persons to suffer. But you've just been describing to me what you'd take, if you had once a good chance, from your husband."

"Oh I'm not talking about my husband!"

"Then whom *are* you talking about?"

Both the retort and the rejoinder had come quicker than anything previously exchanged, and they were followed on Maggie's part by a momentary drop. But she was n't to fall away, and while her companion kept his eyes on her, while she wondered if he were n't expecting her to name his wife then, with high hypocrisy, as paying for his daughter's bliss, she produced something that she felt to be much better. "I'm talking about *you*."

"Do you mean I've been your victim?"

"Of course you've been my victim. What have you done, ever done, that has n't been *for* me?"

"Many things; more than I can tell you — things you've only to think of for yourself. What do you make of all that I've done for myself?"

"'Yourself'?" — She brightened out with derision.

"What do you make of what I've done for American City?"

It took her but a moment to say. "I'm not talking of you as a public character — I'm talking of you on your personal side."

"Well, American City — if 'personalities' can do it — has given me a pretty personal side. What do you make," he went on, "of what I've done for my reputation?"

"Your reputation *there?* You've given it up to them, the awful people, for less than nothing; you've given it up to them to tear to pieces, to make their horrible vulgar jokes against you with."

"Ah my dear I don't care for their horrible vulgar jokes," Adam Verver almost artlessly urged.

"Then there exactly you are!" she triumphed. "Everything that touches you, everything that surrounds you, goes on — by your splendid indifference and your incredible permission — at your expense."

Just as he had been sitting he looked at her an instant longer; then he slowly rose, while his hands stole into his pockets, and stood there before her. "Of course, my dear, *you* go on at my expense: it has never been my idea," he smiled, "that you should work for your living. I would n't have liked to see it." With which for a little again they remained face to face. "Say therefore I *have* had the feelings of a father. How have they made me a victim?"

"Because I sacrifice you."

"But to what in the world?"

At this it hung before her that she should have had as never yet her opportunity to say, and it held her for a minute as in a vise, her impression of his now, with his strained smile, which touched her to deepest depths, sounding her in his secret unrest. This was the moment in the whole process of their mutual vigilance in which it decidedly *most* hung by a hair that their thin wall might be pierced by the lightest wrong touch. It shook between them, this transparency, with their very breath; it was an exquisite tissue, but stretched on a frame, and would give way the next instant if either so much as breathed too hard. She held her breath, for she knew by his

eyes, the light at the heart of which he could n't
blind, that he was, by his intention, making sure —
sure whether or no her certainty was like his. The
intensity of his dependence on it at that moment —
this itself was what absolutely convinced her so that,
as if perched up before him on her vertiginous point
and in the very glare of his observation, she balanced
for thirty seconds, she almost rocked: she might have
been for the time, in all her conscious person, the
very form of the equilibrium they were, in their different ways, equally trying to save. And they were
saving it — yes, they were, or at least she was: that
was still the workable issue, she could say, as she
felt her dizziness drop. She held herself hard; the
thing was to be done, once for all, by her acting now
where she stood. So much was crowded into so short
a space that she knew already she was keeping her
head. She had kept it by the warning of his eyes; she
should n't lose it again; she knew how and why, and
if she had turned cold this was precisely what helped
her. He had said to himself "She'll break down and
name Amerigo; she'll say it's to him she's sacrificing
me; and it's by what that will give me — with so
many other things too — that my suspicion will be
clinched." He was watching her lips, spying for the
symptoms of the sound; whereby these symptoms had
only to fail and he would have got nothing that she
did n't measure out to him as she gave it. She had
presently in fact so recovered herself that she seemed
to know she could more easily have made him name
his wife than he have made her name her husband.
It was there before her that if she should so much as

force him just *not* consciously to avoid saying "Charlotte, Charlotte" he would have given himself away. But to be sure of this was enough for her, and she saw more clearly with each lapsing instant what they were both doing. He was doing what he had steadily been coming to; he was practically *offering* himself, pressing himself upon her, as a sacrifice — he had read his way so into her best possibility; and where had she already for weeks and days past planted her feet if not on her acceptance of the offer? Cold indeed, colder and colder she turned as she felt herself suffer this close personal vision of his attitude still not to make her weaken. That was her very certitude, the intensity of his pressure; for if something dreadful had n't happened there would n't for either of them be these dreadful things to do. She had meanwhile as well the immense advantage that *she* could have named Charlotte without exposing herself — as for that matter she was the next minute showing him.

"Why I sacrifice you simply to everything and to every one. I take the consequences of your marriage as perfectly natural."

He threw back his head a little, settling with one hand his nippers. "What do you call, my dear, the consequences?"

"Your life as your marriage has made it."

"Well, has n't it made it exactly what we wanted?"

She just hesitated, then felt herself steady — oh beyond what she had dreamed. "Exactly what *I* wanted — yes."

His eyes, through his straightened glasses, were still on hers, and he might, with his intenser fixed smile, have been knowing she was for herself rightly inspired. "What do you make then of what I wanted?"

"I don't make anything, any more than of what you've got. That's exactly the point. I don't put myself out to do so — I never have; I take from you all I can get, all you've provided for me, and I leave you to make of your own side of the matter what you can. There you are — the rest is your own affair. I don't even pretend to concern myself —!"

"To concern yourself —?" He watched her as she faintly faltered, looking about her now so as not to keep always meeting his face.

"With what may have *really* become of you. It's as if we had agreed from the first not to go into that — such an arrangement being of course charming for *me*. You can't say, you know, that I haven't stuck to it."

He didn't say so then — even with the opportunity given him of her stopping once more to catch her breath. He said instead: "Oh my dear — oh, oh!"

But it made no difference, know as she might what a past — still so recent and yet so distant — it alluded to; she repeated her denial, warning him off, on her side, from spoiling the truth of her contention. "I never went into anything, and you see I don't; I've continued to adore you — but what's that from a decent daughter to such a father? what but a question of convenient arrangement, our having two houses, three houses, instead of one (you would have arranged for fifty if I had wished!) and my making it easy for you to see the child? You don't claim,

I suppose, that my natural course, once you had set up for yourself, would have been to ship you back to American City?"

These were direct enquiries, they quite rang out in the soft wooded air; so that Adam Verver for a minute appeared to meet them with reflexion. She saw reflexion however quickly enough show him what to do with them. "Do you know, Mag, what you make me wish when you talk that way?" And he waited again while she further got from him the sense of something that had been behind, deeply in the shade, coming cautiously to the front and just feeling its way before presenting itself. "You regularly make me wish I *had* shipped back to American City. When you go on as you do —" But he really had to hold himself to say it.

"Well, when I go on —?"

"Why you make me quite want to ship back myself. You make me quite feel as if American City would be the best place for us."

It made her all too finely vibrate. "For 'us' —?"

"For me and Charlotte. Do you know that if we *should* ship it would serve you quite right?" With which he smiled — oh he smiled! "And if you say much more we *will ship*."

Ah then it was that the cup of her conviction, full to the brim, overflowed at a touch! *There* was his idea, the clearness of which for an instant almost dazzled her. It was a blur of light in the midst of which she saw Charlotte like some object marked by contrast in blackness, saw her waver in the field of vision, saw her removed, transported, doomed.

And he had named Charlotte, named her again, and she had *made* him — which was all she had needed more: it was as if she had held a blank letter to the fire and the writing had come out still larger than she hoped. The recognition of it took her some seconds, but she might when she spoke have been folding up these precious lines and restoring them to her pocket. "Well, I shall be as much as ever then the cause of what you do. I have n't the least doubt of your being up to that if you should think I might get anything out of it; even the little pleasure," she laughed, "of having said, as you call it, 'more.' Let my enjoyment of this therefore, at any price, continue to represent for you what *I* call sacrificing you."

She had drawn a long breath; she had made him do it *all* for her, and had lighted the way to it without his naming her husband. That silence had been as distinct as the sharp, the inevitable sound, and something now in him followed it up, a sudden air as of confessing at last fully to where she was and of begging the particular question. "Don't you think then I can take care of myself?"

"Ah it 's exactly what I 've gone upon. If it was n't for that —!"

But she broke off and they remained only another moment face to face. "I 'll let you know, my dear, the day *I* feel you 've begun to sacrifice me."

"'Begun'?" she extravagantly echoed.

"Well, it will be for me the day you 've ceased to believe in me."

With which, his glasses still fixed on her, his hands in his pockets, his hat pushed back, his legs a little

apart, he seemed to plant or to square himself for a
kind of assurance it had occurred to him he might as
well treat her to, in default of other things, before they
changed their subject. It had the effect for her of
a reminder — a reminder of all he was, of all he had
done, of all, above and beyond his being her perfect
little father, she might take him as representing, take
him as having quite eminently, in the eyes of two
hemispheres, been capable of, and as therefore wishing, not — was it ? — illegitimately, to call her attention to. The "successful" beneficent person, the
beautiful bountiful original dauntlessly wilful great
citizen, the consummate collector and infallible high
authority he had been and still was — these things
struck her on the spot as making up for him in a wonderful way a character she must take into account in
dealing with him either for pity or for envy. He
positively, under the impression, seemed to loom
larger than life for her, so that she saw him during
these moments in a light of recognition which had
had its brightness for her at many an hour of the past,
but which had never been so intense and so almost
admonitory. His very quietness was part of it now,
as always part of everything, of his success, his originality, his modesty, his exquisite public perversity,
his inscrutable incalculable energy; and this quality
perhaps it might be — all the more too as the result,
for the present occasion, of an admirable traceable
effort — that placed him in her eyes as no precious
work of art probably had ever been placed in his
own. There was a long moment, absolutely, during
which her impression rose and rose, even as that of

the typical charmed gazer, in the still museum, before the named and dated object, the pride of the catalogue, that time has polished and consecrated. Extraordinary in particular was the number of the different ways in which he thus affected her as showing. He was strong — that was the great thing. He was sure — sure for himself always, whatever his idea: the expression of that in him had somehow never appeared more identical with his proved taste for the rare and the true. But what stood out beyond everything was that he was always marvellously young — which could n't but crown at this juncture his whole appeal to her imagination. Before she knew it she was lifted aloft by the consciousness that he was simply a great and deep and high little man, and that to love him with tenderness was not to be distinguished a whit from loving him with pride. It came to her, all strangely, as a sudden, an immense relief. The sense that he was n't a failure, and could never be, purged their predicament of every meanness — made it as if they had really emerged, in their transmuted union, to smile almost without pain. It was like a new confidence, and after another instant she knew even still better why. Was n't it because now also, on his side, he was thinking of her as his daughter, was *trying* her, during these mute seconds, as the child of his blood ? Oh then if she was n't with her little conscious passion the child of any weakness, what was she but strong enough too ? It swelled in her fairly; it raised her higher, higher: she was n't in that case a failure either — had n't been, but the contrary; his strength was her strength, her pride was his, and they were decent and competent together. This was all in the answer she finally made him.

"I believe in you more than any one."

"Than any one at all?"

She hesitated for all it might mean; but there was — oh a thousand times! — no doubt of it. "Than any one at all." She kept nothing of it back now, met his eyes over it, let him have the whole of it; after which she went on: "And that's the way, I think, you believe in me."

He looked at her a minute longer, but his tone at last was right. "About the way — yes."

"Well then —?" She spoke as for the end and for other matters — for anything, everything else there might be. They would never return to it.

"Well then —!" His hands came out, and while her own took them he drew her to his breast and held her. He held her hard and kept her long, and she let herself go; but it was an embrace that, august and almost stern, produced for all its intimacy no revulsion and broke into no inconsequence of tears.

IV

MAGGIE was to feel after this passage how they had both been helped through it by the influence of that accident of her having been caught a few nights before in the familiar embrace of her father's wife. His return to the saloon had chanced to coincide exactly with this demonstration, missed moreover neither by her husband nor by the Assinghams, who, their card-party suspended, had quitted the billiard-room with him. She had been conscious enough at the time of what such an impression, received by the others, might in that extended state do for her case; and none the less that, as no one had appeared to wish to be the first to make a remark about it, it had taken on perceptibly the special shade of consecration conferred by unanimities of silence. The effect, she might have considered, had been almost awkward — the promptitude of her separation from Charlotte, as if they had been discovered in some absurdity, on her becoming aware of spectators. The spectators on the other hand — that was the appearance — might n't have supposed them, in the existing relation, addicted to mutual endearments; and yet, hesitating with a fine scruple between sympathy and hilarity, must have felt that almost any spoken or laughed comment could be kept from sounding vulgar only by sounding beyond any permitted measure intelligent. They had evidently looked, the two young wives, like a pair of

276

women "making up" effusively, as women were supposed to do, especially when approved fools, after a
broil; but taking note of the reconciliation would
imply on her father's part, on Amerigo's and on Fanny
Assingham's, some proportionate vision of the grounds
of their difference. There had been something in
the incident, there had been but too much, for each
observer; yet there was nothing any one could have
said without seeming essentially to say: "See, see, the
dear things — their quarrel's blissfully over!" "Our
quarrel? What quarrel?" the dear things themselves
would necessarily in that case have demanded; and
the wits of the others would thus have been called
upon for some agility of exercise. No one had been
equal to the flight of producing off-hand a fictive
reason for any estrangement — to take, that is, the
place of the true, which had so long, for the finer sensibility, pervaded the air; and every one accordingly,
not to be inconveniently challenged, was pretending
immediately after to have remarked nothing that any
one else had n't.

Maggie's own measure had remained all the same
full of the reflexion caught from the total inference;
which had acted virtually by enabling every one present — and oh Charlotte not least! — to draw a long
breath. The message of the little scene had been different for each, but it had been this, markedly, all
round, that it re-enforced — re-enforced even immensely — the general effort, carried on from week to week
and of late distinctly more successful, to look and talk
and move as if nothing in life were the matter. Supremely however, while this glass was held up to her,

had Maggie's sense turned to the quality of the success constituted on the spot for Charlotte. Most of
all, if she was guessing how her father must have
secretly started, how her husband must have secretly
wondered, how Fanny Assingham must have secretly,
in a flash, seen daylight for herself — most of all had
she tasted, by communication, of the high profit involved for her companion. She *felt* in all her pulses
Charlotte feel it, and how publicity had been required,
absolutely, to crown her own abasement. It was the
added touch, and now nothing was wanting — which,
to do her stepmother justice, Mrs. Verver had appeared but to desire from that evening to show with
the last vividness that she recognised. Maggie lived
over again the minutes in question — had found herself repeatedly doing so; to the degree that the whole
evening hung together, to her aftersense, as a thing
appointed by some occult power that had dealt with
her, that had for instance animated the four with just
the right restlessness too, had decreed and directed
and exactly timed it in them, making their game of
bridge — however abysmal a face it had worn for her
— give way precisely to their common unavowed impulse to find out, to emulate Charlotte's impatience;
a preoccupation, this latter, attached detectedly to
the member of the party who was roaming in her
queerness and was, for all their simulated blindness,
not roaming unnoted.

If Mrs. Verver meanwhile then had struck her as
determined in a certain direction by the last felicity
into which that night had flowered, our young woman
was yet not to fail of appreciating the truth that she

had n't after all been put at ease with absolute per-
manence. Maggie had seen her unmistakeably desire
to rise to the occasion and be magnificent — seen her
decide that the right way for this would be to prove
that the reassurance she had extorted there, under the
high cool lustre of the saloon, a twinkle of crystal and
silver, had n't only poured oil on the troubled waters
of their question, but had fairly drenched their whole
intercourse with that lubricant. She had exceeded the
limit of discretion in this insistence on her capacity
to repay in proportion a service she acknowledged
as handsome. "Why handsome?" Maggie would
have been free to ask; since if she had been veracious
the service assuredly would n't have been huge. It
would in that case have come up vividly, and for each
of them alike, that the truth on the Princess's lips
presented no difficulty. If the latter's mood in fact
could have turned itself at all to private gaiety it might
have failed to resist the diversion of seeing so clever
a creature so beguiled. Charlotte's theory of a generous manner was manifestly to express that her stepdaughter's word, wiping out, as she might have said,
everything, had restored them to the serenity of a relation without a cloud. It had been in short by this
light ideally conclusive, so that no ghost of anything
it referred to could ever walk again. What was the
ecstasy of that, however, but in itself a trifle compro-
mising? — as truly, within the week, Maggie had occasion to suspect her friend of beginning, and rather
abruptly, to remember. Convinced as she was of the
example already given her by her husband, and in
relation to which her profession of trust in his mistress

had been an act of conformity exquisitely calculated, her imagination yet sought in the hidden play of his influence the explanation of any change of surface, any difference of expression or intention. There had been, through life, as we know, few quarters in which the Princess's fancy could let itself loose; but it shook off restraint when it plunged into the figured void of the detail of that relation. This was a realm it could people with images — again and again with fresh ones; they swarmed there like the strange combinations that lurked in the woods at twilight; they loomed into the definite and faded into the vague, their main present sign for her being however that they were always, that they were duskily, agitated. Her earlier vision of a state of bliss made insecure by the very intensity of the bliss — this had dropped from her; she had ceased to see, as she lost herself, the pair of operatic, of high Wagnerian lovers (she found deep within her these comparisons) interlocked in their wood of enchantment, a green glade as romantic as one's dream of an old German forest. The picture was veiled on the contrary with the dimness of trouble; behind which she felt indistinguishable the procession of forms that had lost all so pitifully their precious confidence.

Therefore though there was in these days for her with Amerigo little enough even of the imitation, from day to day, of unembarrassed reference — as she had foreseen for that matter from the first that there would be — her active conception of his accessibility to their companion's own private and unextinguished right to break ground was not much less active than before. So it was that her inner sense, in spite of everything, represented him as still pulling wires and controlling currents, or rather indeed as muffling the whole possibility, keeping it down and down, leading his accomplice continually on to some new turn of the road. As regards herself Maggie had become more conscious from week to week of his ingenuities of intention to make up to her for their forfeiture, in so dire a degree, of any reality of frankness — a privation that had left on his lips perhaps a little of the same thirst with which she fairly felt her own distorted, the torment of the lost pilgrim who listens in desert sands for the possible, the impossible plash of water. It was just this hampered state in him none the less that she kept before her when she wished most to find grounds of dignity for the hard little passion which nothing he had done could smother. There were hours enough, lonely hours, in which she let dignity go; then there were others when, clinging with her winged concentration to some deep cell of her heart, she stored away her hived tenderness as if she had gathered it all from flowers. He was walking ostensibly beside her, but in fact given over without a break to the grey medium in which he helplessly groped; a perception on her part which was a perpetual pang and which might last what it would — for ever if need be — but which if relieved at all must be relieved by his act alone. She herself could do nothing more for it; she had done the utmost possible. It was meantime not the easier to bear for this aspect under which Charlotte was presented as depending on him for guidance, taking it from him even in doses of bitterness and yet lost with him in devious depths. Nothing was thus

more sharply to be inferred than that he had promptly
enough warned her, on hearing from her of the precious assurance received from his wife, that she must
take care her satisfaction did n't betray something
of her danger. Maggie had a day of still waiting after
allowing him time to learn how unreservedly she had
lied for him — of waiting as for the light of she scarce
knew what slow-shining reflexion of this knowledge
in his personal attitude. What retarded evolution,
she asked herself in these hours, might n't poor Charlotte all unwittingly have precipitated? She was thus
poor Charlotte again for Maggie even while Maggie's
own head was bowed, and the reason for this kept
coming back to our young woman in the conception
of what would secretly have passed. She saw her, face
to face with the Prince, take from him the chill of his
stiffest admonition, with the possibilities of deeper
difficulty that it represented for each. She heard her
ask, irritated and sombre, what tone, in God's name
— since her bravery did n't suit him — she *was* then
to adopt; and by way of a fantastic flight of divination
she heard Amerigo reply, in a voice of which every
fine note, familiar and admirable, came home to her,
that one must really manage such prudences a little
for one's self. It was positive in the Princess that for
this she breathed Charlotte's cold air — turned away
from him in it with her, turned with her, in growing
compassion, this way and that, hovered behind her
while she felt her ask herself where then she should
rest. Marvellous the manner in which, under such
imaginations, Maggie thus circled and lingered —
quite as if she were, materially, following her unseen,

counting every step she helplessly wasted, noting every hindrance that brought her to a pause.

A few days of this accordingly had wrought a change in that apprehension of the instant beatitude of triumph — of triumph magnanimous and serene — with which the upshot of the night-scene on the terrace had condemned our young woman to make terms. She had had, as we know, her vision of the gilt bars bent, of the door of the cage forced open from within and the creature imprisoned roaming at large — a movement on the creature's part that was to have even for the short interval its impressive beauty, but of which the limit, and in yet another direction, had loomed straight into view during her last talk under the great trees with her father. It was when she saw his wife's face ruefully attached to the quarter to which in the course of their session he had so significantly addressed his own — it was then that Maggie could watch for its turning pale, it was then she seemed to know what she had meant by thinking of her, in the shadow of his most ominous reference, as "doomed." If, as I say, her attention now, day after day, so circled and hovered, it found itself arrested for certain passages during which she absolutely looked with Charlotte's grave eyes. What she unfailingly made out through them was the figure of a little quiet gentleman who mostly wore, as he moved alone across the field of vision, a straw hat, a white waistcoat and a blue necktie, keeping a cigar in his teeth and his hands in his pockets, and who oftener than not presented a somewhat meditative back while he slowly measured the perspectives of the park and broodingly counted (it might have appeared) his steps. There were hours of intensity for a week or two when it was for all the world as if she had guardedly tracked her stepmother, in the great house, from room to room and from window to window, only to see her, here and there and everywhere, *try* her uneasy outlook, question her issue and her fate. Something indubitably had come up for her that had never come up before; it represented a new complication and had begotten a new anxiety — things these that she carried about with her done up in the napkin of her lover's accepted rebuke while she vainly hunted for some corner where she might put them safely down. The disguised solemnity, the prolonged futility of her search might have been grotesque to a more ironic eye; but Maggie's provision of irony, which we have taken for naturally small, had never been so scant as now, and there were moments while she watched with her, thus unseen, when the mere effect of being near her was to feel her own heart in her throat, was to be almost moved to saying to her: "Hold on tight, my poor dear — without *too much* terror — and it will all come out somehow."

Even to that indeed, she could reflect, Charlotte might have replied that it was easy to say; even to that no great meaning could attach so long as the little meditative man in the straw hat kept coming into view with his indescribable air of weaving his spell, weaving it off there by himself. In whatever quarter of the horizon the appearances were scanned he was to be noticed as absorbed in this occupation; and Maggie was to become aware of two or three extraordinary

occasions of receiving from him the hint that he measured the impression he produced. It was not really
till after their recent long talk in the park that she
knew how deeply, how quite exhaustively, they had
then communicated — so that they were to remain
together, for the time, in consequence, quite in the
form of a couple of sociable drinkers who sit back from
the table over which they have been resting their elbows, over which they have emptied to the last drop
their respective charged cups. The cups were still
there on the table, but turned upside down; and nothing was left for the companions but to confirm by
placid silences the fact that the wine had been good.
They had parted positively as if on either side primed
with it — primed for whatever was to be; and everything between them, as the month waned, added its
touch of truth to this similitude. Nothing truly *was*
at present between them save that they were looking
at each other in infinite trust; it fairly wanted no more
words, and when they met during the deep summer
days, met even without witnesses, when they kissed at
morning and evening or on any of the other occasions
of contact that they had always so freely celebrated,
a pair of birds of the upper air could scarce have appeared less to invite each other to sit down and worry
afresh. So it was that in the house itself, where more
of his waiting treasures than ever were provisionally
ranged, she sometimes only looked at him — from end
to end of the great gallery, the pride of the house, for
instance — as if, in one of the halls of a museum, she
had been an earnest young woman with a Baedeker
and he a vague gentleman to whom even Baedekers

were unknown. He had ever of course had his way of walking about to review his possessions and verify their condition; but this was a pastime to which he now struck her as almost extravagantly addicted, and when she passed near him and he turned to give her a smile she caught — or so she fancied — the greater depth of his small perpetual hum of contemplation. It was as if he were singing to himself, *sotto voce*, as he went — and it was also on occasion quite ineffably as if Charlotte, hovering, watching, listening for her part too, kept sufficiently within earshot to make it out as song, and yet by some effect of the very manner of it stood off and did n't dare.

One of the attentions she had from immediately after her marriage most freely paid him was that of her interest in his rarities, her appreciation of his taste, her native passion for beautiful objects and her grateful desire not to miss anything he could teach her about them. Maggie had in due course seen her begin to "work" this fortunately natural source of sympathy for all it was worth. She took possession of the ground throughout its extent; she abounded, to odd excess, one might have remarked, in the assumption of its being for her, with her husband, *all* the ground, the finest clearest air and most breatheable medium common to them. It had been given to Maggie to wonder if she did n't in these intensities of approbation too much shut him up to his province; but this was a complaint he had never made his daughter, and Charlotte must at least have had for her that, thanks to her admirable instinct, her range of perception marching with his own and never falling behind, she

had probably not so much as once treated him to a
rasping mistake or a revealing stupidity. Maggie,
wonderfully, in the summer days, felt it forced upon
her that that was one way, after all, of being a genial
wife; and it was never so much forced upon her as
at these odd moments of her encountering the *sposi*,
as Amerigo called them, under the coved ceilings of
Fawns while, so together yet at the same time so separate, they were making their daily round. Charlotte
hung behind with emphasised attention; she stopped
when her husband stopped, but at the distance of
a case or two, or of whatever other succession of objects; and the likeness of their connexion would n't
have been wrongly figured if he had been thought
of as holding in one of his pocketed hands the end of
a long silken halter looped round her beautiful neck.
He did n't twitch it, yet it was there; he did n't drag
her, but she came; and those betrayals that I have
described the Princess as finding irresistible in him
were two or three mute facial intimations which
his wife's presence did n't prevent his addressing his
daughter — nor prevent his daughter, as she passed,
it was doubtless to be added, from flushing a little at
the receipt of. They amounted perhaps only to a
wordless, wordless smile, but the smile was the soft
shake of the twisted silken rope, and Maggie's trans-
lation of it, held in her breast till she got well away,
came out only, as if it might have been overheard,
when some door was closed behind her. "Yes, you
see — I lead her now by the neck, I lead her to her
doom, and she does n't so much as know what it is,
though she has a fear in her heart which, if you had

the chances to apply your ear there that I, as a husband, have, you would hear thump and thump and thump. She thinks it *may* be, her doom, the awful place over there — awful for *her;* but she's afraid to ask, don't you see? just as she's afraid of not asking; just as she's afraid of so many other things that she sees multiplied all about her now as perils and portents. She'll know, however — when she does know."

Charlotte's one opportunity meanwhile for the air of confidence she had formerly worn so well and that agreed so with her firm and charming type was the presence of visitors never, as the season advanced, wholly intermitted — rather in fact, so constant, with all the people who turned up for luncheon and for tea and to see the house, now replete, now famous, that Maggie grew to think again of this large element of "company" as of a kind of renewed water-supply for the tank in which, like a party of panting gold-fish, they kept afloat. It helped them unquestionably with each other, weakening the emphasis of so many of the silences of which their intimate intercourse would otherwise have consisted. Beautiful and wonderful for her even at times was the effect of these interventions — their effect above all in bringing home to each the possible heroism of perfunctory things. They learned fairly to live in the perfunctory; they remained in it as many hours of the day as might be; it took on finally the likeness of some spacious central chamber in a haunted house, a great overarched and overglazed rotunda where gaiety might reign, but the doors of which opened into sinister circular passages.

THE PRINCESS

Here they turned up for each other, as they said, with
the blank faces that denied any uneasiness felt in the
approach; here they closed numerous doors carefully
behind them — all save the door that connected the
place, as by a straight tented corridor, with the outer
world, and, encouraging thus the irruption of society,
imitated the aperture through which the bedizened
performers of the circus are poured into the ring. The
great part Mrs. Verver had socially played came luckily, Maggie could make out, to her assistance; she had
"personal friends" — Charlotte's personal friends
had ever been, in London, at the two houses, one
of the most convenient pleasantries — who actually
tempered at this crisis her aspect of isolation; and it
would n't have been hard to guess that her best moments were those in which she suffered no fear of
becoming a bore to restrain her appeal to their curiosity. Their curiosity might be vague, but their clever
hostess was distinct, and she marched them about,
sparing them nothing, as if she counted each day on a
harvest of half-crowns. Maggie met her again, in the
gallery, at the oddest hours, with the party she was
entertaining; heard her draw out the lesson, insist on
the interest, snub, even, the particular presumption
and smile for the general bewilderment — inevitable
features these latter of almost any occasion — in a
manner that made our young woman, herself incure-
ably dazzled, marvel afresh at the mystery by which
a creature who could be in some connexions so earn-
estly right could be in others so perversely wrong.
When her father, vaguely circulating, was attended
by his wife, it was always Charlotte who seemed to

bring up the rear; but he hung in the background when she did *cicerone*, and it was then perhaps that, moving mildly and modestly to and fro on the skirts of the exhibition, his appearance of weaving his spell was for the initiated conscience least to be resisted. Brilliant women turned to him in vague emotion, but his response scarce committed him more than if he had been the person employed to see that after the invading wave was spent the cabinets were all locked and the symmetries all restored.

There was a morning when, during the hour before luncheon and shortly after the arrival of a neighbourly contingent — neighbourly from ten miles off — whom Mrs. Verver had taken in charge, Maggie paused on the threshold of the gallery through which she had been about to pass, faltering there for the very impression of his face as it met her from an opposite door. Charlotte, halfway down the vista, held together, as if by something almost austere in the grace of her authority, the semi-scared (now that they were there!) knot of her visitors, who, since they had announced themselves by telegram as yearning to enquire and admire, saw themselves restricted to this consistency. Her voice, high and clear and a little hard, reached her husband and her stepdaughter while she thus placed beyond doubt her cheerful submission to duty. Her words, addressed to the largest publicity, rang for some minutes through the place, every one as quiet to listen as if it had been a church ablaze with tapers and she were taking her part in some hymn of praise. Fanny Assingham looked rapt in devotion — Fanny Assingham who forsook this other friend as little as she forsook either her host or the Princess or the Prince or the Principino; she supported her, in slow revolutions, in murmurous attestations of presence, at all such times, and Maggie, advancing after a first hesitation, was not to fail of noting her solemn inscrutable attitude, her eyes attentively lifted, so that she might escape being provoked to betray an impression. She betrayed one however as Maggie approached, dropping her gaze to the latter's level long enough to seem to adventure, marvellously, on a mute appeal. "You understand, don't you, that if she did n't do this there would be no knowing what she might do?" This light Mrs. Assingham richly launched while her younger friend, unresistingly moved, became uncertain again, and then, not too much to show it — or rather positively to conceal it and to conceal something more as well — turned short round to one of the windows and awkwardly, pointlessly waited. "The largest of the three pieces has the rare peculiarity that the garlands looped round it, which as you see are the finest possible *vieux Saxe*, are n't of the same origin or period, or even, wonderful as they are, of a taste quite so perfect. They've been put on at a later time by a process known through very few examples, and through none so important as this, which is really quite unique — so that though the whole thing is a little *baroque* its value as a specimen is I believe almost inestimable."

So the high voice quavered, aiming truly at effects far over the heads of gaping neighbours; so the speaker, piling it up, sticking at nothing, as less interested judges might have said, seemed to justify the faith with which she was honoured. Maggie meanwhile at the window knew the strangest thing to be happening: she had turned suddenly to crying, or was at least on the point of it — the lighted square before her all blurred and dim. The high voice went on; its quaver was doubtless for conscious ears only, but there were verily thirty seconds during which it sounded, for our young woman, like the shriek of a soul in pain. Kept up a minute longer it would break and collapse — so that Maggie felt herself the next thing turn with a start to her father. "Can't she be stopped? Hasn't she done it *enough?*" — some such question as that she let herself ask him to suppose in her. Then it was that, across half the gallery — for he hadn't moved from where she had first seen him — he struck her as confessing, with strange tears in his own eyes, to sharp identity of emotion. "Poor thing, poor thing" — it reached straight — "*isn't* she, for one's credit, on the swagger?" After which, as held thus together they had still another strained minute, the shame, the pity, the better knowledge, the smothered protest, the divined anguish even, so overcame him that, blushing to his eyes, he turned short away. The affair but of a few muffled moments, this snatched communion yet lifted Maggie as on air — so much for deep guesses on her own side too it gave her to think of. There was honestly an awful mixture in things, and it wasn't closed to her aftersense of such passages — we have already indeed in other cases seen it open — that the deepest depth of all, in a perceived penalty, was that you couldn't be sure some of your compunctions and contortions wouldn't show for ridiculous.

Amerigo that morning for instance had been as absent as he at this juncture appeared to desire he should mainly be noted as being; he had gone to London for the day and the night — a necessity that now frequently rose for him and that he had more than once suffered to operate during the presence of guests, successions of pretty women, the theory of his fond interest in whom had been publicly cultivated. It had never occurred to his wife to pronounce him ingenuous, but there came at last a high dim August dawn when she could n't sleep and when, creeping restlessly about and breathing at her window the coolness of wooded acres, she found the faint flush of the east march with the perception of that other almost equal prodigy. It rosily coloured her vision that — even such as he was, yes — her husband could on occasion sin by excess of candour. He would n't otherwise have given as his reason for going up to Portland Place in the August days that he was arranging books there. He had bought a great many of late and had had others, a large number, sent from Rome — wonders of old print in which her father had been interested. But when her imagination tracked him to the dusty town, to the house where drawn blinds and pale shrouds, where a caretaker and a kitchenmaid were alone in possession, it was n't to see him, in his shirt-sleeves, unpacking battered boxes.

She saw him in truth less easily beguiled — saw him wander in the closed dusky rooms from place to place or else for long periods recline on deep sofas and stare before him through the smoke of ceaseless cigarettes. She made him out as liking better than anything in the world just now to be alone with his thoughts. Being herself connected with his thoughts, she continued to believe, more than she had ever been, it was thereby a good deal as if he were alone with *her*. She made him out as resting so from that constant strain of the perfunctory to which he was exposed at Fawns; and she was accessible to the impression of the almost beggared aspect of this alternative. It was like his doing penance in sordid ways — being sent to prison or being kept without money; it would n't have taken much to make her think of him as really kept without food. He might have broken away, might easily have started to travel; he had a right — thought wonderful Maggie now — to so many more freedoms than he took! His secret was of course that at Fawns he all the while winced, was all the while in presences in respect to which he had thrown himself back with a hard pressure on whatever mysteries of pride, whatever inward springs familiar to the man of the world, he could keep from snapping. Maggie, for some reason, had that morning, while she watched the sunrise, taken an extraordinary measure of the ground on which he would have *had* to snatch at pretexts for absence. It all came to her there — he got off to escape from a sound. The sound was in her own ears still — that of Charlotte's high coerced quaver before the cabinets in the hushed gallery; the voice by which she herself had been pierced the day before as by that of a creature in anguish and by which, while she sought refuge at the blurred window, the tears had been forced into her eyes. Her comprehension soared so high that the wonder for her became really his not feeling the need of wider intervals and thicker walls. Before *that* admiration she also meditated; consider as she might now she kept reading not less into what he omitted than into what he performed a beauty of intention that touched her fairly the more by being obscure. It was like hanging over a garden in the dark; nothing was to be made of the confusion of growing things, but one felt they were folded flowers and that their vague sweetness made the whole air their medium. He had to turn away, but he was n't at least a coward; he would wait on the spot for the issue of what he had done on the spot. She sank to her knees with her arm on the ledge of her window-seat, where she blinded her eyes from the full glare of seeing that his idea could only be to wait, whatever might come, at her side. It was to her buried face that she thus for a long time felt him draw nearest; though after a while, when the strange wail of the gallery began to repeat its inevitable echo, she was conscious of how that brought out his pale hard grimace.

V

THE resemblance had n't been present to her on first coming out into the hot still brightness of the Sunday afternoon — only the second Sunday, of all the summer, when the party of six, the party of seven including the Principino, had practically been without accessions or invasions; but within sight of Charlotte seated far away and very much where she had expected to find her the Princess fell to wondering if her friend would n't be affected quite as she herself had been that night on the terrace under Mrs. Verver's perceptive pursuit. The relation to-day had turned itself round; Charlotte was seeing her come through patches of lingering noon quite as she had watched Charlotte menace her through the starless dark; and there was a moment, that of her waiting a little as they thus met across the distance, when the interval was bridged by a recognition not less soundless and to all appearance not less charged with strange meanings than that of the other occasion. The point however was that they had changed places; Maggie had from her window seen her stepmother leave the house — at so unlikely an hour, three o'clock of a canicular August, for a ramble in garden or grove — and had thereupon felt her impulse determined with the same sharpness that had made the spring of her companion's three weeks before. It was the hottest day of the season, and the shaded siesta, for people all at

296

their ease, would certainly rather have been prescribed; but our young woman had perhaps not yet
felt it so fully brought home that such refinements
of repose among them constituted the empty chair
at the feast. This was the more distinct as the feast,
literally, in the great bedimmed dining-room, the
cool ceremonious semblance of luncheon, had just
been taking place without Mrs. Verver. She had
figured but as the absent victim of a bad headache,
not reported to the rest of the company by her husband, but named directly to Mr. Verver himself, on
their having assembled, by her maid, deputed for the
effect and conscientiously producing it.

Maggie had sat down with the others to viands
artfully iced, to the slow circulation of precious tink-
ling jugs, to marked reserves of reference in many
directions — poor Fanny Assingham herself scarce
thrusting her nose out of the padded hollow into which
she had withdrawn. A consensus of languor, which
might almost have been taken for a community of
dread, ruled the scene — relieved only by the fitful
experiments of Father Mitchell, good holy hungry
man, a trusted and overworked London friend and
adviser, who had taken for a week or two the light
neighbouring service, local rites flourishing under
Maggie's munificence, and was enjoying, as a convenience, all the bounties of the house. *He* conversed
undiscouraged, Father Mitchell — conversed mainly
with the indefinite wandering smile of the entertainers,
and the Princess's power to feel him on the whole
a blessing for these occasions was not impaired by
what was awkward in her consciousness of having,

from the first of her trouble, really found her way without his guidance. She asked herself at times if he suspected how more than subtly, how perversely, she had dispensed with him, and she balanced between visions of all he must privately have guessed and certitudes that he had guessed nothing whatever. He might nevertheless have been so urbanely filling up gaps, at present, for the very reason that his instinct, sharper than the expression of his face, had sufficiently served him — made him aware of the thin ice, figuratively speaking, and of prolongations of tension, round about him, mostly foreign to the circles in which luxury was akin to virtue. Some day at some happier season she would confess to him that she had n't confessed, though taking so much on her conscience; but just now she was carrying in her weak stiffened hand a glass filled to the brim, as to which she had recorded a vow that no drop should overflow. She feared the very breath of a better wisdom, the jostle of the higher light, of heavenly help itself; and, in addition, however that might be, she drew breath this afternoon, as never yet, in an element heavy to oppression.

Something grave had happened somehow and somewhere, and she had, God knew, her choice of suppositions: her heart stood still when she wondered above all if the cord might n't at last have snapped between her husband and her father. She shut her eyes for dismay at the possibility of such a passage — there moved before them the procession of ugly forms it might have taken. "Find out for yourself!" she had thrown to Amerigo for her last word on the ques-

tion of who else "knew," that night of the breaking
of the Bowl; and she flattered herself that she had n't
since then helped him, in her clear consistency, by
an inch. It was what she had given him all these
weeks to be busy with, and she had again and again
lain awake for the obsession of her sense of his uncertainty ruthlessly and endlessly playing with his dignity. She had handed him over to an ignorance that
could n't even try to become indifferent and that yet
would n't project itself either into the cleared air of
conviction. In proportion as he was generous it had
bitten into his spirit, and more than once she had said
to herself that to break the spell she had cast upon him
and that the polished old ivory of her father's inat-
tackable surface made so absolute, he would suddenly
commit some mistake or some violence, smash some
window-pane for air, fail even of one of his blest in-
veteracies of taste. In that way, fatally, he would have
put himself in the wrong — blighting by a single false
step the perfection of his outward show.

These shadows rose and fell for her while Father
Mitchell prattled; with other shadows as well, those
that hung over Charlotte herself, those that marked
her as a prey to equal suspicions — to the idea in particular of a change, such a change as she did n't dare
to face, in the relations of the two men. Or there
were yet other possibilities as it seemed to Maggie;
there were always too many, and all of them things
of evil when one's nerves had at last done for one
all that nerves could do; had left one in a darkness
of prowling dangers that was like the predicament of
the night-watcher in a beast-haunted land who has

no more means for a fire. She might, with such nerves, have supposed almost anything of any one; anything almost of poor Bob Assingham, condemned to eternal observances and solemnly appreciating her father's wine; anything verily, yes, of the good priest as he finally sat back with fat folded hands and twiddled his thumbs on his stomach. The good priest looked hard at the decanters, at the different dishes of dessert — he eyed them half-obliquely, as if *they* might have met him to-day for conversation better than any one present. But the Princess had her fancy at last about that too; she was in the midst of a passage, before she knew it, between Father Mitchell and Charlotte — some approach he would have attempted with her that very morning perhaps to the circumstance of an apparent detachment recently noted in her from any practice of devotion. He would have drawn from this, say, his artless inference — taken it for a sign of some smothered inward trouble and naturally pointed the moral that the way out of such straits was not through neglect of the grand remedy. He had possibly prescribed contrition — he had at any rate quickened in her the beat of that false repose to which our young woman's own act had devoted her at her all so deluded instance. The falsity of it had laid traps compared to which the imputation of treachery even accepted might have seemed a path of roses. The acceptance, strangely, would have left her nothing to do — she could have remained, had she liked, all insolently passive; whereas the failure to proceed against her, as it might have been called, left her everything, all the more that it was wrapped so in confidence. She had to confirm day after day the rightness of her cause and the justice and felicity of her exemption — so that would n't there have been, fairly, in any explicit concern of Father Mitchell's, depths of practical derision of her success?

The question was provisionally answered at all events by the time the party at luncheon had begun to disperse — with Maggie's version of Mrs. Verver sharp to the point of representing her pretext for absence as a positive flight from derision. She met the good priest's eyes before they separated, and priests were really at the worst, so to speak, such wonderful people that she believed him for an instant on the verge of saying to her in abysmal softness: "Go to Mrs. Verver, my child — *you* go: you 'll find you can help her." This did n't come, however; nothing came but the renewed twiddle of thumbs over the satisfied stomach and the full flush, the comical candour, of reference to the hand employed at Fawns for mayonnaise of salmon. Nothing came but the receding backs of each of the others — her father's slightly bent shoulders in especial, which seemed to weave his spell, by the force of habit, not less patiently than if his wife had been present. Her own husband indeed was present to feel anything there might be to feel — which was perhaps exactly why this personage was moved promptly to emulate so definite an example of "sloping." He had his occupations — books to arrange perhaps even at Fawns; the idea of the siesta, moreover, in all the conditions, had no need to be loudly invoked. Maggie was in the event left alone for a minute with Mrs. Assingham, who, after waiting for safety, appeared to have at heart to make a demonstration. The stage of "talking over" had long passed for them; when they communicated now it was on quite ultimate facts; but Fanny desired to testify to the existence, on her part, of an attention that nothing escaped. She was like the kind lady who, happening to linger at the circus while the rest of the spectators pour grossly through the exits, falls in with the overworked little trapezist girl — the acrobatic support presumably of embarrassed and exacting parents — and gives her, as an obscure and meritorious artist, assurance of charitable interest. What was clearest always in our young woman's imaginings was the sense of being herself left for any occasion in the breach. She was essentially there to bear the burden, in the last resort, of surrounding omissions and evasions, and it was eminently to that office she had been to-day abandoned — with this one alleviation, as appeared, of Mrs. Assingham's keeping up with her. Mrs. Assingham suggested that she too was still on the ramparts — though her gallantry proved indeed after a moment to consist not a little of her curiosity. She had looked about and seen their companions beyond earshot.

"Don't you really want us to go — ?"

Maggie found a faint smile. "Do you really want to — ?"

It made her friend colour. "Well then — no. But we *would*, you know, at a look from you. We'd pack up and be off — as a sacrifice."

"Ah make no sacrifice," said Maggie. "See me through."

"That's it — that's all I want. I should be too base —! Besides," Fanny went on, "you're too splendid."

"Splendid?"

"Splendid. Also, you know, you *are* all but 'through.' You've done it," said Mrs. Assingham.

But Maggie only took it from her. "What does it strike you I've done?"

"What you wanted. They're going."

Maggie continued to look at her. "Is that what I wanted?"

"Oh it wasn't for you to say. That was *his* affair."

"My father's?" Maggie asked after an hesitation.

"Your father's. He has chosen — and now she knows. She sees it all before her — and she can't speak or resist or move a little finger. That's what's the matter with *her*," said Fanny Assingham.

It made a picture somehow for the Princess as they stood there — the picture that the words of others, whatever they might be, always made for her, even when her vision was already charged, better than any words of her own. She saw round about her, through the chinks of the shutters, the hard glare of nature — saw Charlotte somewhere in it virtually at bay and yet denied the last grace of any protecting truth. She saw her off somewhere all unaided, pale in her silence and taking in her fate. "Has she told you?" she then asked.

Her companion smiled superior. "*I* don't need to be told — either! I see something, thank God, every day." And then as Maggie might appear to be wondering what, for instance: "I see the long miles of ocean and the dreadful great country, State after State — which have never seemed to me so big or so terrible. I see *them* at last, day by day and step by step, at the far end — and I see them never come back. But *never* — simply. I see the extraordinary 'interesting' place — which I've never been to, you know, and you have — and the exact degree in which she'll be expected to be interested."

"She *will* be," Maggie presently replied.

"Expected?"

"Interested."

For a little after this their eyes met on it; at the end of which Fanny said: "She'll be — yes — what she'll *have* to be. And it will be — won't it? — for ever and ever." She spoke as abounding in her friend's sense, but it made Maggie still only look at her. These were large words and large visions — all the more that now really they spread and spread. In the midst of them however Mrs. Assingham had soon enough continued. "When I talk of 'knowing' indeed I don't mean it as you'd have a right to do. You know because you see — and I don't see *him*. I don't make him out," she almost crudely confessed.

Maggie again took time. "You mean you don't make out Amerigo?"

But Fanny shook her head, and it was quite as if, as an appeal to one's intelligence, the making out of Amerigo had, in spite of everything, long been superseded. Then Maggie measured the reach of her allusion and how what she next said gave her meaning a richness. No other name was to be spoken, and Mrs. Assingham had taken that without delay from her eyes — with a discretion still that fell short but by an inch. "You know how he feels."

Maggie at this then slowly matched her headshake. "I know nothing."

"You know how *you* feel."

But again she denied it. "I know nothing. If I did —!"

"Well, if you did?" Fanny asked as she faltered.

She had had enough, however. "I should die," she said as she turned away.

She went to her room through the quiet house; she roamed there a moment, picking up pointlessly a different fan, and then took her way to the shaded apartments in which at this hour the Principino would be enjoying his nap. She passed through the first empty room, the day nursery, and paused at an open door. The inner room, large dim and cool, was equally calm; her boy's ample antique historical royal crib, consecrated reputedly by the guarded rest of heirs-apparent and a gift early in his career from his grand-father, ruled the scene from the centre, in the stillness of which she could almost hear the child's soft breathing. The prime protector of his dreams was installed beside him; her father sat there with as little motion — with head thrown back and supported, with eyes apparently closed, with the fine foot that was so apt to betray nervousness at peace upon the other knee, with the unfathomable heart folded in the constant flawless freshness of the white waistcoat that could always receive in its armholes the firm prehensile thumbs. Mrs. Noble had majestically melted, and the whole place signed her temporary abdication;

yet the actual situation was regular, and Maggie lingered but to look. She looked over her fan, the top of which was pressed against her face, long enough to wonder if her father really slept or if, aware of her, he only kept consciously quiet. Did his eyes truly fix her between lids partly open, and was she to take this — his forbearance from any question — only as a sign again that everything was left to her? She at all events for a minute watched his immobility — then, as if once more renewing her total submission, returned without a sound to her own quarters.

A strange impulse was sharp in her, but it was n't, for her part, the desire to shift the weight. She could as little have slept as she could have slept that morning, days before, when she had watched the first dawn from her window. Turned to the east, this side of her room was now in shade, with the two wings of the casement folded back and the charm she always found in her seemingly perched position — as if her outlook, from above the high terraces, was that of some castle-tower mounted on a rock. When she stood there she hung over, over the gardens and the woods — all of which drowsed below her at this hour in the immensity of light. The miles of shade looked hot, the banks of flowers looked dim; the peacocks on the balustrades let their tails hang limp and the smaller birds lurked among the leaves. Nothing therefore would have appeared to stir in the brilliant void if Maggie, at the moment she was about to turn away, had n't caught sight of a moving spot, a clear green sunshade in the act of descending a flight of steps. It passed down from the terrace, receding, at

a distance, from sight and carried, naturally, so as to
conceal the head and back of its bearer; but Maggie
had quickly recognised the white dress and the particular motion of this adventurer — had taken in that
Charlotte, of all people, had chosen the glare of noon
for an exploration of the gardens and that she could
be betaking herself only to some unvisited quarter
deep in them or beyond them that she had already
marked as a superior refuge. The Princess kept her
for a few minutes in sight, watched her long enough
to feel her, by the mere betrayal of her pace and direction, driven in a kind of flight, and then understood for herself why the act of sitting still had become impossible to either of them. There came to
her confusedly some echo of an ancient fable — some
vision of Io goaded by the gadfly or of Ariadne roaming the lone sea-strand. It brought with it all the
sense of her own intention and desire; she too might
have been for the hour some far-off harassed heroine
— only with a part to play for which she knew exactly
no inspiring precedent. She knew but that all the while
— all the while of her sitting there among the others
without her — she had wanted to go straight to this
detached member of the party and make somehow,
for her support, the last demonstration. A pretext
was all that was needful, and Maggie after another
instant had found one.

She had caught a glimpse, before Mrs. Verver disappeared, of her carrying a book — made out, half-lost
in the folds of her white dress, the dark cover of a volume that was to explain her purpose in case of her
being met with surprise, and the mate of which pre-

cisely now lay on Maggie's table. The book was an old novel that the Princess had a couple of days before mentioned having brought down from Portland Place in the charming original form of its three volumes. Charlotte had hailed with a specious glitter of interest the opportunity to read it, and our young woman had therefore on the morrow directed her maid to carry it to Mrs. Verver's apartments. She was afterwards to observe that this messenger, unintelligent or inadvertent, had removed but one of the volumes, which happened not to be the first. Still possessed accordingly of the first while Charlotte, going out fantastically at such an hour to cultivate romance in an arbour, was helplessly armed with the second, Maggie prepared on the spot to sally forth with succour. The right volume, with a parasol, was all she required — in addition, that is, to the bravery of her general idea. She passed again through the house unchallenged and emerged upon the terrace, which she followed, hugging the shade, with that consciousness of turning the tables on her friend which we have already noted. But so far as she went, after descending into the open and beginning to explore the grounds, Mrs. Verver had gone still further — with the increase of the oddity moreover of her having exchanged the protection of her room for these exposed and shining spaces. It was not, fortunately, however, at last, that by persisting in pursuit one did n't arrive at regions of admirable shade : this was presumably the asylum the poor wandering woman had had in view — several wide alleys in particular, of great length, densely overarched with the climbing rose and the honeysuckle and converging in separate green vistas at a sort of umbrageous temple, an ancient rotunda, pillared and statued, niched and roofed, yet with its uncorrected antiquity, like that of everything else at Fawns, conscious hitherto of no violence from the present and no menace from the future. Charlotte had paused there in her frenzy or whatever it was to be called; the place was a conceivable retreat, and she was staring before her from the seat to which she appeared to have sunk all unwittingly as Maggie stopped at the beginning of one of the perspectives.

It was a repetition more than ever then of the evening on the terrace; the distance was too great to assure her she had been immediately seen, but the Princess waited with her intention as Charlotte on the other occasion had waited — allowing, oh allowing, for the difference of the intention! Maggie was full of the sense of *that* — so full that it made her impatient; whereupon she moved forward a little, placing herself in range of the eyes that had been looking off elsewhere, but that she had suddenly called to recognition. Charlotte, who had evidently not dreamed of being followed, instinctively, with her pale stare, stiffened herself for protest. Maggie could make that out — as well as, further, however, that her second impression of her friend's approach had an instant effect on her attitude. The Princess came nearer, gravely and in silence, but fairly paused again to give her time for whatever she would. Whatever she would, whatever she could, was what Maggie wanted — wanting above all to make it as easy for her as the case permitted. That was not what Charlotte had wanted the other night, but this never mattered — the great thing was to allow her, was fairly to produce in her, the sense of highly choosing. At first, clearly, she had been frightened; she had n't been pursued, it had quickly struck her, without some design on the part of her pursuer, and what might n't she be thinking of in addition but the way she had, when herself the pursuer, made her stepdaughter take in her spirit and her purpose? It had sunk into Maggie at the time, that hard insistence, and Mrs. Verver had felt it and seen it and heard it sink; which wonderful remembrance of pressure successfully applied had naturally till now remained with her. But her stare was like a projected fear that the buried treasure so dishonestly come by, for which her companion's still countenance at the hour and afterwards had consented to serve as the deep soil, might have worked up again to the surface, might be thrown back upon her hands. Yes, it was positive that during one of these minutes the Princess had the vision of her particular alarm. "It's her lie, it's her lie that has mortally disagreed with her; she can keep down no longer her rebellion at it, and she has come to retract it, to disown it and denounce it — to give me full in my face the truth instead." This for a concentrated instant Maggie felt her helplessly gasp — but only to let it bring home the indignity, the pity of her state. She herself could but tentatively hover, place in view the book she carried, look as little dangerous, look as abjectly mild, as possible; remind herself really of people she had read about in stories of the wild west, people who threw up their hands on certain occasions for a sign they were n't carrying revolvers. She could almost have smiled at last, troubled as she yet knew herself, to show how richly she was harmless; she held up her volume, which was so weak a weapon, and while she continued, for consideration, to keep her distance, explained with as quenched a quaver as possible. "I saw you come out — saw you from my window and could n't bear to think you should find yourself here without the beginning of your book. *This* is the beginning; you 've got the wrong volume and I 've brought you out the right."

She remained after she had spoken; it was like holding a parley with a possible adversary, and her intense, her exalted little smile requested formal leave. "May I come nearer now?" she seemed to say — as to which however, the next minute, she saw Charlotte's reply lose itself in a strange process, a thing of several sharp stages, which she could stand there and trace. The dread, after this space, had dropped from her face; though she still discernibly enough could n't believe in her having in so strange a fashion been deliberately made up to. If she had been made up to at least it was with an idea — the idea that had struck her at first as necessarily dangerous. That it was n't, insistently was n't, this shone from Maggie with a force finally not to be resisted; and on that perception, on the immense relief so constituted, everything had by the end of three minutes extraordinarily changed. Maggie had come out to her really because she knew her doomed, doomed to a separation that was like a knife in her heart; and in the very sight of her uncontrollable, her blinded

physical quest of a peace not to be grasped, something
of Mrs. Assingham's picture of her as thrown for a
grim future beyond the great sea and the great con-
tinent had at first found fulfilment. She had got
away in this fashion — burning behind her almost
the ships of disguise — to let her horror of what was
before her play up without witnesses; and even after
Maggie's approach had presented an innocent front
it was still not to be mistaken that she bristled with
the signs of her extremity. It was n't to be said for
them either that they were draped at this hour in
any of her usual graces; unveiled and all but un-
ashamed, they were tragic to the Princess in spite of
the dissimulation that with the return of comparative confidence was so promptly to operate. How
tragic in essence the very change made vivid, the
instant stiffening of the spring of pride — this for possible defence if not for possible aggression. Pride
indeed had the next moment become the mantle
caught up for protection and perversity; she flung
it round her as a denial of any loss of her freedom.
To be doomed was in her situation to have extravagantly incurred a doom, so that to confess to wretch-
edness was by the same stroke to confess to falsity.
She would n't confess, she did n't — a thousand
times no; she only cast about her, and quite frankly
and fiercely, for something else that would give colour
to her having burst her bonds. Her eyes expanded,
her bosom heaved as she invoked it, and the effect
upon Maggie was verily to wish she could only help
her to it. She presently got up — which seemed to
mean "Oh stay if you like!" — and when she had

moved about a while at random, looking away, looking at anything, at everything but her visitor; when she had spoken of the temperature and declared that she revelled in it; when she had uttered her thanks for the book, which, a little incoherently, with her second volume, she perhaps found less clever than she expected; when she had let Maggie approach sufficiently closer to lay untouched the tribute in question on a bench and take up obligingly its superfluous mate: when she had done these things she sat down in another place, more or less visibly in possession of her part. Our young woman was to have passed, in all her adventure, no stranger moments; for she not only now saw her companion fairly agree to take her then for the poor little person she was finding it so easy to appear, but fell, in a secret responsive ecstasy, to wondering if there were n't some supreme abjection with which she might be inspired. Vague but increasingly brighter this possibility glimmered on her. It at last hung there adequately plain to Charlotte that she had presented herself once more to (as they said) grovel; and that truly made the stage large. It had absolutely, within the time, taken on the dazzling merit of being large for each of them alike.

"I 'm glad to see you alone — there 's something I 've been wanting to say to you. I 'm tired," said Mrs. Verver, "I 'm tired —!"

"'Tired' — ?" It had dropped, the next thing; it could n't all come at once; but Maggie had already guessed what it was, and the flush of recognition was in her face.

"Tired of this life — the one we've been leading.
You like it, I know, but I've dreamed another
dream." She held up her head now; her lighted eyes
more triumphantly rested; she was finding, she was
following her way. Maggie, by the same influence,
sat in sight of it; there was something she was *saving*,
some quantity of which she herself was judge; and
it was for a long moment, even with the sacrifice
the Princess had come to make, a good deal like
watching her from the solid shore plunge into uncertain, into possibly treacherous depths. "I see
something else," she went on; "I've an idea that
greatly appeals to me — I've had it for a long time.
It has come over me that we're wrong. Our real life
is n't here."

Maggie held her breath. "'Ours' — ?"

"My husband's and mine. I'm not speaking for
you."

"Oh!" said Maggie, only praying not to be, not
even to appear, stupid.

"I'm speaking for ourselves. I'm speaking,"
Charlotte brought out, "for *him*."

"I see. For my father."

"For your father. For whom else?" They looked
at each other hard now, but Maggie's face took refuge
in the intensity of her interest. She was n't at all
events so stupid as to treat her companion's question
as requiring an answer; a discretion that her controlled stillness had after an instant justified. "I
must risk your thinking me selfish — for of course
you know what it involves. Let me admit it — I *am*
selfish. I place my husband first."

"Well," said Maggie, smiling and smiling, "since that's where I place mine —!"

"You mean you'll have no quarrel with me? So much the better then; for," Charlotte went on with a higher and higher flight, "my plan's completely formed."

Maggie waited — her glimmer had deepened; her chance somehow was at hand. The only danger was her spoiling it; she felt herself skirting an abyss. "What then, may I ask, *is* your plan?"

It hung fire but ten seconds; it came out sharp. "To take him home — to his real position. And not to wait."

"Do you mean — a — this season?"

"I mean immediately. And — I may as well tell you now — I mean for my own time. I want," Charlotte said, "to have him at last a little to myself; I want, strange as it may seem to you" — and she gave it all its weight — "to *keep* the man I've married. And to do so I see I must act."

Maggie, with the effort still to follow the right line, felt herself colour to the eyes. "Immediately?" she thoughtfully echoed.

"As soon as we can get off. The removal of everything is after all but a detail. That can always be done; with money, as he spends it, everything can. What I ask for," Charlotte declared, "is the definite break. And I wish it now." With which her head, like her voice, rose higher. "Oh," she added, "I know my difficulty!"

Far down below the level of attention, in she could scarce have said what sacred depths, Maggie's inspiration had come, and it had trebled the next moment into sound. "Do you mean *I'm* your difficulty?"

"You and he together — since it's always with you that I've had to see him. But it's a difficulty that I'm facing, if you wish to know; that I've already faced; that I propose to myself to surmount. The struggle with it — none too pleasant — has n't been for me, as you may imagine, in itself charming; I've felt in it at times, if I must tell you all, too great and too strange an ugliness. Yet I believe it may succeed."

She had risen with this, Mrs. Verver, and had moved for the emphasis of it a few steps away; while Maggie, motionless at first, but sat and looked at her. "You want to take my father *from* me?"

The sharp successful almost primitive wail in it made Charlotte turn, and this movement attested for the Princess the felicity of her deceit. Something in her throbbed as it had throbbed the night she stood in the drawing-room and denied that she had suffered. She was ready to lie again if her companion would but give her the opening. Then she should know she had done all. Charlotte looked at her hard, as if to compare her face with her note of resentment; and Maggie, feeling this, met it with the signs of an impression that might pass for the impression of defeat. "I want really to possess him," said Mrs. Verver. "I happen also to feel that he's worth it."

Maggie rose as if to receive her. "Oh — worth it!" she wonderfully threw off.

The tone, she instantly saw, again had its effect: Charlotte flamed aloft — might truly have been believing in her passionate parade. "You've thought *you've* known what he's worth?"

"Indeed then, my dear, I believe I have — as I believe I still do."

She had given it, Maggie, straight back, and again it had n't missed. Charlotte for another moment only looked at her; then broke into the words — Maggie had known they would come — of which she had pressed the spring. "How I see that you loathed our marriage!"

"Do you *ask* me?" Maggie after an instant demanded.

Charlotte had looked about her, picked up the parasol she had laid on a bench, possessed herself mechanically of one of the volumes of the relegated novel and then more consciously flung it down again: she was in presence, visibly, of her last word. She opened her sunshade with a click; she twirled it on her shoulder in her pride. "'Ask' you? Do I need? How I see," she broke out, "that you've worked against me!"

"Oh, oh, oh!" the Princess exclaimed.

Her companion, leaving her, had reached one of the archways, but on this turned round with a flare. "You have n't worked against me?"

Maggie took it and for a moment kept it; held it, with closed eyes, as if it had been some captured fluttering bird pressed by both hands to her breast. Then she opened her eyes to speak. "What does it matter — if I've failed?"

"You recognise then that you've failed?" asked Charlotte from the threshold.

Maggie waited; she looked, as her companion had done a moment before, at the two books on the seat; she put them together and laid them down; then she made up her mind. "I've failed!" she sounded out before Charlotte, having given her time, walked away. She watched her, splendid and erect, float down the long vista; then she sank upon a seat. Yes, she had done all.

BOOK SIXTH

I

"I 'LL do anything you like," she said to her husband
on one of the last days of the month, "if our being here
this way at this time seems to you too absurd or too
uncomfortable or too impossible. We 'll either take
leave of them now, without waiting — or we 'll come
back in time, three days before they start. I 'll go
abroad with you if you but say the word; to Switzer-
land, the Tyrol, the Italian Alps, to whichever of your
old high places you would like most to see again —
those beautiful ones that used to do you good after
Rome and that you so often told me about."

Where they were, in the conditions that prompted
this offer, and where it might indeed appear ridiculous
that, with the stale London September close at hand,
they should content themselves with remaining, was
where the desert of Portland Place looked blank as it
had never looked, and where a drowsy cabman, scan-
ning the horizon for a fare, could sink to oblivion of
the risks of immobility. But Amerigo was of the odd
opinion, day after day, that their situation could n't be
bettered; and he even went at no moment through the
form of replying that, should their ordeal strike her
as exceeding their patience, any step they might take
would be for her own relief. This was, no doubt,
partly because he stood out so wonderfully, to the end,
against admitting, by a weak word at least, that any
element of their existence *was* or ever had been an

ordeal; no trap of circumstance, no lapse of "form," no accident of irritation, had landed him in that inconsequence. His wife might verily have suggested that he was consequent — consequent with the admirable appearance he had from the first so undertaken and so continued to present — rather too rigidly at *her* expense; only, as it happened, she was n't the little person to do anything of the sort, and the strange tacit compact actually in operation between them might have been founded on an intelligent comparison, a definite collation positively, of the kinds of patience proper to each. She was seeing him through — he had engaged to come out at the right end if she *would* see him: this understanding, tacitly renewed from week to week, had fairly received, with the procession of the weeks, the consecration of time; but it scarce needed to be emphasised that she was seeing him on *his* terms, not at all on hers, or that, in a word, she must allow him his unexplained and uncharted, his one practicably workable way. If that way, by one of the intimate felicities the liability to which was so far from having even yet completely fallen from him, happened handsomely to show him as more bored than boring — with advantages of his own freely to surrender, but none to be persuadedly indebted to others for — what did such a false face of the matter represent but the fact itself that she was pledged? If she had questioned or challenged or interfered — if she had reserved herself that right — she would n't have been pledged; whereas there were still, and evidently would be yet a while, long tense stretches during which their case might have been hanging for every eye on her possible, her impossible defection. She must keep it up to the last, must n't absent herself for three minutes from her post: only on those lines assuredly would she show herself as with him and not against him.

It was extraordinary how scant a series of signs she had invited him to make of being, of truly having been at any time, "with" his wife: that reflexion she was not exempt from as they now, in their suspense, supremely waited — a reflexion under the brush of which she recognised her having had, in respect to him as well, to "do all," to go the whole way over, to move indefatigably while he stood as fixed in his place as some statue of one of his forefathers. The meaning of it would seem to be, she reasoned in sequestered hours, that he *had* a place, and that this was an attribute somehow indefeasible, unquenchable, which laid upon others — from the moment they definitely wanted anything of him — the necessity of taking more of the steps than he could, of circling round him, of remembering for his benefit the famous relation of the mountain to Mahomet. It was strange, if one had gone into it, but such a place as Amerigo's was like something made for him beforehand by innumerable facts, facts largely of the sort known as historical, made by ancestors, examples, traditions, habits; while Maggie's own had come to show simply as that improvised "post" — a post of the kind spoken of as advanced — with which she was to have found herself connected in the fashion of a settler or a trader in a new country; in the likeness even of some Indian squaw with a papoose on her back and barbarous beadwork to sell. Maggie's own, in short, would have been sought in vain in the most rudimentary map of the social relations as such. The only geography marking it would be doubtless that of the fundamental passions. The "end" that the Prince was at all events holding out for was represented to expectation by his father-in-law's announced departure for America with Mrs. Verver; just as that prospective event had originally figured as advising, for discretion, the flight of the younger couple, to say nothing of the withdrawal of whatever other importunate company, before the great upheaval of Fawns. This residence was to be peopled for a month by porters, packers and hammerers, at whose operations it had become peculiarly public — public that is for Portland Place — that Charlotte was to preside in force; operations the quite awful appointed scale and style of which had at no moment loomed so large to Maggie's mind as one day when the dear Assinghams swam back into her ken besprinkled with sawdust and looking as pale as if they had seen Samson pull down the temple. They had seen at least what she was n't seeing, rich dim things under the impression of which they had retired; she having eyes at present but for the clock by which she timed her husband, or for the glass — the image perhaps would be truer — in which he was reflected to her as *he* timed the pair in the country. The accession of their friends from Cadogan Place contributed to all their intermissions, at any rate, a certain effect of resonance; an effect especially marked by the upshot of a prompt exchange of enquiries between Mrs. Assingham and the Princess. It was noted on the occasion of that anxious lady's last approach to her young friend at Fawns that her sympathy had ventured, after much accepted privation, again to become inquisitive, and this principle had perhaps never so yielded to that need as on the question of the present odd "line" of the distinguished eccentrics.

"You mean to say really that you 're going to stick here ?" And then before Maggie could answer : "What on earth will you do with your evenings ?"

Maggie waited a moment — Maggie could still tentatively smile. "When people learn we 're here — and of course the papers will be full of it! — they 'll flock back in their hundreds, from wherever they are, to catch us. You see you and the Colonel have yourselves done it. As for our evenings, they won't, I dare say, be particularly different from anything else that 's ours. They won't be different from our mornings or our afternoons — except perhaps that you two dears will sometimes help us to get through them. I 've offered to go anywhere," she added; "to take a house if he will. But *this* — just this and nothing else — is Amerigo's idea. He gave it yesterday," she went on, "a name that as he said described and fitted it. So you see" — and the Princess indulged again her smile that did n't play, but that only, as might have been said, worked — "so you see there 's a method in our madness."

It drew Mrs. Assingham's wonder. "And what then is the name ?"

"'The reduction to its simplest expression of what we *are* doing' — that 's what he called it. Therefore as we 're doing nothing, we 're doing it in the most aggravated way — which is the way he desires." With which Maggie further said: "Of course I understand."

"So do I!" her visitor after a moment breathed. "You've had to vacate the house — that was inevitable. But at least here he does n't funk."

Our young woman accepted the expression. "He does n't funk."

It only however half-contented Fanny, who thoughtfully raised her eyebrows. "He's prodigious; but what is there — as you've 'fixed' it — *to* dodge? Unless," she pursued, "it's her getting near him; it's — if you'll pardon my vulgarity — her getting *at* him. That," she suggested, "may count with him."

But it found the Princess prepared. "She can get near him here. She can get 'at' him. She can come up."

"*Can* she?" Fanny Assingham questioned.

"*Can't* she?" Maggie returned.

Their eyes for a minute intimately met on it; after which the elder woman said: "I mean for seeing him alone."

"So do I," said the Princess.

At which Fanny, for her reasons, could n't help smiling. "Oh if it's for *that* he's staying —!"

"He's staying — I've made it out — to take anything that comes or calls upon him. To take," Maggie went on, "even that." Then she put it as she had at last put it to herself. "He's staying for high decency."

"Decency?" Mrs. Assingham gravely echoed.

"Decency. If she *should* try —!"

"Well —?" Mrs. Assingham urged.

"Well, I hope —!"

"Hope he'll see her?"

Maggie hesitated, however; she made no direct reply. "It's useless hoping," she presently said. "She won't. But he ought to." Her friend's expression of a moment before, which had been apologised for as vulgar, prolonged its sharpness to her ear — that of an electric bell under continued pressure. Stated so simply, what was it but dreadful, truly, that the feasibility of Charlotte's "getting at" the man who for so long had loved her should now be in question? Strangest of all things doubtless this care of Maggie's as to what might make for it or make against it; stranger still her fairly lapsing at moments into a vague calculation of the conceivability, on her own part, with her husband, of some direct sounding of the subject. Would it be too monstrous, her suddenly breaking out to him as in alarm at the lapse of the weeks: "Wouldn't it really seem that you're bound in honour to do something for her privately before they go?" Maggie was capable of weighing the risk of this adventure for her own spirit, capable of sinking to intense little absences, even while conversing as now with the person who had most of her confidence, during which she followed up the possibilities. It was true that Mrs. Assingham could at such times somewhat restore the balance by not wholly failing to guess her thought. Her thought however just at present had more than one face — had a series that it successively presented. These were indeed the possibilities involved in the adventure of her concerning herself for the quantity of compensation Mrs. Verver might still

look to. There was always the possibility that she
was after all sufficiently to get at him — there was in
fact that of her having again and again done so.
Against this stood nothing but Fanny Assingham's
apparent belief in her privation — more mercilessly
imposed or more hopelessly felt in the actual relation
of the parties; over and beyond everything that from
more than three months back of course had fostered
in the Princess a like conviction. These assumptions
might certainly be baseless — inasmuch as there were
hours and hours of Amerigo's time that there was no
habit, no pretence of his accounting for; inasmuch too
as Charlotte, inevitably, had had more than once, to
the undisguised knowledge of the pair in Portland
Place, been obliged to come up to Eaton Square,
whence so many of her personal possessions were in
course of removal. She did n't come to Portland Place
— did n't even come to ask for luncheon on two separate occasions when it reached the consciousness of
the household there that she was spending the day
in London. Maggie hated, she scorned, to compare
hours and appearances, to weigh the idea of whether
there had n't been moments during these days when
an assignation in easy conditions, a snatched interview in an air the season had so cleared of prying eyes,
might n't perfectly work. But the very reason of this
was partly that, haunted with the vision of the poor
woman carrying off with such bravery as she found to
her hand the secret of her not being appeased, she was
conscious of scant room for any alternative image.
The alternative image would have been that the secret
covered up was the secret of appeasement somehow

obtained, somehow extorted and cherished; and the difference between the two kinds of hiding was too great to permit of a mistake. Charlotte was hiding neither pride nor joy — she was hiding humiliation; and here it was that the Princess's passion, so powerless for vindictive flights, most inveterately bruised its tenderness against the hard glass of her question.

Behind the glass lurked the *whole* history of the relation she had so fairly flattened her nose against it to penetrate — the glass Mrs. Verver might at this stage have been frantically tapping from within by way of supreme irrepressible entreaty. Maggie had said to herself complacently after that last passage with her stepmother in the garden of Fawns that there was nothing left for her to do and that she could thereupon fold her hands. But why was n't it still left to push further and, from the point of view of personal pride, grovel lower? — why was n't it still left to offer herself as the bearer of a message reporting to him their friend's anguish and convincing him of her need? She could thus have translated Mrs. Verver's tap against the glass, as I have called it, into fifty forms; could perhaps have translated it most into the form of a reminder that would pierce deep. "You don't know what it is to have been loved and broken with. You have n't been broken with, because in *your* relation what can there have been worth speaking of to break? Ours was everything a relation could be, filled to the brim with the wine of consciousness; and if it was to have no meaning, no better meaning than that such a creature as you could breathe upon it, at your hour, for blight, why was I myself dealt with all for deception? why condemned after a couple of short years to find the golden flame — oh the golden flame! — a mere handful of black ashes?" Our young woman so yielded at moments to what was insidious in these foredoomed ingenuities of her pity that for minutes together sometimes the weight of a new duty seemed to rest upon her — the duty of speaking before separation should constitute its chasm, of pleading for some benefit that might be carried away into exile like the last saved object of price of the *émigré*, the jewel wrapped in a piece of old silk and negotiable some day in the market of misery.

This imagined service to the woman who could no longer help herself was one of the traps set for Maggie's spirit at every turn of the road; the click of which, catching and holding the divine faculty fast, was followed inevitably by a flutter, by a struggle of wings and even, as we may say, by a scattering of fine feathers. For they promptly enough felt, these yearnings of thought and excursions of sympathy, the concussion that could n't bring them down — the arrest produced by the so remarkably distinct figure that, at Fawns, for the previous weeks, was constantly crossing, in its regular revolution, the further end of any watched perspective. Whoever knew, or whoever did n't, whether or to what extent Charlotte, with natural business in Eaton Square, had shuffled other opportunities under that cloak, it was all matter for the kind of quiet ponderation the little man who so kept his wandering way had made his own. It was part of the very inveteracy of his straw hat and his white waistcoat, of the trick of his hands in his pockets,

of the detachment of the attention he fixed on his slow
steps from behind his secure pince-nez. The thing
that never failed now as an item in the picture was
that gleam of the silken noose, his wife's immaterial
tether, so marked to Maggie's sense during her last
month in the country. Mrs. Verver's straight neck
had certainly not slipped it; nor had the other end of
the long cord — oh quite conveniently long! — disengaged its smaller loop from the hooked thumb that,
with his fingers closed upon it, her husband kept out of
sight. To have recognised, for all its tenuity, the play
of this gathered lasso might inevitably be to wonder
with what magic it was twisted, to what tension sub-
jected, but could never be to doubt either of its adequacy to its office or of its perfect durability. These
reminded states for the Princess were in fact states of
renewed gaping. So many things her father knew
that she even yet did n't!

All this at present with Mrs. Assingham passed
through her in quick vibrations. She had expressed
while the revolution of her thought was incomplete
the idea of what Amerigo "ought" on his side, in the
premises, to be capable of, and then had felt her companion's answering stare. But she insisted on what
she had meant. "He ought to wish to see her — and
I mean in some protected and independent way, as he
used to — in case of her being herself able to manage
it. That," said Maggie with the courage of her conviction, "he ought to be ready, he ought to be happy,
he ought to feel himself sworn — little as it is for the
end of such a history! — to take from her. It's as if
he wished to get off without taking anything."

Mrs. Assingham deferentially mused. "But for what purpose is it your idea that they should again so intimately meet?"

"For any purpose they like. That's *their* affair."

Fanny Assingham sharply laughed, then irrepressibly fell back to her constant position. "You're splendid — perfectly splendid." To which, as the Princess, shaking an impatient head, would n't have it again at all, she subjoined: "Or if you 're not it 's because you 're so sure. I mean sure of *him*."

"Ah I 'm exactly *not* sure of him. If I were sure of him I should n't doubt —!" But Maggie cast about her.

"Doubt what?" Fanny pressed as she waited.

"Well, that he must feel how much less than she he pays — and how that ought to keep her present to him."

This in its turn after an instant Mrs. Assingham could meet with a smile. "Trust him, my dear, to keep her present! But trust him also to keep himself absent. Leave him his own way."

"I 'll leave him everything," said Maggie. "Only — you know it 's my nature — I *think*."

"It 's your nature to think too much," Fanny Assingham a trifle coarsely risked.

This but quickened however in the Princess the act she reprobated. "That may be. But if I had n't thought —!"

"You would n't, you mean, have been where you are?"

"Yes, because they on their side thought of everything *but* that. They thought of everything but that I might think."

THE PRINCESS

"Or even," her friend too superficially concurred, "that your father might!"

As to this, at all events, Maggie discriminated. "No, that would n't have prevented them; for they knew his first care would be not to make me do so. As it is," Maggie added, "that has had to become his last."

Fanny Assingham took it in deeper — for what it immediately made her give out louder. "*He's* splendid then." She sounded it almost aggressively; it was what she was reduced to — she had positively to place it.

"Ah that as much as you please!"

Maggie said this and left it, but the tone of it had the next moment determined in her friend a fresh reaction. "You think, both of you, so abysmally and yet so quietly. But it's what will have saved you."

"Oh," Maggie returned, "it's what — from the moment they discovered we could think at all — will have saved *them*. For they're the ones who are saved," she went on. "We're the ones who are lost."

"Lost — ?"

"Lost to each other — father and I.'" And then as her friend appeared to demur, "Oh yes," Maggie quite lucidly declared, "lost to each other really much more than Amerigo and Charlotte are; since for them it's just, it's right, it's deserved, while for us it's only sad and strange and not caused by our fault. But I don't know," she went on, "why I talk about myself, for it's on father it really comes. I let him go," said Maggie.

"You let him, but you don't make him."

333

THE GOLDEN BOWL

"I take it from him," she answered.

"But what else can you do?"

"I take it from him," the Princess repeated. "I do what I knew from the first I *should* do. I get off by giving him up."

"But if he gives you?" Mrs. Assingham presumed to object. "Does n't it moreover then," she asked, "complete the very purpose with which he married — that of making you and leaving you more free?"

Maggie looked at her long. "Yes — I help him to do that."

Mrs. Assingham hesitated, but at last her bravery flared. "Why not call it then frankly his complete success?"

"Well," said Maggie, "that's all that's left me to do."

"It's a success," her friend ingeniously developed, "with which you've simply not interfered." And as if to show that she spoke without levity Mrs. Assingham went further. "He has made it a success for *them* —!"

"Ah there you are!" Maggie responsively mused. "Yes," she said the next moment, "that's why Amerigo stays."

"Let alone that it's why Charlotte goes." And Mrs. Assingham, emboldened, smiled. "So he knows —?"

But Maggie hung back. "Amerigo —?" After which, however, she blushed — to her companion's recognition.

"Your father. He knows what *you* know? I mean," Fanny faltered — "well, how much does he

334

know?" Maggie's silence and Maggie's eyes had in fact arrested the push of the question — which for a decent consistency she could n't yet quite abandon. "What I should rather say is does he know how much?" She found it still awkward. "How much, I mean, they did. How far" — she touched it up — "they went."

Maggie had waited, but only with a question. "Do you think he does?"

"Know at least something? Oh about *him* I can't think. He's beyond me," said Fanny Assingham.

"Then do you yourself know?"

"How much — ?"

"How much."

"How far — ?"

"How far."

Fanny had appeared to wish to make sure, but there was something she remembered — remembered in time and even with a smile. "I've told you before that I know absolutely nothing."

"Well — that's what *I* know," said the Princess.

Her friend again hesitated. "Then nobody knows — ? I mean," Mrs. Assingham explained, "how much your father does."

Oh Maggie showed she understood. "Nobody."

"Not — a little — Charlotte?"

"A little?" the Princess echoed. "To know anything would be, for her, to know enough."

"And she does n't know anything?"

"If she did," Maggie answered, "Amerigo would."

"And that's just it — that he does n't?"

"That's just it," said the Princess profoundly.

335

On which Mrs. Assingham reflected. "Then how is Charlotte so held?"

"Just *by* that."

"By her ignorance?"

"By her ignorance."

Fanny wondered. "A torment —?"

"A torment," said Maggie with tears in her eyes.

Her companion a moment watched them. "But the Prince then —?"

"How *he's* held?" Maggie asked.

"How *he's* held."

"Oh I can't tell you that!" And the Princess again broke off.

II

A TELEGRAM in Charlotte's name arrived early — "We shall come and ask you for tea at five if convenient to you. Am wiring for the Assinghams to lunch." This document, into which meanings were to be read, Maggie promptly placed before her husband, adding the remark that her father and his wife, who would have come up the previous night or that morning, had evidently gone to an hotel.

The Prince was in his "own" room, where he often sat now alone; half a dozen open newspapers, the *Figaro* notably, as well as the *Times*, were scattered about him; but with a cigar in his teeth and a visible cloud on his brow he appeared actually to be engaged in walking to and fro. Never yet on thus approaching him — for she had done it of late, under one necessity or another, several times — had a particular impression so greeted her; supremely strong, for some reason, as he turned quickly round on her entrance. The reason was partly the look in his face — a suffusion like the flush of fever, which brought back to her Fanny Assingham's charge, recently uttered under that roof, of her "thinking" too impenetrably. The word had remained with her and made her think still more; so that at first as she stood there she felt responsible for provoking on his part an irritation of suspense at which she had n't aimed. She had been going about him these three months, she perfectly knew, with a maintained idea — of which she had never spoken to him; but what had at last happened was that his way of looking at her on occasion seemed a perception of the presence not of one idea but of fifty, variously prepared for uses with which he somehow must reckon. She knew herself suddenly, almost strangely glad to be coming to him at this hour with nothing more abstract than a telegram; but even after she had stepped into his prison under her pretext, while her eyes took in his face and then embraced the four walls that enclosed his restlessness, she recognised the virtual identity of his condition with that aspect of Charlotte's situation for which, early in the summer and in all the amplitude of a great residence, she had found with so little seeking the similitude of the locked cage. He struck her as caged, the man who could n't now without an instant effect on her sensibility give an instinctive push to the door she had n't completely closed behind her. He had been turning twenty ways, for impatiences all his own, and when she was once shut in with him it was yet again as if she had come to him in his more than monastic cell to offer him light or food. There was a difference none the less between his captivity and Charlotte's — the difference, as it might be, of his lurking there by his own act and his own choice; the admission of which had indeed virtually been in his starting at her entrance as if even this were in its degree an interference. That was what betrayed for her practically his fear of her fifty ideas, and what had begun after a minute to make her wish to repudiate or explain. It was more wonderful than she could have told; it was for all the world as if she was succeeding with him beyond her intention. She had for these instants the sense that he exaggerated, that the imputation of purpose had fairly risen too high in him. She had begun, a year ago, by asking herself how she could make him think more of her; but what was it after all he was thinking now? He kept his eyes on her telegram; he read it more than once, easy as it was, in spite of its conveyed deprecation, to understand; during which she found herself almost awestruck with yearning, almost on the point of marking somehow what she had marked in the garden at Fawns with Charlotte — that she had truly come unarmed. She did n't bristle with intentions — she scarce knew, as he at this juncture affected her, what had happened to the only intention she had come with. She had nothing but her old idea, the old one he knew; she had n't the ghost of another. Presently in fact, when four or five minutes had elapsed, it was as if she positively had n't so much even as that one. He gave her back her paper, asking with it if there were anything in particular she wished him to do.

She stood there with her eyes on him, doubling the telegram together as if it had been a precious thing and yet all the while holding her breath. Of a sudden somehow, and quite as by the action of their merely having between them these few written words, an extraordinary fact came up. He was with her as if he were hers, hers in a degree and on a scale, with an intensity and an intimacy, that were a new and a strange quantity, that were like the irruption of a tide loosening them where they had stuck and making

339

them feel they floated. What was it that, with the rush of this, just kept her from putting out her hands to him, from catching at him as in the other time, with the superficial impetus he and Charlotte had privately conspired to impart, she had so often, her breath failing her, known the impulse to catch at her father? She did however just yet nothing inconsequent — though she could n't immediately have said what saved her; and by the time she had neatly folded her telegram she was doing something merely needful. "I wanted you simply to know — so that you may n't by accident miss them. For it's the last," said Maggie.

"The last?"

"I take it as their good-bye." And she smiled as she could always smile. "They come in state — to take formal leave. They do everything that's proper. To-morrow," she said, "they go to Southampton."

"If they do everything that's proper," the Prince presently asked, "why don't they at least come to dine?"

She hesitated, yet she lightly enough provided her answer. "That we must certainly ask them. It will be easy for you. But of course they're immensely taken —!"

He wondered. "So immensely taken that they can't — that your father can't — give you his last evening in England?"

This was for Maggie more difficult to meet; yet she was still not without her stop-gap. "That may be what they'll propose — that we shall go somewhere together, the four of us, for a celebration — except that to round it thoroughly off we ought also to have

Fanny and the Colonel. They don't *want* them at tea, she quite sufficiently expresses; they polish them off, poor dears, they get rid of them beforehand. They want only *us* together; and if they cut us down to tea," she continued, "as they cut Fanny and the Colonel down to luncheon, perhaps it's after all for the fancy of their keeping their last night in London for each other."

She said these things as they came to her; she was unable to keep them back even though as she heard herself she might have been throwing everything to the winds. But was n't that the right way — for sharing his last day of captivity with the man one adored? It was every moment more and more for her as if she were waiting with him in his prison — waiting with some gleam of remembrance of how noble captives in the French Revolution, in the darkness of the Terror, used to make a feast or a high discourse of their last poor resources. If she had broken with everything now, every observance of all the past months, she must simply then take it so — take it that what she had worked for was too near at last to let her keep her head. She might have been losing her head verily in her husband's eyes — since he did n't know all the while that the sudden freedom of her words was but the diverted intensity of her disposition personally to seize him. He knew as little that this was her manner — now she *was* with him — of beguiling audaciously the supremacy of suspense. For the people of the French Revolution assuredly there was n't suspense; the scaffold, for those she was thinking of, was certain — whereas what Charlotte's telegram

341

announced was, short of some incalculable error, clear liberation. Just the point however was in its being clearer to herself than to him; her clearnesses, clearances — those she had so all but abjectly laboured for — threatened to crowd upon her in the form of one of the clusters of angelic heads, the peopled shafts of light beating down through iron bars, that regale on occasion precisely the fevered vision of those who are in chains. She was going to know, she felt, later on — was going to know with compunction doubtless on the very morrow, how thumpingly her heart had beaten at this foretaste of their being left together: she should judge at leisure the surrender she was making to the consciousness of complications about to be bodily lifted. She should judge at leisure even that avidity for an issue which was making so little of any complication but the unextinguished presence of the others; and indeed that she was already simplifying so much more than her husband came out for her next in the face with which he listened. He might certainly well be puzzled, in respect to his father-in-law and Mrs. Verver, by her glance at their possible preference for a concentrated evening. "But it is n't — is it?" he asked — "as if they were leaving each other?"

"Oh no; it is n't as if they were leaving each other. They're only bringing to a close — without knowing when it may open again — a time that has been, naturally, awfully interesting to them." Yes, she could talk so of their "time" — she was somehow sustained; she was sustained even to affirm more intensely her present possession of her ground. "They have their reasons — many things to think of; how can one tell? But there's always also the chance of his proposing to me that *we* shall have our last hours together; I mean that he and I shall. He may wish to take me off to dine with him somewhere alone — and to do it in memory of old days. I mean," the Princess went on, "the *real* old days before my grand husband was invented and, much more, before his grand wife was: the wonderful times of his first great interest in what he has since done, his first great plans and opportunities, discoveries and bargains. The way we've sat together late, ever so late, in foreign restaurants, which he used to like; the way that, in every city in Europe, we've stayed on and on, with our elbows on the table and most of the lights put out, to talk over things he had that day seen or heard of or made his offer for, the things he had secured or refused or lost! There were places he took me to — you would n't believe! — for often he could only have left me with servants. If he should carry me off with him to-night for old sake's sake to the Earl's Court Exhibition it will be a little — just a very, very little — like our young adventures." After which while Amerigo watched her, and in fact quite because of it, she had an inspiration to which she presently yielded. If he was wondering what she would say next she had found exactly the thing. "In that case he'll leave you Charlotte to take care of in our absence. You'll have to carry *her* off somewhere for your last evening; unless you may prefer to spend it with her here. I shall then see that you dine, that you have everything, quite beautifully. You'll be able to do as you like."

She could n't have been sure beforehand and really

had n't been; but the most immediate result of this speech was his letting her see that he took it for no cheap extravagance either of irony or of oblivion. Nothing in the world of a truth had ever been so sweet to her as his look of trying to be serious enough to make no mistake about it. She troubled him — which had n't been at all her purpose; she mystified him — which she could n't help and comparatively did n't mind; then it came over her that he had after all a simplicity, very considerable, on which she had never dared to presume. It was a discovery — not like the other discovery she had once made, but giving out a freshness; and she recognised again in the light of it the number of the ideas of which he thought her capable. They were all apparently queer for him, but she had at least with the lapse of the months created the perception that there might be something in them; whereby he stared there, beautiful and sombre, at what she was at present providing him with. There was something of his own in his mind to which she was sure he referred everything for a measure and a meaning; he had never let go of it from the evening, weeks before, when, in her room after his encounter with the Bloomsbury cup, she had planted it there by flinging at him, on the question of her father's view of him, her determined "Find out for yourself!" She had been aware, during the months, that he had been trying to find out and had been seeking above all to avoid the appearance of any evasions of such a form of knowledge as might reach him with violence, or with a penetration more insidious, from any other source. Nothing however had reached him; nothing he could at all conveniently reckon with had disengaged itself for him even from the announcement, sufficiently sudden, of the final secession of their companions. Charlotte was in pain, Charlotte was in torment, but he himself had given her reason enough for that; and, in respect to the rest of the whole matter of her obligation to follow her husband, that personage and she, Maggie, had so shuffled away every link between consequence and cause that the intention remained, like some famous poetic line in a dead language, subject to varieties of interpretation. What renewed the obscurity was her strange image of their common offer to him, her father's and her own, of an opportunity to separate from Mrs. Verver with the due amount of form — and all the more that he was in so pathetic a way unable to treat himself to a quarrel with it on the score of taste. Taste in him as a touchstone was now all at sea; for who could say but that one of her fifty ideas, or perhaps forty-nine of them, would n't be exactly that taste by itself, the taste he had always conformed to, had no importance whatever? If meanwhile at all events he felt her as serious, this made the greater reason for her profiting by it as she perhaps might never be able to profit again. She was invoking that reflexion at the very moment he brought out, in reply to her last words, a remark which, though perfectly relevant and perfectly just, affected her at first as a high oddity. "They're doing the wisest thing, you know. For if they were ever to go —!" And he looked down at her over his cigar.

If they were ever to go in short it was high time, with her father's age, Charlotte's need of initiation, and the general magnitude of the job of their getting settled and seasoned, their learning to "live into" their queer future, it was high time they should take up their courage. This was eminent sense, but it did n't arrest the Princess, who the next moment had found a form for her challenge. "But shan't you then so much as miss her a little? She's wonderful and beautiful, and I feel somehow as if she were dying. Not really, not physically," Maggie went on —"she's naturally so far, splendid as she is, from having done with life. But dying for us — for you and me; and making us feel it by the very fact of there being so much of her left."

The Prince smoked hard a minute. "As you say, she's splendid, but there is — there always will be — much of her left. Only, as you also say, for others."

"And yet I think," the Princess returned, "that it is n't as if we had wholly done with her. How can we not always think of her? It's as if her unhappiness had been necessary to us — as if we had needed her, at her own cost, to build us up and start us."

He took it in with consideration, but he met it with a lucid enquiry. "Why do you speak of the unhappiness of your father's wife?"

They exchanged a long look — the time that it took her to find her reply. "Because not to —!"

"Well, not to —?"

"Would make me have to speak of *him*. And I can't," said Maggie, "speak of him."

"You 'can't' —?"

"I can't." She said it as for definite notice, not to

346

be repeated. "There are too many things," she never-theless added. "He's too great."

The Prince looked at his cigar-tip, and then as he put back the weed: "Too great for whom?" Upon which as she hesitated, "Not, my dear, too great for you," he declared. "For me — oh as much as you like."

"Too great for me is what I mean. I know why I think it," Maggie said. "That's enough."

He looked at her yet again as if she but fanned his wonder; he was on the very point, she judged, of ask-ing her why she thought it. But her own eyes main-tained their warning, and at the end of a minute he had uttered other words. "What's of importance is that you're his daughter. That at least we've got. And I suppose that if I may say nothing else I may say at least that I value it."

"Oh yes, you may say that you value it. I myself make the most of it."

This again he took in, letting it presently put forth for him a striking connexion. "She ought to have *known* you. That's what's present to me. She ought to have understood you better."

"Better than you did?"

"Yes," he gravely maintained, "better than I did. And she didn't really know you at all. She doesn't know you now."

"Ah yes she does!" said Maggie.

But he shook his head — he knew what he meant. "She not only doesn't understand you more than I, she understands you ever so much less. Though even I —!"

347

"Well, even you?" Maggie pressed as he paused.

"Even I, even I even yet —!" Again he paused and the silence held them.

But Maggie at last broke it. "If Charlotte does n't understand me it's because I've prevented her. I've chosen to deceive her and to lie to her."

The Prince kept his eyes on her. "I know what you've chosen to do. But I've chosen to do the same."

"Yes," said Maggie after an instant —"my choice was made when I had guessed yours. But you mean," she asked, "that she understands *you*?"

"It presents small difficulty!"

"Are you so sure?" Maggie went on.

"Sure enough. But it does n't matter." He waited an instant; then looking up through the fumes of his smoke, "She's stupid," he abruptly opined.

"O-oh!" Maggie protested in a long wail.

It had made him in fact quickly change colour. "What I mean is that she's not, as you pronounce her, unhappy." And he recovered with this all his logic. "Why is she unhappy if she does n't know?"

"Does n't know —?" She tried to make his logic difficult.

"Does n't know that *you* know."

It came from him in such a way that she was conscious instantly of three or four things to answer. But what she said first was: "Do you think that's all it need take?" And before he could reply, "She knows, she knows!" Maggie proclaimed.

"Well then what?"

But she threw back her head, she turned impatiently

away from him. "Oh I need n't tell you! She knows enough. Besides," she went on, "she does n't believe us."

It made the Prince stare a little. "Ah she asks too much!" That drew however from his wife another moan of objection, which determined in him a judgement. "She won't let you take her for unhappy."

"Oh I know better than any one else what she won't let me take her for!"

"Very well," said Amerigo, "you'll see."

"I shall see wonders, I know. I've already seen them and am prepared for them." Maggie recalled — she had memories enough. "It's terrible" — her memories prompted her to speak. "I see it's *always* terrible for women."

The Prince looked down in his gravity. "Everything's terrible, cara — in the heart of man. She's making her life," he said. "She'll make it."

His wife turned back upon him; she had wandered to a table, vaguely setting objects straight. "A little by the way then too, while she's about it, she's making ours." At this he raised his eyes, which met her own, and she held him while she delivered herself of something that had been with her these last minutes. "You spoke just now of Charlotte's not having learned from you that I 'know.' Am I to take from you then that you accept and recognise my knowledge?"

He did the enquiry all the honours — visibly weighed its importance and weighed his response. "You think I might have been showing you that a little more handsomely?"

"It is n't a question of any beauty," said Maggie; "it's only a question of the quantity of truth."

"Oh the quantity of truth!" the Prince richly though ambiguously murmured.

"That's a thing by itself, yes. But there are also such things all the same as questions of good faith."

"Of course there are!" the Prince hastened to reply. After which he brought up more slowly: "If ever a man since the beginning of time acted in good faith —!" But he dropped it, offering it simply for that.

For that then when it had had time somewhat to settle like some handful of gold-dust thrown into the air, for that then Maggie showed herself as deeply and strangely taking it. "I see." And she even wished this form to be as complete as she could make it. "I see."

The completeness had clearly after an instant struck him as divine. "Ah my dear, my dear, my dear —!" It was all he could say.

She was n't talking however at large. "You've kept up for so long a silence —!"

"Yes, yes, I know what I've kept up. But will you do," he asked, "still one thing more for me?"

It was as if for an instant it had with her new exposure made her turn pale. "Is there even one thing left?"

"Ah my dear, my dear, my dear!" — it had pressed again in him the fine spring of the unspeakable.

There was nothing however that the Princess herself could n't say. "I'll do anything if you'll tell me what."

"Then wait." And his raised Italian hand, with its play of admonitory fingers, had never made gesture more expressive. His voice dropped to a tone—! "Wait," he repeated. "Wait."

She understood, but it was as if she wished to have it from him. "Till they've been here, you mean?"

"Yes, till they've gone. Till they're away."

She kept it up. "Till they've left the country?"

She had her eyes on him for clearness; these were the conditions of a promise — so that he put the promise practically into his response. "Till we've ceased to see them — for as long as God may grant! Till we're really alone."

"Oh if it's only that —!" When she had drawn from him thus then, as she could feel, the thick breath of the definite — which was the intimate, the immediate, the familiar as she had n't had them for so long — she turned away again, she put her hand on the knob of the door. But her hand rested at first without a grasp; she had another effort to make, the effort of leaving him, of which everything that had just passed between them, his presence, irresistible, overcharged with it, doubled the difficulty. There was something — she could n't have told what; it was as if, shut in together, they had come too far — too far for where they were; so that the mere act of her quitting him was like the attempt to recover the lost and gone. She had taken in with her something that within the ten minutes, and especially within the last three or four, had slipped away from her — which it was vain now, was n't it? to try to appear to clutch or to pick up. That consciousness in fact had a pang, and she bal-

anced intensely for the lingering moment and almost
with a terror of her endless power of surrender. He
had only to press, really, for her to yield inch by inch,
and she fairly knew at present, while she looked at
him through her cloud, that the confession of this
precious secret sat there for him to pluck. The sensation was for the few seconds extraordinary; her weakness, her desire, so long as she was yet not saving herself, flowered in her face like a light or a darkness.
She sought for some word that would cover this up;
she reverted to the question of tea, speaking as if they
should n't meet sooner. "Then about five. I count on
you."

On him too however something had descended; as
to which that exactly gave him his chance. "Ah but
I shall see you —! No?" he said, coming nearer.

She had, with her hand still on the knob, her back
against the door, so that her retreat under his approach must be less than a step, and yet she could n't
for her life with the other hand have pushed him
away. He was so near now that she could touch him,
taste him, smell him, kiss him, hold him; he almost
pressed upon her, and the warmth of his face —
frowning, smiling, she might n't know which; only
beautiful and strange — was bent upon her with the
largeness with which objects loom in dreams. She
closed her eyes to it, and so the next instant, against
her purpose, had put out her hand, which had met his
own and which he held. Then it was that from behind
her closed eyes the right word came. "Wait!" It was
the word of his own distress and entreaty, the word
for both of them, all they had left, their plank now on

the great sea. Their hands were locked, and thus she said it again. "Wait. Wait." She kept her eyes shut, but her hand, she knew, helped her meaning — which after a minute she was aware his own had absorbed. He let her go — he turned away with this message, and when she saw him again his back was presented, as he had left her, and his face staring out of the window. She had saved herself and she got off.

III

LATER on in the afternoon, before the others arrived, the form of their reunion was at least remarkable: they might in their great eastward drawing-room have been comparing notes or nerves under menace of some stiff official visit. Maggie's mind, in its restlessness, even played a little with the prospect; the high cool room in its afternoon shade, its old tapestries uncovered, the perfect polish of its wide floor reflecting the bowls of gathered flowers and the silver and linen of the prepared tea-table, drew from her a remark in which this whole effect was mirrored, as well as something else in the Prince's movement while he slowly paced and turned. "We're distinctly bourgeois!" she a trifle grimly threw off as an echo of their old community; though to a spectator sufficiently detached they might have been quite the privileged pair they were reputed, granted only they were taken as awaiting the visit of Royalty. They might have been ready, on the word passed up in advance, to repair together to the foot of the staircase — the Prince somewhat in front, advancing indeed to the open doors and even going down, for all his princedom, to meet, on the stopping of the chariot, the august emergence. The time was stale, it was to be admitted, for incidents of magnitude; the September hush was in full possession at the end of the dull day, and a couple of the long windows stood open to the balcony that

overhung the desolation — the balcony from which
Maggie, in the springtime, had seen Amerigo and
Charlotte look down together at the hour of her return
from the Regent's Park, near by, with her father, the
Principino and Miss Bogle. Amerigo now again, in
his punctual impatience, went out a couple of times
and stood there; after which, as to report that nothing
was in sight, he returned to the room with frankly
nothing else to do. The Princess pretended to read;
he looked at her as he passed; there hovered in her
own sense the thought of other occasions when she
had cheated appearances of agitation with a book.
At last she felt him standing before her and then
raised her eyes.

"Do you remember how this morning when you
told me of this event I asked you if there were anything particular you wished me to do? You spoke
of my being at home, but that was a matter of course.
You spoke of something else," he went on while she
sat with her book on her knee and her raised eyes;
"something that makes me almost wish it may happen. You spoke," he said, "of the possibility of my
seeing her alone. Do you know, if that comes," he
asked, "the use I shall make of it?" And then as she
waited: "The use is all before me."

"Ah it's your own business now!" said his wife.
But it had made her rise.

"I shall make it my own," he answered. "I shall
tell her I lied to her."

"Ah no!" she returned.

"And I shall tell her you did."

She shook her head again. "Oh still less!"

355

With which therefore they stood at difference, he with his head erect and his happy idea perched in its eagerness on his crest. "And how then is she to know?"

"She is n't to know."

"She's only still to think *you* don't — ?"

"And therefore that I'm always a fool? She may think," said Maggie, "what she likes."

"Think it without my protest — ?"

The Princess made a movement. "What business is it of yours?"

"Is n't it my right to correct her — ?"

Maggie let his question ring — ring long enough for him to hear it himself; only then she took it up. "'Correct' her?" — and it was her own now that really rang. "Are n't you rather forgetting who she is?" After which, while he quite stared for it, as it was the very first clear majesty he had known her to use, she flung down her book and raised a warning hand. "The carriage. Come!"

The "Come!" had matched for lucid firmness the rest of her speech, and when they were below in the hall there was a "Go!" for him, through the open doors and between the ranged servants, that matched even that. He received Royalty, bareheaded, therefore, in the persons of Mr. and Mrs. Verver, as it alighted on the pavement, and Maggie was at the threshold to welcome it to her house. Later on, upstairs again, she even herself felt still more the force of the limit of which she had just reminded him; at tea, in Charlotte's affirmed presence — as Charlotte affirmed it — she drew a long breath of richer relief. It was the strangest, once more, of all impressions; but what she most felt for the half-hour was that Mr. and Mrs. Verver were making the occasion easy. They were somehow conjoined in it, conjoined for a present effect as Maggie had absolutely never yet seen them; and there occurred, before long, a moment in which Amerigo's look met her own in recognitions that he could n't suppress. The question of the amount of correction to which Charlotte had laid herself open rose and hovered for the instant only to sink conspicuously by its own weight; so high a pitch she seemed to give to the unconsciousness of questions, so resplendent a show of serenity she succeeded in making. The shade of the official, in her beauty and security, never for a moment dropped; it was a cool high refuge, the deep arched recess of some coloured and gilded image, in which she sat and smiled and waited, drank her tea, referred to her husband and remembered her mission. Her mission had quite taken form — it was but another name for the interest of her great opportunity: that of representing the arts and the graces to a people languishing afar off and in ignorance. Maggie had sufficiently intimated to the Prince ten minutes before that she needed no showing as to what their friend would n't consent to be taken for; but the difficulty now indeed was to choose, for explicit tribute of admiration, between the varieties of her nobler aspects. She carried it off, to put the matter coarsely, with a taste and a discretion that held our young woman's attention, for the first quarter of an hour, to the very point of diverting it from the attitude of her overshadowed, her almost superseded companion. But

Adam Verver profited indeed at this time even with his daughter by his so marked peculiarity of seeming on no occasion to *have* an attitude; and so long as they were in the room together she felt him still simply weave his web and play out his long fine cord, knew herself in presence of this tacit process very much as she had known herself at Fawns. He had a way, the dear man, wherever he was, of moving about the room, noiselessly, to see what it might contain; and his manner of now resorting to this habit, acquainted as he already was with the objects in view, expressed with a certain sharpness the intention of leaving his wife to her devices. It did even more than this; it signified, to the apprehension of the Princess, from the moment she more directly took thought of him, almost a special view of these devices, as actually exhibited in their rarity, together with an independent, a settled appreciation of their general handsome adequacy which scarcely required the accompaniment of his faint contemplative hum.

Charlotte throned, as who should say, between her hostess and her host, the whole scene having crystallised, as soon as she took her place, to the right quiet lustre; the harmony was n't less sustained for being superficial, and the only approach to a break in it was while Amerigo remained standing long enough for his father-in-law, vaguely wondering, to appeal to him, invite or address him, and then in default of any such word selected for presentation to the other visitor a plate of *petits fours*. Maggie watched her husband — if it now could be called watching — offer this refreshment; she noted the con-

summate way — for "consummate" was the term she
privately applied — in which Charlotte cleared her
acceptance, cleared her impersonal smile, of any betrayal, any slightest value, of consciousness; and then
felt the slow surge of a vision that at the end of another
minute or two had floated her across the room to
where her father stood looking at a picture, an early
Florentine sacred subject, that he had given her on
her marriage. He might have been in silence taking
his last leave of it; it was a work for which she knew
he entertained an unqualified esteem. The tenderness
represented for her by his sacrifice of such a treasure had become to her sense a part of the whole in-
fusion, of the immortal expression; the beauty of his
sentiment looked out at her always, from the beauty
of the rest, as if the frame made positively a window
for his spiritual face: she might have said to herself
at this moment that in leaving the thing behind him,
held as in her clasping arms, he was doing the most
possible toward leaving her a part of his palpable self.
She put her hand over his shoulder, and their eyes
were held again together by the abiding felicity; they
smiled in emulation, vaguely, as if speech failed them
through their having passed too far: she would have
begun to wonder the next minute if it were reserved
to them, for the last stage, to find their contact, like
that of old friends reunited too much on the theory of
the unchanged, subject to shy lapses.

"It's all right, eh?"

"Oh my dear — rather!"

He had applied the question to the great fact of the
picture, as she had spoken for the picture in reply,

but it was as if their words for an instant afterwards symbolised another truth, so that they looked about at everything else to give them this extension. She had passed her arm into his, and the other objects in the room, the other pictures, the sofas, the chairs, the tables, the cabinets, the "important" pieces, supreme in their way, stood out, round them, consciously, for recognition and applause. Their eyes moved together from piece to piece, taking in the whole nobleness — quite as if for him to measure the wisdom of old ideas. The two noble persons seated in conversation and at tea fell thus into the splendid effect and the general harmony: Mrs. Verver and the Prince fairly "placed" themselves, however unwittingly, as high expressions of the kind of human furniture required æsthetically by such a scene. The fusion of their presence with the decorative elements, their contribution to the triumph of selection, was complete and admirable; though to a lingering view, a view more penetrating than the occasion really demanded, they also might have figured as concrete attestations of a rare power of purchase. There was much indeed in the tone in which Adam Verver spoke again, and who shall say where his thought stopped? "*Le compte y est.* You've got some good things."

Maggie met it afresh — "Ah don't they look well?" Their companions, at the sound of this, gave them, in a spacious intermission of slow talk, an attention, all of gravity, that was like an ampler submission to the general duty of magnificence; sitting as still, to be thus appraised, as a pair of effigies of the contemporary great on one of the platforms of Madame Tussaud. "I'm so glad — for your last look."

With which, after Maggie — quite in the air — had said it, the note was struck indeed; the note of that strange accepted finality of relation, as from couple to couple, which almost escaped an awkwardness only by not attempting a gloss. Yes, this was the wonder, that the occasion defied insistence precisely because of the vast quantities with which it dealt — so that separation was on a scale beyond any compass of parting. To do such an hour justice would have been in some degree to question its grounds — which was why they remained in fine, the four of them, in the upper air, united through the firmest abstention from pressure. There was visibly no point at which, face to face, either Amerigo or Charlotte had pressed; and how little she herself was in danger of doing so Maggie scarce needed to remember. That her father would n't by the tip of a toe — of that she was equally conscious: the only thing was that since he did n't she could but hold her breath for what he would do instead. When at the end of three minutes more he had said, with an effect of suddenness, "Well, Mag — and the Principino?" it was quite as if *that* were by contrast the hard, the truer voice.

She glanced at the clock. "I 'ordered' him for half-past five — which has n't yet struck. Trust him, my dear, not to fail you!"

"Oh I don't want *him* to fail me!" was Mr. Verver's reply; yet uttered in so explicitly jocose a relation to the possibilities of failure that even when just afterwards he wandered in his impatience to one of the long windows and passed out to the balcony she asked herself but for a few seconds whether reality, should she follow him, would overtake or meet her there. She followed him of necessity — it came absolutely so near to his inviting her, by stepping off into temporary detachment, to give the others something of the chance that she and her husband had so fantastically discussed. Beside him then, while they hung over the great dull place, clear and almost coloured now, coloured with the odd sad pictured "old-fashioned" look that empty London streets take on in waning afternoons of the summer's end, she felt once more how impossible such a passage would have been to them, how it would have torn them to pieces, if they had so much as suffered its suppressed relations to peep out of their eyes. This danger would doubtless indeed have been more to be reckoned with if the instinct of each — she could certainly at least answer for her own — had n't so successfully acted to trump up other apparent connexions for it, connexions as to which they could pretend to be frank.

"You must n't stay on here, you know," Adam Verver said as a result of his unobstructed outlook. "Fawns is all there for you of course — to the end of my tenure. But Fawns so dismantled," he added with mild ruefulness, "Fawns with half its contents and half its best things removed, won't seem to you, I'm afraid, particularly lively."

"No," Maggie answered, "we should miss its best things. Its best things, my dear, have certainly been removed. To be back there," she went on, "to be back there —!" And she paused for the force of her idea.

"Oh to be back there without anything good —!"

But she did n't hesitate now; she brought her idea forth. "To be back there without Charlotte is more than I think would do." And as she smiled at him with it, so she saw him the next instant take it — take it in a way that helped her smile to pass all for an allusion to what she did n't and could n't say. This quantity was too clear — that she could n't at such an hour be pretending to name to him what it was, as he would have said, "going to be," at Fawns or any-where else, to want for *him*. That was now — and in a manner exaltedly, sublimely — out of their compass and their question; so that what was she doing while they waited for the Principino, while they left the others together and their tension just sensibly threat-ened, what was she doing but just offer a bold but substantial substitute? Nothing was stranger more-over, under the action of Charlotte's presence, than the fact of a felt sincerity in her words. She felt her sincerity absolutely sound — she gave it for all it might mean. "Because Charlotte, dear, you know," she said, "is incomparable." It took thirty seconds, but she was to feel when these were over that she had pronounced one of the happiest words of her life. They had turned from the view of the street; they leaned together against the balcony rail, with the room largely in sight from where they stood, but with the Prince and Mrs. Verver out of range. Nothing he could try, she immediately saw, was to keep his eyes from lighting; not even his taking out his cigar-

THE GOLDEN BOWL

ette-case and saying before he said anything else:
"May I smoke?" She met it for encouragement
with her "My dear!" again, and then while he struck
his match she had just another minute to be nervous
— a minute that she made use of however not in
the least to falter, but to reiterate with a high ring,
a ring that might, for all she cared, reach the pair
inside: "Father, father — Charlotte's great!"

It was not till after he had begun to smoke that
he looked at her. "Charlotte's great."

They could close upon it — such a basis as they
might immediately feel it make; and so they stood
together over it quite gratefully, each recording to
the other's eyes that it was firm under their feet.
They had even thus a renewed wait as for proof of it;
much as if he were letting her see, while the minutes
lapsed for their concealed companions, that this was
finally just why — but just *why!* "You see," he presently added, "how right I was. Right, I mean, to
do it for you."

"Ah rather!" she murmured with her smile. And
then as to be herself ideally right: "I don't see what
you would have done without her."

"The point was," he returned quietly, "that I
did n't see what *you* were to do. Yet it was a risk."

"It was a risk," said Maggie — "but I believed in
it. At least for myself!" she smiled.

"Well *now*," he smoked, "we see."

"We see."

"I know her better."

"You know her best."

"Oh but naturally!" On which, as the warranted
364

truth of it hung in the air — the truth warranted, as
who should say, exactly by the present opportunity
to pronounce, this opportunity created and accepted
— she found herself lost, though with a finer thrill
than she had perhaps yet known, in the vision of all
he might mean. The sense of it in her rose higher,
rose with each moment that he invited her thus to
see him linger; and when, after a little more, he had
said, smoking again and looking up, with head
thrown back and hands spread on the balcony rail,
at the grey gaunt front of the house, "She's beautiful, beautiful!" her sensibility reported to her the
shade of a new note. It was all she might have wished,
for it was, with a kind of speaking competence, the
note of possession and control; and yet it conveyed
to her as nothing till now had done the reality of
their parting. They were parting, in the light of it,
absolutely on Charlotte's *value* — the value that
was filling the room out of which they had stepped
as if to give it play, and with which the Prince on his
side was perhaps making larger acquaintance. If
Maggie had desired at so late an hour some last conclusive comfortable category to place him in for dis-
missal, she might have found it here in its all coming
back to his ability to rest upon high values. Somehow, when all was said, and with the memory of her
gifts, her variety, her power, so much remained of
Charlotte's! What else had she herself meant three
minutes before by speaking of her as great? Great for
the world that was before her — *that* he proposed she
should be: she was n't to be wasted in the application
of his plan. Maggie held to this then — that she

was n't to be wasted. To let his daughter know it he had sought this brief privacy. What a blessing accordingly that she could speak her joy in it! His face meanwhile at all events was turned to her, and as she met his eyes again her joy went straight. "It's success, father."

"It's success. And even *this*," he added as the Principino, appearing alone, deep within, piped across an instant greeting — "even this is n't altogether failure!"

They went in to receive the boy, upon whose introduction to the room by Miss Bogle Charlotte and the Prince got up — seemingly with an impressiveness that had caused Miss Bogle not to give further effect to her own entrance. She had retired, but the Principino's presence by itself sufficiently broke the tension — the subsidence of which, in the great room, ten minutes later, gave to the air something of the quality produced by the cessation of a sustained rattle. Stillness, when the Prince and Princess returned from attending the visitors to their carriage, might have been said to be not so much restored as created; so that whatever next took place in it was foredoomed to remarkable salience. That would have been the case even with so natural, though so futile, a movement as Maggie's going out to the balcony again to follow with her eyes her father's departure. The carriage was out of sight — it had taken her too long solemnly to reascend, and she looked a while only at the great grey space on which, as on the room still more, the shadow of dusk had fallen. Here at first her husband had n't rejoined

her; he had come up with the boy, who, clutching
his hand, abounded, as usual, in remarks worthy of
the family archives; but the two appeared then to
have proceeded to report to Miss Bogle. It meant
something for the Princess that her husband had thus
got their son out of the way, not bringing him back
to his mother; but everything now, as she vaguely
moved about, struck her as meaning so much that
the unheard chorus swelled. Yet *this* above all —
her just being there as she was and waiting for him
to come in, their freedom to be together there always
— was the meaning most disengaged: she stood in
the cool twilight and took in all about her where it
lurked her reason for what she had done. She knew
at last really why — and how she had been inspired
and guided, how she had been persistently able, how
to her soul all the while it had been for the sake of
this end. Here it was then, the moment, the golden
fruit that had shone from afar; only what *were* these
things in the fact, for the hand and for the lips, when
tested, when tasted — what were they as a reward?
Closer than she had ever been to the measure of her
course and the full face of her act, she had an instant
of the terror that, when there has been suspense,
always precedes, on the part of the creature to be
paid, the certification of the amount. Amerigo knew
it, the amount; he still held it, and the delay in his
return, making her heart beat too fast to go on, was
like a sudden blinding light on a wild speculation.
She had thrown the dice, but his hand was over her
cast.

He opened the door however at last — he had n't

been away ten minutes; and then with her sight of
him renewed to intensity she seemed to have a view
of the number. His presence alone, as he paused to
look at her, somehow made it the highest, and even
before he had spoken she had begun to be paid in
full. With that consciousness in fact an extraordinary
thing occurred; the assurance of her safety so making
her terror drop that already within the minute it had
been changed to concern for his own anxiety, for
everything that was deep in his being and everything
that was fair in his face. So far as seeing that she
was "paid" went he might have been holding out the
money-bag for her to come and take it. But what
instantly rose for her between the act and her acceptance was the sense that she must strike him as waiting for a confession. This in turn charged her with
a new horror: if *that* was her proper payment she
would go without money. His acknowledgement
hung there, too monstrously, at the expense of Charlotte, before whose mastery of the greater style she
had just been standing dazzled. All she now knew
accordingly was that she should be ashamed to listen
to the uttered word; all, that is, but that she might
dispose of it on the spot for ever.

"Is n't she too splendid?" she simply said, offering
it to explain and to finish.

"Oh splendid!" With which he came over to her.

"That's our help, you see," she added — to point
further her moral.

It kept him before her therefore, taking in — or
trying to — what she so wonderfully gave. He tried,
too clearly, to please her — to meet her in her own

way; but with the result only that, close to her, her face kept before him, his hands holding her shoulders, his whole act enclosing her, he presently echoed: "'See'? I see nothing but *you*." And the truth of it had with this force after a moment so strangely lighted his eyes that as for pity and dread of them she buried her own in his breast.

THE END